ELMHURST PUBLIC LIBRARY

A Green Mountain Romance

"You're a very nice guy."

"This is what I'm trying to tell you."

Her laughter broke the tension that had grown and multiplied during the intense conversation. His smile lit up his handsome face, and Megan couldn't resist him when he looked at her that way. She put her hand around his nape and drew him in for a kiss. "He cooks, he irons, he bakes *and* he makes dreams come true."

"You forgot balances the books and makes you come multiple times every night. What can I say, babe? I'm a Renaissance man."

"And he's funny and cute and sexy and adorable."

"All those things? You shouldn't let a guy like that get away. You might regret it for the rest of your life."

"Yes, I'm quite sure I would."

Praise for the Green Mountain Romances

"Force introduces readers to a local Vermont family that will warm the heart and make them nostalgic for their own hometowns. . . ." —*Debbie's Book Bag*

"Now this is how contemporary romance is done." —*Cocktails and Books*

"Marie truly just has a way of telling a story that draws you in, and never lets you go. Not even when you reach the end of the book." —*Guilty Pleasures Book Reviews*

"Marie Force has written a fabulous story that pulls at your heartstrings as you flip the pages, devouring every single word!" —*Fresh Fiction*

Berkley titles by Marie Force

ALL YOU NEED IS LOVE
I WANT TO HOLD YOUR HAND
I SAW HER STANDING THERE
AND I LOVE HER

AND I
LOVE HER

Marie Force

ELMHURST PUBLIC LIBRARY
125 S. Prospect Avenue
Elmhurst, IL 60126-3298

BERKLEY BOOKS, NEW YORK

THE BERKLEY PUBLISHING GROUP
Published by the Penguin Group
Penguin Group (USA) LLC
375 Hudson Street, New York, New York 10014

USA • Canada • UK • Ireland • Australia • New Zealand • India • South Africa • China

penguin.com

A Penguin Random House Company

AND I LOVE HER

A Berkley Book / published by arrangement with the author

Copyright © 2015 by HTJB, Inc.
Excerpt from *A Day in the Life* by Marie Force copyright © 2015 by HTJB, Inc.
Excerpt from *You'll Be Mine* by Marie Force copyright © 2015 by HTJB, Inc.
Penguin supports copyright. Copyright fuels creativity, encourages diverse voices,
promotes free speech, and creates a vibrant culture. Thank you for buying an authorized
edition of this book and for complying with copyright laws by not reproducing, scanning,
or distributing any part of it in any form without permission. You are supporting writers
and allowing Penguin to continue to publish books for every reader.

BERKLEY® is a registered trademark of Penguin Group (USA) LLC.
The "B" design is a trademark of Penguin Group (USA) LLC.

For information, address: The Berkley Publishing Group,
a division of Penguin Group (USA) LLC,
375 Hudson Street, New York, New York 10014.

ISBN: 978-0-425-27549-8

PUBLISHING HISTORY
Berkley mass-market edition / March 2015

PRINTED IN THE UNITED STATES OF AMERICA

10 9 8 7 6 5 4 3 2 1

Cover photographs: *Couple in Bed* © Yuri Arcurs/Istock;
Open Window © Sinelyov/Shutterstock.
Cover design by George Long.
Interior text design by Kelly Lipovich.

This is a work of fiction. Names, characters, places, and incidents either are the product
of the author's imagination or are used fictitiously, and any resemblance to actual persons,
living or dead, business establishments, events, or locales is entirely coincidental.

If you purchased this book without a cover, you should be aware that this book is
stolen property. It was reported as "unsold and destroyed" to the publisher, and neither
the author nor the publisher has received any payment for this "stripped book."

CHAPTER 1

———◄❦►———

Business opportunities are like buses,
there's always another one coming.

—Sir Richard Branson, founder of Virgin Group

When her sister and brother-in-law said they wanted to talk to her at the diner Monday evening, Megan Kane assumed they were going to tell her they were finally expecting the niece or nephew she'd wanted for as long as they'd been married. But the words that came from Brett and Nina in stuttering, halting sentences had nothing to do with babies.

"Moving overseas."

"Selling the diner."

"So sorry to do this to you."

"It was an amazing opportunity."

"We couldn't say no."

"You can come with us." Nina seemed crushed to be delivering this news to her "baby" sister, who was almost twenty-eight and hardly a baby anymore. "I'd love that. We could run around and explore together while Brett is at work. It would be so fun."

Megan shook off the shock and found her voice. "No. You've been taking care of me since you were twenty-two, Neen. It's time to go live your life. I'll be fine."

"We really do mean it when we say you should come with us," Brett said. He was always so kind to her, never once in all these years acting as if her tight bond with his wife was a problem for him.

"I can't do that. I can't crash your party. I've been around your necks long enough as it is."

"You're hardly around our necks, Megan," Nina said. "We could have so much fun! Would you think about it before you automatically say no? Please?"

"Fine." Megan said what her sister needed to hear. "I'll think about it."

"Great!" Nina said, beaming with pleasure at the small victory.

"If you decide to stay here, we'll help you find another job," Brett said. "Maybe the new owners of the diner would want to keep you on. They'd be crazy not to."

He'd been a terrific brother-in-law to her since he married her sister nine years ago. A teacher at a nearby boys' prep school, he'd apparently applied for overseas positions in the past but they'd never materialized until now.

Work at Nina's Diner without Nina? Unthinkable. "I'll figure something out. You guys don't need to worry about me."

"Of course we'll worry about you, Meg." Nina reached for her sister's hand across the table. "I don't know how *not* to worry about you."

"It's probably time I got a life of my own." Megan tried to stay calm even as she panicked on the inside. Not see Nina every day? Unbearable. "Mom and Dad would be horrified if they knew I was still living in the garage apartment."

"They'd be proud of you."

"No, they'd be proud of *you*, but you deserve it. You've created such a wonderful business here, and now you have this fantastic opportunity to travel. I'd never hold you guys back from doing what you want."

Brett's relief was so visible he practically sagged under the weight of it. Obviously, they'd worried about telling her their news. "You really can come with us if you want to, Megan," he said. "It would be great to have you in France."

"I'd love to come visit while you're there, but this is home." In reality, *Nina* was home to her, not Butler or the house where they'd once lived with their parents, but Megan kept those thoughts to herself.

"You said you'd think about it!" Nina said.

"Neen, I can't just go traipsing off to France, as fun as that sounds. I need to figure out my life and what I'm going to do with it. I can't do that in France. I don't want either of you to worry about me. I swear I'll be fine."

"Are you sure?" Nina asked tearfully. "You'd tell me if you didn't mean that, wouldn't you?"

"I'm very sure." Megan kept her emotions out of it—for now anyway. "This could turn out to be a good thing for me. It'll give me the kick in the butt I've needed to move on." Megan had been marching in place for more than ten years, since the snowy night they lost their parents in a car crash during her senior year of high school.

Nina had been her rock ever since, acting as mother, father and big sister all rolled into one. The sisters had held on to each other for all these years, and the thought of everyday life without Nina was unfathomable to Megan.

"If you agree, we're going to rent the house," Brett said, "but the garage apartment is all yours for as long as you want or need it. We told the Realtor the garage wasn't part of the deal."

"Of course I agree. No sense the house sitting vacant when you could be making some money." Her brother-in-law's sweetness nearly broke her emotional dam, but she refused to cry in front of them. Since there were going to be tears—and lots of them—she had to get out of there immediately. No way would she make them feel bad about something they were so excited about. Knowing she was on borrowed time where the tears were concerned, Megan gathered up her belongings and stood. "I'll see you guys in the morning."

"Let me drive you home," Nina said.

"That's okay. I could use the fresh air after being inside all afternoon." They'd used their afternoon and evening "off" to do their monthly deep clean of the diner.

"You're sure you're all right?" Nina asked.

Megan bent to kiss her sister's cheek. "I'm fine, and I'm thrilled for both of you."

Nina held her tight for a minute. "Love you, Meggie."

Megan couldn't remember the last time Nina had called her by her childhood nickname. "Love you, too."

Feeling as if she'd been set adrift, untethered from the one sure thing in her life, Megan stepped out of the diner, taking a moment to breathe in the fresh, clean early-autumn air. The tears she'd managed to contain in front of Nina and Brett broke loose in sobs that had her looking for a place to hide until the storm passed.

She crossed the street and ducked behind the Green Mountain Country Store, planning to hide out until Brett and Nina left for home.

The last thing she wanted was for them to see her crying, and nothing short of a miracle would help her keep it together tonight.

After another twelve-hour marathon in front of the computer, Hunter Abbott stood and stretched out the kinks in his shoulders and back. As the chief financial officer for the Green Mountain Country Store and other Abbott family businesses, Hunter worked pretty much all the time. If it weren't for the pressing need for food that his body demanded every few hours, he'd probably work around the clock.

It wasn't like he had anything better to do. And wasn't that a sad, pathetic fact of his life?

His stomach let out an unholy growl that had him checking the time on his computer. Nine ten. With the diner closed today, that left pizza as his only option in town at this hour. He dialed the number to Kingdom Pizza from memory and ordered a small veggie and a salad. If he was resorting to eating junk, at least it was somewhat healthy. Before his twin sister, Hannah, had remarried over the summer, Hunter might've headed for her house to bum some dinner and conversation. But with Nolan now living with Hannah and the two of them in starry-eyed newly wedded bliss, Hunter steered clear.

He turned off his computer and glanced at the stack of files still awaiting his attention. Bring them home or leave them for tomorrow? After a brief internal debate, he shut off the light and left them. His tank was running on empty, and tomorrow would bring more of the same.

In the outer office, he was surprised to find the light still on in his sister Ella's office. He went over to knock on her door. "You're working late."

"As are you."

"Except I always do. What's your excuse?"

"Getting some new products entered into the system, and dealing with a pile of paperwork that never seems to get smaller no matter what I do."

"I hear you there. So much for being self-employed, huh?"

She smiled at him, but he noted a hint of sadness in her eyes that caught him by surprise. Ella was one of the most joyful people he'd ever known—always happy and upbeat.

"Everything okay?"

"Sure. Why do you ask?"

"You just seemed . . . I don't know . . . sad or something for a second there."

"I'm fine. No need to worry."

"Okay then." Hunter took a step back, planning to leave, but there it was again—the sadness he'd seen before. "You know if there's anything wrong, you can come to me, right? We may see each other a thousand times a day, but I'm right over there if you need me. No matter what it is."

"Thank you, Hunter. That's very sweet of you. I know you want to take care of everything for all of us, but some things . . . Well, some things can't be managed. They are what they are."

More confused than ever, Hunter wasn't sure whether he should stay and try to force the issue or give her some space to deal with whatever was bothering her. "I'm here, El. I'm right here. Don't suffer in silence."

Her smile softened her face. "I'll see you tomorrow."

"Do you want me to wait for you so you're not here alone?"

"No. I've got another hour or so, and I can lock up."

"Give me a quick call to let me know you got home okay."

"Hunter . . ."

"What? You'll always be my little sister, so call me."

"I'm only four years younger than you."

"And I vividly remember the day you were born."

"Freak."

Hunter chuckled at the predictable comment. His family teased him every day about his photographic memory and ability to recall facts and figures from years ago that should've been impossible to remember. Sometimes he wished he could forget some of the crap that rattled around in his brain, but it was his lot in life to be a walking, talking data warehouse. "See you in the morning."

"Have a good night."

"Call me."

"Go!"

Hunter went down the stairs thinking about what Ella had said about him wanting to take care of things for everyone. Perhaps it was also his lot in life as the oldest of the ten Abbott siblings, but he wanted the people he loved to be happy and their problems to be few, even if that meant taking on more than his share of the load.

Hannah had been after him recently to work less and play more. If only he could think of something he'd rather do than work.

Totally pathetic. He knew it, but damn if he could figure out how to snap out of the rut he'd fallen into. When had he become an all-work, no-play stick in the mud? If he were being honest with himself, he'd been in the rut for a long time, probably since he graduated from college and joined the family business full time. College had been the last time he'd been truly free of responsibility and obligation.

Thinking about the blissful college days had him remembering his late brother-in-law Caleb, Hannah's first husband, who'd died in Iraq seven years ago. If he came back to life and saw how ridiculously out of balance Hunter's life had become, he'd raise holy hell.

Raising holy hell was on Hunter's mind as he stepped into the cool darkness and waited for the motion-sensitive light to come on. Once it did, he turned to lock the door behind him. Ella would see to setting the alarm system.

Leaving her alone at the store made him anxious, but he would check on her if she didn't remember to call him.

A sound to his left had him stopping to listen. Was that sniffling? "Who's there?"

"It's me, Megan. I'm sorry to scare you."

That voice . . . It cut through him like a knife slicing butter. Every nerve ending in his body stood up to take note of her nearness, which happened every damned time he came into any kind of contact with her. "Megan," he said in a voice that was barely a whisper. "What're you doing here in the dark?"

"Hiding out."

"Why? Are you hurt? What's wrong?" True to form, he wanted to make things right for her, no matter what it took. His heart beat quickly, as if he'd been running for miles, and his hands were suddenly sweaty and clammy. He'd never understand why this particular woman provoked such a strong reaction in him every time he laid eyes on her—or in this case, heard tears in her voice as she spoke in the dark.

"Nothing's wrong. I just needed a minute. Sorry to trespass on your property. I'll get out of your way."

"Wait. Don't go." The words came out sounding far more desperate than he'd intended. "At least let me drive you home."

"That's all right. I can walk."

"I wouldn't mind at all."

She stepped into the light, and the sight of her tear-ravaged face broke his heart. What could possibly be so wrong?

"It's out of your way."

"I've got nowhere to be." He watched her expressive face as she pondered his offer. Her lips pursed, which brought her cheekbones into sharper relief against the pale skin on her face. *Exquisite* was the word that came to mind whenever he looked at her, which was as often as he could. Until recently she'd had a major crush on his brother Will, but that had no bearing whatsoever on how he felt about her. He looked at her, and he wanted. It was that simple.

Except she barely knew he was alive, which was a problem.

"If you're sure you don't mind," she said after an impossibly long pause.

"I really don't."

"Thank you."

She walked with him to his silver Lincoln Navigator and stood by his side as he held the passenger door and waited for her to get settled.

As he got into the driver's side, his growling stomach reminded him of the takeout order. "Have you had dinner?" The words were out before he could take the time to overanalyze the situation.

"Not yet."

"I have a pizza and salad on order. I'd be happy to share."

"I don't know if I could eat."

"Come along and keep me company?"

"Um, sure. Okay." She reached into her purse, withdrew a tissue and wiped her eyes.

"Are you going to tell me why you were crying?"

"Do I have to?"

"Of course not." He was surprised that she would think he'd try to force it out of her. "But I'm told I'm a good listener."

She had no reply to that, so he turned the key to start the engine, lowering the windows a bit to get some air.

"I probably stink from cleaning the diner," she said.

"No, you don't." As he drove, he thought of a thousand things he'd like to say to her, but none were the sort of things a guy blurted out when he finally had a moment alone with the woman he desired.

How exactly did you tell a woman who barely knew you were alive that you thought about her constantly? That seeing her upset killed you. That wanting her kept you awake at night. How did you tell her it didn't matter if she had once been obsessed with your brother? That there was nothing you wouldn't do to see her smile, to see her pale blue eyes light up with joy?

How could he say any of that and not sound like a total creep?

He couldn't, so he kept his mouth shut and hoped he wouldn't do something embarrassing like hyperventilate from the overwhelming effort it took not to say all of it.

CHAPTER 2

*To think is easy. To act is difficult. To act
as one thinks is the most difficult.*

—Johann Wolfgang von Goethe, German writer
and statesman

Hunter pulled into the parking lot at Kingdom Pizza
and said he'd be right back. When he'd asked her to
keep him company, Megan assumed he'd want to eat at the
restaurant, but now she watched him pay for takeout through
big plate-glass windows and wondered what he had planned.

The cashier said something that made Hunter laugh as he
returned his wallet to the back pocket of his black pants. His
white pinstriped dress shirt stretched across broad shoulders
that tapered down to a narrow waist. Since she'd much rather
check out Hunter Abbott than think about her own woes,
Megan let her gaze travel down over what looked to be a tight,
muscular ass and long legs.

As she'd spent most of her adult life longing for his
brother Will, she hadn't given Hunter all that much thought.
He was, she decided, every bit as good-looking as Will, but
in a different sort of way. Where Will was brawny and out-
doorsy and rugged, Hunter was equally muscular and fit, but
his appearance was far more refined.

Will had lighter coloring than Hunter, who had dark, wavy hair and intense brown eyes. As she watched Hunter turn away from the counter and head for the door with his purchases in hand, something Will had said recently chose that moment to pop into her mind. *You're focusing on the wrong Abbott brother.*

What did that mean?

Megan was still thinking about that when she leaned over the fancy SUV's center console to open the driver-side door for him.

"Thanks." He handed her the pizza box and another bag, which she held on her lap.

The smell of the herbs and spices had her mouth watering. Half an hour ago, she couldn't have imagined eating anything, and now she was suddenly starving.

"Do you mind if we take it back to my place?"

"Um, no, I guess not."

You're focusing on the wrong Abbott brother.

During the long years of her not-so-secret obsession with Will Abbott, she'd created a mental catalog of all the things she knew about him. However, when it came to Hunter Abbott, her catalog was empty in comparison. She knew hardly anything about him other than the fact that he was the oldest of the ten Abbotts and worked as the chief financial officer for his family's company.

He came into the diner twice a day for coffee—at the exact same times every day—but unlike some of his more boisterous siblings, Hunter tended to keep to himself, observing rather than participating when joined at the diner by his family members.

The two of them had rarely exchanged more than a few words when he ordered food and she brought it to him. Except for one time recently when she'd asked him about Cameron moving in with Will, and he'd suggested she go out with someone else—him perhaps—to get her mind off Will. *The wrong brother . . .*

A few minutes later, he pulled into the driveway of a

well-kept tan colonial with black shutters several blocks from Elm Street.

"This is yours?"

"Uh-huh."

"I love this house and the garden. I had no idea you lived here."

"I thought everyone in this town knew where everyone else lived."

"I spend too much time at the diner listening to everyone's business to pay much attention to where they all live."

"Good point." He relieved her of the pizza box and bag. "Come on in."

The words were spoken casually, but when he opened the car door and the overhead light came on, she couldn't miss the intense way he looked at her.

You're focusing on the wrong Abbott brother.

What did Will know that she didn't? Suddenly, she wanted the answer to that question even more than she wanted a slice of the mouthwatering pizza. Hunter took the pizza and bag and waited for her to come around the truck before he led her to the front door, where he used his key and then stepped aside to let her go in ahead of him.

The house was dark except for a small light in the kitchen, and it smelled fresh and clean, like lemons and maybe laundry detergent. She probably should've expected that a man who dressed the way Hunter did wouldn't live like a typical bachelor. And when he flipped on a light in the living room, she saw there was nothing typical about this bachelor pad.

"Toss your stuff anywhere."

His sofa and love seat were tan with dark brown trim. The tables were black and the usual life clutter nonexistent. On the fireplace mantel was a single framed photo of his family along with several candlesticks with thick cream-colored candles. The walls held framed prints by a Vermont photographer whose work Megan recognized.

She put her sweater and purse on the chair inside the door and followed him into the kitchen.

What am I doing here? The thought nearly stopped her in her tracks as she entered a fully renovated kitchen that had black appliances, matching granite countertops and funky teardrop lights suspended over an island.

"Have a seat." He gestured to one of the two bar stools tucked under the extended edge of the countertop. "I ordered a veggie and got several slices of cheese, too. What's your preference?"

"Either is fine. I didn't expect you to share your dinner with me."

"I'm happy to share." He put a slice of each kind on her plate and pushed it across the counter to her. "Wine? Beer? Soda? Water?"

"I'll take a beer if you have an extra."

"Coming right up." He opened two bottles—with an opener, no twist-offs for him—and handed one to her.

She glanced at the label, which she didn't recognize. Naturally, it was something imported and classy, like him.

He joined her at the bar, sliding onto the other stool and offering to share his salad.

"No, thanks. The pizza is more than enough."

They ate in silence, and Megan appreciated that he didn't push her to talk about what had upset her earlier. Being with him on this little detour from her regular routine had helped to briefly take her mind off the bomb Nina and Brett had dropped on her earlier.

The whole thing came rushing back to her in one big wave of sadness that made it difficult to swallow her pizza. She took a sip of beer and closed her eyes, hoping to contain the emotional firestorm that threatened to erupt again at any second.

Megan opened her eyes to find Hunter watching her, and Will's words once again bounced around in her brain. *You're focusing on the wrong Abbott brother.* Looking into Hunter's deep brown eyes, which were filled with concern and compassion and something else she couldn't easily identify, Megan was filled with an awareness of Hunter as a man for the first time. Until right that second, he'd been a customer, a guy she knew from town, Will's brother.

She cleared her throat and took another sip of her beer. "Nina and Brett are selling the diner."

His expression changed in a heartbeat from compassionate to shocked. "What?"

"He's been offered a teaching position in France for the new school year. They're leaving next week. Apparently, the person the school originally hired had to decline at the last minute, so they have very little time to get there."

"Megan . . ."

"The diner is closing."

"And you just found this out?"

She nodded. "After we cleaned."

"You were crying. Behind the store."

"Maybe a little."

He pushed his plate away, apparently having lost interest in the food, and reached for her hand. "Are you okay?"

She glanced down at their joined hands and shrugged. "I will be. It's just a job. I suppose I can find another one somewhere."

"That's not what I meant. Your sister . . . You two are close, and she'll be leaving. Soon."

Damn it, he had to say that. He had to home in on the part of the situation that had truly broken her heart, and she was going to cry again if she didn't get out of there immediately. She withdrew her hand and stood, nearly tipping over the stool in her haste. "Thank you so much for the pizza and the company. I'm just going to . . . I'll go now."

He stood and took hold of her elbow. "Don't go. Not now. Not when you're upset."

She shook her head. "You've had a long day. You don't need an emotional female blubbering all over you."

"Please," he said, the note of longing in his tone impossible to deny, "don't go. Let me help."

The wrong brother, the wrong brother, the wrong brother . . .

Megan blinked rapidly, wishing intently that she were a stronger person, the kind who didn't fall apart over news that tipped her world upside down.

And then Hunter's arms were around her, and he was

holding her, the scent of fine, expensive cologne filling her senses, making her forget, if only for a second, that her heart was breaking.

"I stink like ammonia and bleach, and you smell like Nordstrom."

His laughter rumbled through his body, making her smile despite the tears that threatened to spill over at any second. "You don't smell like either of those things."

Was he . . . sniffing her hair? And was she really tipping her head to give him better access?

"You smell like jasmine and lilies. I love the smell of jasmine. It's one of my favorite things in the summer."

His gruff words sent a tingle of sensation down her backbone, which settled in a throb between her legs that made her gasp with surprise.

Hunter released her abruptly. "I'm sorry. I didn't mean . . ." He stared at her.

"You didn't." She wanted to beg him to hold her some more, to make her feel like he had for that brief second before she overreacted and ruined the moment. Summoning courage she wouldn't have thought she had, she took a small step toward him and put her hands on his waist, above his black leather belt.

"Megan . . ."

She looked up at him, noting the slashes of color that had appeared in the area of his cheekbones as well as the raw heat in his gaze. "It felt good to have you hold me, Hunter. Would you do it again?"

He blew out a deep breath and drew her into his arms, holding her so tightly she could barely breathe.

If Will had been the wrong Abbott brother, was Hunter the right one? The thought, which moved through her mind like a bullet whizzing toward its target, nearly made her laugh when a second ago she'd been on the verge of tears.

What am I doing here?

She forced the question from her mind and leaned into his embrace as well as the comfort he offered so willingly.

His ringing phone interrupted the moment. He tensed for

a second before he released her, seeming reluctant to let go. "I need to grab that. I'm waiting for a call from my sister."

"Sure," she said, embarrassed now by the way she'd blatantly asked him to hold her. Her hands dropped from his waist, and she looked down as she linked her index fingers.

"Hey, El." Hunter sounded rushed and abrupt. "You're home? Okay, thanks for calling. See you tomorrow." He ended the call and turned back to Megan. "Sorry about that. Now where were we?"

She shook her head. "It's okay. I'll be fine. It was just . . . tonight." Shrugging, she added, "The news sort of blindsided me."

"Of course it did." He took her hand, apparently comfortable touching her now that she'd all but begged him to, and led her into the living room, where he sat on one of the sofas and drew her down next to him. "You're losing your sister from your daily life, not to mention your job. That would upset anyone."

"I want to be happy for her," Megan said softly. "She's done so much for me."

"Tell me." He tucked a strand of her hair behind her ear. "I want to know you."

Sitting next to him in his lovely home with his appealing masculine scent filling her senses and his kindness touching her heart, Megan wanted to know him, too.

"You know our parents were killed in a car accident the winter of my senior year of high school."

"Yes, I remember. I don't know if I ever told you how truly sorry I was for you and Nina. Your folks were great people."

His kind words nearly brought her to tears again. "Thank you for saying that. Yes, they were. It was an awful time, but somehow we got through it together. Nina was a senior in college, but she came home to be with me, and she never left. She finished her degree over the summer. Then, when she and Brett got married, they took the house, and I moved to the garage apartment. I've been there ever since. She opened the diner, I went to work for her and the years just sort of passed in a blur. And now . . . Now I'm not sure what I'll do." Megan ran her damp hands over the soft denim of her jeans. Talking about the darkest days of her life never got any easier, even ten years later.

"I'm sure the thought of her moving away has to be so upsetting for you."

"It is, but I'm also feeling selfish for wishing she wouldn't go while at the same time I'm happy for her to have this incredible opportunity. Crazy, right?"

"Not at all. She's your anchor. It's only natural you'd feel this way at the thought of her so far away. I'd die if Hannah moved away from me."

She smiled at his attempt to make her feel better. Had she ever noticed what a nice guy he was? "I feel like a big baby weeping over the fact that my sister is moving overseas."

"I think you're being really hard on yourself. For one thing, the news shocked you because you hadn't been expecting it. For another, you and Nina share a special bond that will be changed by this, even if it's a good change. For her at least."

"It's a good change for me, too. It's time for me to shake things up a bit. Maybe I'll finally go to college or find a job with more potential or something. After the way I reacted to Will falling for Cameron, I'm sure you'd all like to see the last of me. With Nina leaving and my job going away, there's no reason to stay."

"That's not true. There's a very good reason to stay."

CHAPTER 3

*I like thinking big. If you're going to be thinking
anything, you might as well think big.*

—Donald Trump, business magnate

The words had been said before he took a second to consider the implications of laying it all on the line. Sitting
next to her on his sofa, her hand curled around his, Hunter
wanted to keep her there forever. Listening to her talk, her
nearness spinning him up in knots, he wanted her like he'd
never wanted another woman.

He'd sensed the fragility beneath the tough veneer she
showed the world, and now that he'd seen the fragility first-
hand, he wanted to fix things for her, to make her smile again,
to make her *happy*. Why he wanted that so badly he couldn't
begin to know. It just *was*, the way Hannah was his twin, Molly
and Lincoln were his parents and Butler was his home.

She looked at him, her head tilted ever so slightly in
inquiry. "Are you going to tell me this very good reason I
should stay?"

"I, um . . ." Hunter Abbott didn't stutter. He didn't fum-
ble over his words, or at least he never had before. Until
Megan Kane's crystal blue eyes seemed to see right through
the smooth exterior *he* showed the rest of the world. "I don't
want you to go."

"Why?"

Shaking his head, he laughed softly. "Damned if I know."

His words hung in the air between them, almost like a gauntlet he'd thrown down, hoping she'd pick it up and run with it. Did she understand what he was saying? Perhaps not, which was why he tried to think of a better way to say it. "I like you, Megan. I have for a while now."

"You like me . . . as in . . ."

"I *like* you. A lot."

"Why?" she asked, wide-eyed. "I'm not even nice most of the time."

Her blunt comment made him laugh again. "We all have our moments."

"I have more than most. I've been awful to Cameron, for one thing. I'm trying to be a better person."

"I heard you apologized to her."

"I did."

"That's good of you."

"I was wrong to treat her that way. It wasn't her fault he fell for her."

"No, it wasn't."

She glanced at him, and the hesitance he saw in her eyes made him want to hold her again and never let her go. "You like me even though I used to like him?"

"That never mattered to me, although I often wished you might someday consider his older, wiser and much more handsome brother."

Her laughter surprised and delighted him. He'd never heard her laugh like that before, and he *loved* it. He loved that he'd made it happen and wanted to do it again.

"So you *used* to like him," he said tentatively. "As in past tense?"

"Yes, past tense. He's crazy about Cameron, and so is everyone else." She shrugged it off, as if it hadn't hurt her to watch Will fall for Cameron. "He said something to me recently . . . about how I was focusing on the wrong Abbott brother."

Hunter was so shocked to hear this that he didn't know

what to say. Will had tried to help his cause with Megan? That was news to him.

"Was he talking about you?"

"Yeah, I think he was."

"Is this why you asked me out a couple of months ago? You said it might help me to get over Will if I went out with someone else. I told you I didn't think going out with Will's brother would help me get over him."

"I remember," he said, grimacing. It hadn't been funny at the time. Rather, it had felt like the final nail in his coffin where she was concerned. He'd left the diner that day feeling as if he had a better chance of winning a million bucks in the lottery than he did of ever getting Megan to notice him as anything other than her beloved's brother.

"Did I hurt your feelings that day?"

"You crushed me." After a pause, he smiled so she'd know he was teasing her. Sort of.

Her lips parted, her eyes widened and he wanted to kiss her so badly he burned with it. "I'm sorry."

"I was teasing. I wasn't totally crushed. Just kinda."

"I didn't know. I've been so oblivious, and I feel terrible."

"That's not why I told you. I don't want you to feel terrible. I wanted you to know. That's all."

"That's *all*? Like that's the end of it?"

"I'm hoping it's just the beginning of it."

Megan struggled to absorb the shock of hearing Hunter admit he was interested in her. Romantically interested. Hunter Abbott of the Green Mountain Country Store Abbotts. The man who dressed like an advertising executive on Madison Avenue in New York rather than an accountant on Elm Street in Butler. He was smart, quiet, handsome, intense and currently looking at her in a way that made Megan's skin feel unusually warm.

She had to put a stop to this. How had it even happened? One minute they were eating pizza and the next they were talking about him being interested in her. She'd never thought of him that way. For so long, the only man she'd wanted had been his brother Will, who had never thought of her as anything other than the waitress he talked to at the diner.

To hear that Will's brother had harbored secret feelings for her while she harbored not-so-secret feelings for Will was . . . Well, she didn't know exactly what word to use to describe how strange that was.

She stood up. "I need to go."

"Because of what I said?"

"Because I can't process this on top of everything else that's already happened tonight. My brain feels like it's spinning or something."

"I'm sorry. I didn't tell you that to upset you more than you already were. I just . . . I wanted you to know."

"You didn't upset me."

"Let me drive you home."

"That's not necessary. I can walk. It's not that far."

"It's dark and cold, Megan. Let me drive you. Please?"

"Fine. Okay. Thanks."

He went to get his jacket and returned with his keys. Neither of them said anything as he followed her out to the driveway, where he again held the car door for her and waited for her to get settled.

Megan watched him walk around the front of the SUV and get into the driver's side.

Hunter put on his seatbelt but made no move to start the car. After a long silence, he cleared his throat. "I know I already said it, but I really am sorry. Tonight was not the night to have this conversation."

She turned in her seat so she could try to make out his face in the inky darkness. "I want you to know I'm flattered. I truly am. And I'd like to talk about it. Sometime. Just not tonight. If that's okay."

"It's okay."

"Are you mad?"

"No," he said with a small laugh as he turned the key to start the engine. "I'm sort of oddly relieved that you know."

"So you've . . . felt this way, about me . . . for a while, then?"

"Yes."

"How long?"

"I don't know."

"How can you not know?"

"I don't remember not feeling this way."

"Hunter! I've known you for years!"

After another long pause, he said, "I thought we weren't going to talk about this tonight."

Megan had so many questions suddenly running around in her mind, but he was right. She'd put a stop to the conversation, so it wasn't fair to restart it just because she had questions.

He drove to her house, which was located about a mile past his parents' house on the way to Butler Mountain.

"I can get out here."

Hunter pulled up to the curb. "I suppose it would be useless to offer to walk you to the door."

"It would," she said with a smile, "but thank you for asking and for the pizza and the ride. And everything."

"No problem."

"We'll talk about it, Hunter. I promise."

"I'll hold you to that. You know where to find me."

"Yes, I do." She got out of the car and headed for the garage apartment at the end of the long driveway, aware of him watching her even though he couldn't see her.

Hunter Abbott. Though his revelations had added to the emotional turmoil swirling inside her, Megan couldn't stop thinking about the sincerity she'd felt coming from him. She'd been focused on Will for so long that the thought of another man being interested in her was something that would take some time to process.

As she showered and changed into cozy flannel pajamas, Megan thought about Hunter and everything she'd learned about him during the eventful evening they'd spent together.

She got into bed thinking more about his confession than she was about the impending changes in her life that had upset her in the first place. Snuggling into bed, she relived every minute she'd spent with him, from the second he found her crying in the dark outside the store until he dropped her off at home.

He'd been so thoughtful and caring, scooping her up and taking her home with him, feeding her and listening to her cry over her sister's surprising news. And when he'd held her for that all-too-brief moment in the kitchen, the last thing on her mind had been her feelings for his brother.

She could still remember how good he'd smelled and how great his strong arms had felt around her. The tingle of desire she'd experienced in his arms had taken her completely by surprise, and once again, she really wished she hadn't ruined the moment by gasping. What might've happened if she had handled it better?

Now she would never know, but she fell asleep hoping she might get another chance to find out.

Hunter returned home to a ringing phone and ran to answer it.

"Hey there," a female voice said.

Hunter had no idea who it was until she started speaking again.

"I wanted to let you know that Tom has the kids this weekend if you want to get together."

Oh God, Lauren . . .

"Hunter? Are you there?"

"Yeah, I'm here. Sorry, just getting home and ran for the phone."

"It's been a while. I thought it might be fun."

It was always fun with Lauren, but that was all it had ever been or ever would be. After holding Megan in his arms, however briefly, he had no desire to spend time with any other woman. "I wish I could, but this weekend is crazy." In truth he didn't have any plans, but he hoped that would change between now and then.

"Do you?"

"What?" he asked, not following where she was going with the question.

"Wish you could?"

"Lauren . . ."

"Do you have someone else, Hunter?"

He ran his fingers through his hair repeatedly, wishing he could think of a way to get out of this conversation without hurting her feelings. She'd been a good friend to him for a couple of years. "I, um . . . I might. I don't know."

"You don't know? What does that mean?"

"It means," Hunter said with a sigh, "I can't see you anymore."

"You aren't sure if you have someone else, but you can't see me anymore. You realize how crazy that sounds, don't you?"

"Yes."

"Are you sure?" The question was tinged with sadness that made him feel bad.

He thought of Megan's gorgeous face, her teary blue eyes and the way she'd felt in his arms. "I'm sure." He was sure of nothing more than he wanted a chance with her, and that could never happen as long as he was still seeing Lauren on occasion.

"I'm really sorry to hear that. I thought we had a fun thing going."

"It was fun."

"So that's it? We're done?"

"I don't know what you want me to say." He eyed the left-over pizza still sitting on his counter, his stomach turning at the sight of it. Then he realized she was crying, and he felt like total shit. "Lauren, come on. We were never about anything more than a good time. I thought you knew that."

"I did know that, but that doesn't mean I don't have feelings for you."

"I wish I knew what to say, but I don't."

"Were you going to tell me that we were done?"

"I guess I'm a little confused here. I wasn't aware that we were in any kind of relationship, per se. We dated here and there, but that was the extent of it."

"That's not all we did."

"We had *fun*. Didn't we?"

"Yes, but—"

"No buts. That's all it was. Fun. Please don't make it into something more serious than that because we both know it wasn't."

"I'm going to go now."

"Lauren—"

"Bye, Hunter." When the line went dead he pressed the Off button and returned the cordless phone to the cradle. With his hands flat against the granite countertop, he tried to figure out how this night had gotten so far out of control in the course of two hours.

"At least I'm not stuck in my usual rut," he said with a laugh that turned to a grimace when he recalled the hurt in Lauren's voice. His conscience was clear where she was concerned. They'd had an uncommitted, once-in-a-while arrangement that usually revolved around the one weekend a month when her young kids were with their father.

He liked Lauren and had enjoyed the time they'd spent together, but he didn't think of her between visits. He didn't count the days or the weeks until he could see her again. Hell, he hardly even talked to her except for on the weeks they saw each other. He had nothing at all to feel guilty about, and she knew it. He'd intentionally kept his friendship with Lauren uncommitted and casual because he had feelings for someone else. So why did he feel like the world's biggest asshole after the conversation with her?

He wished he could call Hannah and air it out with her, but it was too late to call her. She'd know just what to say to make him feel better and to help him figure out what his next move with Megan ought to be. He stashed the leftover pizza in the fridge and wiped down the countertop before trudging upstairs, unbuttoning his shirt as he went.

Hunter stripped down to boxers, brushed his teeth and got into bed, his mind still whirling from the eventful evening. His thoughts kept coming back to that all-too-brief moment when he'd held Megan close to him and felt the click of two halves coming together in a perfect fit. He could still recall the scent of jasmine that had surrounded her, making him want to get even closer to her.

God, he had it bad for her, and the thought of her leaving town made him crazy. Mindful of her huge crush on Will, he hadn't acted on his feelings for her, but he'd always known she was right across the street, working every day at the diner, close by even if she had no idea how he felt about her.

He thought about the possibility of buying the diner from Nina and Brett. If only they hadn't just agreed to acquire additional acreage to expand the family's sugaring facility to accommodate expected demands from the new website. Between that and the cost of the website, the family business couldn't afford to take on something else. Not right now anyway. He needed time to pull the financing together, but time was the one thing he didn't have where Megan was concerned.

Hunter had money of his own put away, but it probably wasn't enough to buy the diner, and besides, how would that keep Megan in town? Hadn't she said it was time to shake things up? To maybe go to college? To get a "real" job?

He couldn't stand the panic that seized him at the thought of her slipping away before he ever had a chance to really know her. Lying awake for hours that night, he ran the numbers in his head but couldn't seem to arrive at a place where he could afford to solve all her problems by keeping the diner "in the family."

What if he found a way and she wasn't interested in continuing to work there with her sister out of the picture? And what in the hell did he know about managing a restaurant anyway? Not much, but he could learn. He could figure it out if it meant keeping her around.

He was already working sixteen hours a day to keep up with the demands of the family's vast business interests. What were a couple more hours if it meant the woman he cared for might stay in Butler rather than going God knows where to find this so-called real life she'd been missing out on?

By the time the sun began to streak between the slats in the blinds, Hunter was no closer to a solution, but he was more determined than ever to do *something*, *anything* to keep her from leaving town.

CHAPTER 4

━━◀◆▶━━

The cynic says, "One man can't do anything."
I say, "Only one man can do anything."

—John W. Gardner, former secretary of health,
education and welfare

Hunter waited until he was fairly certain Nolan would've left for the garage before he headed to Hannah's in the morning. He'd given up on sleep at about five A.M. and had a full pot of coffee in him by the time he pulled up to the stately Victorian where Hannah lived with her new husband.

Today he needed his sister and closest friend to tell him what the hell to do.

Hunter groaned when he saw Nolan's truck still parked in the driveway. He should've been long gone by now. Since it was a workday and Nolan would be heading out soon, it was probably safe to knock on the door. At least he hoped so . . .

He missed Hannah. She hadn't gone anywhere, but he'd tried to give her some space since she and Nolan had gotten together, which had left him on the outside looking in. The situation was reminiscent of when she and Caleb had first been together in high school and then in college at the University of Vermont when he'd had the miserable misfortune of being their unwanted third roommate. And hadn't those been good times? Thankfully Will had joined them the next year to save him from having to be alone with the lovebirds.

As Hunter used the big brass knocker on the door and heard it echo inside the house, he yearned for the "old days" when he could walk right into his sister's house without having to worry about seeing something that couldn't be unseen. Although, he was thrilled to see his sister happy again after suffering through the agonizing loss of Caleb, a man they'd all loved and respected. She'd chosen a great guy in Nolan, another close friend of Hunter's, and he couldn't be happier for both of them.

That didn't mean, however, that he didn't miss the ability to talk to his sister any time he wanted or needed to.

The door swung open, and Nolan greeted him in the uniform shirt he wore to work along with a pair of black jeans and work boots. His brother-in-law looked frazzled.

"Everything okay?" Hunter asked.

"Hannah's not feeling great today."

"Oh." Hunter was about to ask him to tell Hannah he'd call her later.

"Come in." Nolan walked away as he said the words, so Hunter followed him inside, closing the door behind him.

Nolan led him into the kitchen, where Hannah was seated at the table, wearing a robe and sipping a cup of tea. She was pale and had dark circles under her eyes that had Hunter immediately concerned for her health and that of her unborn child.

"Hey." She forced a weak smile for her brother. "What brings you out so early?"

Nolan stood next to Hunter, hands on his hips, the picture of agitation as he studied his wife.

"I was hoping to talk to you, but we can do it another time if you're not feeling well."

"I'm fine," she said with a pointed look for her husband. "Go to work."

"Stop trying to get rid of me."

"I'm not trying to get rid of you, but you've got a busy day at the garage, and I'm fine."

"You're not fine. You can't stop puking."

"Am I puking right now?"

"Hannah . . ."

"Nolan. Go to work."

"Fine. Call me if it gets worse."

"I will."

"Will you really?"

"Nolan!"

He leaned in to kiss her, lingering long enough for Hunter to find a picture on the wall that needed his full attention. "I'll be home to check on you at lunchtime."

"It's practically lunchtime now."

"I'll be back."

"Thanks for the warning. I'll make sure my boyfriend is gone by then."

"You're hilarious when you're not puking."

"And you're leaving so I can talk about what a pain you are to my brother."

"He was my best man. He wouldn't dare let you get away with that, would you, Hunter?"

"Um, well, she was my twin long before I was your best man."

The comment earned Hunter a bright, beaming smile from his sister.

"Should've known," Nolan muttered before he kissed Hannah again and headed for the mudroom.

They heard the garage door go up and come down and his truck start in the driveway.

"Go make sure he's really gone," Hannah said. "Yesterday he faked me out, came back in five minutes later and caught me puking again." She waved her hand. "Go check."

"Yes, ma'am. Is there anything else I can do for you, ma'am?"

"Just that."

Hunter did as she asked and went to look out the window of the sitting room, which overlooked the empty driveway. Returning to the kitchen, he said, "He's gone."

"Finally! He's driving me crazy."

"He's worried about you. So am I. You look like hell."

"Aww, shucks. Thanks! I'm pregnant, not dying. Vomit happens, especially in the first trimester." When she'd postponed the planned Labor Day opening of the new inn for war widows, named in Caleb's honor, she'd told her family it was because she was feeling so crappy. They'd also put off their planned move to Nolan's house, which would free up the Victorian to serve as the new inn.

"Seems to be happening a lot. What does the doctor say?"

"She said the same thing I did—it happens. She's keeping an eye on me with weekly appointments to make sure I don't get dehydrated." This was said as if it were no big deal to be so sick.

"You're all . . ." He waved his hand as he searched for the word he needed. "Zen or something. What the hell is wrong with you that you don't care that you're puking the day away?"

Laughing, she said, "I don't care about the puking. As long as the baby is fine—and he or she is doing great—that's all I care about. At the end of all of this, I get a *baby*. I really want this baby, and I'm willing to do whatever I have to."

Despite her pallor, despite the dark circles, she positively glowed with joy. "I'm happy for you, Hannah banana. It's nice to see you excited again and looking forward to something."

"I'm so excited it's not even funny." She rested her hand over her still-flat abdomen. "How will I *survive* for seven more months until I can meet this little person?"

"You never were known for your patience. I still remember being your lookout while you opened all your Christmas presents and rewrapped them. I used to be terrified we were going to get caught, but you always said the risk was worth it."

"I still say that."

The risk is worth it. Was it, he wondered?

"What's on your mind, Hunter?"

"Last night was kind of crazy."

She got up, poured him a cup of coffee, grimacing at the smell, and brought it to him before rejoining him at the table.

"Thanks. Why do you brew this stuff if you can't stand the smell of it?"

"My husband needs it to function, and I need him to function so I don't have to."

"Gotcha."

"Crazy how?" she asked, getting back to his initial statement.

"I worked late, and when I came out, Megan was there and she was crying."

"Wait. Megan was where? At the store?"

"Sitting on the back steps."

"In the dark? By herself?"

"Yeah. Nina and Brett are selling the diner and moving overseas so he can take a job teaching at a school in France. They'd just told Megan."

"Oh damn. Wow. She took it hard, huh?"

Nodding, he said, "I talked her into letting me give her a ride and feed her dinner, which we did at my house."

"You had her at your house?"

"Just long enough to eat some pizza and talk a little." *And to hug her*, he thought, but didn't say. That seemed too personal to share with anyone, even Hannah.

"Still. You had her at your house. That's a big development."

"She talked about moving away, finding a 'real' job and maybe going to college. She never got to do that because her parents died and everything got derailed."

"I remember that. Such a sad time for them."

"I can't let her leave town, Hannah. What'll I do if she leaves before . . . Well, before I get a chance with her?"

"Ah, so that's why you look like you haven't slept."

He stood because he couldn't remain seated any longer and contain the energy that zipped through him at lightning speed. The pot of coffee he'd consumed earlier only added to his edginess.

"How was I supposed to sleep when all I could think about was how I can convince her to stay?"

"Does she know how you feel about her?"

"Sort of."

"What does that mean?"

"I told her I liked her. A lot. And that I have for some time."

"You came right out and said that?"

"Yeah, I did. Was that the wrong thing to say?"

The last thing he expected Hannah to do was laugh, but she dissolved into uncontrollable giggles.

Infuriated and panic-stricken over the possibility that he might've done the wrong thing with Megan, Hunter propped his hands on his hips. "What the *hell* is so funny?"

"You are," she said between deep breaths and more laughter. "I've never seen you so flustered over a woman before. It's hilarious. You're always so perfect and put together, and today you're a hot mess. I love it."

"Stop your laughing and tell me what to *do*, will you, please?"

Hannah took a deep breath and wiped the tears from her eyes. "Fight for her, Hunter. If she's what you want, and I think she is, then make sure there's no way she doesn't know that."

"How do I do that?"

"First of all, tell her in no uncertain terms that you will be seriously bummed if she moves away. Then ask her out. Take her somewhere amazing. Treat her like a queen. You know what you need to do."

"She's really upset about Nina leaving and her job and everything."

"Then give her something else to think about. She'll appreciate that."

"You really think so?"

Hannah nodded. "It's the right thing to do if you're interested in her. I've never understood why you haven't asked her out before now. It's not like you're an ugly troll or anything. Thankfully, you grew out of your troll phase, and you're rather nice to look at these days."

He couldn't help but laugh at that. "Gee, thanks."

"I think you're gorgeous and wonderful and classy and charming and successful and smart and no woman will *ever* be worthy of you, in my humble opinion. You do know all that, don't you?"

"Well, shit, no, I didn't." And she'd given him a lump in his throat the size of an orange by saying it.

She stood and came over to him, reaching up to put her hands on his shoulders. "Every bit of it is true. Any woman would be lucky to have you, and if she's the one you want, then *go get her.*"

"It's not that simple, Han."

"Maybe it is."

"Until very recently, she had her heart set on Will. Don't forget that."

"She knows as well as anyone that her interest in him is—and always was—futile."

"She said as much last night. Even used the past tense to describe her crush on him."

"So what's stopping you from making a move?"

"I don't know, but something is."

"What're you afraid of?"

Leave it to Hannah to ask the tough questions. "Trying and failing. It feels more significant with her for whatever reason." He forced himself to look at her. "Lauren called me last night wanting to get together this weekend, and I told her I couldn't see her anymore."

"What did she say?"

"She cried."

"Oh, yikes. So she was attached?"

"I guess, although I don't see how she could be. I haven't even seen her in a month or more."

"She was probably holding out hope that your occasional thing would turn into more."

"Maybe. I don't know. I never led her on, Han. I swear I didn't."

"I believe you."

"She knew it wasn't going anywhere."

"Okay, so you've ended it with her, and Megan said she no longer has feelings for Will. That leaves me to wonder— *again*—what's standing in the way of you asking her out?"

"Nothing, I guess, except for this gigantic fear that she'll say no again."

"Wait, *whoa!* *Again?* You've asked her out before?"

"Once. Sort of."

"Explain. Immediately."

"Are you always this way or is it pregnancy hormones?"

"Always, as you well know." She waved her hand, urging him to come clean.

"It was a while ago. Couple of months, I guess, when Will was in New York helping Cameron move. She asked me if it was true they were moving in together and I said it was, and she got really upset. I told her it might help if she went out with someone else to get her mind off him. And yes, I know how pathetic that was, so you don't need to tell me. I suggested she might go out with me."

"What did she say?" Hannah asked, riveted. "And why have you not told me this before?"

"I don't tell you *everything.*"

"Since when do you not tell me everything?"

"Since *you* have stuff *I* don't want to hear."

"Fair enough," she said with a laugh. "But you still haven't told me what she said."

"Something to the effect of how does going out with his brother help her to forget about Will."

"Ouch."

"Right? That hurt, and afterward, I started to feel like maybe it wasn't going to happen with her no matter how badly I wanted it to."

"Am I allowed to play devil's advocate?"

"Why do you think I came here? I need you to tell me what to do."

"Which I find funny since you've never needed me to tell you what to do with women before."

"Because they never mattered as much as this one does."

"Are you in love with her, Hunter?"

The question made him feel like he'd been electrocuted or something equally unpleasant. "I don't know. How the hell am I supposed to know that when I've only ever hugged her once and—"

Hannah's eyes got very large. "*When* did you hug her?"

"It might've happened last night. When she was at my house."

"How am I supposed to work under these conditions when I'm only getting half the information?"

"Hannah . . . *Please*. Stop torturing me and *tell me what to do*."

"You need to stop torturing *yourself* and go for it. Tell her you want her and make it happen. Be relentless the way you are in business. Give her no choice but to fall for you the way you've fallen for her."

"What if she wants nothing to do with me? What if she's making plans, right now, to move away from here?"

"She's here today, and time's a-wasting. The diner closes between two and four every day. Where are you going to be at two o'clock today?"

The thought of showing up at her work and making a stand paralyzed him, which wasn't something he could recall ever happening before. He was known for being decisive and direct in his dealings with the people in his life—both personally and professionally. How was it possible that one woman could turn him into an impotent mute?

"Hunter. Answer me. Where are you going to be at two today?"

"At the diner."

"And what are you going to say to her?"

"I'm going to tell her I'd like to take her out the next time she has a free night, preferably tonight."

"That's right."

"And what will you say if she tells you she's busy?"

"I'll ask her when she will not be busy."

"Good. See, you can do this."

"What if I can't? What if I look at her and nothing comes out, and she thinks I'm an idiot?"

She gave him a peculiar look and for a second he thought she might be about to puke again.

"What? Why're you looking at me like that?"

"I've known you for thirty-five years, and I've never seen you like this. Ever. You're always the picture of calm, cool competence. To see you all unglued over a woman, well . . . It's different and probably long overdue."

"Don't get too excited yet. There's still time for me to screw this up in any number of ways."

"You're not going to screw it up. It's too important to you. Think of it like a business arrangement and treat it the way you would something for work."

"Because there's nothing more romantic than an accountant with debits and credits on his mind."

Smiling, she hugged him. "Do me a favor and don't mess this up. I'd hate to see you unhappy, and if you mess it up, you'll be unhappy."

Returning her embrace, he said, "I'll try not to."

"Now go do what you've got to do, and then call me and tell me everything. Well, everything that's not gross."

"I really hope there's some gross stuff before long."

"Eww. Go fight for what you want, and stop overthinking it. Just *do* it."

"You make it sound so simple, yet I recall having to practically shove you into the arms of a very enthusiastic mechanic who was *all* about you."

"We're not talking about me. We're talking about you."

"It's much more fun to talk about you, and besides you knew he'd be happy to hear you were into him. I have no idea how she feels about me."

She gave him a push toward the door. "Then go find out."

"I'm going."

"Good luck."

"Thanks."

"Not that you need it."

"Yes, I do need it. Don't jinx me."

She'd steered him all the way to the front door before he managed to turn around. She was freakishly strong for a girl, but then she always had been.

"Can I ask you one more thing?" he said hesitantly.

"Sure."

"Do you like her? Megan?"

"I don't know her very well."

"What you know of her . . ."

"I've seen her at her worst with Cameron, but I've also seen her apologize for that. I had a talk with her recently, and—"

"Back up. You had a talk with her? *When?* What did you say? Why?"

"That's four questions," Hannah said with a laugh. "I talked to her because I wanted to get to know her better."

"Why did you do that?"

"Because I knew you were interested in her, and I wanted to make an effort. For your sake."

"Thank you for doing that."

"So to answer your question, I don't dislike Megan. I feel sorry for everything she's been through, losing her parents the way she did. I can't imagine life without Mom and Dad, and we're thirty-five. I'd like to give her the benefit of the doubt at this point, but I'll be honest with you. She's going to need to prove herself worthy of my amazing brother. I'm willing to give her a chance because I want you to have absolutely everything and anything you want."

"Love you best of all, Hannah," he whispered gruffly, moved by her words, her devotion and the intense connection they'd shared their entire lives.

"Love you best of all, too. More than you'll ever know."

He hugged her and kissed her forehead. "Don't give Nolan too rough a time about being concerned for you. He loves you almost as much as I do."

"Yeah, yeah, whatever. He's a pain. Keep me posted on what happens with Megan, but leave out the gross stuff."

"You're jinxing me," he said as he walked down the stairs and headed for his SUV thinking about gross stuff and hoping there'd be something to report.

CHAPTER 5

*You've got to say, I think that if I keep working
at this and want it badly enough I can
have it. It's called perseverance.*

—Lee Iacocca, former chairman of
Chrysler Corporation

Hunter left Hannah's, thinking about everything she'd said. As an accountant and the fiduciary steward for his family's business interests, he was extremely risk averse. He didn't take unnecessary chances. He didn't gamble. As a rule, he didn't risk anything he couldn't afford to lose.

So taking a gamble on Megan went against everything he believed in, especially because he had no way to do his due diligence, to fully investigate all his many questions and options before he put his heart on the line with her.

Perhaps he was overanalyzing the whole situation, which wouldn't be the first time he'd done that. He couldn't help the way he was wired, and that wiring had served him well in his professional life. However, his instincts, which he usually trusted implicitly, were telling him that his overanalyzing tendencies might not be useful to him in this case.

He arrived at the office late, which was also not like him. Hunter was a stickler for family members setting the right example for the rest of their employees and insisted everyone get to work on time. So when he walked in to find an impromptu family staff meeting going on in the outer office, he wasn't surprised to see his siblings check their watches—even the ones who didn't wear watches.

"Yes, thank you," he said without actually looking at any of them as he headed to his office. "I know I'm late. First time for everything."

"And you look like hell, too," Will said. "What gives?"

"Nothing."

"Something," his sister Charley said, making the others laugh.

"Leave him alone," Ella said, earning a permanent place in Hunter's heart. "He gets to be human like the rest of us once in a while."

"No, he doesn't," Charley said. "If he becomes human, the whole operation will fall apart."

"I can *hear* you," Hunter said from his office.

"I intended for you to hear me," Charley retorted in her usual pain-in-the-ass fashion.

"Don't you people have work to do?" Hunter asked.

"You're not the boss of us," Charley said.

"Dad! Tell them to work!"

"Kids, get to work," Lincoln said from his office. "You're making your brother mad."

"Who's mad?" Elmer Stillman asked as he came up the stairs and into the reception area.

"Hunter," Charley said. "Rolled out on the wrong side of the bed this morning and was *late* to work."

"You don't say," Elmer replied. "It's the end of the world as we know it."

"Right?" Will asked with a laugh. "That's what we said, too."

"I expect better from you, Gramps," Hunter said, even though he was amused by his grandfather's contribution to the expected abuse. Sometimes working with family members truly sucked. Most of the time, however, it didn't.

Elmer came to his door, eyes twinkling with mirth. "I apologize profusely."

"Yeah, yeah," Hunter said with a grin. "The damage is done."

"May I come in for a minute?"

"Of course."

Elmer closed the door, which surprised Hunter.

"Everything okay?"

"Oh sure. I just have some personal business I'd like to discuss with you."

"What kind of personal business?"

"The financial kind."

"That's what I'm here for."

"And you do a damned fine job of it. You know how proud I am of you, don't you?" Before Hunter could form a reply to the unexpected compliment, Elmer continued. "Smartest kid I ever met grew up to be the sharpest, savviest man I know."

Hunter swallowed hard, unprepared for the wallop of emotion that accompanied such effusive words from a man he worshiped. "Thank you, Gramps. Means the world to me coming from you."

"It's all true. Every word. I trust your judgment, and I need some advice."

"Whatever I can do."

"I've got some money I'm looking to invest. I'm trying to find the right opportunity, but I'll be damned if I know where to look."

Hunter was immediately riveted by the possibility that his grandfather's desire to invest in something could keep Megan in Butler. However, he pushed that thought aside because acting in *his* best interest wouldn't necessarily be in his grandfather's best interest.

"Do you have any ideas of what you might like to do?" Hunter asked.

"I'm thinking a small business maybe. Something that could use the boost that comes with new capital, but I'd need you to help me hire someone to oversee the actual business. I'm enjoying my retirement too much to get bogged down in the details again."

"Right," Hunter said, tapping his mechanical pencil against his lip as he contemplated the convergence of ethics and desire. What to do? "I heard of one business in town that's closing unless they find new owners."

"Which one?"

"The diner."

"Yes, I heard that, too. Something about Brett and Nina moving overseas . . ."

Hunter eyed his grandfather warily. "What're you up to?"

"Up to? I'm talking to you about an investment I'd like to make. How does that make me up to something?"

"The timing is interesting."

"How so?"

"The whole town is probably abuzz with the news that Brett and Nina are leaving, and suddenly you're interested in investing in a business, something that could use an influx of capital. It's . . . curious."

"I still don't understand why."

Elmer was a formidable opponent when it came to sparring, and Hunter knew when he was outmatched by a master. He had no doubt his grandfather was up to *something*, but because it suited his own agenda, Hunter decided to play along.

"So you want to buy the diner?"

"Thought crossed my mind."

"And you didn't think to just say that when you first came in here?"

"I didn't want to limit my options if you knew of a better opportunity."

Elmer never blinked, yet Hunter still sensed he was being played. "Have you approached Brett and Nina?"

"Not yet. I was hoping you might handle that for me."

"I'll look into it," Hunter said casually even though his heartbeat accelerated at the possibility of a solution that might keep Megan around. If his grandfather bought the diner, they could hire her to run it for them or at least work there if she wasn't interested in management. Unless she had other plans altogether, a thought that left him feeling deflated.

Elmer withdrew a piece of paper from his pocket and handed it over to Hunter. "Offer them this."

Hunter unfolded the paper, his eyes bugging at the zeros. "You can't just go in there and make them a blind offer. We have to do our due diligence."

"Our due what?"

"*Diligence.* We need financial statements and an inspection of the building and equipment. We need profit and loss information for the last five years and . . ." At the sight of his grandfather's perplexed expression, Hunter stopped himself. "Didn't you once run a business?"

"Yeah, but we did it the old-fashioned way." Elmer winked at him. "A handshake was good enough."

"That's not good enough for me."

"Figured as much."

"Where've you been hiding all this money?"

"In tin cans I buried in the backyard. Where else?"

Hunter gaped at him. "Are you kidding me?"

"Yep," Elmer said with a deep guffaw. "You don't know everything, young man. I got a few secrets here and there."

"Apparently," Hunter said, equal parts annoyed and amused. "Do your due doodoo or whatever it is, and keep me posted."

"*Diligence*, and I will."

"Excellent." Elmer stood and headed for the door, a jaunty bounce in his step.

As his grandfather went out, his brother Will came in after exchanging greetings with Elmer. "What's he up to?" Will asked.

"Your guess is as good as mine," Hunter said. "But he's definitely up to something."

Will laughed. "Watch out. When he meddles, people end up engaged and living together and married."

Will's words set off a powerful sense of yearning in Hunter, for things he hadn't known he wanted before spending time with Megan the night before. He wanted *more*. He wanted to get to know her—what she liked and didn't like, what she enjoyed, what made her smile, what made her happy.

"Hunter? Where'd you go?"

He realized he'd zoned right out of the conversation. "Sorry. Did you need me for something?"

"I need your help with a very personal project."

Intrigued, Hunter said, "What kind of project?"

Will looked over his shoulder to make sure no one could hear him. "I want to buy an engagement ring for Cameron, but I have no idea where to begin."

"Oh wow, that's big news. Congrats."

"Thanks."

"You could ask Colton. He's probably better versed on diamonds and rings than I am."

"I can't tell him out of fear of it getting back to Cameron through Lucy."

"Lucy would never say anything."

"Still, it's kind of personal, and the fewer people who know the better. I want Cam to be completely surprised, and I want to get it right with the ring, which is where you come in. Will you help?"

"Of course. When do you want to go?"

"Maybe Saturday? I scouted out some jewelry stores in Rutland."

"I can do that." Hunter glanced up at his brother. "So you're really going to do this, huh?"

"I really am, and I can't wait to ask her. She's . . . Well, she's everything, and I want her to know that."

"I'm happy for you, Will. Truly. She's fantastic. We all love her."

"Yeah," Will said with a goofy smile that Hunter might've made fun of if he hadn't been so incredibly envious of his brother's obvious happiness. "She's pretty great."

"So Saturday it is."

"Thanks, Hunter. I really appreciate your help."

"Anytime. Let me ask you something . . ."

"Sure, what's up?"

"Did you really tell Megan she was focusing on the wrong Abbott brother?"

Before his eyes, Will seemed to squirm. "Maybe . . ."

"Did you do that to help me out or to get her off your back?"

"Some of both—not that she was ever 'on my back,' as you put it. She was a little much with Cam a few times, and I wanted that to stop. She was acting like a jealous ex when there was never anything between us."

"There really wasn't?"

"We made out once at a party the summer after she graduated. One minute we were talking about what she'd been through losing her parents, and she was crying and then her tongue was down my throat. It lasted all of five minutes. For me anyway."

"Her crush on you lasted ten years."

"I never encouraged it."

"How come?"

"I don't know. I just . . . I wasn't into her that way. She's a nice girl and everything—well, most of the time she is. I cut her some slack because of what she's been through, but the last time she got bitchy with Cam right in front of me. I'd had enough at that point."

Hunter thought about what Will had said and wondered why Megan had spent so much time yearning for a man who'd shown so little interest in her.

"What's going on, Hunter? Why all the questions about Megan?"

"I wanted to better understand what went on between the two of you."

"Why?"

"Because I'm going to ask her out."

"Oh. Really?"

"Yes, really."

"What brought this on all of a sudden?"

"It's hardly all of a sudden. At least not for me."

"I had no idea you were into her until Cameron figured it out and told me. I hope I never did anything to, you know, make it harder for you."

Hunter grunted out a laugh. "You being alive makes it harder for me with her."

"Yeah, sorry about that."

He waved off Will's apology. "No worries. You have a couple of other redeeming qualities."

"Just a couple?"

"Don't push your luck."

"I'll quit while I'm ahead and let you get some work done. Good luck with Megan."

"Thanks." After Will left, Hunter stared at the piles of folders and papers on his desk that required his attention. But rather than dive into work the way he usually did, he sat behind his desk and stared off into space thinking about the important question he needed to ask Megan, how he should ask it and what she might say.

News traveled with the speed of wildfire in a small town, and Butler was no exception. By the time the diner opened that morning, all their regulars already knew Brett and Nina were moving overseas and the diner was closing down after the weekend. Moving from table to table, refreshing coffee and taking orders the way she did every day, Megan did her best to dodge the endless questions about what she would do now that her sister—and her job—were going away.

Over the course of the first hour they were open, Megan must've said a hundred times that she was happy for her sister and Brett to have the opportunity to live overseas and no, she didn't know what her plans were after the diner closed.

As the breakfast rush started in earnest, Megan was too busy to answer questions, which was just as well because she'd run out of answers, and her emotions were swinging all over the place.

"Megan!" Butch, the cook, was never the jolliest of fellows, especially first thing in the morning, but he'd been extra surly this morning after Nina broke the news to him that his job was going away—soon.

Megan scurried toward the open window where several plates of pancakes and eggs waited for her to deliver them.

Butch grunted at her. "Move your ass, will you?"

"I'll move my ass if you shut your mouth."

He grunted again, half laugh, half aggravation, which meant business as usual between them.

She secretly loved Butch, who was big and burly with sleeve tattoos on both arms and bulky muscles, all of which he loved to show off by wearing tank tops year-round, even when it was freezing outside. Though they bickered nonstop most days, she knew there was nothing he wouldn't do for her, which he frequently proved when he fixed her car for free or gave her rides when it was snowing, allowing her to keep her eyes closed while she breathed deeply and tried to forget that she was in a car in the snow—her least favorite place to be. There wasn't much she wouldn't do for him either.

Butch was someone she would miss when the diner closed. Their relationship defied easy definition—it was part brother-sister, part angry coworker, part dysfunctional relative. He was a member of the family she and Nina had put together in the years since they lost their parents, and he was important to both of them. Nina had cried when she told him her news, which had made Megan cry, too. She felt like she was losing her family all over again as the closing of the diner loomed large in the immediate future, like a dark, threatening cloud.

Megan moved through the diner, tending to seventeen tables at once without having to think too much about what she was doing. Nina manned the register and kept the coffee pots full while busing tables, dealing with customers and handling takeout orders.

The three of them had a good groove, one that had worked well for years. It was funny, Megan thought, as she refilled the mugs of Hunter's grandfather, Elmer Stillman, and his friends Cletus Wagner and Percy Flanders, how you don't think much about the people in your daily life until they aren't going to be in your life anymore. People like Mr. Stillman, who always made her laugh with his homespun sayings about everything from coffee to moose to love.

And had she just thought of him as *Hunter's* grandfather rather than Will's? That was a first. Although Hunter hadn't been far from her thoughts all morning as she relived the night before over and over again. What he'd said to her, how he'd said it, the way he'd looked at her and the tenderness he'd shown her . . . It had all been so . . . unexpected.

Despite the usual morning chaos in the diner, exacerbated by Brett and Nina's news, she kept expecting him to walk through the door and realized she was watching for him, hoping to see him again sooner rather than later. He'd missed his usual seven-fifteen muffin run, which had her wondering if he'd skipped breakfast altogether.

"Are you all right, honey?" Mr. Stillman asked kindly—and quietly.

Megan realized she'd been standing by their table holding the coffeepot for at least a minute if not two. "I'm sorry to space out on you, and yes, I'm fine."

"Must've come as a surprise to you to hear your sister and her husband are moving overseas."

"It did."

"You'll miss her."

"Very much."

"Lots of people in this town care about you. I hope you know that."

"I do, thank you." He was such a dear, sweet man, and she would miss seeing him every day.

"My son's a lawyer in St. J," Percy said. "Looking for a new office manager. I can put in a word for you if you're interested."

"That'd be great. Thanks." The thought of driving all the way to St. Johnsbury in winter weather made her feel ill, but she was in no position to turn down any job opportunities. She wrote down her phone number on a slip from her order pad and handed it to Percy. "Have him give me a call if he'd like to."

"I'll do that."

She thought about her conversation with Elmer and Percy as she counted her tips after the lunch rush had come and gone with no sign of Hunter. Maybe he'd had a change of heart after last night. Maybe spending time with her one on one had shown him there was nothing all that special about her and he'd moved on. Surely a successful, self-assured man who looked like him could have any woman he wanted.

The thought made her sag into the booth she'd chosen in the far back corner, away from where Brett and Nina were having lunch and whispering with excitement about their big adventure. Butch had gone home after lunch but would be back in a couple of hours to cook dinner. Megan was done for the day. Two other waitresses took alternating days on the dinner shift.

They had a routine they followed, a routine that would be interrupted when the diner ceased to be the center of their existence. What would she do without this place to come to every day? That thought made her feel panicky. It wasn't the money that worried her. Their parents' life insurance had ensured that she and Nina were quite comfortable, so technically she wouldn't have to work right away. The diner had been about much more than earning a living to both of them for as long as Nina and her husband had owned it.

Now it was about to disappear from her life almost as suddenly as her parents had. If she stayed here any longer, she was going to cry again, and she wouldn't do that to Nina or Brett. She refused to rain on their exciting parade. Collecting the cash from the tabletop, she shoved the rolled bills into her purse and headed for the door.

"I'll see you at home."

"Are you okay?" Nina asked, tuned into her as always.

"Yep. Just got a couple of things to do, and now's as good a time as any." In truth, she had nothing to do, and after the diner closed, she'd have days full of nothing to do until she figured out her next move. Thinking of the empty, pointless days ahead brought back the panicked feeling as she pushed through the door and nearly smashed into Hunter, who was on his way in.

He reached out to grab her, keeping them both from tumbling down the stairs. "Whoa. What's the rush?" Hunter took a closer look at her, slipped an arm around her shoulders and guided her down to the sidewalk. "Walk. Talk. Tell me what's wrong."

How could he know with just a quick glance that she was teetering on the edge of another meltdown? He didn't give her time to answer him before he guided her along the sidewalk, his arm around her shoulders drawing inquisitive looks from people they encountered along the way—people who knew them both and were clearly stunned to see them together.

And were they *together* or was he just being nice again? How the heck was she supposed to know? But God it felt good to be surrounded by him and the scent of class that clung to him in the form of cologne that was probably ridiculously expensive. She barely knew him but had no doubt he didn't go for the cheap stuff. That wasn't him.

His arm was heavy and muscular around her, holding her against his side as he walked with no apparent destination in mind. As they passed Nolan's garage, Hunter's new brother-in-law stopped what he was doing to watch them go by. Hunter didn't seem to notice Nolan watching them, but Megan did.

They continued along Elm Street, past the art gallery and coffee shop, the pizza place and the barn where Hunter's brother Lucas did his woodworking. As usual, Lucas was out front, watching the world go by as he created his masterpieces. When he saw his oldest brother with his arm slung around Megan's shoulders, Lucas froze, his mouth open in surprise as they went by. Hunter seemed as oblivious to Lucas as he'd been to Nolan. His entire focus was on her and wherever he was taking her.

Megan had to admit it felt pretty good to be scooped up by Hunter Abbott and escorted through town with his arm around her. At some point during their walk—or forced march or whatever you wanted to call it—she'd forgotten that she'd been on the verge of tears when she left the diner.

With the way things happened in Butler, by the time she returned to the diner in the morning, the questions would've shifted from the diner closing to what was she doing with Hunter Abbott's arm around her. That thought brought a small smile to her face as she ventured a glance up at him. His handsome face was set in an unreadable expression. It stayed that way until they reached the playground at the far end of town, where he directed her to a bench and encouraged her to sit.

CHAPTER 6

⮞◀◆▶⮜

*The entrepreneur always searches for change,
responds to it, and exploits it as an opportunity.*

—Peter F. Drucker, management consultant

He came down next to her, his arm stretched along the back of the bench as he turned to face her. "Now tell me what's wrong."

She wasn't sure if it was the swift walk through town, his nearness or the intense way he looked at her that left her breathless. She suspected it had far more to do with his nearness and the way he looked at her than with the walk.

"Same thing as last night. It was a tough day at the diner. The word is out that we're closing, and people are upset."

Hunter reached out to tuck a strand of her hair behind her ear, the gesture so tender and intimate that Megan found herself wanting to lean into him again, to breathe in that scent, to let him comfort her, to make her feel something other than devastated by yet another sudden, unexpected change in her life.

"You were about to cry when you nearly crashed into me, weren't you?"

She stared at him, amazed by how well he understood her. "Maybe." Megan cleared her throat and forced herself to look at him. "I'm not usually so quick to cry. It's just this whole thing has been . . . It's hard to imagine life without the diner. I know it's just coffee and eggs to the rest of town, but to me . . . To Nina and me, it's been like a family."

"I understand that. I feel the same way about the people who work with us at the store and the customers. They're part of my life the same way my parents and siblings and grandfather are."

She appreciated that he understood why she was upset and didn't seem to judge her for being emotional about a diner, of all things. "Your grandfather was very sweet to me this morning, but then he always is. He's one of my favorites."

"Funny you should say so today of all days."

"Why?"

"He came to see me this morning. Apparently, he's interested in speaking to Brett and Nina about buying the diner."

"He is? Really? So he would be the new owner?"

"If they can work out a deal."

"He wants to *work* there?"

Hunter laughed. "Not exactly. He wants me to run it—me and you, if you're interested."

"Oh," Megan said, stunned and slightly euphoric at the possibility. "So like we would work there together?"

"Sort of. In his perfect scenario, you'd do what Nina does now, you'd hire someone to wait tables and I'd help you with the business stuff. If you were interested in my help, that is. I'd probably need you more than you'd need me. I have no idea how to run a restaurant."

"Why would your grandfather want to do that? He's retired and enjoying his life."

"Don't let on that I told you, but I think it has something to do with him wanting you to spend time with me."

"I don't understand," she said, though her heart beat a little faster at the way he looked at her when he said that. His expression was one of amusement and exasperation and affection.

"He's a bit of a matchmaker in his spare time, and he's tuned into the fact that I'm interested in you, so he's trying to make it a bit easier on me—and he's trying to make sure you don't run away before we have a chance to spend some time together."

"And he *told* you this?"

"Nope. I know him and what he's been up to lately with my siblings."

"What's he been up to?"

"It's not only him. It's my dad, too. The two of them think we don't know they've decided we need some help in the romance department if they ever want to have grandchildren and great-grandchildren. They brought Cameron to town hoping she'd connect with one of us, and you know how that worked out. They messed with Hannah's battery so she'd have no choice but to call Nolan."

Megan laughed at the thought of the two older men tinkering with a battery to move a romance along. "That's really devious."

"They're good. I've got to give them credit. They arranged for Colton to spend a week in New York City when they found out he was interested in Lucy, and now they're engaged."

"So it's your turn?"

"Something like that." He raised a rakish eyebrow in an expression that made her mouth go dry. "How do you feel about being shamelessly manipulated?"

"I do love your grandfather, and your dad is really nice, too."

"For a couple of schemers, they're pretty cool."

"Your grandfather is really planning to buy the diner so you and I might . . ." Her face heated with embarrassment. She had no idea how to phrase her question.

"Have a chance to spend some time together? Yeah, exactly."

"Isn't that a lot of money for him to spend on matchmaking?"

"He probably sees it as a 'kill-two-birds-with-one-stone' opportunity. The diner is an established business, and with the store's website going live soon, we should have an uptick in visitors who'll need somewhere to eat while they're in town. And if it means he gets to throw you and me together at the same time, it's a win-win for him."

"Were you coming to talk to Brett and Nina when I almost crashed into you?"

"Among other things."

"What other things?"

"I had something I wanted to ask you."

"What?"

Was it her imagination or did he seem nervous?

"I wondered if you might go out with me. Like on a date. A real date."

"Oh." As she stared at his handsome face and the dark eyes staring back at her, awaiting her reply, Megan experienced a flutter of anticipation and that odd tingle of desire that reminded her of the night before when he'd put his arms around her.

"You're kind of killing me here," he said with a small grin. "It took all my courage to ask you that, and now you're leaving me hanging."

"You were really nervous about asking me out?"

"Incredibly nervous."

"Why?"

"Because you might say no."

She could see now he was truly worried about her turning him down, and felt herself melt at the thought of such an amazing guy being nervous about asking her out. "I'd love to go out with you, Hunter, but you should know . . ."

"What should I know?"

"I don't want to get serious with anyone. I'm just not wired that way, and it's important you know that at the outset. The last thing I'd want is to hurt you or—"

He laid a finger gently over her lips. "Let me worry about me. I'm talking about dinner, not a lifetime commitment."

Acute embarrassment made her face go hot. "I didn't mean to make it into more, it's just . . . I . . . I want to be fair to you."

As if she hadn't spoken, he said, "When do you want to go out? Tonight?"

Megan laughed at his overly eager reply. "Sure." How was it possible she'd been about to cry a few minutes ago and now he had her laughing? He was cute and funny and it would be fun to spend some time with him—as long as it was fun and nothing more than that. "I could do something tonight. What do you have in mind?"

He opened his mouth to reply but then closed it. "I have no idea. I hadn't gotten past the asking part."

She covered her mouth so he wouldn't see her laughing at him.

"Smooth, huh? I finally work up the nerve to ask you out and haven't got the first idea of where to take you."

"I'm sure you'll think of something between now and later."

"I will. I promise."

"It's really nice of you to ask."

"It's really nice of you to say yes." He reached for her hand and then looked up at her. "Is this okay?"

How had she never noticed how sweet and sexy he was? Not in the same way as his brother, but different in a good way. "It's okay."

"Should we go talk to your sister about the diner?"

"We can do that."

"You'll stay, won't you? If we keep the diner open. You'll stay?"

She stared at him, startled by the intense way he looked at her. "Is that why you're doing this?"

"I'd be lying if I said I wasn't interested in keeping you in town." After a pause, he added, "Does that bother you?"

"No," she said softly. "It flatters me, but I meant it when I said I don't want to be serious with anyone."

"I heard you. So you're interested in helping to keep the diner open?"

"I'm not sure what I'm going to do." She looked away from him, noticing the people on the sidewalk who were taking an interest in the two of them sitting close to each other on the park bench. News of this conversation would be all over town, if it wasn't already. "Since Nina told me she was leaving, I've been thinking a lot about what I should do next."

"What do you want to do?"

"That's just it. I don't know. Percy said something about a job in St. J, but that's a long shot. I don't have the experience they probably want."

"Well, helping us at the diner would buy you some time to think about it, among other things."

"What other things?"

"You'd get to hang out with me." Standing, he gave her a gentle tug to encourage her to come with him. She expected him to release her hand, but he tucked it into the crook of his elbow and headed back the way they'd come.

"You're making a rather public declaration."

"Am I?"

"You know you are."

"Do you care?"

"No, not really."

"There isn't anyone else, is there?"

"You know there isn't. When would I have had time for a boyfriend when I was so busy dreaming about your brother?"

Hunter winced. "How about we not talk about that?"

"I'm sorry. I didn't mean to hurt your feelings."

"You didn't, but what guy wants to feel like he's competing with his brother?"

"You're not competing with him."

"No?"

She shook her head. "There was never anything between us except for me and my imagination."

"I hope there'll be much more than that between you and me. I have a pretty active imagination when it comes to you."

She stopped walking and turned to him. "I'm worried you didn't hear what I said before." His words along with his nearness made her feel overly warm as they walked along the sidewalk. People were staring at them, not that Hunter seemed to notice.

"I heard you, and I understand you believe you're incapable of anything that smacks of serious. But I don't want you to have any doubts that I'm interested, and I want to get to know you better."

"What if you don't like what you find out about me?"

"That's not going to happen."

"How can you be so sure?"

"Well, obviously I can't be totally sure, but I have a good feeling where you're concerned."

"What kind of good feeling?"

"The kind that tells me to trust my instincts, that it'll be well worth my time to get to know you."

"And these instincts are reliable or have been in the past?"

"Extremely."

"It must be nice to have an internal compass to guide you. Where can I get one of them?"

"You can borrow mine any time you need it."

The comment made her laugh for the third—or was it the fourth—time since they left the diner. He was charming and smooth, but not in a creepy way. No, he was smooth in the way of a man who knew himself and was comfortable in his own skin. She was finding that to be an exceptionally appealing quality.

Outside the diner, Hunter straightened his arm and put his hand on her lower back to guide her inside. He did this so naturally, like he did it all the time, or like he wanted to.

She was still processing those thoughts when they entered the diner, where Nina was seated at a table going through a stack of papers with the checkbook, a calculator and her ever-present cup of coffee on the table.

"Hey," she said. "Thought you went home. Oh, hi, Hunter."

"Hi, Nina."

Nina took a closer look as if trying to determine exactly where Hunter's hand was on her sister's back—upper or lower. Definitely lower. Nina's mouth fell open and her eyes widened, but she tamped down her reaction before it could venture into the realm of embarrassing.

"What's up?" Nina asked.

"Hunter would like to talk to you about the diner."

Nina gestured for them to join her on the other side of the booth.

He let her go in ahead of him. Megan wondered if he purposely sat close enough to her that his thigh was pressed against hers.

"What about the diner?" Nina looked from Megan to Hunter and then back to her sister, a million questions reflected in her dark brown eyes. Whereas Megan had gotten their father's cool patrician coloring, Nina was a replica of their Italian mother, right down to the dark curls and olive-toned skin that Megan had envied all her sunburned life.

"On behalf of my grandfather, I'm inquiring about the potential purchase of the diner."

Nina's eyes lit up with surprise and what looked like pleasure. "Oh, that's wonderful! Except—and don't take this the wrong way because I love Elmer—is he really up for running a business at this point in his life?"

"Hell no," Hunter said with a laugh. "He's delegating that to me, which is why I'm here talking to you rather than him."

"So how would this work exactly?"

"Our thought was to hire Megan to run the place for us, and she could hire someone to replace her." Hunter didn't let on that it was *his* plan, not *their* plan. His grandfather had never mentioned Megan's name.

"Interesting," Nina said, again letting her gaze dart between them.

To his credit, Hunter never blinked as he withstood Nina's scrutiny. Megan knew this because she was watching him almost as intently as Nina was. Megan wanted to lean into him, to breathe in that cool, expensive scent, and wished he'd put his arm around her again. She'd liked that and wondered if he'd do it again later when they went out together.

The thought of going out with him, on a real date, gave her butterflies in her belly—the good kind of butterflies, the excited-about-something kind of butterflies.

"Megan?"

She realized Nina had been speaking to her while she'd been off with the butterflies. "Sorry. What did you say?"

"I asked if you're up for running this place."

"I'm sure I could be. As I told Hunter when he talked to me about it earlier, it could give me something to do while I figure out my plans."

Only because Hunter was sitting so close to her did Megan feel his body go tense. What was that about?

"Naturally," he said, "we'd like to see the financials, including the profit and loss, and have the building and equipment inspected before we make an official offer."

"I understand. I'll need a day or two to get the financial info together. You're welcome to schedule the inspection in the meantime. If you could make it between two and four P.M., I'd appreciate that."

"Will do."

"I'll drop everything off to you when I have it."

"Could you let me know if you receive other interest? We'd like to be considered serious contenders."

"Absolutely. Thank you for this and for including Megan in your plans."

Hunter looked at her then, smiling with such warmth and tenderness that Megan nearly swooned. No man had ever looked at her quite that way. "I'd better get back to my other job before they fire me," he said. "I'll see you later?"

"Yes. I'll call you when I get home."

He withdrew his wallet from his back pocket, took out a card and borrowed Nina's pen to write something on the back of it. Then he held it out to Megan. "I'll be at the office until about seven. That's my extension." He flipped it over to reveal the number he'd put on the back. "And then at home."

She took the card from him, letting her fingers brush against his and enjoying the flash of awareness in his eyes from that fleeing contact. What would it be like . . . *Okay, don't go there.* Not with Nina watching this entire transaction and about to pounce on her with a thousand questions.

"Okay," Megan said as Hunter got up to leave. The butterflies were doing the backstroke in her belly, making her feel fluttery and overly warm.

"Talk to you then. See you, Nina."

"Bye, Hunter. I'll be in touch."

"Look forward to it."

With a last smile for Megan, he left the diner, the bells on the door jingling as he went out.

After a brief pause, Nina said, "Start talking. Right now."

CHAPTER 7

Live daringly, boldly, fearlessly.

—Henry J. Kaiser, industrialist

Amused by her sister's directive, Megan thought about making Nina drag it out of her, but she was equally eager to talk about what'd happened, and Nina would always be her first choice of confidants. "He asked me out."

"When?"

"Just now. In the park."

"Oh my God! That's awesome. He's so hot. Crazy hot."

"You think so?"

"Are you *serious*? Everyone thinks so. Look at him—all class and buttoned-down hotness. I bet he's a wild man in bed."

"Nina! You did not just say that!" And Megan would never admit to anyone that she found the thought of Hunter being a wild man in bed incredibly arousing.

"Don't even try to tell me you haven't thought of that."

"Well, not exactly in those terms, but now that you mention it . . ."

Nina's loud laughter echoed off the walls of the empty diner. "Good for you, Meggie. He's a great guy. You couldn't ask for better."

"Don't get all excited. I already told him I'm not looking

for anything serious." The thought of not being able to have these conversations with her sister whenever she needed to threatened to ruin her good mood, so Megan didn't let her mind go there. Not today. Not when she had something fun to look forward to for once.

"Why would you say that to him before you even go out with him?"

"Because." Megan tried not to squirm under her sister's intense glare. No one saw right through her the way Nina did. "I don't want it. It's not my style, and he'd be crazy to fall for me."

"May I say something that might make you mad, but I still think it needs to be said?"

"How can I resist after that intro?"

Nina pushed aside the paperwork, the calculator and her precious coffee mug to reach across the table for Megan's hands. "The crush you had on Will."

Will was about the last thing Megan wanted to talk about after making plans with his brother. "What about it?"

"I have a theory about that."

"Which is?"

"This is the part that's going to make you mad. I've wanted to say this for a long time, but it was never the right time. Now that you've got a date with Hunter, I think you need to hear it."

"When have you ever held back with me?"

"Only when I was afraid I might hurt you."

"You've opened Pandora's box now. You may as well put it out there."

"This is my opinion and only my opinion, but I think you were using Will as a way to avoid real relationships with other guys. As long as you had yourself convinced he was the one for you, you could hide behind him almost like a shield to keep anyone from getting too close."

Skewered by Nina's assessment, Megan stared out the window. Was that true? Had she really done that? If she had, it wasn't a conscious thing that she'd set out to do intentionally.

Nina took a deep breath, released Megan's hands only long enough to secure her dark curls behind her ears—something she did when she was nervous—and pressed on. "And I know why you did it."

"Oh please. Don't stop now."

"You're pissed. I knew you would be, and I'm really sorry, but I think you did it so you'd never be hurt again the way you were when we lost Mom and Dad. And I understand that. Believe me, I do. If I hadn't already been involved with Brett when they died, I might've done exactly the same thing to avoid ever again feeling the way I did then."

Megan was unable to contain the tears that slid down her cheeks. "So you're saying I created an imaginary boyfriend for myself so I wouldn't make the mistake of having real feelings for someone else?"

"Yes. Exactly."

Megan wiped away the tears, irritated by them.

"You're mad, right?"

"No."

"It's okay if you are. I'd understand that."

Megan picked up the spoon sitting next to Nina's mug and flipped it between her fingers. "You're not wrong, but I didn't do it intentionally. I never said to myself, 'If you fall into a mad, crazy crush with Will Abbott, who has no real interest in you, you'll be able to avoid the possibility of getting hurt with someone else.' It wasn't like that."

"I know it wasn't, honey. And the only reason I even brought it up is because I've seen the way Hunter looks at you."

Megan sat up straighter. "You have? When? Why didn't you say anything?"

"I've noticed Hunter's interest in you for years now, and I didn't say anything because you weren't ready to hear it. Not until recently when you seemed to accept that Will is in love with someone else, and you can't hide behind him anymore."

"I wasn't doing that! I wasn't hiding. I was right here every day, out in the open."

"With your Will shield out in front, making you unapproachable to Hunter or anyone else who might've been interested. You put off the 'keep away' vibe. It was loud and clear. Then Will went and fell in love, and suddenly you can't use him that way anymore, and you've become more accessible—and more vulnerable."

"What the hell, Nina? Did you go to shrink school when I wasn't paying attention or something?"

"Nope," Nina said with a smirk. "I speak Megan."

Megan suddenly felt very sorry for herself. "Who's going to speak Megan when you're in France?"

Nina crossed her arms and sat back against the booth, a satisfied smile on her face. "Perhaps the oh-so-sexy and oh-so-interested Hunter Abbott?"

The thought of that sent a lightning rod of heat through Megan, making all the most important parts of her tingle with anticipation. "I shouldn't even go out with him if he's that interested in me."

"Ahhh," Nina said, her smile wide and knowing. "If the pink in your cheeks is any indication, you like the idea of him being that interested in you."

"It's flattering. I won't deny that. Like you said, he's a really nice guy, but he deserves someone who can give him what he needs. He's a 'forever' kind of guy, and that's so not me."

"And easy on the eyes."

"Did you hear anything I just said?"

"I heard it, and I hate that you have yourself convinced that it's not going to work out before you even have your first date with him. I want you to give him a *real*, honest chance, Megan. I want you to put aside all the fears about what *might* happen and go for it. Let him in. He obviously cares for you very much, and you'd be safe with him."

"Does the thought of me being with him make it easier for you to leave?"

"Hell yes it does. I almost talked Brett out of taking the job because I was so afraid to leave you alone. But he reminded me that you're going to be twenty-eight soon, and eventually we'll have to cut the cord. I really am sorry to do this to you so suddenly. That wasn't the plan at all. It just happened that way."

"I know, and Brett's right. It is time. As long as I could hide behind you and Will and everything that was keeping me safe, I wasn't under any pressure to take chances." She forced herself to meet her sister's gaze. "I miss them every day."

"Oh, honey, so do I. Every single day. We'll always miss them. But I want you to have what they had, what I have with Brett. I don't want you to be so afraid of losing someone again that you don't give your heart to anyone."

"What if I take this big risk you're advocating with Hunter, and then something happens to him, too?"

"That's always a possibility. What is it that Elmer likes to say? 'Life is a fatal illness.'"

Megan smiled at that. Elmer Stillman was a font of wisdom and corny sayings, and Megan adored him.

"But Hunter is a young guy," Nina continued, "with most of his life still ahead of him. You can either take a chance that it's all going to be fine or continue to hide out. I'll support you no matter what you do, but you should know I'm rooting for Hunter."

"Hey! That's not fair. You're *my* sister!"

Nina shrugged, her smile smug and satisfied. "And I'm on Team Hunter all the way."

"Traitor."

"Not at all. How much you want to bet you'll be thanking me some day for taking his side?"

"I've learned not to challenge you on these things. It always costs me money."

"Ha!" Nina laughed. "That's why I'm the much older and wiser sister."

"Whatever."

Nina propped her chin on her upturned fist. "So where's he taking you? I bet it's somewhere amazing and classy with white tablecloths and candles."

The thought of that pushed Megan into panic mode. "I have nothing to wear to a place like that!"

"Then let's go shopping."

"You don't have time."

"For this, I'll make time. Let's go."

Megan allowed Nina to take her by the hand and march her out of the diner. If nothing else came of this outing, at least she'd be prepared for her big date—and she'd get to spend some precious time with her beloved sister.

Hunter was completely useless for the rest of the day. With financial statements for the month of August due at the end of the week, he needed to focus. In fact, if he was a day or two late with the financials, no one would notice but him. But he prided himself on his timely reporting and didn't want to get in the habit of dropping the ball. At the end of the day, he attended the weekly staff meeting, which often turned into a family bitch session about what was going on throughout the company.

He usually took advantage of the meeting to ask questions about everyone's ongoing projects, but today, all he wanted to ask was where he should take Megan on their momentous date. Tapping his mechanical pencil against his lip, he ran through all the nice places he could think of, dismissing one after the other as not quite right for what he had in mind.

"Hunter," his father said, barking out his name.

Hunter snapped out of his thoughts to find everyone looking at him. "What?"

"Are you listening?"

"No, not really."

They stared at him.

"What the hell is wrong with you this week?" Charley asked.

"Truthfully, I have a date tonight, and I have no idea where to take her. It's an *important* date, so it has to be somewhere really good. What do you guys think?"

A cloud of stunned silence descended upon the normally rowdy group.

"An important date," Charley said, breaking the silence after a full minute of everyone staring at him. "With *who*?"

Hunter was already regretting the huge error he'd made by telling them about the date. "Megan."

"Ohkhh," Ella said. "You finally asked her out?"

"Megan-from-the-diner *Megan*?" Wade asked.

"Yes," Hunter said, not sure he liked his brother's tone.

"Isn't she kinda, I don't know, sort of . . . cranky?" Wade asked.

If looks could kill, the one Hunter sent his younger brother would've finished him off. "You did hear me say I'm going out with her, right?"

Behind her hand, Charley snorted with laughter.

"Sorry," Wade said, but he didn't look sorry. Not one bit sorry.

"Megan has turned over a new leaf recently," Will said. "She's been very pleasant and friendly, and I'm glad you finally asked her out. You've wanted to for a long time."

Hunter wanted to hug Will for giving Megan such a ringing endorsement, especially in light of his own history with her, such as it was. "Thank you," he said gruffly.

Will nodded and then sat back in his chair. "Where should you take her?"

"How much time do you have?" Lincoln asked.

"Um, a couple of hours, I guess. Typical date."

"So you couldn't take her over to Burlington for dinner and then stay at the lake?"

"Overnight?" Hunter asked, even as the idea of spending a night alone with Megan made him want to drool. Among other things.

Lincoln shrugged. "It's not like you two are kids. You're both mature adults."

"It's our *first* date, Dad. I hardly think suggesting an overnight in Burlington is going to get me a second date."

"You never know," Will said, rubbing his whisker-roughened jaw thoughtfully.

Cameron came rushing into the conference room, out of breath and flushed. "Sorry I'm late. I was up on the mountain with Colton, and we got sidetracked."

"Doing what?" Will asked with a scowl.

Cameron patted his face indulgently. "Nothing that will get me in trouble with you or him in trouble with Lucy. We were reviewing the images for the website and trying to choose the best ones. I couldn't believe how late it'd gotten. What'd I miss?"

"Hunter has a date with Megan," Will said, "and he can't figure out where to take her. Dad suggested dinner in Burlington and staying at the lake."

Cameron zeroed in on Hunter. "You have a date with Megan! This is huge news!"

"Am I the only one who had no idea he liked her?" Wade asked.

"Not the only one," Charley said.

"I told you that," Hunter said.

"Um, no you didn't. I think I would've remembered."

Their mother, Molly, came breezing into the conference room. "Remembered what?"

Lincoln jumped up to greet his wife with a hug. "What brings you here, my love?"

She put her arms around him and leaned into his embrace. "I'm looking for you."

"You found me."

"Tell me what we're talking about," Molly said, homing in on the fact that something was up. Her antennae were always well calibrated where her children were concerned.

"Hunter's got a date with Megan," Will said.

Hunter wished he could rewind the last ten minutes and transport himself out of this room, away from the office and the store, to a place where he wasn't surrounded by people who wanted to know every detail of his life. But it was his own fault they were up in his grill. He'd all but invited them by blurting out his plans with Megan. He never should've told them he had the date in the first place. Since the meeting was all but over, he gathered his stuff and stood.

"Where're you going?" Charley asked. "We haven't figured out where you should take her yet."

"I'll take care of it myself," Hunter said. "Forget I said anything."

"Right . . ." Charley sat back in her chair and smiled smugly. "As if."

As the others laughed at Charley's comment, Hunter took the opportunity to exit the conference room. In his office, he dropped the files on his desk he'd taken to the useless meeting and turned off his computer, more than ready to end this unproductive day.

CHAPTER 8

◄►

Long-range planning works best in the short term.

—Doug Evelyn, museum director

Molly came into Hunter's office and shut the door behind her.

"Not you, too," Hunter said.

"I haven't come to pile on."

"That's a relief."

"I have a suggestion."

"I'm listening."

"Get in the car and drive. Go off without a plan and see where the road takes you."

Hunter tugged at his collar, which suddenly felt tight and restrictive. "That's not how I roll."

"Oh, I know," she said, laughing, "but it's also not at all like you to tell your siblings you have a date and are conflicted about where to take her."

Hunter sat in his chair and let out a deep breath. "True. Nothing about this is typical."

A satisfied smile stretched across his mother's face.

"What?"

"It's just nice to see, that's all."

"What's nice to see?"

She pushed off the door and came around his desk to lean against it. "You, taking a chance on something you can't fully analyze and dissect ahead of time."

"I hate that I can't do that."

Molly tossed her head back and laughed. "I bet you do."

"Glad you find it so funny."

"It's not funny so much as it is amusing and endearing." She rearranged his hair the way she had nearly every day of his life growing up. Despite her best efforts, his hair continued to do its own thing. It had been years, decades perhaps, since she'd tried to tame it. "I love seeing you all in knots over a woman."

"She's . . . She's special. I don't want to screw it up."

"She's very special."

"You really think so?" Hunter couldn't believe how desperate he was for his mother's approval, even though he certainly didn't need it at his age.

"I really do. I'll never forget how gracefully she and Nina handled their crushing loss. When they had to be dying inside, they made sure the funeral portrayed the wonderful people Rick and Lori were."

Needing something to do with all the energy coursing through him, Hunter rubbed at the late-day stubble on his jaw. "I don't think she's ever gotten over it."

"Who would? I'm almost sixty years old and my father is still at the center of my life. The day he isn't there anymore . . . Well, I don't have to tell you."

"No, you don't." The thought of life without Elmer Stillman was like trying to imagine a day without sunshine. "He's considering buying the diner, you know."

"He's *what*?"

"He's in discussions to buy the diner."

"Why?"

"The truth?"

She raised the formidable eyebrow that had kept ten children straight all their lives.

"I think he's doing it because he knows I'm interested in Megan and wants to keep her in town."

"Are you shitting me?"

Hunter had a formidable eyebrow of his own that served as his reply.

"That old schemer," Molly said with a bark of laughter. "He sure has been busy lately."

"With some help from your husband."

"What do you know?"

"Just that the two of them seem to have taken it upon themselves to 'help us along' in the romance department. They think they're so clever, but they're not really fooling anyone."

"You can't argue with their results though. A wedding, an engagement and a shack-up all in one year. Not bad."

"Not bad at all, and I get the feeling they're looking to add me to their list of successes."

"Are you bothered by that?"

"Not as much as I would be if I hadn't been waiting forever for this chance with Megan. I spent a sleepless night trying to figure out how we could buy the diner to keep her in town, and then along came Gramps with a solution to my problem. I can't say that bothered me much at all."

Molly smiled at him. "What did Megan have to say about it?"

"That it would give her some time to figure out her next move." As he said those words, a sinking feeling came over him. The thought of her moving on to something—or some-one—else made him feel ill. "She's been right across the street all this time, and I couldn't work up the nerve to ask her out."

"Because you knew she was interested in Will."

"Partially. But also because it's always seemed more significant with her. I don't know why. I don't even know her all that well when it comes right down to it. I just know how I feel when she's around."

"You need to trust that feeling, Hunter."

"I'm trying to, but she's already warning me off her."

"How so?"

"She said she's not interested in being serious with anyone."

"She's scared, honey. She's already lost so much in her

life that she's put up brick walls all around her heart to keep the hurt out."

"What if I can't get past those walls?"

"You've always been an excellent climber," she said, grinning. "From the time you were nine months old and already escaping from your crib. If you want her badly enough, and I think you do, you'll find a way over the walls."

"You don't think I'm a fool for getting involved with someone who's already told me she doesn't want what I want?"

"I think you'd be a fool not to try, but you need to do so fully aware that she might not change her mind about what she wants—and what she doesn't."

Lost in thought, he once again tapped his mechanical pencil against his lip. "I like your idea of getting in the car and taking off somewhere with her."

"You don't always have to have a plan. Remember that."

"I might need a reminder from time to time."

"There's no place in matters of the heart for spreadsheets or pie charts."

"What?" he asked, horrified.

"Sorry to be the bearer of bad news, but I have to say it does *my* heart good to see you taking a chance with yours. It's about time."

"What if . . . What if I take this huge gamble on her, and she decides to leave town or that I'm not the one for her or something equally unfortunate."

"That's always a risk, but if she decides to leave town you could always go with her."

"How do I do that when my job and my entire life are here?"

"I know I speak for your father when I tell you neither of us would ever want you to feel like you were stuck here out of some sense of obligation to the family. Even if the whole operation would fall apart without you."

He grunted out a laugh, because that was true.

"You're fantastic at what you do, and Dad and I are extremely grateful for and proud of your contributions here. But that doesn't mean the family business is a life sentence. As much as it would pain us to see you go, we'd figure it out.

You're a grown man, Hunter, as well as a wonderful son and brother and an outstanding asset to the business. All that said, you have a right to your own life, too, and we'd never stand in the way of that."

Touched by what she'd said, he looked up at her. "I love this job. You know that. I'd never want to leave it."

"Hopefully it won't come to that, but keep your options open. If you feel for this woman what I think you do, you'll want her to be happy, too. In fact, her happiness could very well become the most important thing to you."

"If I feel the way you think I do. What does that mean?"

"L-o-v-e."

Hunter blanched at that. "I *like* her, Mom. Did you hear me say I barely know her? Did you hear me say she's already told me she doesn't want to get serious?"

Molly shrugged and gave him the trademark grin that let him know she could see right through his bullshit. She'd always been scarily perceptive when it came to her children. "Keep telling yourself that. I've got to run and get ready for a date of my own." She winked at him. "Your dad is taking me out tonight."

"I want that." The words were out before he could stop them.

"Want what?"

"What you guys have."

Her face softened as she gazed at him with unabashed love. "I want that for you, too, honey. Clearly your father and grandfather want it, too. If you want it, *go get it*. Stop hiding out in this office behind your computer and your spreadsheets. Go out there and *live*, Hunter."

Unable to deny the truth behind her words, he said, "I'm trying."

"Good. Keep me posted on how it's going."

"That's not happening. I've already told you all too much."

"Too late to turn back now." She kissed his cheek and headed for the door. "Cat's out of the bag, my friend."

"Mom?"

Molly turned back to face him. "Yes?"

"Thank you."

"My pleasure, sweetheart. Good luck tonight. I'll be hoping to hear you had a wonderful time."

"Thanks again."

Hoping to avoid any further involvement from his nosy siblings, Hunter left the office and headed home to wait for Megan's call.

CHAPTER 9

In all realms of life it takes courage to stretch your limits, express your power, and fulfill your potential.

—Suze Orman, financial guru

Megan stared at the phone. She was under no obligation to call him. In fact, with the diner closing soon, she could slip out of town and avoid the emotional farewell with Nina and Brett as well as the diner's many loyal patrons. Who would miss her if she left without saying good-bye?

Hunter would. The two words echoed through her mind loud and clear. He'd been so nice to her, and it pained her to think of hurting him by blowing him off when they had plans. Wouldn't it be better to walk away now before anything happened between them?

As much as Megan yearned to make some changes in her life, she wasn't at all prepared to risk the sort of things she'd be endangering by entering into a real relationship with a man, especially someone like Hunter, who knew what he wanted and went after it with single-minded purpose.

Being at the center of that single-minded purpose had been flattering. She couldn't deny that, but she'd hidden behind her fictional boyfriend for all those years for good reason. She'd rather be alone than ever again hurt like she had after losing her parents.

"It's not fair to him," she whispered, smoothing a hand over the skirt of the subtly sexy black dress Nina had talked her into buying. She'd been excited earlier, wondering what Hunter would think of the dress as well as the three-inch heels she'd bought to wear with it. Megan couldn't remember the last time she'd had an occasion that called for heels. Nina had been excited, too, pushing Megan up the stairs to her apartment to get ready for her big date that wasn't going to happen now.

Taking a deep breath and trying to suppress the disappointment that threatened to overwhelm her, she called the number he'd written on the back of his business card.

He answered on the second ring, sounding out of breath. "Hello?"

That one breathless word conveyed a world of anticipation, which made her feel terrible all over again for what she was about to say to him.

"Megan? Are you there?"

"Yes, I'm here."

"What's wrong?"

"I, um . . . I wanted to tell you . . ."

"Are you home?"

"Yes, but . . ."

"I'll be right there."

The line went dead before she could reply. For a brief moment, she thought about leaving before he got there but dismissed that idea almost as quickly as she'd had it. He was a nice guy. At the very least, he deserved the truth. Or some version of it that would convince him she was a lousy bet in the romance department.

She sat on the edge of her sofa, acutely aware of how fast her heart was beating as she waited for him. He didn't live that far from her, so she wasn't surprised to hear heavy footsteps on the stairs that led to her apartment ten minutes later.

He rapped on the door. "Megan?"

Summoning a calm exterior even as her interior swirled

around like a washing machine on the spin cycle, Megan crossed the small room and pulled open the door.

Whatever Hunter had been about to say died on his lips as he took in her outfit. "Wow," he said on a long exhale. "You're stunning."

"Thank you," she said, unnerved by the compliment and the heat she saw in his gaze as he stared at her. "Come in."

He followed her inside, closing the door behind him. "I had things I was going to say, but I can't seem to remember any of them."

Megan knew a moment of pure feminine power when she realized she'd rendered him all but speechless with the outfit as well as the time she'd spent on her hair and makeup.

Hunter took a look around at her tiny but cozy living space. "I love your place."

"Thanks. It's small, but it's home."

He gestured to the crowded bookshelves that occupied one wall of her living room. "You like to read."

"My favorite thing to do." Escaping into imaginary worlds took her far away from her own life. "I have thousands more on my e-reader."

"I like to read, too." He pushed off the door and came closer to her, his nearness and that incredible scent that came with him making her heart go crazy again. Tonight he wore a black sweater with dark jeans, managing to look sexy and well put together at the same time. "One of my favorite things to do."

Being alone with him, even knowing she was totally safe with him, made her feel nervous and jumpy. It had been years, a decade in fact, since she'd been completely alone with a man—if you could call the boys she'd dated then "men." They were boys compared to the man who stood before her now, eating her up with his hungry gaze.

"Hunter, I wanted to tell you . . ."

He closed the small distance between them, took her hand and led her to the sofa, where he sat beside her. Having him right next to her, looking at her the way he always did, it was almost impossible to form the words she needed.

"What do you want to tell me?"

She couldn't continue to look at him and say what needed to be said, too. "You've been really nice to me, and I appreciate that. But I . . ."

"Please don't tell me you don't want to go out tonight. You'll crush me."

Startled by the passion she heard in his voice, she forced herself to look at him. "You have no idea what you're getting into with me."

"I want to know. Tell me what I'm getting into."

She shook her head. "I wish things were different, but it would be better for you—"

"No, it wouldn't. Never having the chance to know you would not be better for me."

"How can you say that? You don't know—"

"Then tell me. Tell me all the awful things I don't know, and I'll decide for myself if any of them are deal-breakers for me. Give me a chance, Megan. That's all I'm asking for." As he spoke, he brushed dampness from her face, which was how she knew she was crying. "Sweetheart, please . . . Talk to me. Let me in. I want so badly to know you—the real you, not the cool, collected woman you show the rest of the world. I want to know *Megan*."

Hearing him call her sweetheart made her melt on the inside. Her father had called her that, and she liked the sound of it coming from Hunter. Megan wiped her face, determined to put her emotions on ice and convince him he could do better than a woman who was broken on the inside.

Hunter put his arm around her and drew her in close to him.

Though being so close to him didn't do a damned thing for her intention to end this before it went any further, she couldn't seem to resist the comfort he offered so willingly. With her face resting against his chest, Megan was grateful for the opportunity to gather her thoughts without having to look at the incredibly insightful brown eyes that seemed to see right through her.

"After my parents died," she began in a small voice, "I was a bit of a mess."

"Of course you were. Anyone would be."

"I did a lot of stupid things. With guys. A lot of guys."

His hand was big and warm on her arm, and he didn't seem to breathe while he waited to hear what she would say next.

"Things I'm ashamed of now."

"That was a long time ago, Megan. You were young and grief-stricken and running from the pain. I don't judge you for what you did then. I don't know how anyone could."

"This went on for a while, until the night I kissed Will at a party."

Only the slight tightening of his grip on her arm indicated his reaction to hearing about her kissing his brother. He remained silent.

"After that I sort of fixated on him. Nina and I talked about it earlier, and she said if I were supposedly 'in love' with Will, that kept me from messing around with other guys. I poured everything into my fixation on him. Nina made me see . . ."

"What did she make you see?"

"That as long as I had myself convinced Will was the one for me, I could justify keeping other men at a distance."

"So there hasn't been anyone else in all that time?"

"No."

"How long ago did you kiss Will?"

"The summer I graduated from high school. Ten years ago."

"Oh, Megan," he said with a sigh. "I'm so sorry for your terrible loss and all the pain it's caused you, but you don't need to be afraid of me. I promise you don't need to put up walls to keep me out."

"That's very nice of you to say, but I think it might be easier if I just continue on the way I've been. I can't hide behind Will anymore, and I know that. I'm really happy for him. He's a great guy, and he deserves to be happy."

"Yes, he does, but so do you. You may deserve it more than anyone I know."

"You deserve it, too, Hunter. You deserve better—"

"No." He moved slightly to his left, his finger under her

chin compelling her to look at him. "Don't say I deserve better than you."

"You do."

"No," he said, more forcefully this time.

Before she could begin to gauge his intentions, he was leaning in closer, his lips brushing against hers, softly, slowly, sweetly.

Megan whimpered. "Hunter . . ."

"Kiss me."

She raised her hand to his smooth face and pressed her lips to his. So much for her good intentions to cut him loose. How had she ended up kissing him on her sofa?

"God, you're so sweet," he whispered against her neck, the heat of his breath sending goose bumps down her back. "I knew you would taste so sweet." Then he was back for more, this time adding subtle touches of his tongue to her bottom lip that had her leaning in, desperate to be closer to him.

She curled her arms around his neck and made him gasp when she brushed her tongue against his.

His groan made his entire body vibrate. He tipped his head, seeking a better angle, his hand buried in her hair to keep her from getting away.

Megan had forgotten what it was like to be held by a man, to be kissed and touched this way. But no man had ever managed to take her away from all her worries and fears the way Hunter Abbott was doing. She wanted to kiss him until he was all she could think about.

Without taking the time to consider what she was doing or how she'd intended to stop this before it started, she brought him with her when she reclined against the sofa pillows. Never breaking the kiss, Hunter followed her lead, coming down on top of her, his body fitting intimately against hers.

She took advantage of the opportunity to run her fingers through his wavy dark hair, which she discovered was softer than it looked.

"Megan," he said when he came up for air. "I didn't mean

for things to get so . . . heated." When he would've pulled back from her, she stopped him.

"Don't go. Not yet."

He leaned his forehead against hers, looking down at her with desire and confusion and questions she could see he wanted to ask but didn't.

"I was going to tell you I can't do this, and then we were kissing, and now I can't remember why I was going to say that."

His laugh was deep and rich, and she loved that she'd made him laugh. She loved the way the laughter lit up his eyes and softened his demeanor. "I understand you're afraid to have a real relationship. All I'm asking is that you give me—and us—a chance."

"What is it about me that you find so interesting? I'm kind of boring when it comes right down to it."

"You're not boring at all. I've always suspected that under that cool façade a complex woman was waiting to get out. All I can tell you is I like how I feel when you're around."

"How do you feel?"

"Excited, interested, distracted, stupid."

"Stupid? *You?* You're like the smartest person I know."

"Not when you're around. So many times I've wanted to ask you out, but I couldn't bring myself to say the words, to ask the question. That makes me feel really stupid."

"You're not. Not at all. Although you may be if you get involved with me."

"I wish you wouldn't say stuff like that about the woman who makes me feel all those things." He kissed her nose and then her lips. "I've got another thing to add to the list of things you make me feel." Pressing his erection into her belly, he said, "Aroused."

Megan closed her eyes, trying to process all the things he was saying and all the emotions that accompanied his words.

"I didn't intend to begin our first date this way," he said. "Not that I'm complaining—at all. Best first date I've ever had."

"We haven't gone anywhere yet."

"And it's still the best ever."

"Doesn't take much to make you happy." Megan went with her trademark sarcasm to hide her emotional reaction to just about everything he said to her.

"You call being able to hold you and kiss you not much? To me it's incredible." He kissed her again, as if he couldn't stop now that he'd started. "And just think, we've already gotten the awkward 'will we or won't we' first-kiss business out of the way, so we won't have to worry about that all night."

"Thank goodness."

"So you'll go out with me and no more about not being good enough or deserving enough or deciding things for me without my input?"

What else could she say to that other than, "Okay."

Hunter felt like he'd dodged a bullet. He'd driven to Megan's house like a man possessed. He'd guessed what she'd been about to say and hadn't given her a chance to say it. On the ride to her house, he'd tried to think of the words he would need to persuade her to give him a chance. He hadn't expected to end up making out with her on the sofa, but as he'd said to her, he certainly wasn't complaining.

Every minute he spent with her, no matter what they were doing, confirmed what he'd suspected for some time now— there could be something special between them. Listening to her share her worries and hearing the pain in her voice had made something inside him rise up in protest, wanting to ensure she never felt that way again.

Hearing that she'd tried to outrun her pain by giving herself to other guys had made him want to kill someone, not that he'd let her see that. No, the worst thing he could ever do is let her think he was judging her when he wasn't. How could he pretend to know what it had been like to suddenly lose the two most important people in her life at the tender age of eighteen?

If she'd found a way to manage the pain, so be it. That was then, this was now, and hearing how she'd reacted to the aftermath of her loss only made him more determined to make sure nothing ever hurt her again.

"Where're we going?" she asked, breaking a lengthy silence.

Drawn out of his thoughts by her question, Hunter glanced over at her. "I don't know yet. I thought we'd take a ride and see what looks good to us."

In the faint light coming from the dashboard, he thought he saw her smile. "I figured you'd have this evening planned down to the last minute."

"Usually I would, but tonight I wanted to do something different and be more spontaneous."

"Spontaneous. Is that painful for you?"

"Why do I have a feeling you're making fun of me?"

"I would never do that."

"Yes, I think you would." He loved to see her playful side emerging. She was always so serious and contained. Now he knew why. She kept a tight rein on her emotions as a shield against being hurt again. Understanding that about her was like being given the keys to her inner workings. He would guard and protect those keys with everything he had for as long as he was lucky enough to have her in his life.

"You're awfully quiet over there, which makes me wonder what you're thinking about."

"I'm thinking about you, which I do a lot."

"What in particular?" she asked.

"That I'm glad you told me what you did earlier."

"I'm ashamed of what I told you. I wish you didn't know that about me."

"It's part of who you are, and I want to know who you are. I want to understand you, because if I understand you, I can make sure I don't do anything to hurt you."

After a long pause, she said, "Since last night . . . I've felt like I'm living in some sort of fairy tale or something."

"The one where the handsome, dashing accountant scoops you up and takes you away from all your troubles?"

"Yes, that's the one."

He hadn't expected such a serious reply to his teasing

comment, but it pleased him deeply to know she felt that way. Reaching across the center console, he took her hand and had to remember he was driving when she curled both her hands around his.

Hunter kept his eyes on the road, even though he preferred looking at her. He wanted to know what she was thinking, but he didn't ask. There'd be time for that later. Right now he wanted to enjoy having her riding next to him, holding his hand with an entire evening stretched out before them to spend any way they wished to.

He decided there was definitely something to be said for spontaneity when it involved her.

They drove for a long time through dark, winding mountain roads. Hunter had no idea where they were and didn't care. A touch of a button on the GPS could get them home, but for the moment, he was rather enjoying being "lost" with Megan.

A roadside tavern appeared in the headlights. "What do you think?"

"Looks good to me."

Hunter signaled and then pulled off the road, laughing when he saw the name of the place: Pig's Belly Tavern and Publick House. "You can tell our grandchildren I brought you to the Pig's Belly Tavern for our first date."

"It'll make for a good story."

Her comeback filled him with foolish hope for a future with her that was far from assured. *Don't get ahead of yourself. First date. Go slow.* Reluctantly, he withdrew his hand from her grasp to shut off the engine. "Wait for me. I'll come around for you."

As he walked around the car, he repeated the "go slow" refrain. But after holding her and kissing her—and having her kiss him back so enthusiastically—it wasn't easy. All he could think about was when he might get to kiss her again. He opened the passenger door and held it for her as she turned to him.

"Hunter?"

"Yes?"

"Do you think, before we go in there, you might want to . . ." She looked at him expectantly. "Kiss me again?"

He reached up to kill the dome light before he put his arms around her and forgot all about going slow when he realized her enthusiasm more than equaled his. His knees went weak under him, and his blood felt like it was on fire as it rushed through his veins. Then her hands were under his sweater on his back, moving restlessly.

"God, Megan," he said when he had no choice but to breathe. "You have no idea what you do to me."

"What do I do? Tell me."

"You make me forget this is our first date." He kissed her neck and made her moan when he dragged his tongue over her soft skin. "You make me want like I've never wanted anything or anyone." More kisses, until he reached her earlobe, which he bit down on, just hard enough to make her gasp. "You make me want you in my bed or your bed or the first bed we can find, and I haven't even bought you dinner yet."

Her husky, lusty laugh made him harder, if that was possible. "You bought me pizza last night."

"That's true. I did." He kissed her again, already addicted to the sweet taste of her. "But pizza doesn't make for as good a story as the Pig's Belly Tavern."

"No, it doesn't."

"You aren't a vegetarian, are you? Because if you are, I'm not sure the Pig's Belly is the place for you."

"I was way back when, but I'm not anymore."

"That's a relief."

"You suppose it's all pig all the time here?"

"I don't know about you, but I'm dying of curiosity." He could tell he surprised her when he lifted her right out of the SUV, bumped the door closed behind him and then let her slide down the aroused front of him.

"Nice move."

"Thanks. Wait till you see the rest of them."

"I can't wait."

Hunter drew in a deep breath, releasing it in rattling increments.

"What?" she asked. "Did I say the wrong thing?"

"Hardly. You said the exact right thing. I'm still trying to believe I'm really here with you, that I can touch you and kiss you and put my arm around you outside the Pig's Belly. I've wanted to do all of that for so long. You have no idea how long."

"I'm glad you finally got to come to the Pig's Belly," she said with a sly smile as she looked up at him.

Hunter laughed. "The Pig is the least of it, as you well know."

"I'm still trying to believe you really feel that way about me."

"I really do."

"You still haven't said why."

"Some things can't be easily explained. They just *are*."

"And this just *is* for you?"

"Yes, you are." He put his arms around her again, drew her in close to him and kept his eyes open and fixed on her as he brought his lips down on hers for a sweet, undemanding kiss that was better than the best sex he'd had with anyone else. And when she curled her arms around his neck and leaned into him, pressing her body against his suggestively, he came damn close to saying to hell with the Pig.

"Food first," he said. "More kissing later."

"Mmm," she said against his lips, making him want to beg for mercy. "Promise?"

"Most definitely."

"Okay then." She dropped her arms from around his neck. "Hunter?"

"Yeah?"

"I really like kissing you and everything, but I still don't want this to be a big deal between us. You said you don't want to hurt me . . . I don't want to hurt you either. There's no reason we can't have a lot of fun together without it getting serious."

"I've been warned. It's all good."

"You're sure?"

"Very sure." Hunter kept his arm around her and tried to will his raging erection into submission before they got to the tavern entrance. "Wait." He dropped his arm from around her shoulders. "I need a minute."

"What? Oh." She pressed her hand to her mouth, but that didn't do much to muffle the sound of her laughter.

"It's not funny."

"Yes, it is."

With her laughter only making his problem worse, he ran his fingers through his hair and walked in circles, thinking about accounts payable and receivable and every other unsexy thing that came to mind. But none of those images could trump the one of Megan, sitting in his passenger seat, asking him to kiss her. That would stay with him long after this first date was a distant memory.

It took a while, but Hunter finally felt as if he could walk into the restaurant without embarrassing himself or Megan. He gestured for her to lead the way.

"Are you sure?" she asked in that teasing tone he was already growing to love. He hadn't expected that from her, but what might've annoyed him coming from one of his siblings was perfect coming from her.

"As sure as I'll ever be."

CHAPTER 10

—◄►—

*Look well to this day. Yesterday is but a dream
and tomorrow is only a vision. But today well
lived makes every yesterday a dream of
happiness and every tomorrow a vision
of hope. Look well therefore to this day.*

—Francis Gray

The Pig's Belly was more or less what Hunter expected—more in the sense that it was crowded, and less in the way of atmosphere, of which there was none. At least not what he'd consider atmosphere.

"This is great." Megan smiled at the huge bronze statue of a full-bellied pig standing upright that greeted them inside the door. "How have I never heard of it?"

"Can't imagine." Seeing her bright smile, Hunter decided atmosphere was overrated if all it took to make her happy was a big bronze pig.

They were shown to a table and handed menus that featured pig, pork and more pig.

"I'm torn between the ribs and the pig's feet," he said after reviewing the limited menu.

"Don't overlook the pork chop."

"Always a favorite."

"I'm thinking about the knuckles myself."

"Really?" he asked, sort of horrified at the thought of actually eating pig knuckles—or watching her do it.

She laughed at the face he made at her. "No, not really."

"Thank goodness."

"I'm going with ribs. Seems safe enough."

"Make that two."

They ordered the ribs with sides of fries, coleslaw and baked beans along with two draft beers.

"I'm going to tell the grandchildren you got the knuckles," Hunter said after their beverages arrived.

"I'll tell them you got the testicles."

He nearly snorted beer out his nose. "That wasn't on the menu."

She shrugged. "You think they'll check?"

"Good to know you're not above making things up to suit your agenda."

"I've been doing that since I was a little kid."

"Making things up?"

Nodding, she said, "Stories of all kinds."

"Do you write?"

"One of my other favorite things to do. I've been writing all my life."

Fascinated by the revelation, Hunter leaned in closer so he could hear her better. He didn't want to miss a thing. "What sort of stories?"

"All kinds. Romance, mostly, but some fantasy and science fiction stuff, too."

"Have you done anything with them?"

She shook her head and took a sip from her glass. "It's a hobby. Nothing more." Returning the glass to the table, she glanced at him, as if there were something else she wanted to say.

Under the table, he reached for her hand. "Tell me."

Hesitating, she fixated on the rough-hewn wooden wall on the far side of the room. "I'd planned to go to Middlebury to study writing. Before."

He understood that she meant before her parents were

killed. Her life was divided into before and after. "Why didn't you go? Was it because of the money?"

"No, they left us in pretty good shape with the insurance and their savings. It was more because I lost the desire to write for a really long time afterward. It didn't seem to make much sense to go to school for it if I couldn't do it."

"It came back eventually?"

"Yeah. Took years though, and by then it was too late."

"It's never too late. You know that, don't you?"

"It was too late for Middlebury. I was never a big fan of school to begin with, and the thought of going back now is extremely unappealing. Who knows if I would've been able to cut it there anyway? One of the last conversations I had with my dad was him telling me I needed better study habits if I was going to survive there and me arguing that I was good enough to get in, so that had to count for something."

Hunter watched her try to shake off the unpleasant memory.

"Sorry." She forced a smile. "Didn't mean to drag down the mood."

"You didn't. Not at all. I want to hear about your parents. I'd like to know them as much as I'd like to know you."

"That's really nice of you. They were good people, even if I liked to fight with them."

"That's your job when you're a teenager."

"Still . . . I wish I'd done less of it. If I'd known I had so little time with them . . ."

Hunter's heart ached for her when he realized that not only was she still dealing with her grief after all this time, but a sizable amount of guilt, too. "I knew who they were, but I didn't know them all that well. I can't help but think they wouldn't want you dwelling on the bad times. I'm sure there were lots of good times, right?"

"There were. I played competitive soccer when I was a kid, and we traveled all over the place to games and tournaments. Those trips were always fun. And we went to Disney once, the year Nina graduated from high school. She hated it, but I loved it. We also did a lot of skiing together. My dad was crazy into skiing. That's why we lived in Vermont, because he liked to ski so much."

"He came to the right place."

"Yeah, but it's ironic when you think about how he died." She picked up a small plastic frame from the table, her eyes widening before she laughed. "Check it out! 'Drink too much at the Pig's Belly? Not to worry. Ask for the key to our Fantasy Suite upstairs and spend the night as our guest. Arrive alive—don't drink and drive.' What do you suppose the Fantasy Suite at the Pig's Belly is like?"

"I'm tempted to drink too much so we can find out," Hunter said.

Megan signaled for their waitress. "Could we have two more beers, please?"

The waitress glanced at their unfinished drinks. "Sure."

Stunned, Hunter could only stare at Megan in wonder. "What're you up to?" he asked, more amused and bewitched by her with every passing minute. She'd gone from talking about the saddest time in her life to laughing with abandon in the course of a few seconds.

"Trying to teach you to be spontaneous."

"I like learning from you, but please tell me you're not a fan of that *Bachelor* show with the ridiculous fantasy suites."

"Okay, I won't."

"Not you, too! My sisters are addicted to it. It's the stupidest thing ever."

"I can think of stupider things. In fact, now that the diner is closing, maybe I should try out to be a contestant."

"You're not doing that."

"Who says?"

Once again he had the distinct feeling that she was making fun of him and enjoying it. "I say."

"That's kind of bossy for someone who's not allowed to be serious about me."

"I'm the oldest of ten kids. Bossy is my business."

"Are you always like that?"

"Sometimes more than others."

"Like when?"

"You really want to know?" he asked.

"I wouldn't have asked if I didn't really want to know."

He leaned in close to her, pressing his lips against her ear. "I'm *really* bossy in bed."

A tremble went through her that he felt because he was sitting so close to her. "Is that right?"

"Uh-huh."

"Bossy how?"

Hunter's cock pressed insistently against his fly as he brought her in even closer to him. "I know what I want, and I know how to get it, but only after you get what you want." He kissed her cheek and then her temple. "Does it turn you on to hear that?"

"Um, yeah . . ."

Laughing, he squeezed her shoulder, thrilled to be with her, to be talking to her about things he'd never said out loud to anyone before. He didn't talk about what he liked to do in bed. Usually, he just did it. Judging by the rock-hard erection currently making him extremely uncomfortable, there was something to be said for talking about it. In an effort to get through dinner without embarrassing himself, he said, "Tell me other things about you I don't know."

"Let's see . . . My favorite color is yellow, my favorite movie is *The Princess Bride*, my favorite book—ever—is *Gone With the Wind*, a wretched, awful, over-the-top disaster of a story, but I love it anyway. My favorite band is the Beatles—"

"Wait, does my dad know that?"

"Of course he does. We talk about it all the time."

"I should've known. Favorite song of theirs?"

"Duh, 'Yellow Submarine.' "

Hunter laughed at the witty comment and the face she made to go along with it. "Naturally."

"What's your favorite Beatles song?"

"Would I lose points if I told you I'd be happy if I never heard another Beatles song again for the rest of my life?"

"Yes, you would," she said in all seriousness.

"Fine, if you're going to be that way and I have to pick one . . . I'd have to say 'And I Love Her.' "

She stared at him for a long, breathless, charged moment and then licked her lips, igniting him all over again. "That's a good one."

Their food arrived, forcing him to focus on something other than the desire that throbbed through his body like an extra heartbeat. He'd wanted other women before, but nothing could compare to the kind of yearning that came from being so close to Megan. Being able to touch her and hold her and kiss her and talk with her and laugh with her was making him crazy for more.

"This is so good," Megan said, her mouth full of tender meat.

Hunter glanced over at her, smiling at the streak of barbecue sauce on her face as he removed it with a napkin.

She sent him a sheepish grin. "Ribs might not have been the best first-date choice."

"Go ahead and get messy. I'll be happy to clean you up."

"You surprise me."

He froze midbite. "How so?"

"You come across all buttoned-down and serious, but you're not only that. You're also fun and funny and . . ."

"And what?" he asked, desperate for her to finish the thought.

"Kinda dirty—in a good way."

Hunter put the rib he'd been about to eat back on his plate and wiped his hands and face before leaning in to kiss her. "I can be *really* dirty with the right inspiration."

Her eyes heated with interest and curiosity and desire.

"Is this moving too fast for you?" he asked.

"As long as you really heard me about the not-getting-serious thing, it's not moving too fast for me. How about you?"

"Definitely not. I feel like I've been waiting forever to be able to spend this kind of time with you, without knowing for sure that I'd ever get to."

"Why did you wait so long if you felt that way?"

"I tried once, if you'll recall . . ."

She winced. "Sorry about that. I thought you were just being nice. I didn't think you really wanted to go out with me."

"I really did, and I still do. Even more so than I did before, if that's possible."

"I want you to know," she said haltingly, "being with you, last night and tonight, has been so special, and you've helped to make what would've been a very difficult week for me much more bearable than it would've been otherwise."

"I'm glad I could do that for you. Why do I hear a 'but' coming?"

"If things don't work out with the diner, I'm probably going to have to move to find another job. There aren't that many other options in Butler."

"You could look in St. J or other towns close by without moving, couldn't you?" The thought of her leaving town right when he was finally getting the chance to know her made him edgy and anxious.

"I could." She wiped her face and took a drink of her beer. "But I won't."

"Why not?"

After a long pause, she said, "I'm afraid to drive in the snow, so that sort of limits my options when it comes to working in Vermont. I need to be able to walk to work in the winter."

He pushed his plate away, no longer interested in eating, and put his arm around her. "If you find a job in another town, I'll drive you there and pick you up all winter."

"You can't commit to that."

"Yes, I can. I'm self-employed. I can do whatever I want to."

"Still, you have a business to run and obligations."

"If it means keeping you close to me, Megan, I'd do it in a heartbeat."

"You're very sweet, but that's sounding an awful lot like a guy looking to get serious with a woman."

"I've got to be honest with you."

"Okay."

"I really did hear what you said earlier, but I do want to be serious about you. I know you've got stone walls up around your heart, and I understand why. You should know I plan to scale those walls."

Her lips parted as she began to say something that never materialized.

"Is that okay?"

"Do I have a choice?"

"Always. But you're going to have to tell me right now if you want to call this off. Otherwise, I'll be climbing the walls, effective immediately."

She laughed nervously, but she looked at him in a way that made him feel warm all over. "You don't mince words, do you?"

"No point to mincing words. I want you. I've wanted you for a long time. I don't see any reason to pretend otherwise."

"You're sort of freaking me out right now."

"I'm sorry. I don't mean to. We can go if you want to." He started to signal for the check, but she stopped him with her hand over his.

"I don't want to go."

Hunter felt like his entire life and any chance he had at being truly happy had come down to this moment. "So what you're saying . . ."

"Is I have no idea what I'm doing here with you, but I'm having fun for the first time in a really long time. And I don't want to go home."

He released a deep breath he hadn't realized he'd been holding. "Will you do me a favor? Will you not make any plans to move without talking to me first? I know I have no right to ask that of you on our first official date, and it's selfish of me to want to keep you close. But if you talk to me, maybe we can find a way to work it out short of you moving."

"I'll talk to you about it."

"Hopefully my grandfather's offer on the diner will go through, and you can still work there. If you want to, that is. I don't want you to feel obligated."

"I don't. But Nina's plans have me thinking about what else I might like to do."

"Will you talk to me about that, too?"

She nibbled on her bottom lip as she pondered his question. "Yes, I'll talk to you about it." She glanced over at him. "It's kind of flattering that you care enough to want to help me figure this out."

"I do, Megan. I care. I want to be involved. I want us to figure it out together."

As they finished eating, Hunter noticed people beginning to migrate toward a back room. "Wonder what's going on back there."

Megan turned to look. "I hope they aren't sacrificing pigs or something."

"Want to check it out?"

"If you do."

Hunter signaled for their check and then opened the wet wipes that had come with the ribs, handing one to Megan and using the other to make sure his face was free of sauce. Retrieving his wallet, he withdrew a credit card, put it on the check and handed it back to the waitress.

"Thanks for dinner," Megan said. "It was great."

"It was much better than expected."

His words were nearly drowned out by the music that was now coming from the back room. Raising a brow in her direction, he laughed at the expression on her face.

"Pigs gone wild."

"Sounds like it."

They had to practically shout to be heard over the music.

Hunter signed the credit card slip and put the card and receipt in his wallet. Hannah teased him about keeping every piece of paper he'd ever come into contact with, but if he should ever be audited—personally or professionally—he was ready.

With his hand low on Megan's back, he escorted her to the adjoining room, which was crowded with people dancing up a storm to the rockabilly band that included two fiddlers currently locked in a frenetic duel as the crowd cheered them on.

"This is awesome," Megan said, her lips close to his ear so he could hear her.

He slid his arm around her waist and held her while they watched the musicians. The music reminded him of Mumford and Sons, a band he'd seen in Boston a few months ago.

When he woke up this morning, he hadn't expected to end up in a place called the Pig's Belly, but with Megan in his arms, her soft, fragrant hair brushing against his chin, there was nowhere else on earth he'd rather be.

CHAPTER 11

—◆—

*You must be the change you wish
to see in the world.*

—Mahatma Gandhi

Surrounded by Hunter's strong arms and the incredibly appealing scent that made her want to burrow her nose into his neck to get closer to it, Megan was content. And it was all because of him. She'd enjoyed peeling back the layers of his strictly business exterior to find a sexy, hot-blooded guy underneath his polished veneer.

In all the years of her forced exile from men and dating, she hadn't missed any of it. But a few passionate kisses with Hunter had unleashed the kind of desire she'd never experienced before. Knowing he was so totally into her was a huge turn-on. None of the boys she'd dated had been so tuned into her or interested in what she thought or said. Like most teenage boys, they'd been after one thing and one thing only. She'd given it to them because it had given her temporary respite from the unrelenting pain of her loss. She'd been young and stupid and broken.

Everything about this newfound connection with Hunter was different. For one thing, he was the first genuine man she'd dated. The others had been boys compared to him.

Hearing him say he was bossy in bed had made her want to drag him upstairs to one of those fantasy suites and see what he meant by that.

With his hand flat on her belly, his fingers pointing downward, one of them positioned just above her pubic bone, Megan wanted to rise up on her tiptoes to force his hand down to where she'd come alive since he kissed her earlier. But after what she'd told him about her past, would he think she was easy if she made a move like that?

Perhaps, but did she care if he thought that? Not as much as she probably should have, and that was because he'd been so open about how much he liked her. Before she could give it too much thought or consideration, she tapped on the arm he had around her, which immediately loosened to release her.

"I'm going to the restroom. Be right back."

"I'll be here."

Three little words that said so much. Tapping into her inner reserve of spontaneity, she kissed him, touching her tongue ever so briefly to his bottom lip before leaving him wide-eyed and unsatisfied. The expression on his face was priceless as she turned away from him and made her way through the crowd to the reception area. Though her back was now to him, she could *feel* him watching her.

This might turn out to be a huge mistake, but she was willing to risk it because he'd made her feel so safe with him—safe to be herself, to take a few chances, to let go of her painful past and imagine something different for herself. What he'd said about scaling the walls she'd put up around her heart had been incredibly sweet.

"May I help you?" the hostess asked.

"I was wondering about the rooms upstairs."

"Ahh, yes. I take it you saw the notice on your table."

"I did, and I'm intrigued. My boyfriend has had a couple of beers, and I was thinking it might be better to stay put tonight." She tried not to think about the fact that she was due at work at seven the next morning. Hopefully, Nina would forgive her if she was a little late. What would Nina do? Fire her? That thought, along with what she was doing to surprise Hunter, made Megan feel giddy and lighthearted, two emotions that had been in short supply in her life until recently.

"That's why we have them. I'd be happy to set you up. All I need is a license and a credit card that won't be charged unless there's damage or theft."

"Sure, no problem." Casting a watchful eye in the direction of where she'd left Hunter, she handed over the requested items.

Five minutes later she had a key to Room 3 on the second floor. Giggling to herself as she imagined his reaction, she made a quick trip to the ladies' room before rejoining him and putting her arms around him from behind, which made him startle and then relax when he realized it was her.

"Did you miss me?"

"Terribly."

"Want to dance?"

"Um, well, I'm not a very good dancer," he said.

"That's not true."

"How do you know?"

"I saw you at the last Grange dance. You were moving just fine when you and your brothers were taunting Will by dancing with Cameron."

"You saw that, huh?"

"Yep."

"I was hoping no one saw that."

"Well, I did, so now your secret is out." She took his hand and dragged him through the crowd to the dance floor, where people were partying like it was a Friday night rather than a Tuesday. No one seemed to care what day of the week it was as they moved to the fast-paced music. In his conservative sweater and dark jeans, Hunter looked wildly out of place among flannel, T-shirts, faded jeans and an occasional tank top, but he didn't seem to care that he stood out in the crowd.

He would stand out in any crowd. The aura of class he projected without even trying wasn't something he could just decide to shed. Megan would bet he was classy even when he was naked, a thought that had her giggling madly.

"Am I that funny?" he asked, shouting to be heard over the music.

"Not that. Something else."

He scowled playfully at her and pulled her in tight against him. Despite the faster-than-ever music, he moved her slowly, looking down at her the whole time. In a sea of writhing bodies and loud music, all she could see was him. She moved closer, bringing her lower body into contact with his.

With his erection pressed into her belly, his eyes closed and his jaw tightened.

Megan curled her hand around his nape, bringing his head down to her.

His lips were soft and persuasive against her neck, making her strain against him, needing to get closer.

"What do you say we get out of here?" she asked right against his ear so he could hear her over the loud music.

"And go where?"

"I'll show you." She took his hand and led him off the dance floor, through the restaurant to the stairs the hostess had pointed out earlier.

"What're you up to?" he asked.

"Since you won't let me go on *The Bachelor*, this was my only chance to check out a fantasy suite. You wouldn't deny me that, would you?"

"Um, no. Most definitely not."

She withdrew the keycard from her purse and held it up for him to see.

"Where did that come from?"

"I told the hostess my boyfriend had too much to drink, and she was happy to put us up for the night."

"Was she now? For the whole night?"

"Uh-huh. Checkout is at eleven."

With his hands on her hips, he peppered her neck with kisses that made her laugh. "I think I'm going to be late for work tomorrow. Again."

"I have to work at seven."

"Can you call in sick?"

"I might have to. I was thinking earlier that Nina can't exactly fire me."

"True."

At the door to the room, she turned to face him, feeling vulnerable and uncertain about what had seemed like such a great idea a few minutes ago. "I'm sending mixed messages here, aren't I?"

"I'm good with that."

She smiled at his hasty reply. "I'm serious, Hunter."

"You said you don't want to get serious," he said, his smile teasing.

"And yet I go get a key for one of these rooms and bring you up here like a brazen—"

He kissed the words right off her lips. "We're having fun. That's all we're doing tonight. And I *love* your surprise."

"In that case . . ." Megan pushed the door open and stopped short at the sight before her. The room was *gorgeous*. A four-poster bed with a white eyelet coverlet, a gas fireplace, a cozy sitting area in front of the fireplace, shiny knotty pine floors.

"The Pig's Belly continues to astound me," Hunter said.

"I know!" Megan went to check out the bathroom and let out a happy squeal at the sight of a huge tub with built-in jets. "And this is *free*? Why aren't people in Butler talking about this place?"

"Let's make a solemn vow right now to tell no one about it."

"Agreed." All at once the nerves reappeared, making her wonder what he really thought about her orchestrating such a romantic interlude on this, their first real date. Maybe she shouldn't have been quite so spontaneous.

"What's wrong?"

"I'm hoping you aren't really thinking that I'm . . . You know . . ."

"Beautiful?" He took a step toward her. "Adventuresome?" Another step. "Sexy as hell?" One more step to bring him face-to-face with her. "Exactly what I need?"

Flustered by what he'd said and how he'd said it, Megan

smiled but shook her head. "As nice as all of that is, it's not what I meant."

"I know, but I'm not thinking about anything other than those things. Whatever happened in the past is in the past. This is a clean slate, and you've thoroughly blown my mind tonight in all the best ways possible."

"I have? Really?"

"Absolutely." Raising his hands to cradle her face, he kissed her softly and thoroughly, blowing *her* mind with only the light brush of his lips against hers.

Megan reached for him, her hands landing at his waist and closing the remaining distance between them.

He kissed her for a long time, soft, sweet, sexy undemanding kisses that went a long way toward calming the nerves that had nearly derailed her spontaneous gesture. "What're you thinking right now?" he asked.

"At this very second?"

"Uh-huh."

"I'm wondering how you knew just what to say and do to calm me down when I'd started to second-guess myself. And mostly I'm wondering where you came from all of a sudden."

He smiled down at her. "It's hardly all of a sudden. I've been right across the street all this time waiting and hoping I might have a chance to be with you like this. And I knew what to say because I could see you were about to panic about what you'd done and what I might think of it."

Megan rested her head against his chest, sighing when he wrapped his arms around her. How nice it was to be with a man who seemed to understand her so effortlessly. That was certainly a first.

"What do you say we get a little more comfortable?" he asked after a long silence.

"I hope you know I didn't do this expecting, well, anything. I sort of did it without thinking it all the way through to this moment when we're both trying to figure out what's going to happen."

"Nothing has to happen. I'm happy to have more time to

spend with you, to be off on this little departure from my real life with you. Anything else that happens is a bonus, so don't feel any pressure coming from me."

"You don't have to feel any pressure either," she said, smiling.

"Oh please," he said with a big, sexy grin, "pressure me. Make my day, my year, my *life* complete."

"You're funny, Hunter Abbott. I never would've guessed that."

"Wait till you see the rest of my hidden qualities." After waggling his brows playfully, he tugged his sweater up and over his head and kicked off his shoes. When she had removed her shoes, too, he led her to the bed, where they stretched out next to each other.

Turning to face him, Megan noticed the logo for the Seventh Annual Capt. Caleb M. Guthrie Memorial Road Race on the T-shirt he'd worn under the sweater. "Did you do the run they just had?"

Nodding, he said, "I do it every year."

"I'd like to do it one of these years. I'm always working, but I love to run. And I know he was your friend."

"One of my best friends and former roommate as well as my brother-in-law."

"I'm sorry you lost him."

"Thanks. It was a very difficult time. Still is in many ways."

"Always will be. It took me a while after I lost my parents to realize it's not something you ever 'get over.' You learn to live with it, but it's always a part of who you are."

He nodded in agreement. "I've seen that with Hannah, too. She's really happy with Nolan now, but I know she still thinks about Caleb and misses him all the time."

"Nolan is a great guy. I think it's so sweet how he waited for her to be ready to fall in love again."

"I doubt Hannah would've taken a second chance with anyone but him. They're perfect together."

"What was their wedding like? I didn't hear too much about it, but the town sure was quiet that weekend with everyone in Burlington."

"It was . . . very touching and emotional. We're thrilled to see her moving forward with Nolan and excited about their baby. But days like that are such a reminder about who isn't here anymore and never will be again. Caleb's parents and brother were there and all his best friends, who are Hannah's friends, too, and Nolan's. It was a happy day, but it was bittersweet in many ways. I know Hannah and Nolan would agree."

"You're close with her? Your sister?"

"Extremely. She's my twin, you know that, right?"

"I'm not sure if I knew that. Of course I'm well aware that your younger brothers are twins because they're always trying to confuse me as to who is who when they come into the diner. They're such flirts."

Hunter uttered a low growl that surprised her. "I'll kick their asses if they flirt with you."

"That I'd like to see. You do know there're two of them, right?"

"So what? I've been kicking their asses since they were little brats."

"Sure you have."

"You don't believe me?"

"Not for one second do I believe you ever beat up your little brothers."

"I didn't beat them up, per se, but rather I put a hurt on them from time to time when they needed to be reminded who's boss."

"Such a badass," she said, laughing.

"Shhh, don't tell anyone. The whole accountant thing is my disguise. Kind of like Clark Kent was a reporter."

"Now you're comparing yourself to Superman?"

"If the cape fits . . ."

"You're too funny."

"You think it's easy being the oldest of ten kids? It's like being the dictator of a banana republic."

"And you love every minute of it."

"I do. For the most part."

"You have an amazing family. You're so lucky."

"And I know it. Believe me. Sometimes they drive me

nuts, but I'm always thankful for them. You should come to Sunday dinner at my mom's. Talk about a banana republic. It's full-on chaos."

The thought of joining his family for a big chaotic dinner filled Megan with yearning to be part of them, but the yearning was quickly extinguished when she recalled the awful way she'd treated Cameron. "I'm sure they wouldn't want me there."

"Why would you say that?"

"I reacted badly when Will started seeing Cameron. I'm ashamed of the way I treated her. She has every right to hate me. Him, too, for that matter."

"They don't hate you, Megan."

"Still, I bet they hardly want to sit across from me at Sunday dinner."

"They wouldn't care at all if you were there."

"How do you know that?"

"They're so happy it's disgusting. Nothing and no one can bring them down." He tucked a strand of hair behind her ear. "Can you keep a huge secret?"

"Of course I can. If you only knew the stuff I hear during a single shift. I could ruin lives."

"Note to self: Stay on Megan's good side."

"You know it. Now what's the big secret?"

"He's going to propose to her. I'm going with him Saturday to pick out a ring."

"That's really exciting. I'm happy for him. He's a good guy, and he deserves to be happy."

"Does it upset you to hear he's getting engaged?"

"Not as much as it would have a couple of months ago." She placed her hand over his, which he had laid flat on the bed. "In fact, I'm starting to feel a little grateful to her."

"Why's that?"

"Because if she hadn't come along and forced me to give up on my crush on Will, I might've missed out on the fact that his very sexy older brother was interested in getting to know me better."

He raised a brow, and the gesture transformed his face from handsome to rakish. "Very sexy, huh?"

"Yep."

"What're you doing all the way over there?"

"Just waiting for you to invite me over there."

"Dear Megan, please come closer to me. Love, Hunter. How's that?"

"Hmm, I'm not convinced you really want me to."

"Let me try again then. Dear Megan, please come over here and kiss me before I die from wanting you to. Much love, Hunter. Better?"

Was it possible for a heart to do somersaults and still keep beating? "Much love?"

"Could be. You'll have to come over here to find out."

"Well, since you asked me so nicely . . ." She scooted across the big bed until she was several inches from him. "Good?"

"Not quite." He put his arm around her and brought her the rest of the way until her body was tucked in tight against his. "Now *that* is much better."

"Is it kind of crazy that we're in this room together at a place called the Pig's Belly with the floor vibrating from the music downstairs?"

"One of the craziest things I've ever done."

"Me, too."

"And the best first date I've ever had."

"Same."

He stared into her eyes for a long, breathless moment before he kissed her, groaning as their lips came together.

Megan reached for him, trying to bring him closer, which was how he ended up on top of her.

Breaking the kiss, he looked down at her. "Is this okay?"

Rather than answer him with words, she put her arms around him and tangled her legs with his to keep him from getting away.

"You have no idea how badly I want you."

She raised her hips ever so slightly, making him groan again when she pressed against his erection. "I have a small idea."

"Hey! There's nothing *small* about it."

Megan's laughter was quickly muffled by devouring kisses,

sweeping thrusts of his tongue and his hand under her dress, flat against the back of her leg, branding her with his heat. She squirmed under him, trying to move things along, but Hunter wouldn't be rushed.

"Easy, honey. We've got all night."

The thought of a full night with him only made her more restless.

He pulled back from her all of a sudden, kneeling between her legs and pushing her dress up and over her head, leaving her only in a black thong and matching satin bra, her breasts spilling over the top.

Hunter licked his lips as he zeroed in on her breasts before bending to kiss the upper slope of one and then the other. "You're so beautiful, Megan. I've thought so for such a long time."

He made her feel more beautiful than she had ever felt before with the way he looked at her and in the worshipful way he kissed and touched her. When she released the front clasp on her bra, his gorgeous brown eyes went wide with shock and then dark with desire. "You love to surprise me, don't you?"

"It *is* sort of fun."

"I like your idea of fun." He pushed the bra aside and cupped her breasts, staring down at them.

"What's wrong?"

"Not one damned thing. Just savoring the view." Lowering his head, he took her left nipple into his mouth while pinching the right one lightly between his fingers.

Megan grasped a handful of his hair. She'd forgotten how it felt to be consumed by desire, not that she'd ever felt anything even close to this. Her nipples were incredibly sensitive, and he was making her crazy—until he stopped all of a sudden and rolled off her, leaving her aroused and stunned by his withdrawal.

CHAPTER 12

—◆◆—

You only have to do a very few things right in your life so long as you don't do too many things wrong.

—Warren Buffett

Lying on his back, breathing heavily, Hunter propped an arm over his eyes.

"What's wrong?"

"Nothing."

"Um, okay." A thousand thoughts went through her mind in the time it took for him to lower his arm and reach for her.

"I'm sorry."

"Why did you stop?"

He twirled a lock of her hair around his finger. "Because I want you too much, and I'm afraid if I show you how much, I'll freak you out and send you running from me."

Flooded with relief to know he hadn't changed his mind about wanting her, Megan placed her hand on his cheek, compelling him to look at her.

He turned his face into her hand, kissing her palm and setting off a whole new wave of need.

"You won't freak me out."

"You don't know that for sure. It's been a long time for you, and I'm feeling . . ."

"How are you feeling?"

"Out of control. And I'm never out of control. Ever."

"Maybe there's a first time for everything," she said, ridiculously flattered to know she'd done that to him. Megan tugged on his T-shirt. "Take this off."

"We should probably stop."

"Do we have to?"

"No, but you need to understand what I mean by out of control."

"Make me understand."

"I can be kind of . . . demanding . . . during sex."

"So you said earlier." Megan swallowed hard as her entire body heated with interest and curiosity and desire that settled into an intense throb between her legs. "Demanding in what way?"

"I like to be in charge, and with you . . ." He cupped her breast and ran his thumb over her nipple. "Just touching you like this was like lighting a live fuse. It's never happened that fast before."

"Would you ever hurt me in any way?"

He blanched, his eyes widening and his mouth moving silently. "No," he said softly. "Not in a million years would I ever hurt you. I just don't want to scare you by showing you how crazy you make me."

"You make me pretty crazy, too."

"Yeah?"

She nodded and again pulled on his T-shirt, urging him to take it off, which he did, revealing a lanky, muscular chest covered with just the right amount of soft dark hair. His abs were ripped and well defined, which came as a surprise.

"Do all accountants have such impressive abs?"

He snorted out a laugh. "How the hell would I know?"

"You must work out a lot."

"I do wilderness survival training with my brothers, so I have to work out just about every day in the gym I have in my basement so they don't show me up when we train."

"God forbid."

"Exactly."

Megan bent over him and kissed his neck, throat and chest, making a path to those impressive abs that rippled under her lips.

He buried his fingers in her hair, tightening them into fists as she moved farther down, following the trail of dark hair that led to the waistband of his jeans. "Megan . . ."

"Maybe if we take the edge off, you won't be so scary with this loss-of-control issue you seem to have." As she spoke, all the reasons she'd thought it was a bad idea to get involved with him were swept away on a wave of desire so strong she could barely breathe for wanting him. She unbuttoned and unzipped his pants, pushing them down to reveal silk boxers that made her laugh. "Why am I not surprised?"

"What's so funny?"

"You. You're classy right down to the silk boxers."

"Haven't you ever felt silk against your most important parts?"

"Can't say that I have."

He caressed her face. "We'll have to rectify that. Immediately. Then you won't be laughing."

"You're going to buy me underwear?"

"Sweetheart, I'm going to buy you *silk* underwear. Only the best."

"I'll look forward to that." She kissed his stomach, working her way from one side to the other and then back down to where his cock strained against dark silk. "Will you promise me something?" she asked.

"Anything."

"That no matter what we do here, you won't think less of me because of it."

"I could never think less of you for wanting to be with me this way. I feel like all the best fantasies I've ever had are happening right in front of me. How could I ever think less of you?"

"I don't do this sort of thing. At least not anymore."

"I know. You told me, and I believed you. Trust me, if you'd been with anyone else in the last couple of years, I would've known. I've been a little . . . obsessed."

Megan smiled widely. "Really?"

"Yeah, really. Not like a stalker or anything . . . It hadn't come to that. Yet."

She loved that he made her laugh, he made her hot and he made her courageous all at the same time.

"We could stop right now, and that would be fine, too," he said. "I'd be quite content if I got to hold you while you sleep."

"Would you?"

He nodded.

"But wouldn't this make it difficult for you to sleep?" She caressed his hard length, dragging the silky fabric back and forth until he was pressing desperately against her palm. Then she raised the waistband up and over, leaving it to rest on his shaft.

"Christ, Megan. You're making me feel like a horny teenager."

Pushing her hand inside his boxers, she wrapped her fingers around his cock and stroked while bending over him to run her tongue around the head. "Did anyone do this for you when you were a horny teenager?"

"I wish," he said with a pained laugh.

Megan wished she were doing this for the first time with him. She wished she'd saved herself for a man who appreciated her the way he did. Back then, she'd been so out of control, so determined to outrun the relentless pain that always came rushing back the minute she was left alone again with her own thoughts.

"What're you thinking?"

She looked up at him. "That I wish I'd never done this before so you could be my first."

"I'll be the first one who matters."

Snagged in his adoring gaze, Megan had trouble looking away. Then he surged in her hand, harder than he'd been before, reminding her of what she'd started. Reluctantly, she dropped her eyes and tried to show him what his kindness had meant to her.

She drew him in, pushing his underwear down as she went. As he bumped against the back of her throat, she squeezed the base with her hand and swirled her tongue around the head.

"Holy shit," he said, hissing as he throbbed and lengthened in her mouth. He fisted tight handfuls of her hair, holding on tight as she withdrew and then took him deep again, cupping his balls with her free hand. *"Megan . . ."*

"Hmm?" As she let her lips vibrate against his cock, she absolutely loved that she'd made Hunter Abbott swear.

"Fuck. Stop. If you don't want me to . . ."

She didn't stop. Rather she stepped up her game, sucking and stroking and licking until his hips lifted off the bed and he came with a groan that echoed through his body and into her mouth. Megan swallowed and stroked him gently until he sagged back into the mattress, seeming totally spent. She cleaned him up with her tongue, kissing her way up to his stomach, which quivered violently under her lips.

His arms came around her, holding her head to his chest, his breathing deep and strained, his heart beating rapidly. "That was incredible. Thank you."

She'd never had a guy thank her for doing that before. "Figures you're polite, even in bed."

"Especially in bed."

"Why am I not surprised?"

"That doesn't mean I can't get down and dirty, too."

"Oh really? Do tell."

"I'd rather *show.* Just give me a minute to recover, and then it's on."

Megan closed her eyes, smiling at the promise she heard in his voice. "Mmm, can't wait."

Hunter's mind—among other things—was completely blown. She'd rocked his entire universe with what she'd done, but *watching* her do it . . . That had been the single most erotic moment of his life. He'd relive it over and over again. And now, with her warm soft body curled up to his, his cock cradled between her breasts, all he wanted was more of her.

"Are you tired?" It was now after midnight, and she'd been up since the crack of dawn to work the breakfast shift.

"Not as tired as I should be." To make her point, she dragged her breasts up over his chest, sending a surge of lust to his recently satisfied cock.

He tucked her hair behind her ears. "What time did you get up yesterday?"

"Five. Same time I'm always up—even on days off. My internal alarm goes off at the same time every day."

"Well, that kind of sucks."

"You know it. On Mondays, when I get to sleep in, I never make it past five."

His hands moved down her back until he was cupping her ass cheeks. "Maybe you just need to be properly worn out."

"Right. Like working eight hours a day doesn't do that?"

"You work too hard."

She shrugged. "It's not like I have anything better to do."

"Yes, you do."

"Like what?"

"Your writing, for one thing. Me, for another."

"You?" she said, laughing. "Doing you is better than working. I'll give you that."

"Wow, thanks. Nicest compliment I've ever received."

Her quiet laughter made him smile as a wave of contentment unlike anything he'd ever experienced had him wishing this night at the Pig's Belly would last forever.

"If the sale of the diner goes through, I'd like to make it so you have to work less than you do now."

She raised her head, propping her chin on the hand she laid flat on his chest. "Why would you do that?"

"So you'll have more time to write and work on things that truly matter to you. And selfishly, so you can spend time with me. If you want to, that is."

"I'd like that. This has been the best night."

"For me, too, and not just because of the fantasy-suite portion of the program. I like talking to you as much as I like being able to touch you and kiss you and make you moan."

"Is there anyone who's going to be heartbroken over you being here with me?"

"Disappointed maybe, but not heartbroken. And I wouldn't be here if I hadn't already ended anything else that matters before I went out with you." He put his arms around her.

"So you ended something to go out with me?"

"Something casual."

"But you ended it because of me?"

"Yes."

"When?"

"Last night."

Her smile did amazing things for her entire face, making her glow with the kind of happiness he'd never seen from her before. "I wish I'd known, Hunter. All that time you felt this way, and I never knew."

"You weren't ready to know. Until Will met Cameron, and you accepted it wasn't going to happen with him, you wouldn't have given me a chance."

"No," she said, sighing, "I wouldn't have, and how foolish that seems now."

"Doesn't matter anymore. All that matters is right here. Right now. And you were well worth the wait." With her kiss-swollen lips hovering just above his, Hunter wanted to pinch himself to make sure he wasn't dreaming this whole thing. "You totally took control of things just now and made me your bitch."

"I did, didn't I?"

"You seem awfully proud of yourself."

"With good reason."

He tightened his arms around her and turned them so he was on top. "Now it's my turn." Gazing down at her, he touched his lips to hers. "After this, after tonight . . . You're mine. You know that, don't you?"

Her expression was impossible to read. "What does that mean exactly?"

"It means that you're not doing this with anyone but me." He pressed his cock against the V of her legs to make his point. "It means that I feel possessive where you're concerned, and not in a creepy way, but in a caring way. I want you to be happy, and I want to be the one who makes you happy." Hunter's heart pounded with anxiety and fear as he waited to hear what she would say.

"I can live with that. And P.S., I don't want to do *this* with anyone but you."

"Damn straight you don't."

"I wasn't expecting our resident mild-mannered accountant to be so alpha."

"Don't let the pocket protector deceive you. Next order of business . . . I had a physical two months ago, and I'm totally safe. I can show you the report from Dr. Edwards if you want to see it."

"I believe you."

"What about you?"

"I'm safe because I haven't had sex in ten years, but I'm not on birth control if that's what you're asking me."

"It is. Since we intend for this to be an entirely monogamous relationship, how would you feel about rectifying that in the next little while?"

"I might be convinced. You're already calling this a relationship, huh?"

"Hell yes I am. I finally have the woman I've craved in my arms and in my bed—"

"I'm actually in the Pig's bed."

"With the big bad wolf," he said with an exaggerated growl that made her laugh. "If that's not a relationship, I don't know what is."

"I . . ." Her brows furrowed, and she bit her bottom lip adorably.

Hunter kissed her, forcing her to release her abused lip. "What? Just say it. Whatever you're thinking, I want to know."

She looked up at him with those amazing sky-blue eyes, and he knew he wanted to see them every day for the rest of his life. "I don't know if I'll be any good at this relationship business. I've never done it before."

"We'll figure it out together. I haven't done it in a long time, and none of the others mattered the way you do, so there's no comparison."

"Why do I matter so much?"

"I can't explain why I feel the way I do when I look at you. I only know I've never felt this way before about anyone else. And I have a sneaking suspicion I wouldn't ever feel this way about anyone but you."

"That's a lot of pressure."

"No pressure. I promise."

She raised a brow that called him out on his shit.

He grinned. "Okay, maybe a little pressure," he said, pressing his cock against her rhythmically. "But only the good kind."

"You're incorrigible."

"If you say so. Right now, what I am mostly is dying from wanting to make love to you."

"I'm not saying no."

"We don't have any condoms."

"Don't all guys have at least one in their wallet, especially a guy who's as ruthlessly organized as you are?"

"Chalk it up to a rare case of unpreparedness. I thought we were having dinner. Never in my wildest dreams did I imagine this night unfolding the way it has."

"Your wildest dreams need to get a little wilder."

"Clearly," he said with a snort of laughter.

She tapped on his shoulder. "Let me up."

"Do I have to?"

"Just for a minute. I'll be right back."

"All right," he said reluctantly as he moved off her and propped his head on his hand to watch her get up. Bare except for the thong that left her gorgeous ass on full display as she walked into the bathroom, she was so fucking sexy. Long and lean and toned . . . His mouth watered in anticipation of all the many ways he planned to express his desire for her.

"Ah-ha," she said from the bathroom. "The Pig doesn't disappoint."

"I'm almost afraid to ask . . ."

If the back view of her had been amazing, the front side was jaw-dropping as she emerged from the bathroom, her luscious breasts bobbing as she moved, her light pink nipples requiring his full attention until she revealed the strip of condoms she'd been hiding behind her back. "Along with toothbrushes, toothpaste, razors, shaving cream and anything else we might need."

"They stock the bathrooms with condoms. Get out of here."

She made a feint toward the door. "Okay, I'm going."

"Don't you dare! Get your sexy ass over here, and bring your new friends."

Laughing, she crossed the room and fell into his outstretched arms. Their lips came together in a kiss that could only be called epic—tongues and teeth and hands . . . Everywhere he could reach. He wanted to devour her and rock her world so thoroughly that she'd never have a reason to look at any other man for the rest of her life.

A tall order for any guy, but Hunter was up to the challenge as he broke the kiss and arranged her under him. He took the condoms from her, pleased to see there were six of them. That might be enough for what he had in mind. "Hands over your head."

She swallowed hard, her eyes big and round, her lips puffy and damp from their kisses, but she did as he directed.

CHAPTER 13

The only limits are, as always, those of vision.

—James Broughton

Hunter focused on the spot on her neck where her pulse throbbed and ran his tongue over it, reveling in the knowledge that she was excited and ready for whatever he might ask of her. "Hold on to the headboard if you need to, but your hands stay there, okay?"

She licked her lips, and that slight movement of her tongue made his dick harder than it had ever been—and they were just getting started.

"Anytime you say the word *stop*, we stop. But if you say it, make sure you mean it, because it's game off. Got me?"

Wrapping her fingers around the iron bars that made up the headboard, she nodded.

"Are you comfortable?"

Her legs moved restlessly, which made her breasts bounce. "For the most part."

"Where are you uncomfortable?"

"You know!"

He cupped her mound, pressing his fingers between her folds. "Here?"

Megan lifted her hips. *"Yes."*

Hunter teased her for a full minute, loving the way she moved almost desperately against his fingers. "We'll come back to that."

"Ugh, that's not nice."

"Oh, baby, I'm going to be so nice to you."

"Yeah, yeah. So far all I'm getting is a lot of talk."

"I love that saucy mouth of yours." Hunter cupped her breasts and sucked her nipple into his mouth, using his tongue and teeth.

She went wild under him, which made him want to skip over all the preliminaries and go straight to the main event. Instead, he gave the other side the same attention before moving down to place strategic kisses on her belly, making a straight line to her core, kissing her through the strip of satin that covered her. The scent of her desire and the knowledge that she was so wet for him tested the fragile hold he had on his control.

Even though he'd warned her, he didn't want to scare her or turn her off by acting like a rutting beast the first time he made love to her. Thank goodness she'd taken the edge off with the incredible blow job. Otherwise, he'd be out of his mind by now. With his thumbs under the strings around her hips, he eased her panties down her legs and discarded them behind him. Placing his hands on her knees, he spread her legs apart.

Other than a thin strip of pale blonde hair, she was bare before him.

She lifted her hips off the bed, all but begging him to do something. "Hunter . . ."

"I'm here, sweetheart. Just admiring the incredible view."

"Stop looking and start *doing*."

"Look at who's being bossy now."

"Hunter!"

Chuckling, he kissed his way slowly and torturously from her knee to her thigh, taking little nibbles as he went until he reached her center. "Should I do the other side, too? I wouldn't want that leg to feel left out."

"If you do, I'll kill you." Her voice sounded frustrated and aroused and so sexy it wasn't even funny.

He opened her to his tongue and set out to make her as crazy as she was making him. Using his tongue, teeth and fingers, he drove her up and over the first peak before she knew what hit her. And then he did it again. By the time he was ready to move on, she was panting and sweating and quivering.

"Look at me," he said, hovering now above her.

She forced her eyes open.

"Everything okay in there?"

"All is well. Very, very well."

"Excellent. Ready for more?"

"There's *more*?"

"Much more."

"I'm ready."

He kissed her and sat back on his knees to roll on the condom, returning to his new favorite place between her spread legs when he was suited up.

"Can I touch you now?" she asked.

"I wish you would."

She brought her arms down from over her head and wrapped them around his neck, hugging him. "That was incredible."

"From where I was, too."

"You really like doing that?"

"I love doing that, but only when it's you."

"You're just saying that."

"No, I'm not. It's not always my favorite thing to do, but with you, it could become my new favorite thing." As he spoke, he nudged at her opening with his cock, working his way in slowly, knowing it had been a while for her. And oh, *God*, was she tight and hot and wet.

His entire body trembled from the effort it took to go slow, to take his time, to not lose control before she was ready to take him. "Feel okay?"

"Burns a little bit."

"Want me to stop?"

"No." To make her point, she curled her hands over his ass and nearly triggered his release by pulling him into her.

Then she gasped, and they both froze.

"Easy, baby. Nice and easy. Try to relax."

"Hard to relax when I'm being invaded."

He laughed, which made him falter in his effort to go slow and retain control. Withdrawing, he started over, moving in tiny increments until he felt her begin to relax even as her flesh contracted around his, making him see stars. Being inside her was the most incredible feeling he'd ever experienced.

Curving his hands under her shoulders, he dropped his forehead to rest on hers, his eyes closed and his heart pounding so hard he could hear the staccato beats, one right after the other.

She lifted her hands to his head, combing her fingers through his hair and then down to massage his shoulders.

"Megan . . ."

"Hmm?"

"This is my favorite moment of my entire life so far. I just thought you should know that."

She looked up at him, her expression one of amazement. "I think it's mine, too."

"I need to move."

"It's okay. You can."

"Are you sure? It doesn't hurt?"

"No, it doesn't hurt. I just feel very . . . full."

The comment sparked the fire inside him, and he began to move faster, withdrawing almost completely before filling her again.

Her nails dug into his ass, which was like gas on an already burning flame. He positively ignited, losing himself in her, in the feel of her soft skin against his, her breasts mashed against his chest and her legs wrapped around his hips. There was nothing else but her. There would never be anything else but her. That thought was crystal clear to him in the midst of the best sex of his life. This went so far beyond the word *sex* that Hunter didn't even know what to call it.

Love. It was love and lust and desire and passion. He'd never felt all those things at the same time before, and the combination was overwhelming. He reached between them to make sure she was with him when he finally let go and gave in to the powerful need to come.

She cried out as she came, her tight channel gripping his cock so hard he saw stars as he followed her into paradise.

He kissed her as he came, his tongue tangling with hers until he couldn't last another second without breathing. "Holy shit," he whispered when he could speak again. Every inch of his body tingled in the aftermath. Somehow he'd always known it would be incredible with her, but nothing could've prepared him for the reality of what it had been like to make love to her. "Megan . . ."

"Yeah?" Her voice was hoarse and sexy sounding.

"You wiped me out."

"I think you might've killed me."

"I didn't hurt you, did I?"

"Not at all. You made me feel like it was my first time, because it's never been like that before."

"I'm so glad to hear that." He kissed her and felt himself begin to harden again inside her. "I think we should call in sick to work tomorrow."

"That might be the best idea you'll ever have."

"No, bringing you to the Pig's Belly was the best idea I'll ever have."

She laughed and drew him into another kiss.

CHAPTER 14

There are no secrets to success. It is the result of preparation, hard work, and learning from failure.

—General Colin Powell, former secretary of state

No matter what time Will Abbott arrived in the office, and he was a fairly early riser, their office manager, Mary, was always there first. He was convinced after years of trying to beat her to work that she had some sort of monitoring device on him to tell her when he was on his way so she could get there first.

Today was no exception.

"Honestly, Mary, how do you do it?"

After years of answering that question, she said the same thing she always did. "I'll never tell." She'd worked for the Abbott family business for more than thirty years and was one of their most valued employees—and a good friend to all of them.

"I'm going to figure it out one of these days."

"Keep trying. There was a message from Hunter on my voicemail. He's not coming in today."

That news stopped Will in his tracks. "What did he say?"

"Just that he won't be in today."

"And nothing else?"

"Nothing else. Oh, and this came from Nina across the street." She handed him a big white envelope. "She said it's the paperwork Hunter requested about the diner's financial status. Could you put it on his desk for me?"

"Why is Hunter inquiring about the diner's financial status?"

"How would I know? You did hear it's for sale though, didn't you?"

"Yeah, but he didn't say anything to the rest of us about buying it."

"Perhaps he's only looking into it at this point."

"Maybe."

Will put the paperwork on Hunter's desk and went into his own office to prepare for a meeting with a new cheese supplier who was coming in to talk with him this morning. They were expanding their Vermont Made line in anticipation of the website going live by the end of the year.

Charley appeared at his door an hour later, looking grumpy as always first thing in the morning. "You got a minute?"

"Uh-huh." Will looked up from the information the supplier had sent him. "What's up?"

Charley came in and dropped into Cameron's chair, sucking down a huge sip of her coffee. "This thing with Hunter and Megan. What do you think of it?"

"I think it's great. He's been into her for a long time."

"But wasn't she into *you* until very recently?"

"She had a thing for me, but there was never anything to it. She's moved on."

"To our brother. That doesn't worry you at all?"

"Why would it worry me?"

"*Because* you don't want to see him get hurt by a woman who might be using him to get to you?"

"How is she going to 'get to me'? It's quite apparent to anyone and everyone who knows me that I'm off the market."

"Who knows what she's thinking? It wouldn't be unheard of for a woman to use one man to get closer to another."

"You're not giving him enough credit, Charl. He's no fool."

"I was in high school with her—a year ahead of her, but I knew her. I was dating this guy for a while, but he dumped me for her because I wouldn't sleep with him and she would."

"So we're going to hold something against her that happened more than ten years ago?"

"I'm just saying . . . We should keep an eye on her and make sure she's not using him or something."

"I get that you're worried about him, and I'm sure he'd appreciate the concern, but you need to stay out of it. He's a grown man who knows what he wants. If he's found it with her, leave him alone. And leave her alone, too."

"You don't need to be so bitchy about it," she said.

Pot, meet kettle, Will thought, but kept the thought to himself. "I'm not being bitchy. I'm just saying it's none of our business."

"Since when? Why does he get a free pass when everyone else's business is fair game around here?"

"I'm not saying give him a free pass. Feel free to bust his balls to your heart's content, but don't drag up shit from ten years ago when we were all young and stupid to plant doubts in his mind that he doesn't need right now. That's all I'm saying."

"You've gone soft."

"Someday it might happen to you, too."

"Doubtful," she said disdainfully.

"I pity the fool who has the good fortune to fall for you," Will said with a teasing grin.

"He'd have to be a fool."

Will laughed. "Go away and let me work, and keep your nose out of Hunter's business."

"Does he know you've appointed yourself his guard dog?"

"I'm nobody's guard dog, but I've been where he is right now. It's hard enough to navigate a new relationship without everyone scrutinizing your every move."

"He's going to bring on his own scrutiny. He's late again."

"He's not coming in today. He left a message for Mary."

Charley's mouth fell open. "He actually *called out of work*? Hunter Abbott. Our brother?"

"The one and only."

"And Megan wasn't at the diner when I stopped for coffee. Holy shit! This is a four-alarm scandal!"

"No, it isn't, Charley."

"Get real. In Butler, this counts as headline news, and you know it. I love how he called Mary when he knew she wouldn't be here, rather than having to talk to one of us."

"Can you blame him? He's never called out before, so he probably didn't even know what to do."

"He knew exactly what he was doing," Charley said.

"Who knew what they were doing?" Lincoln asked as he joined them, dogs in tow and coffee in hand.

"Hunter called out for the day," Charley said.

Lincoln's face showed a moment of delight that he quickly curbed. "Did he now?"

"And Megan's not at the diner," Charley added with a salacious smile.

"Really. Well . . . That's interesting."

Charley pounced. "Right? That's what I'm trying to tell Will."

"And I'm trying to tell her to relax and leave him alone," Will said.

"Not a bad idea," Lincoln said. "You might want to take your brother's advice."

Charley rolled her eyes in a way that encompassed them both. "Whatever." She left the office, probably headed to find someone more willing to gossip about Hunter than Will and their father were.

"How about that?" Lincoln asked when he was alone with Will.

"Not you, too."

"I'm happy for him. It's about time he did something about his feelings for Megan."

"I'm happy for him, too. So happy for him I plan to leave him alone so he can enjoy it without *all* of us bugging him."

"You've become wise in your old age, William."

"Whatever you say. Let me ask you—what's up with Hunter

looking into buying the diner? How can we swing that on top of the website and the new acreage?"

Lincoln bent to scratch Ringo behind the ears. "He's looking into buying the diner? That's news to me."

"Look me in the eye and say that."

"Say what?"

Exasperated, Will said, "I don't believe for a minute that you know nothing about this. What're you up to now?"

"I'm not up to anything. Have you also become suspicious in your old age?"

"I have good reason to be. You've been like a matchmaking fool lately, thinking we don't know what you're up to."

"Again I have to say I don't know what you're talking about."

"Again I have to say look me in the eye when you say that."

"You're being suspicious when there's no place for suspicion. We'll let Hunter clear this up for us when he comes back tomorrow. Until then, no point speculating."

"Right," Will said. "No point."

"Got to get to work." Lincoln scooted out of the office with Ringo and George in hot pursuit.

Will had barely returned his attention to the information about the cheese vendor when Cameron came rushing in, coffee in hand. They never had gotten around to finding her an office of her own. Why bother when he was more than happy to share his space with her? Every time he laid eyes on her, he fell more deeply in love with her. Today was no exception.

"Megan was a no-show at the diner this morning," Cameron reported, her eyes big and her smile even bigger. "*Where* is Hunter?"

"Your guess is as good as mine."

"Shut the front door! Are you serious? He's a no-show, too?"

"You heard it here first."

"Oh my God! This is fantastic news!"

"You really think so? After the way she treated you?"

Cameron waved a hand. "What do I care? She was sad to

lose out on a chance with you, and after having a chance with you, I can't say I blame her."

"Shut the door and come here."

The small private smile she reserved just for him was one of his favorites. She closed the door and came around the desk, stepping between his legs. "Yes?"

Will held out his arms to her.

She put the coffee cup on the desk and came down on his lap, curling her arms around his neck. "What can I do for you?"

"This." With one hand cupping her sweet ass, he kissed her like he hadn't seen her in a year, as if he hadn't woken up with her that morning and engaged in slow, sexy morning lovemaking before leaving her to sleep a little longer while he got an early start.

"Mmm," she said against his lips. "What brought this on?"

"I missed you."

"For the one hour you were away from me?"

"I miss you when I'm away from you for one minute."

"You've got a bad case, Mr. Abbott."

"You bet I do, and it's all your fault."

She nuzzled his neck and kissed the spot below his ear that made him rock-hard every time, as she well knew.

"*Cameron*. It's not nice to do that to me here."

"I hate to point out that you started it."

"You started it by crashing into our moose and making me fall in love with you."

She giggled softly. "Let's blame it on Fred."

"It really is his fault."

"Thank God for Fred," she said with a sigh.

He tightened his hold on her. "I keep thinking it's not possible for anything to feel as good as I do when I'm with you."

"I have the same thoughts."

"No regrets about moving away from your life in the city to live with me?"

She raised her head off his shoulder to meet his gaze. "Not one single regret. Best thing I ever did."

"Yes, it was."

"We need to work so we can get through the day and go home together."

Will groaned with agony over the hours that stretched out ahead of them before they could truly be alone—or as alone as they ever were with his dogs, Trevor and Tanner, underfoot. "How about a nooner?"

She squirmed on his lap, making him groan for a whole other reason. "That could be arranged."

"I'll never make it until then."

"Be strong." She laid a kiss on him that made him want to beg for mercy—and a time machine that would make it noon right now. Then she got up and moved to her chair on the other side of his desk, pulling her laptop from the messenger bag that went everywhere with her.

She switched into work mode effortlessly while he was still firmly stuck in I-want-sex-and-I-want-it-now mode. "Get to work, Will," she said without taking her eyes off the laptop screen.

"I'd rather watch you work."

"You need to get ready for your meeting with the cheese lady."

"I'm far more prepared for my meeting with you."

She bit her lip to hold back a smile. "Work now, William. Play later."

"Life isn't fair," he muttered as he forced his attention back to the prospectus from the cheese lady. Despite his protestations to the contrary, he was finding life to be exceptionally fair lately—and sweeter than he ever could've imagined. He couldn't wait to ask Cameron to marry him, but first he had an important phone call to make. The thought of that call curbed what was left of his libido and filled him with an unreasonable amount of anxiety.

CHAPTER 15

—◄►—

Yesterday's home runs don't win today's games.

—Babe Ruth, baseball player

" *I can't.*"

"We've got one condom left." From behind her, Hunter cupped her breasts and tweaked Megan's nipples, making her moan. "You wouldn't want him to feel left out, would you?"

"Since when are condoms male?"

"They're certainly not female, and don't try to change the subject."

"You aren't tired of this subject yet?"

While continuing to toy with her nipple, he tore open the condom wrapper with his teeth and rolled it on with his free hand. "I'm never going to be tired of this subject."

"Hunter . . ."

With his hand under her leg, he pulled it back to rest on his hip, opening her to him. "Are you too sore, honey?"

"I was too sore after the second time."

"So the sixth time won't make anything worse. That's what you're saying, right?"

"This is madness," she said with a nervous laugh.

"Utter madness, and the single best night of my whole life."

She covered the hand he had on her breast with her own. "Mine, too."

"Was it really or are you just saying that because you feel you have to?"

"Definitely because I feel I have to."

Laughing, Hunter pinched her nipple and pressed only the tip of his cock into her. By now he knew to expect the way her tight channel contracted around him, forcing him to bite down hard on his lip to keep from losing it like an unseasoned boy rather than a man who'd never truly made love before the night he'd spent lost in her.

"*Hunter*," she said on a long exhale that did nothing to help him control the need to plunder.

"Talk to me. Tell me how it feels."

"Incredible. You know that."

"Does it hurt?"

"No." She reached behind her and cupped his ass, pulling him into her.

"Would you tell me if it did?"

"No."

"Megan . . ."

"Shut up and finish what you started, will you?"

"If you're going to be that way about it." She made him laugh, she made him crazy, she made him forget everything that didn't involve her and she made him want to shirk his responsibilities for the first time in his adult life. Grasping her hips, he turned them so she was facedown and he was on top of her. On his knees, he pulled her up until she was on hers, too, and then entered her fully.

"Oh God," she whispered.

He watched her hands roll into fists above her head. "Too much?"

"No! Don't stop."

Hunter didn't need to be told twice. With her fully on board, he let go and let loose, pounding into her like he hadn't had sex in a year, rather than five times in the last twelve hours. Just like their previous encounters, this felt like the first time all over again. He was officially addicted to being inside her.

"Megan," he said on a choppy moan, "you feel so good."

Her legs fell open wider, and she met his every thrust with the press of her ass against his abdomen. Knowing this was going to be over quickly, he reached around to press his fingers against her clit, sending her into another screaming orgasm that triggered his. By his count, that was eight for her and six for him. He'd be lucky to ever walk again and could only imagine how she must feel.

He lay on top of her, pinning her to the bed as aftershocks beat through them both, making him want to stay right here, in this moment, forever.

"We need to go home," she muttered after a long period of silence.

"We're moving into the Pig's Belly. Welcome home, baby."

She snorted with laughter that made her tighten around his cock. As if he hadn't just come like a madman, he felt himself begin to harden again. Was it possible to break your cock from too much sex?

"No way! Out with you! We're not doing it again. I'll be crippled."

Laughing, he kissed his way down her back as he withdrew from her, ending with a gentle bite to each of her delicious cheeks that made her squeal. He went into the bathroom to deal with the condom and ran a washcloth under warm water. Before leaving the bathroom, he turned on the bathtub faucet, pouring in some of the bubble bath the Pig had been good enough to provide. Hunter left the bathroom and found her right where he'd left her, facedown on the bed, eyes closed, lips red and puffy from hours of kissing.

He caressed her back and bottom. After the night they'd spent together, he was officially addicted to her ass as well as a few other important parts of her. "Turn over, honey."

"Don't wanna move."

"You'll like this."

"No more."

"I heard you. I think my penis is sprained anyway."

That made her laugh as she turned over, her eyes meeting his in the bright light of day for the first time. Her cheeks flushed with what might've been embarrassment, but she never looked away.

"Good morning," he said, leaning in to kiss her.

"Morning."

With his hand on her inner thigh, he said, "Open up."

"You've got to be kidding me."

"Just do it. You'll be glad you did."

"That's what you said after the fourth time."

He laughed and shook his head at her saucy comeback. He'd expected her to be hot in bed—in fact, he'd spent an inordinate amount of time thinking about what she might be like in bed only to discover the real thing was far better than anything he could've imagined. But her humor had been unexpected and amazingly refreshing.

Without breaking the intense gaze, she let her legs fall open.

Hunter tried to remember that this was about caretaking and not about sex, but damn was it hard to keep from drooling at the sight of her swollen pink flesh, still slick with the remnants of her release. Swallowing hard, he pressed the warm washcloth into her cleft and held it against her sensitive tissue.

Megan's eyes closed, and she moaned with pleasure. "That feels so good."

"I've got something that would feel even better."

She opened one blue eye, and the way she looked at him let him know he'd better not be thinking what she thought he was thinking.

"Not that, you sex-crazed nympho."

"Me. Right. If I'm a sex-crazed nympho, what does that make you?"

"A Megan-crazed nympho."

His reply drew a big smile from her. "You're very cute in the morning." She reached up to run her fingers over the stubble on his jaw. "I like you this way."

Having her look at him that way and say such things made him light-headed and incredibly hopeful that they'd started something in this room that might turn out to be far more than a fantasy for both of them. "What way?"

"Unshaven, uncombed, un-put-together. I've never seen you like that."

He turned his face into her hand and pressed a kiss to the palm. "I'll have to let myself go more often."

"That'd be fine with me."

Sliding his arms under her shoulders and knees, he lifted her from the bed.

She let out a squeak of surprise. "Seriously? What're you doing? You're going to sprain something else carrying me around."

"You're light as a feather for a tough guy like me."

"Sure I am. Where're you taking me?"

"Since we're both bare-ass naked, not far."

"That's a relief."

He carried her into the bathroom and deposited her into the bubbles that now reached the halfway point of the deep claw-footed tub. When he would've stood to leave her to soak, she grabbed hold of his hand. "Plenty of room for two."

"Scoot forward." Hunter got in behind her, sinking into the warm, fragrant water with a sigh of pleasure. "That feels so good."

"Sure does."

He shut the water off and put his arms around her.

She took his hands and linked their fingers. "Hunter?"

"Hmm?"

"What happens after we leave here and go back to our real lives?"

"This is our real life now."

"It's not just a fantasy?"

"Not for me it isn't. For me it's the best reality I've ever had."

"I still can't believe you feel that way about me."

"You'd better start believing it because I have no intention of not feeling this way about you." He pushed her damp hair aside, kissing her neck and along the tendon that led to her shoulder. "I want us to go home and be together as much as we can."

"So it wasn't just about what happened last night and this morning for you?"

The question hit him like a fist to the gut. Did she really think that?

She rested her head on his shoulder and looked up at him. "Hunter?"

"No, it wasn't about the sex, even if it was the best sex I've ever had in my life. It was about you and being with you and getting to know you and finding out—finally—that all my instincts where you're concerned were spot on. The sex was awesome, amazing, life-changing. But if all we'd done was talk and sleep in the same bed, I'd feel exactly the same way I do now."

"And how do you feel?"

"Captivated. Enthralled. Devastated."

"Why devastated?"

"Because I didn't act on my attraction to you ages ago. Because I was too damned afraid that you'd shoot me down. I should've done something about it sooner."

"You were right last night when you said I wouldn't have been ready."

"Do you feel ready now?"

"I don't know."

"What don't you know?"

"I'm still afraid."

"Of what?"

"Of letting myself feel all these things for you and then having something happen to you or to us . . ."

"Nothing's going to happen."

"You can't possibly know that."

"I know that wild horses and a team of mules couldn't drag me away from you after spending an incredible night with you. There's nothing in this world that would make me not want to be with you."

"You don't know that."

"I do know that."

"What if . . ." She bit her lip, trying to think of how to say what she wanted to ask him.

"What if what?"

"What if 'your Cameron' comes crashing into town, and you take one look at her and realize she's the one you're meant to be with?"

"Megan," he said, sighing, "I've already met the one I'm meant to be with. That's what I've been trying to tell you. Didn't I do a good enough job of showing you how ruined I'd be if you told me this was a one-night stand?"

"I don't want it to be a one-night stand."

"Thank goodness." With their hands still joined, he crossed one arm over the other and wrapped them around her. "I detect a note of hesitancy, however."

"I'm not hesitant about you. It's just that I have no idea what's going to happen now that Nina is leaving, with the diner and everything."

"Nothing has to be decided today or tomorrow or even next week, right?"

"Right."

"So try to relax and chill. It'll work itself out."

"Is that what you would do in my situation? Relax and chill?"

Hunter laughed at the insightful comment. "Probably not."

"Didn't think so."

"How is it that you already know me so well?"

"I suppose I've been getting to know you for a while now. Do you realize you come in at the exact same time every morning and every afternoon?"

"I do?"

"Yep. And you always order the same thing—a tall coffee with cream and two sugars and a grilled corn muffin at seven fifteen every morning. Just the coffee at one forty in the afternoon."

"I do like my coffee."

"Right at one forty every weekday without fail."

"Because you close at two."

"You sell coffee in your own store."

"So? Yours is better and plus, you're not the one doling it

out in our store, although you could if you wanted to. If you decide you're done with the diner and waitressing, we'll find a job for you at the store. If you want to work there, that is."

"That's very sweet of you, but wouldn't your family find it a bit bizarre if we go out on one date and then suddenly I'm working there?"

"We'll be going out on far more than one date, and we created an entire department for Will's girlfriend. I doubt anyone would say too much about hiring mine."

"Your girlfriend . . . You're already giving me a promotion, and I'm not even on the payroll yet."

The comment was flippant, but he knew she had to be reeling from him using that word to describe her. "I want you to be my girlfriend, Megan. I haven't had one—an official girlfriend—since college. I know it's a stupid term right out of high school, but call it whatever you want to—girlfriend, significant other, lover—"

She let out a shriek. "No! Not *lover*. I hate when people call each other that. We get it already. You're sleeping together and feel the need to broadcast it to the world. 'Oh, he's my *lover*.' Gag."

Hunter rocked with silent laughter. "Tell me how you really feel. You don't have to call me your lover as long as you're willing to *be* my lover."

"Ewww." She pulled her hands free and put them over her ears. "Stop using that word. It's like *panties* and *moist* and *ointment* and *congealed* and *excrete*." She shuddered. "Horrible words."

"I've never met anyone who had word phobias."

"Now you have. Do not use those words around me."

"So what you're saying is I can never tell you that my lover's moist panties congealed—"

Her hand over his mouth ended the sentence prematurely. "Do *not*."

He nibbled playfully on her fingers. "I can't believe you didn't want to hear the rest of my sentence, and how did we get from me calling you my girlfriend to congealed ointment?"

"Hunter! I'm serious! Those words gross me out."

"How about these words?" He whispered every filthy, sexy word he could think of in her ear. "Are they allowed?"

"Those are fine," she said primly.

"Your system is screwed up. You know that, don't you?"

"My system, my rules."

"What other rules do you have?"

"You'll have to wait and see."

"I can't wait. I want to know everything there is to know about you."

"You make me sound so complicated, when I'm anything but."

"I wouldn't say that. Since we left home last night, I found out you're a writer, you're funny, you hate the word *lover* and you got into Middlebury. I found out that you have a very sexy mole right here." He pointed to the spot to the right of her belly button. "I found out what makes you come—I love watching you come, by the way—and I found out you snore."

"*What?* I do not snore!"

"Yes, you do. Little tiny snores. Very cute."

"You're making that up."

"Okay, then. If that's what you want to believe . . ."

She crossed her arms. "I'm never sleeping with you again."

"Yes, you are. Tonight, in fact. I want you in my bed."

"Not if you're going to tell me I snore!"

"Then I won't tell you. I'll enjoy it in silence."

"I may need to reconsider this whole thing in light of these revelations."

"Please don't do that." Hunter pushed her arms aside and cupped her breasts, teasing her nipples gently.

She arched into him, wincing.

"Hurts?"

"Little bit. They got one hell of a workout last night." She turned over to face him.

Hunter put his arms around her and looked down at her lovely, rosy skin, made even more so by the heat of the bath.

"I had a really great time," she said. "Thank you."

Touched by her sincerity, he said, "Thank *you*."

"We should probably get going. Nina is leaving in a couple of days, and I want to spend as much time with her as I can."

And just that quickly, the bubble they'd been in all night burst. Hunter felt her withdrawal keenly. If he'd had his way, they would've stayed here all day or at least until the Pig kicked them out of its belly.

Megan stood to get out of the tub, and Hunter offered his hand to guide her and then followed. He released her hand only to give her a towel and to wrap one around his waist. Then he reached for her again. "This is only the beginning, Megan."

She smiled up at him, but she didn't reply.

He could only hope she felt the same way.

CHAPTER 16

————◆————

*If you did not look after today's business then
you might as well forget about tomorrow.*

—Isaac Mophatlane, businessman

H ours later, Hunter pored over the information Nina
had provided that outlined the diner's financial situation. No matter how he spun the data, however, the results
were always the same—the diner was operating in the red.
Brett and Nina had bought the building at the peak of the
real estate market and were carrying a hefty mortgage. That,
coupled with the high cost of food and the relatively low
prices Nina charged her customers, made for a less-than-
profitable picture.

In addition to the financial news, the inspection performed
that afternoon by his cousin Noah, a contractor, had yielded a
number of costly upgrades that needed to be done to bring the
building up to code. Nina and Brett were lucky they hadn't
been subjected to a fire department inspection in the last year.
According to Noah, the hood over the grill had to be replaced
immediately. Noah had told him it would be nearly impossible to insure the building without that upgrade.

Hunter took his role as the family's fiduciary steward
seriously. Regardless of his personal desire to keep Megan

close by, he couldn't, in good conscience, encourage his grandfather to invest his hard-earned money in the diner, knowing what he did now about the financial picture.

Running his fingers through his hair until it stood on end, Hunter tried to find a way to make the numbers work. He needed this to work. If it didn't, what reason would Megan have to stay in town?

The thought of her leaving after the night they'd spent together made him feel sick and sweaty, as if he had some sort of flu or something. With tremendous reluctance, he picked up the phone to call his grandfather.

"Hey, it's Hunter," he said when Elmer answered.

"Ah, just the man I was hoping to hear from. What's the good word?"

"I'm afraid there isn't one."

"What do you mean?"

"The numbers don't add up, Gramps."

"Speak to me."

Hunter launched into a detailed explanation as to why it didn't make financial sense for his grandfather to sink his money into the diner.

"Are these challenges you speak of insurmountable?"

The night without sleep suddenly caught up to him, and Hunter was exhausted at the thought of what needed to be done to turn things around at the diner. "Not completely, but normally when you invest in a business you do so because you feel it will be beneficial to you financially. I can't promise that'll be the case here. In fact, it could be the exact opposite of beneficial."

Elmer was quiet long enough that Hunter wondered if he was still there. "Gramps?"

"I'm here. Just thinking." After another long pause, Elmer said, "Have you ever heard the story of how my father came to open the store?"

Hunter pinched the top of his nose, trying to ward off an exhaustion-fueled headache he felt coming on. He loved his grandfather beyond all reason, but he didn't have the patience at the moment for one of his stories. All he wanted was to see Megan again, but since she'd asked for a few hours with her sister, he was giving her some space. Hunter sat back in his desk chair, prepared to settle in for a few minutes. "Yes, I've heard it."

"I don't think you've heard the whole thing." Elmer loved nothing more than to spin a yarn, and now was no different. "You know the store opened during the Depression when things were hard—really hard. Nothing you imagine can do justice to how bad it was. My first memories were of my mother crying over the fact that she couldn't buy meat. 'How am I to feed my babies if I can't buy meat?' I heard her ask my father one night. It didn't register to me at the time that things were that bad. I figured it out much later, as an adult, when I had a family of my own to feed. I tell you this to give you context of what kind of moxie it took for my father, in that environment, to say, hey, let's open a business that requires a significant investment in inventory."

Despite his exhaustion, despite his desire to move the clock forward to when he could be with Megan again, Hunter was riveted by his grandfather's story.

"My mother was vehemently opposed. They argued about it, and they didn't often argue, especially in front of us. But they argued about the store. My father's position was that he could fill a need for people in the Northeast Kingdom."

"She didn't agree?"

"She agreed it was a good idea. What she couldn't handle was that opening the doors would take every dime they had along with some they didn't. She was afraid of what would become of us if the store failed."

"I've never heard all this."

"It's not something my father liked to talk about. He was crazy about my mother, and the fact that they disagreed so profoundly over this was hard on him."

"But he convinced her."

"Eventually, but it cost him. It cost *them.* I have to give my mother credit. Even though she didn't agree with opening the store, she threw herself into helping him make it work. And they worked around the clock. She had him put a stove and refrigerator in the storeroom so she could cook for us when they had to work late. We had beds back there, too. We practically lived at the store for the first year. And at the end of that year, it was rather apparent to all of us that the store was going to fail."

Hunter could barely breathe. He'd never heard that either. The literature on display at the store told an entirely different story of the family business that didn't include any flirtations with failure. "What happened?"

"The Christmas tree farm happened."

"How so?"

"My father heard a rumor that the owners of the farm had defaulted on the mortgage and abandoned the property. So he went to the bank and worked out a deal to take on the mortgage, beginning in January. That was in October. He called in everyone he knew to harvest the trees. My mother ran the store while he harvested trees until he couldn't move because he was so sore from the backbreaking work. The sale of the trees that Christmas brought in the cash he needed to save the store and make the first mortgage payment on the tree farm. As you well know, we've run the farm ever since."

"And it continues to be a cash cow every holiday season."

"Never more so than that first year. The point of all this, my boy, is that all business, fundamentally, is a risk. Nothing ventured, nothing gained. Jimmy Carter said, 'Go out on a limb. That's where the fruit is.'"

"So you're saying the diner is the fruit?"

"I'm saying it could be the next Christmas tree farm. But if we don't try, we'll never know."

"I'll make the offer."

"You've done your due diligence, son, and you've done it thoroughly the way you always do. The decision was mine and mine alone, just as it's my decision to tell you to make the offer in your name, not mine."

"Gramps," Hunter said, flabbergasted. "It's your money. I can't do that."

"Why not? It's my money. I can do with it what I want, can't I?"

"Of course you can, but—"

"No buts. What's mine is yours. Make the offer and have it come from you. It'll give me great pleasure to watch you turn that place into another Christmas tree farm. I have every confidence you can do it."

Hunter wished he had the same confidence in himself. What did he know about running a restaurant?

As if he'd read Hunter's mind, Elmer said, "If my father could figure out what he needed to know under the conditions he faced when he opened the store *and* make it work, so can you."

"Well, thanks for the vote of confidence. I'll do my best to make you proud."

"You always do. Every day of your life, you've made me proud."

"Thank you," he said, humbled by his grandfather's effusive love.

"Let me know how it goes with the offer."

"I will."

"I happened to hear you took Megan out last night. I hope you had a nice time."

"Yeah." Hunter smiled at what had to be the understatement of his lifetime. "We had a nice time."

"Glad to hear it. I like that girl. She's feisty and isn't afraid to say it like it is."

"That about sums her up."

"She'd be good for you. I've always thought so."

"Always? How long is always?"

"For about as long as you've thought she'd be good for you. It might come as a shock to you to learn that not much gets by me."

Hunter laughed hard. "That would hardly come as a shock to any of us."

Elmer's guffaw kept the smile on Hunter's face long after they'd said their good-byes. His grandfather was truly one of the most uniquely authentic people in Hunter's life, and the story he'd told him was one that Hunter would never forget.

* * *

Megan sat at the foot of Nina's bed and sorted through a basket of socks, helping her sister pick out which ones to take and which ones to put in storage. The task helped to quiet her mind, which had been racing on overtime since she awoke that morning in Hunter Abbott's arms after the most incredible night of her life.

"You're awfully quiet over there," Nina said as she worked on the closet. "What're you thinking about?"

"Nothing much."

"You're not going to tell me what happened on a date that lasted all night? You're not going to tell me why you actually called out of work for the first time . . . ever?"

"Sorry I left you shorthanded at the last minute."

"Who cares about that? We coped. Talk to me about what happened with Hunter."

"We had a really nice time." And wasn't that putting it mildly? She'd never had a better time with any man.

Nina plopped down next to her on the floor. "That's *it*? That's all you're going to say? You spend more than twelve hours in the company of one of the hottest guys in town—hell, in the *state*—and that's all you've got to say? It was *nice*?"

"You think Hunter Abbott is hot, Neen?" Brett said from the doorway. "You never told me that."

Megan cracked up laughing. "Busted."

"Go away, Brett. I'm digging for information that she'll never give me if you're in the room."

"*Pardonnez-moi.*" He'd been driving them crazy with the French all afternoon. "But I just wanted to ask your opinion." He held up two pairs of dress shoes. "Take or don't take?"

"Take them both and go away."

"Just gonna be me and you after Wednesday. Don't forget that."

"I'm not forgetting, but I'm also not going to be forgiving

if you don't buzz off and let me snoop into my sister's love life, so *au revoir*."

Megan put her hand over her mouth to keep from laughing out loud.

"Now you're making me want to stay."

"Brett!"

"Fine, I'm going, but you have to tell me what she says later."

"You'd better not tell him," Megan said after Brett left them alone.

"So far there's nothing to tell," Nina said glumly. "You gotta give me something."

Megan hesitated for a moment, not wanting to say too much but needing to talk it out with someone, and Nina would always be her first choice. The thought of her being so far away in France when Megan needed her . . .

"Don't do that. Don't make that face. We'll Skype and FaceTime and talk every day just like we always do. There'll never be a time when I'm unavailable to you. Ever."

Like always, her sister had said exactly what she needed to hear. Megan leaned in to her one-armed embrace and rested her head on Nina's shoulder.

"We went for a drive when we left here last night. Ended up at a tavern on the side of the road called the Pig's Belly."

"Sounds . . . romantic."

Megan laughed. "Not so much, except the food was amazing, and there was this band playing, so we danced, and then they had rooms upstairs for people who drink too much, except they aren't just 'rooms.' They call them fantasy suites, like on *The Bachelor*."

"Seriously? In a place called the Pig's Belly?"

"I know! We said the same thing."

"Go on . . ."

"We were having a really great time, so we decided to stay. And that's what happened." Ever since he dropped her off at home earlier with a chaste kiss and a promise to call her later, she'd thought about him constantly.

"No way! You are not getting off that easy. You have to tell me the rest."

Brett came to the door again. "Don't shoot the messenger, but Hunter is here looking for you, Megan."

Her entire body tingled with awareness just from hearing he was downstairs waiting for her.

"Oh my goodness," Nina said. "You lit up like a firecracker on the Fourth of July."

Megan leaned in to kiss Nina's cheek. "I'll let you finish up here. Gotta go."

"You'll be in to work in the morning?"

"Of course I will. Where else would I be?"

"*Soooo* much I could say to that."

Eager to see Hunter, she patted Brett's shoulder as she passed him in the doorway and headed down the stairs at the house where she'd grown up. It would be weird to have other people living in it, but it didn't make sense to let it sit empty when Brett and Nina could make some money from the rental.

While he waited for her in the living room, Hunter studied the display of her old school photos on the wall.

"Hey," she said.

He turned and smiled, and her entire world tipped upside down in the span of a second, all because of a smile that reminded her of the intimacy they'd shared the night before. Every muscle in her body ached from what they'd done, but she couldn't wait to do it again.

"You were so cute." He pointed to the picture of her in full ballet regalia. "Adorable."

"That was taken at the pinnacle of my dance career."

"How old were you?"

"Eight, I think. It was a short-lived passion."

He jammed his hands into the pockets of his jeans. Tonight he'd worn faded denim that hugged his muscular legs and other important places. He also hadn't gotten around to shaving, which only added to his over-the-top appeal.

Knowing they weren't alone, and Nina was probably

listening to everything they said, Megan put her hands in her own pockets, trying to resist the urge to run to him, to kiss him, to touch him.

"I hope it's okay I came here. You didn't answer the door at your place."

"Of course it is. If I'm not there, I'm usually here. Or I was. I won't be coming here for much longer." She looked around at the living room that still looked exactly the way her mother had left it—for a few more days anyway. Movers were coming on Saturday to pack everything into crates that would go into storage until Megan and Nina were ready to deal with it.

"Are you okay?"

"Yeah." She pushed back the melancholy that had hovered close to the surface all afternoon while she helped Nina pack. "It's just strange to think of other people living here."

"You could move in here and rent out the garage apartment."

"We talked about that, but they could get more for the house, and what do I need with all this space? I like my apartment." She was rambling and she knew it, so she made an effort to shake off the blues about Nina's move so she could focus on him. "Anyway, how are you?"

"I'm good. Much better now that I'm with you again."

She melted inside every time he said things like that. "Did you go to work?"

"For a couple of hours." His brows furrowed, but he seemed to remember where he was, and the exasperated look disappeared. "Are you hungry?"

"I could eat. Then again, I can always eat."

"Want to grab something?"

"That's what you said last night and look where that got me."

At her mention of last night, he flashed a sexy grin that made her melt in a completely different way. After last night, she was amazed that her girl parts could still tingle like that. In reality, the numbness had worn off the minute she heard he was downstairs waiting for her.

"No Pig's Belly tonight. How about we hit the grocery store, and I cook for you at my house?"

"You cook?"

"I cook, I bake and I iron. Got anything to say about that?"

"Um, nothing other than can you bake me chocolate chip cookies?"

"Please," he said with a scoff. "I could do that by the time I was eight."

"I'll confess to being aroused by this information."

"That's all it takes?" Smiling, he held out his hand to her. "Shall we?"

Megan eyed his outstretched hand with barely restrained desire to feel his skin brushing up against hers. She couldn't remember ever wanting to touch another human being as badly as she wanted to touch him right then. "Neen," she called up the stairs. "I'm going out."

"Don't forget to come home."

She smiled at Hunter. "I might, so don't wait up." Then she took his hand and drew in a deep breath when he gave a gentle tug that brought her in tight against his chest. He kissed her cheek and then her lips. "Sorry," he whispered, "but I was about to die from wanting to do that."

"I was about to die from wanting you to."

"Let's get out of here."

He led her out of the house to the passenger side of his SUV and held the door for her. When she was seated, he leaned in to kiss her again, lingering when her hand came around his neck to keep him there. What she'd intended to be a quick kiss became something else altogether when his tongue swept into her mouth as he grasped her hair. He withdrew from her in small increments until his lips were merely touching hers.

"Holy moly," he whispered, his eyes closed.

She caressed his face, giving special attention to the stubble he'd left on his jaw because she'd told him she liked it. "I like how you say hello."

Laughing, he put his arms around her, hugging her

tightly. "I couldn't wait to see you. Did I give you enough time with your sister?"

"Just enough. I can only do so much to help them. They have to decide what they're taking and what they're leaving."

Hunter kissed her again, buckled her in and closed the door.

Megan watched him walk quickly around the front and kept her eyes on him as he got into the driver's side and caught her looking at him. "What?"

"Just enjoying the view."

He rested his hand on the wheel and stared into the darkness. "I was afraid I'd come to see you and everything would've changed again."

"Why would you be afraid of that?"

"Last night was . . . intense and incredible. It meant so much to me to be with you that way, and I hoped . . ."

"It meant just as much to me, if that's what you were worried about."

"It was."

"I haven't been able to think about anything but you and last night since you dropped me off earlier."

He released a long, ragged deep breath that sounded an awful lot like relief to her. "I haven't thought about much of anything else either."

Megan was equally relieved to hear that, and when he reached across the center console for her hand, she gladly offered it.

CHAPTER 17

---

*Success in business requires training and discipline
and hard work. But if you're not frightened
by these things, the opportunities are just
as great today as they ever were.*

—David Rockefeller, banker and philanthropist

They drove over the one-lane covered bridge on the way out of town.

"That's where I grew up," he said, nodding to Hells Peak Road.

"Everyone knows about the Abbotts and their red barn full of kids."

"You can get away with a lot in life when you grew up in a barn."

Laughing, she said, "How'd you end up a fashionista when you grew up in a barn?"

"I like nice clothes. Why does everyone have to make a thing of that?"

"Because no other man in town dresses like he just stepped out of the pages of *GQ*."

"That's their problem. Not mine."

"True, and for the record, I'm not complaining. I think

you always look really nice. I thought so long before yesterday, too."

He smiled at her. "Is that right?"

"Uh-huh."

"Goddamn it." Hunter swerved to avoid a huge dark object in the middle of the road. "What the hell is Fred doing out at this hour?"

"Doesn't he do his best work at night?"

"Yeah, just ask Cameron."

"I thought people in town would hate her for running into Fred," Megan confessed as they drove around the immovable town moose, tooting at him as they went by. "Instead they fell in love with her."

"She's a really nice person. There's nothing about her not to like."

"That's what I hear."

"You might like her, too, if you give her a chance."

"I wouldn't blame her if she never speaks to me again after the way I acted when she first started seeing Will. I'm ashamed of how I behaved with her."

"It's in the past now. You apologized. She and Will accepted it, and they've moved on. You should, too."

"Yes, I suppose."

"Besides, I want you to come to dinner at my parents' house on Sunday."

"*This* Sunday?" Megan asked, her voice squeaking.

"Why not?"

"Um, well, I, ah . . . Let me get back to you on that." The thought of going completely public with his big and boisterous family so soon after they started seeing each other made her stomach ache with nerves.

They rode to the grocery store in comfortable silence, which was a revelation in and of itself. In her past dating life, she'd always felt the need to fill the silences with some sort of mindless chatter because she worried about the guy losing interest in her. With Hunter, there seemed to be no risk of that happening.

Relaxing into the soft leather seat, she pretended to look out the window while Hunter drove to the grocery store on the outskirts of town. But really, she took every chance she got to look at him.

"What're you in the mood for?" he asked while they waited at a red light at the entrance to the parking lot.

Megan was on the verge of a suggestive reply when bright lights filled the windshield as a car came straight for them across the divided highway. Before she could get out the scream that tore from her chest, Hunter floored the accelerator. The SUV shot forward, through the red light and into the intersection, missing a direct hit by the out-of-control car, which landed in a ditch by the side of the road.

Hunter turned into the parking lot and took the first empty space he could find. "What the hell?"

She couldn't seem to get air to her lungs.

He tuned into her distress, released his seatbelt and came across the center console to her. "Megan, sweetheart, look at me."

Trying to contain the panic, she forced her gaze to meet his.

"Breathe." He placed his hands on her shoulders and gave her a small shake. "*Breathe*, Megan."

She forced air into her lungs, which seemed to relax the stranglehold on her chest. Once she was able to breathe again, she broke down into sobs. "I'm sorry."

"Oh God, honey, don't be sorry." Somehow he managed to fold himself into the small space in front of her and gather her into a tight embrace.

"Scared me."

"I know." He ran his hand over her hair. "It's okay. We're both fine, and I'm so sorry you were scared."

Despite his soothing tone, she couldn't seem to stop crying as the close call kept replaying in her mind. Wanting to think about anything other than what had nearly happened, she burrowed into the curve of his neck and breathed in the sexy, masculine scent she'd become addicted to in the course of one memorable night.

The sound of sirens and the red flash of emergency lights were a reminder of just how close they'd come to potential disaster.

"I'm right here," he said. "Hold on to me for as long as you need to."

"I feel so stupid. Nothing actually happened, and I can't stop crying."

"Please don't say that. You have every reason to be upset." He pulled back from her and wiped the tears from her cheeks and then kissed her softly.

Looking down at him, her tears became laughter when she realized how he'd twisted and contorted his long legs to fit in the small space.

"What's so funny?" he asked, seeming baffled by her seesawing emotions.

"You're going to be crippled if you sit like that for much longer."

"I'm fine. Are you?"

She used her sleeve to wipe the remaining dampness from her face. "I am now. Sorry I overreacted."

"You didn't." He took her by the chin and looked into her eyes. "It scared the hell out of me, too, and I haven't lost the two people I love best in a car crash."

"You get it."

"I got it as it was happening."

She looked around him to the scene playing out in the intersection. "Do you suppose anyone was hurt?"

"I hope not. They're in good hands with the paramedics." He tucked her hair back behind her ears. "Do you want me to take you home?"

She shook her head. "Let's continue with our plans."

"Are you sure?"

"I'm sure."

"I might need to be surgically extracted from the car."

Megan giggled and opened the door, sliding out of the car and then reaching out to help him.

Groaning, Hunter unfolded himself and then jumped around in the parking lot to get the blood flowing to his extremities again. "Note to self: Get a car that allows front-seat snuggling."

"Thank you," she said softly.

He put his arm around her, kissed her temple and walked with her into the store, where people were talking about the crash at the intersection.

"Did you hear if anyone was hurt?" Hunter asked the manager, who was watching the action across the parking lot.

"From what someone heard on the police radio, they think the guy in the car that crashed had a stroke or other medical emergency, but he's alive and talking to them."

"Wow," Hunter said.

Megan shuddered as she remembered the close call. "Hope he'll be okay."

Hunter kept his arm around her while she pushed the cart through the produce aisle. Despite the recent scare and subsequent meltdown, Megan wanted to purr from the pleasure of his nearness, the heavy weight of his arm on her shoulder, making her feel safe and cherished at the same time.

They decided on salad, chicken he'd cook on the grill and potatoes.

"Do you drink OJ in the morning?" Hunter asked.

"Sometimes."

"Let's get some."

"You're making a lot of assumptions, Mr. Abbott."

He raised a brow as he looked down at her. "Am I?"

Her entire body, which was still sore and tender from the night before, tingled with awareness of how this evening would probably end. "No, not really."

"We need to check out the ice cream aisle, too."

"A man after my own heart."

"Yes, he certainly is."

The comment, while flippantly delivered, made her heart flutter and her body heat with desire. How he managed to do that with only a few words was a mystery to her. They turned the corner to the ice cream aisle and came face-to-face with Mrs. Andersen, one of Butler's resident busybodies.

"Oh," she said, obviously delighted to have nearly crashed

into them with her cart. "Hello, Hunter. Megan." She looked from him to her and then to him again. "Hunter and Megan." She clapped her hands gleefully. *"Together.* Isn't this something?"

To his credit, Hunter kept his arm around her, which told Megan he didn't care in the least that Mrs. Andersen had caught them together or that she'd be back in Butler within the hour to spread the news about them through town with the speed of a drought-fueled wildfire.

"How are you, Mrs. Andersen?" he asked, always polite.

"Just fine, Hunter. And you?"

He squeezed Megan's shoulder. "More than fine. In fact, I'm fantastic. Never better."

Way to throw gas on the fire, Megan thought as she subtly nudged his ribs with the elbow that was plastered to his side.

"We've got to get going," Hunter said. "See you soon."

"Yes, you will," Mrs. Andersen said. Her round face wore a delighted smile when they moved past her.

"Fine, fantastic, never better," Megan said in a mimicking tone the minute they were clear of big ears.

"You liked that, huh?"

"The words *gas* and *fire* went through my mind when you said that."

"She does like to spread the good word. That's for sure."

"We made her year with this encounter."

"Good," he said, "because this 'encounter' as you call it has made my year, too. In fact, I think it's possible it's made my life."

"You really like me that much?"

"I adore you."

Right there, in the middle of the ice cream aisle, with prying eyes all around them, Megan turned to him and kissed him square on the lips without a care in the world as to who might see them. He adored her. What could be better than that?

CHAPTER 18

———◄✦►———

Life is too complicated not to be orderly.

—Martha Stewart, businesswoman

It turned out, his chocolate chip cookies were almost better than being adored by him. She ate four of them, one right after the other. His company and attention had helped her to bounce back from the earlier scare. She'd enjoyed the dinner they'd prepared together as well as the cookies he'd made while she nursed a glass of wine and watched him bake.

"I take it you approve of my cookies?"

"Oh my God. *Approve?* Yes, I approve. I want more."

"You're going to get sick."

"What a way to go."

With the kitchen cleaned to his exacting standards, he took off the apron he'd worn to amuse her and hung it on a hook by the oven. Bringing the bottle of chardonnay with him, he went around the counter to join her on the other stool and topped off her glass.

"Are you trying to get me drunk so you can take advantage of me?"

"Do I need to get you drunk so I can take advantage of you?"

"Hardly. I think I proved how easy I am last night."

"Easy?" He laughed. "Yeah, right. You put me through hell, woman."

"I did not."

"Um, yeah, you did. Do you know how many times I've had to order a second cup of coffee because I was so hard from watching you run around the diner that I'd embarrass myself if I got up to leave?"

"That's not true!"

"It's absolutely true. I would sit there and try to think about anything other than how badly I wanted to kiss you and touch you and . . . I wanted more than anything to be able to talk to you."

"You talked to me all the time."

"About what I wanted to eat or whether I wanted more coffee. I wanted to talk about *you.* I wanted to know what you think about, what you care about, what you dream about, what you look like first thing in the morning."

She cringed.

He tapped on the furrow between her brows. "Don't do that. I've seen what you look like first thing in the morning, and it's a thing of beauty."

"Right . . . Sure, it is."

"Megan, look at me."

She forced herself to look into eyes that seemed to see right through her. With any other man, she might feel exposed or vulnerable, but Hunter made her feel safe and wanted in a way that was all new to her.

"You're beautiful, inside and out," he said, right before he kissed her. Then he leaned his forehead against hers and took hold of her hand. "Want to see the rest of my house?"

"Any part in particular?"

"I thought I'd show you my piano."

Because she hadn't been expecting him to say that, she laughed. "You play the piano?"

"Yep. Not very well, but well enough to accompany Nolan when he sang to my sister at their wedding."

"He did? Oh wow, that must've been amazing. What did he sing?"

Keeping his hold on her hand, he led her into the room he used as an office where his upright piano sat against the wall. " 'I Won't Let Go' by Rascal Flatts."

"I love that song. What did Hannah think?"

"She cried. We all did. It was amazing. Until he asked me to accompany him, I didn't even know he could sing. He's got an incredible voice."

"What a perfect song, considering the circumstances."

"I thought so, too."

"Will you play for me sometime?"

"Anytime. But I don't sing. Ever."

"Sounds like there's a story behind that."

"No story, but if my siblings are to be believed, I sound like cats fighting when I sing."

Megan cracked up. "Nice."

"It's a tough crowd, especially for the oldest and wisest."

She rolled her eyes and followed him up narrow stairs to the second floor. He showed her the guest room and guest bathroom. Everything was perfectly clean and orderly, nicely decorated and visually appealing. She expected nothing less from him.

"And now for the main event," he said, leading her into his room, which was done in shades of blue with red accents.

"This is really nice. I love your house. I can tell you put a lot of time into making it yours."

"I've painted every square inch of the place. It was a mess when I first moved in. Took about two years of nights and weekends to get it the way I wanted it."

"You cook, you bake, you iron, you balance the books, you paint. Is there anything you can't do?"

He put his arms around her and cupped her bottom, drawing her in tight against his arousal. "You left out a few of my favorite skills." Nuzzling her neck, he made her crazy with only the touch of his lips against her fevered skin.

Megan couldn't seem to get close enough to him. She wanted to drown in his rich, appealing scent. She wanted to feel, again, the way he'd made her feel the night before when he'd treated her like the most precious thing in his life. It was a heady feeling, she'd discovered, to be on the receiving end of that kind of attention from a man who was as sweet as he was sexy.

"What're you thinking right now?" he asked against her ear, making her tremble.

"That I like the way I feel when I'm with you."

"How do you feel?"

"Safe, happy, amused, aroused, intrigued."

"Don't forget adored."

"How could I forget that?"

"Don't forget that. Don't forget any of it. I love that you feel all of that when you're with me. I feel the same way. I can't get enough of you." He undressed her slowly and reverently, worshiping each new bit of skin as he revealed it. His kisses and caresses set her on fire and had her clutching a handful of his thick dark hair as he kissed his way down the front of her, kneeling before her to remove her jeans and panties. Watching him remove them made her forget she hated that word.

He ran his hands up the back of her legs, cupped her bottom and drew her in closer until his face was flush against her belly.

Her legs trembled while she waited to see what he would do. She combed her fingers through his hair, loving how soft it was. "You're overdressed for this party," she said, hoping to move things along when he seemed perfectly content to stay right where he was while she burned for more.

Hunter squeezed her bottom and then dragged two fingers through the dampness between her legs, making her gasp when he touched her swollen clitoris. "Are you sore from last night, honey?"

Her head fell back and her lips parted from the incredible pleasure of his touch. "Mmm. So sore."

"I'm sorry about that. I'd never want to hurt you."

"You didn't. It's a good kind of sore."

"Sit back on the bed." He helped to arrange her the way he wanted her with her bottom at the edge of the mattress, her legs spread.

Megan was already on the brink of explosive release and he'd barely touched her. And then he pressed her legs farther apart with his hands on her inner thighs and bent to give her his tongue in soft, soothing caresses that made her cry out from the pleasure that zipped through her body.

"Hurt?"

"No. God, no. It's incredible."

He did it again and again and again, licking and teasing and coaxing with only his tongue.

She came twice, one right on top of the other, the second time nearly giving him a bald spot from the frantic way she pulled his hair.

"I could do this all night," he said after her second orgasm.

"Get naked and come here," she said when she could speak again.

"I'm happy right here."

She laughed nervously at the idea of him actually pleasuring her all night. She had no doubt he'd do it if he thought she wanted him to. "Hunter, please. I want you."

Never taking his eyes off her, he stood and unbuttoned his shirt, letting it slide off his broad shoulders. The T-shirt under it followed, landing on the floor.

As he reached for the button to his jeans, Megan sat up and pushed his hands away. "Let me." She pulled the button free and slowly unzipped him, a task that was made difficult by the rock-hard erection behind the zipper. Pushing the jeans and another pair of silk boxers over his hips, Megan leaned in to take him into her mouth.

"Oh God," he whispered as his cock hit the back of her throat.

Megan let it stay there for a full minute before she withdrew and did it again, this time adding her tongue to the mix.

"I didn't think I'd ever come again after last night, and you've already got me right there."

"Do it," she whispered against the tip, making him arch into her. She took him in again, grasping his ass and digging her fingers into the dense muscle.

He cried out, pumping his release into her mouth.

Megan sucked hard, triggering a second wave.

"Holy fucking shit," he whispered.

Knowing she'd once again made the oh-so-classy Hunter Abbott swear made her smile as she slowly released him from her mouth.

He came down on top of her, driving his tongue into her mouth and squeezing her breasts.

Megan wrapped her legs around his hips and felt his recently satisfied cock begin to harden again. "That was fast," she said.

"I'm always hard when you're around. Always."

He kissed her everywhere and had her on the verge of begging when he rolled off her, breathing hard but keeping a tight grip on her hand.

"What's wrong?" she asked.

"You're sore. We should stop. And you have to work early. You have to be tired."

What she was, Megan thought, was incredibly turned on. With that in mind, she sat up and opened the drawer in his bedside table.

"What're you looking for?"

"Condoms."

"Bathroom. Medicine cabinet."

"Stay put."

"Couldn't move if my life depended on it."

She got up and went into the bathroom that adjoined his bedroom and found the condoms right where he'd said they would be. Remembering what had happened last night with six of them, she took half as many tonight and returned to where she'd left him, laid out on the bed, fully erect and absolutely gorgeous. Before her eyes, he got even bigger.

Megan tore open the packet, and with her lip between her teeth, she concentrated on rolling it down his length. Satisfied with her work, she straddled him and leaned over to kiss him.

"We don't have to. I don't want to hurt you."

"You won't."

"Megan . . ."

Another thought occurred to her then. "Unless you don't want to."

"Said no guy ever when a gorgeous babe like you is naked in his bed."

He was so free with the compliments, and she loved them all. She loved that she turned him on so thoroughly, and that he wanted her so badly was a huge turn-on to her as well. Because she was, in fact, still sore from their sexual marathon the night before, she took him in slowly, loving the way his eyes closed, his lips parted, his jaw throbbed and his fingers dug into her legs as he fought for control that she wasn't prepared to surrender.

Taking him in wasn't the easiest thing she'd ever done. Despite how well he'd prepared her, her abused tissues fought the invasion, and for a minute or two she didn't think she could do it. But she forced herself to relax, to recall the incredible pleasure she'd found in his arms last night and again tonight.

Hunter cupped her breasts, playing gently with her tender nipples, which helped to ease his entry below. "Nothing has ever felt this good, Megan. Ever."

"For me either," she said breathlessly. And it was true. Sure, she'd had way too much sex when she was younger, but what she'd done then and what she was doing now with him could hardly be compared. Everything about this was different, and it had been from the beginning. He was different, and she was falling in love with him one minute at a time even if she hadn't planned to let that happen.

It was truly astonishing to her that he could've been so close and yet so far away all this time, and the idea that she could've missed out on this, on him, was truly humbling.

Ten full minutes after they started, she finally was able to take him completely inside her, and for a long moment, he stayed perfectly still even as he gritted his teeth from the effort. "Okay?" he asked, sounding tortured.

"So good."

"Move, Megan. Please . . . Move."

With her hands flat against his chest, Megan began to

swivel her hips, slowly at first and then faster as her body yielded to the invasion. Soon, soreness was forgotten, overtaken by the pleasure they found together.

He took hold of her hands and drew them up and over his head, bringing her down close enough to kiss him. The thrust of his tongue, the rub of her nipples against his chest hair and the fullness within her had her climbing again.

Needing air, she tore her lips free and sucked in greedy gulps. Without missing a beat, Hunter rolled them over so he was on top, pressing into her rhythmically but gently at the same time. "Feel good?"

She looked up to find him gazing down at her with those soft brown eyes that *saw* her the way no one ever had before. "Amazing."

"For me, too."

Under him, she squirmed, trying to get closer, needing him deeper. "Hunter . . ."

"I've got you, honey." Seeming to know what she needed better than she did, he hooked his arm under her left leg and bent it to her chest, opening her fully to his deep strokes. He got the angle just right, making her moan.

"Let me hear you. There's no one around. You can be as loud as you want."

He bumped up against her clit, and she cried out.

"Again." He did it again and again until she screamed from the orgasm that ripped through her.

She felt it everywhere, from the tips of her fingers to the bottoms of her feet and most intensely in the place where they were joined.

He pushed into her hard and fast, and then came with a shout that triggered another wave for her.

Four orgasms in thirty minutes was another first for her. With him warm and heavy on top of her and throbbing with aftershocks inside her, Megan knew a rare moment of perfect contentment, and it was all because of him.

CHAPTER 19

The true entrepreneur is a doer, not a dreamer.

—Nolan Bushnell, engineer and entrepreneur

Since there was no time to spare before Nina and her husband left town, Hunter used his morning coffee stop to set up a meeting with her for that afternoon, after the diner closed at two. Like always, the diner was full of people enjoying coffee and breakfast when Hunter came in at quarter after seven.

Megan caught his eye immediately, smiling and pointing to her wrist, letting him know he was right on schedule. He loved that no one in the diner knew she'd left his bed just over an hour ago. She made him want to shake things up, to bust out of the rut he'd been in for the thirteen years since he'd graduated from college. Until recently, the rut had worked well for him. But now he wanted to examine life outside the lines.

He'd begun his new experiment by not shaving again that morning. Two days in a row broke all his personal records, and his siblings would be all over him about it when they saw him. He planned to explain the stubble by telling them he was growing a beard. Let them wonder. The idea of him being even slightly unpredictable was preposterous to everyone who knew him, which made it fun to embrace the unexpected.

That it made Megan happy was the ultimate payoff. All she'd had to say was that she liked him with some stubble, and he'd put down his razor.

He chose a spot at the counter that gave him a full view of the diner and Megan as she went from table to table, talking, refilling mugs and smiling. She was smiling a lot. Did he dare to think he might have something to do with that? God, he hoped so.

Nina poured him a mug of coffee and slid the creamer and sugar across the counter.

"Can we talk later?" he asked.

"Sure."

"My office after the lunch rush?"

"I'll be there."

"Thanks."

Megan worked her way to his end of the counter and slid onto the stool next to him. "Could you hand me a mug, Neen?"

Her sister put one on the counter in front of her.

"Thanks." Megan poured the last of the coffee in the pot she'd used for refills into her own mug and stirred in cream.

Hunter fought off a powerful urge to lean over and plant a long wet one on her in front of the hometown audience.

She glanced at him, as if she knew what he was thinking, and said, "Don't."

"Please?"

"No."

"Megan."

She giggled behind her hand. *"Hunter."*

"Yes?"

"Don't act so innocent. I know better."

"Mmm, yes, you do."

"You're now officially five minutes over your allotted breakfast time."

"Don't tell my dad. He'll dock my pay."

"Wouldn't you be the one to dock your pay?"

"Yeah," he said, scratching at the stubble on his chin, "I guess I would."

"So you can stay for another five minutes?"

"That can be arranged."

"Good, because there's something I want to show you in the office. Can you come see?"

Hunter tried to get a read on whether she actually had something she wanted to show him or if she wanted to be alone with him. Like a lovesick fool, he hoped it was the latter. "Lead the way." He followed her into the kitchen, past Butch, the cook, who stopped what he was doing to give him a once-over. There was a dude Hunter wouldn't want to screw with. He nodded to Butch, but the cook never so much as blinked.

Megan led him into a cramped office that had a desk, a chair and not much else. Squeezing around him, she closed the door to Butch's prying eyes.

"What did you want to show me?"

"I made that up so I could do this." She drew him down and into a kiss. "Before you did it in front of everyone."

Hunter pinned her against the closed door and tipped his head to kiss her again. "You surprise the hell out of me, you know that?"

"Why? Because I wanted to kiss you as badly as you wanted to kiss me?"

"Yeah. I keep feeling like I'm going to wake up, and I'm still going to be wishing I could touch you like this." To make his point, he cupped her breasts through her thin cotton T-shirt and felt her nipples harden immediately.

She returned the favor by caressing the erection that pressed insistently against his zipper. "You feel very much awake to me."

All the air left Hunter's body in one long, low sound that was part exhale, part moan.

The sound of a bell ringing snapped Hunter out of the desire-induced stupor.

"Megan!" Butch barked. "Pick up!"

"He's such an ass," she said, right before she initiated another kiss that involved tongue this time.

Hunter was actually weighing whether they could pull off a quickie in the office when the bell began to ring incessantly.

"Megan!"

"I don't have any orders in, and he knows it. I'm going to kick his ass."

"Is he into you?" Hunter asked. The thought had never before occurred to him, and the possibility left him reeling.

"No! He's like a brother to me and Nina."

"Does he know that?"

"Yes, Hunter," she said, exasperated. "He's very protective of us."

The bell continued to ring repeatedly, which had to be annoying the patrons by now.

"Damn him," Megan said, the second before she threw open the door. "What the hell, Butch?"

"You're working."

"I'm taking a break!"

"Not in there alone with him you're not."

"I'm going to be twenty-eight years old in a week. Leave me the hell alone."

"No."

"Yes!"

Hunter made a mental note of her upcoming birthday as well as the cleaver Butch held in his left hand. "I'll see you later?"

Megan never blinked in her stare-down with Butch when she said, "Don't go yet."

Hunter stood awkwardly by her side until she finally ended the staring contest.

"Leave me alone, Butch. I mean it." She took Hunter by the hand and all but dragged him out of the kitchen and back into the crowded diner right as Hannah and Nolan came through the door. They stopped short at the sight of Megan dragging Hunter around by his hand.

"Well," Hannah said with a big smile for her brother, "looks like things are going well with you two lovebirds."

Megan immediately released his hand. "I, um, I should get back to work."

"I've got it, Meg," Nina said. "Hang out with your friends."

Though she had no good reason to be nervous, the thought of "hanging out" with Hunter's twin sister and her husband filled her stomach with angry bats. She missed the butterflies.

His hand on her lower back helped to calm her as they followed Hannah and Nolan to a booth in the back of the diner.

Conversations halted and the volume dropped considerably as every patron stopped what they were doing to watch them walk by. No doubt Mrs. Andersen had already told the whole town she'd seen them together at the grocery store. In Butler, walking through the diner with Hunter Abbott's hand on her lower back counted as a public coming-out party.

She appreciated that Hunter guided her into the side of the booth that put their backs to the prying eyes of the town. Across from them, Hannah, already glowing from her pregnancy, positively beamed at her brother.

"You two are so cute together," Hannah said.

"Cut it out, Han."

Megan glanced at him and was surprised to see him looking tense and out of sorts. "What's wrong?" Was he embarrassed to have been caught with her by his sister? Was he not ready to make such a public declaration in front of the town? Did he not want people to know about them? The thoughts rifled through her mind one after the other, making her feel dizzy.

"Nothing. Sorry." He put his arm around her and pulled her in tight against him, kissing the top of her head.

Megan's face flamed with embarrassment as Hannah and Nolan watched with increasing amazement and curiosity.

"I take it things are going well?" Hannah asked.

"Hannah!" Hunter and Nolan said together.

"Leave them alone, babe," Nolan said with a sympathetic look for Hunter.

"Like everyone left us alone when we were first dating?" Hannah asked her husband.

"That was different," Hunter said.

"How so?" Hannah asked.

Had Megan ever noticed before how much the two of them looked alike? Right down to their expressions, the warmth in their brown eyes and their silky dark hair. She was the female version of Hunter and obviously shared his dry sense of humor.

"That was you. This is me. So it's different."

Hannah's ringing laughter had her husband smiling at her mirth. "You're so full of shit your eyes are brown," Hannah said.

"That must be why your eyes are brown, too."

She stuck her tongue out at him, and Megan held back a laugh she knew Hunter wouldn't appreciate. They were too cute together. Pressed up against him, his arm heavy and strong around her, his incredibly appealing scent filling her senses, Megan felt herself relax ever so slightly. It felt good to be held in public by him, to sit with the sister who meant the world to him and have him tell his twin, with only his arm around Megan's shoulders, that she mattered to him.

Wanting to let him know she appreciated his public display of affection, she put her hand on his leg and felt his entire body tense.

"I hope he's treating you well, Megan," Hannah said.

"I give up," Nolan said, smiling at Hunter. "Sorry, man."

"It's all right. She can't help herself."

"That's right, I can't," Hannah said. "So, Megan, all is well?"

Amused by Hunter's obvious distress and annoyance, she smiled up at him. "All is well."

"That's it? That's all I'm going to get?"

"Hannah . . ." Hunter's low growl was full of warning.

"So you've given up shaving, too? I don't think I've seen you with stubble since college. I've got to say, it looks good on you. Kind of rugged and sexy. Don't you think, Megan?"

"Did you just refer to your own brother as rugged and sexy?" Nolan asked his wife.

"So what about it? Just because he's my brother doesn't

mean I don't have eyes. He's a good-looking guy. Don't you think, Megan?"

"I'm going to kill you, Hannah," Hunter said, "and I'm going to make it hurt."

"Oh hush," Hannah said, clearly undeterred by Hunter's irritation. "I'm talking to Megan. Leave me alone."

"I'm sorry about her," Hunter said. "She's been a pain in my ass since about four minutes after I was born."

Megan could no longer contain her laughter. It was indeed hilarious to see the calm, cool, collected Hunter handed his ass by his twin. Spending more time with Hannah was now at the top of Megan's to-do list.

"Don't encourage her by laughing. You can't think she's funny and be with me, too."

"Well," Megan said, "it was nice knowing you."

Hannah dissolved into laughter and raised her fist to Megan, who gave it a bump. As she did, she met the dark-eyed gaze that was so much like Hunter's, and detected a hint of respect coming from Hannah. Until that moment, Megan hadn't realized how desperately she wanted Hunter's family to like her, especially Hannah, who was so important to him.

Nina arrived at their table with four mugs, looking harried and frazzled. "Sorry for the delay. Coffee for everyone?"

"Decaf for me," Hannah said, with obvious distaste.

"Do you need help, Neen?" Megan asked.

"Nope. I got it."

When they all had steaming mugs in front of them, Hannah shifted her attention back to Hunter. "What's this I hear about the family buying this place?"

"Gramps is thinking about buying it."

"Is that right?" Nolan said. "That's cool, huh?"

"Yeah, except he expects me to oversee the whole thing like I've got nothing else to do."

"If anyone can do it, you can," Hannah said.

"We'll have to make some changes, but—"

Megan sat up straighter. "What kind of changes?"

"A few structural things."

"Like what?"

"I should really talk to Nina about this."

"Nina will be gone in a couple of days, and you said you want me to help you run this place if the sale goes through. Doesn't that give me the right to know what kind of changes you have planned?"

"She's got you there," Hannah said, earning another glare from her brother.

"For one thing," Hunter said tentatively, "the hood over the grill needs to be replaced. It failed the inspection."

"Oh. Okay. That's doable. What else?"

"We might have to look at the pricing."

"What about it?"

"At the moment, the diner is operating in the red because the cost of the food is higher than what Nina is charging."

"So you want to raise the prices."

"Possibly."

"Do you know how many people eat here every day because they can't afford to eat anywhere else?" Before he could reply, she continued. "Do you know how many of them come here because they have no one to talk to at home and can find a family of sorts here while they eat meals they couldn't otherwise afford? It's not all about money here. It never has been, and if that's what you're about, you might want to save your grandfather's money and yourself the trouble of buying the place. We'd be better off to let it close down than to try to turn it into something fancy and refined. There's more to the story here than what you'll find in the numbers." He stared at her, and she had no idea what he was thinking. "I need to get back to work. Hannah, Nolan, nice to see you."

Embarrassed by her outburst, but not at all embarrassed by what she'd said, Megan slipped out of his embrace, got up and walked away.

"I like her," Hannah said with a dreamy sigh. "I like her *so* much."

"So do I." Still reeling from Megan's passionate speech,

Hunter never would've guessed her true feelings about the diner and its clientele until she'd so thoroughly schooled him.

Hannah leaned across the table. "Now tell us everything, and leave nothing out."

"I'm not doing that, Han."

"Come on! You've gotta give me something. Who was more up in our business when we first started dating than you were?"

"That was different," Hunter said. "You'd been through so much after losing Caleb. I was just being . . . protective."

"Do you think I feel any less protective toward you? Just because you haven't lost a spouse doesn't mean I wouldn't claw the eyes out of any woman who dared to hurt you."

"She's not going to hurt me. She's amazing. It's everything I always hoped it would be and a few things I never dared to imagine."

Hannah's mouth fell open and her eyes bugged. "Oh. My. God. You're in love with her."

"I have been for years." Admitting that to himself at the same time he admitted it to Hannah was amazingly freeing. Of course he was in love with her. How could he not be?

"Dude, I know the feeling," Nolan said. With a smile for his wife, he added, "Nothing better than finally having everything you've ever wanted."

"I wouldn't say I'm quite there yet, but I'm closer than I was a week ago."

Hannah blinked, and Hunter realized she was trying not to cry. "Hannah . . ."

"Don't mind her," Nolan said. "She cries over insurance commercials these days."

"That commercial was sad!" Hannah wiped away tears that cascaded down her cheeks. "And how is it wrong for me to feel weepy about seeing my favorite person in the whole wide world so happy?"

"Gee, thanks," Nolan muttered under his breath.

"It's a twin thing," Hannah told her husband. "You wouldn't understand." When she reached across the table, Hunter gave her his hand. "I'm going to be honest with you for a minute here."

"And this is new how?"

"Shut up and listen to me, will you please?"

"I'm listening." Despite her meddling and the current histrionics, she was his favorite person in the whole world, too, and she knew it.

"For a long time, I didn't like her very much."

"Hannah—"

"Hear me out. I didn't like her because she could be edgy and bitchy at times. We've all seen that. That said, I also didn't know her very well. Sure, I see her all the time when I come in here, but I didn't *know* her."

"And now you do?"

"I know her better than I used to. I've had a few really fun conversations with her lately, and I've decided she uses the bitchy edgy thing as a defense mechanism."

Hunter had already figured that out for himself, but far be it from him to stop Hannah when she was on a roll. He sat back to listen to what else she had to say.

"I've come to the conclusion that she's actually very sweet and often funny, too."

"Anything else?"

Her eyes flooded with tears again. "I think . . . it's possible . . . she might be good enough for you."

Hunter laughed.

"Don't laugh. I'm being serious!"

"I know you are, and I appreciate your endorsement. I'm sure Megan will, too."

"I want you to be happy, Hunter. That's all I've ever wanted for you."

"I'm happy, Han, so you can stand down."

"Call me crazy," Nolan said, "but Megan seemed sort of pissed just now."

"I'll fix it with her." After what they'd shared over the past few days, Hunter felt fairly confident they could withstand an occasional bump and get past it. "We're good, and I need to get back to work."

"So do I," Nolan said. To Hannah, he said, "Want me to take you home?"

"I do not," Hannah said indignantly. "I'm perfectly capable of driving myself. Cameron is coming over to go over the final plans for the grand opening of Guthrie House, so I've got a full day ahead of me."

"One that includes a nap, right?"

"I'll have no choice about that."

Nolan smiled and kissed her as if Hunter weren't sitting three feet from them watching the whole thing.

Hunter dropped a ten-dollar bill on the table. "And that's my cue to get the hell out of here."

"We're right behind you."

Megan was nowhere to be seen as Hunter left the diner, but he knew he'd see her later when they'd have the opportunity to work out their differences about the pricing. It went against everything he believed in as an accountant and a businessman to allow a business to be intentionally unprofitable. Surely there were some concessions they could make that would allow the diner to continue to assist those in need while also making a profit. He refused to believe it wasn't possible to have it both ways.

CHAPTER 20

*To the degree we're not living our dreams,
our comfort zone has more control of
us than we have over ourselves.*

—Peter McWilliams, self-help author

Hunter emerged from the diner with Hannah and Nolan to find a crowd outside the store. In the middle of the crowd was Fred the moose.

"What's he up to now?" Nolan asked.

"I don't know, but I want to see," Hannah said.

Nolan took hold of her arm. "None of that moose-whisperer business. You hear me? You're pregnant, and if he ever knocked you down . . ."

Hannah waved off his concern. "Oh stop. He's a pussycat."

"She'll be the death of me," Nolan said to Hunter as Hannah marched ahead of them across Elm Street toward the moose.

"Don't let her be. She needs you to live for a good long time. We all do."

"I was joking."

"I wasn't." Hunter tried very hard to never think about the awful days, weeks and months that followed Caleb's death in Iraq. He had spent many a night holding his sister while she sobbed, sleeping next to her because he was afraid she might harm herself to escape the pain, all the while keeping a tight grip on his own grief so he could be there for her.

It had taken a full year for Hunter to feel confident enough in Hannah's stability to let her spend a night alone in the big house she'd inherited from Caleb. That first night, alone in his house in the dark of night, he'd finally shed his own tears for the brother-in-law he'd loved.

Now, following Hannah and her new husband across the street to the store, Hunter was deeply, profoundly grateful to see her happy again with Nolan, expecting her first child and glowing with the kind of joy that had been so much a part of who she'd been before Caleb's death snuffed the light from her eyes.

Nolan's love had reignited that light, and no one was happier to see it again than Hunter.

"Oh for crying out loud, Fred." Hannah marched through the crowd on the sidewalk to the front porch of the store, where Fred had Cameron trapped against the rail. His two front hooves were on the lowest step and his massive body was between her and the sidewalk.

"Hannah!" Nolan said sharply.

His wife proceeded as if he hadn't said anything.

"Oh jeez," Hunter muttered. He didn't often take sides against his twin, but he was firmly on Team Nolan in this case. "Hannah!"

"Fred," Hannah said. "Come down from there and leave Cameron alone. Right now."

Fred let out an obnoxiously loud moo that made more than a few of the townspeople startle. Cameron's usually robust complexion was now stark white as she stared down the moose she'd hit with her car on the way into town the night she arrived from New York City. Since then, Fred had taken an unusual amount of interest in poor Cam, who would always be known in Butler as "the girl who hit Fred."

"Fred." Hannah stood off to the side of the giant moose, looking small and vulnerable. Behind her, Nolan was prepared to do battle to protect his wife, even if that meant getting between her and the moose, who responded to the sound of her voice with a gentle moo and a nuzzle for her outstretched hand. "That's a good boy. Go see Colton up on the mountain. He always has treats for you. And leave Cameron alone. I like her."

Seeming chastened by Hannah's scolding, Fred backed away from the porch. The crowd parted to let him through.

Hunter noticed Cameron wavering on the porch and took the stairs two at a time to get to her before she fell over. "It's okay." He put his arms around her. "Fred's moved on."

"Only thanks to Hannah the moose whisperer." Cameron leaned into him. "Why is he so interested in me? He's looking for revenge, right?"

"Nah." Hunter gave her a quick hug, hoping to calm her. "He's a passive kind of guy."

"Right." Her hands were shaking as she pushed hair back from her face. "Passive."

Will came pushing through the crowd and rushed up the stairs.

Hunter stepped aside to give his brother room.

"What happened?" Intensely focused on his girlfriend, Will took a visual inventory to make sure she was okay.

"Fred happened. Again. I was coming out the door, and it was like he was waiting for me or something. He sort of pinned me against the rail so I couldn't leave, and I was too scared to turn my back on him to go inside."

"He's getting more audacious all the time," Will said.

"He wasn't at all threatening," Hannah said.

"Easy for you to say!" Cameron replied. "He doesn't have a bone to pick with you."

Will put his arms around Cameron. "Come here, baby."

The crowd around them began to disperse, leaving only Hunter, Hannah and Nolan to witness the tender moment between Will and Cameron.

Will drew back from her, kissing her forehead. "Sorry he scared you."

"It's okay. I'm starting to get used to him. Kinda."

"Were you on your way to my house?" Hannah asked.

Cameron nodded. "Not sure if I can drive though. My hands are shaking like crazy."

"I'll drive you," Hannah said. "Will can pick you up later, right?"

"Sure," Will said. "Just give me a call when you're ready."

"Okay." Cameron released a shaky deep breath. "I'll do that. Sorry for the drama, everyone."

"Don't be sorry," Hannah said. "Fred can be an intimidating character when he wants to be, but he would never, ever hurt you. You know that, right?"

"I think so."

"He doesn't believe in revenge," Hunter added.

"How do you know that? He seems rather bent on revenge where I'm concerned."

"Underneath his intimidating exterior, Fred's a pacifist," Hunter said. "He's a make-love-not-war kind of guy."

"And you know this how?" Cameron asked with a healthy dose of skepticism.

"My twin is a moose whisperer," Hunter said. "I'm on the same frequency."

That made them all laugh, as he'd hoped it would, and Cameron seemed noticeably less rattled after a good laugh. "I'm fine," she assured Will. "Go on back to work, and I'll call you when I'm done at Hannah's."

Will kissed her, lingering as he whispered something that made her eyes light up with pleasure.

Hunter looked away, giving his brother some privacy and tuning into the talking-to Hannah was getting from her husband, who was not at all pleased with her for confronting Fred.

"One wrong move, and you're on your ass with a two-ton moose stepping on you—and the baby."

"He'd never hurt me." The dismissive wave of her hand further infuriated Nolan. "He's my friend."

"He is *not* your friend. *I* am your friend. Cameron is your friend. *Fred* is a wild animal."

"You're not going to be my friend much longer if you keep yelling at me."

"I'm not yelling!"

"Hunter, is he yelling?"

"He's speaking loudly."

"See?" Hannah said. "Hunter agrees with me."

"You're impossible," Nolan said. "I'm going back to work. Go home and stay away from that moose, do you hear me?"

Hannah gave him a warm, loving smile. "Yes, dear."

"She's pacifying me, isn't she?" Nolan asked Hunter.

"I would say that's an accurate assessment."

"You're no help to me whatsoever, by the way. Some best man you turned out to be."

"Hey! I gave an awesome toast. Everyone said so."

"For all the good that does me now. You're always going to take her side, aren't you?"

"I'm afraid so. That's just how we roll."

Hannah giggled and gave Hunter a kiss on the cheek. "Love you best of all," she said loud enough for Nolan to hear.

"Anyone know a good lawyer?" Nolan asked as he walked away, shaking his head as he crossed the street to the garage.

"That wasn't nice, Han."

"Oh please. He's always blustering at me about being careful and staying away from anything remotely dangerous. If he had his way, I'd be swaddled in bubble wrap until the baby comes."

"I might be on his side on that one."

"No way. You can't change sides. Doesn't work like that." She curled her hand around his arm. "You're mine." Hannah cleared her throat loudly. "Hey, public-display-of-affection-that's-driving-away-the-customers, are you ready to go?"

"Yeah, yeah." Cameron patted Will on the chest as she left him with one last kiss. "See you later."

"Yes, you will."

After the two women walked away, arm in arm, chatting like old friends, Will came down the stairs to join Hunter. "I think I'm going to have a talk with Dude about Fred." Gertrude "Dude" Danforth, known in town as Snow White, was widely believed to be responsible for the relative taming of Fred the moose. "He really scared her this time. I don't like that."

"What do you suppose Dude can do about it?"

"How the hell do I know? But someone's got to do something. He can't keep confronting Cameron the way he has been since the night she got here."

"He does have good reason to keep an eye on her," Hunter reminded Will.

"What good reason does he have? He was standing in the middle of the road where he didn't belong when she hit him in the dark. How is that her fault?"

"Have you tried telling him that?"

"Now you're just mocking me."

"Do ya think?"

"If you want to play that way, tell me how your first date with Megan turned into an all-nighter."

"That's all right. I'm good. In fact, I need to get to work. Talk to you later?"

"Yeah, yeah. You'll talk to me later all right."

Hunter went up the stairs and into the store before Will could dig in on his quest for information about Megan. Let him wonder.

CHAPTER 21

*All good businesses are personal. The best
businesses are very personal.*

—Mark Cuban, owner of the Dallas Mavericks

For a long time after Hunter walked—or ran—away, Will stood on the front porch of the store, thinking about Fred and Cameron and the phone call he needed to make. Now was a good time to get that taken care of. Cam was out of the office for the next few hours and wouldn't be back until she called him to come get her.

So why were his feet all but cemented to the front porch when he should've been upstairs in his office with the door closed taking care of something he'd been putting off for days now?

Because he was a yellow-bellied coward. That's why. Patrick Murphy had already given Will his blessing. Months ago, in fact, back when Will first met him and professed his intentions to marry Cameron, eventually. That was before she moved to Vermont to live with him. It was before he knew the complete and utter bliss of everyday life with her. It was before he knew what it was like to wake up with her each morning and go to bed with her every night. After a few months of the kind of happiness he'd never dared to dream about, he was ready to make a lifetime commitment to her.

Because she was Patrick's only child and beloved daughter, he owed him the courtesy of a heads-up that a proposal was imminent. Didn't he? Yes, of course he did. So why did the idea of calling Cameron's father intimidate the living hell out of Will? *And we're right back to that yellow-bellied-coward thing again*, he thought, as he took a seat in one of the rockers on the porch.

The gorgeous fall day had people out and about in town, tourists venturing into the store and Elm Street jammed with cars. Autumn in Vermont was second only to ski season in terms of activity. People came from all over to see the foliage that would peak later in the month and into early October. They were far enough north that the color exploded earlier here, and from now until mid-October, the store and the town would be busy.

Thinking about leaves and seasons and tourists was just another way of putting off the dreaded phone call. He was still sitting there ten minutes later when George and Ringo came up the stairs ahead of his dad, who stopped at the sight of Will in one of the rockers.

The dogs came over to greet him, and his dad took the chair next to his. "What brings you out here, son?"

He scratched both dogs behind the ears. "Fred the moose and another confrontation with Cameron."

"Is that right? He's not letting up on her, huh?"

"Nope. Tell me this, Dad. Truthfully, do you think I need to be worried he's going to hurt her?"

"Not for one second. He's not that kind of guy."

"That's what everyone says, but he's freaking her out. And who's to say he won't suddenly turn on her? Just because he's always been a sweet guy doesn't mean he always will be."

"True, but has it occurred to you that he might have a crush on her?"

"A crush."

"Sure. Why not? Moose have feelings, too, and old Fred

knows a pretty girl when he sees one. Maybe he's carrying a torch for her."

"That's so far beyond weird I don't even know what to do with it."

"It's better than thinking he's out to hurt her, isn't it?"

"Yeah, I guess so." The thought of Fred having an actual crush on Cameron was preposterous enough to be funny. He couldn't wait to share his dad's theory with her. "Could I ask you something else?"

"Anything."

"It's kind of personal and not to be repeated."

"All right."

"Could I maybe get you to sign a waiver that would ensure your silence?"

"William," Lincoln said, laughing, "I understand my well-earned reputation for being a gossip, but I *am* capable of keeping important secrets when the need arises."

"Can you provide references to prove this? Because I'm unable to remember a single instance in the history of my life when you sat on something juicy—and this is as juicy as it gets."

"Now you have to tell me."

"Swear to God you won't repeat it?"

"Swear to God, hope to die, stick a needle in my eye."

Knowing that was the best he could hope to get, he took a deep breath and released it. "I'm going to propose to Cameron."

"Ahh, buddy, that's fantastic news." Lincoln's smile stretched across his face and lit his blue eyes with unrestrained glee. "I adore her. We all do."

"As do I." When he thought about how his life had changed since that memorable night in the mud last spring, Will realized that before he met her, he'd lacked the imagination to dream up the reality that was his life today. He hadn't known it was possible to love anyone the way he loved her. He planned to tell her so when he asked the most important question he'd ever ask anyone.

He'd asked the question once before and had been rebuffed,

in what he now viewed as a near miss. He'd be forever grateful that Lisa had said no to his proposal because her rejection had led him to the love of his life. This time he had no doubt whatsoever he'd get the answer he wanted.

"So what do you want to ask me?"

"Earlier this year, when I was in New York, I had a moment alone with Patrick. I told him then I planned to propose to Cam when the time was right and asked for his blessing, which he gave me."

Lincoln nodded in approval. "That's the right thing to do."

"Now that it's actually about to happen though, I'm thinking I should let him know. Do you agree?"

Rocking back and forth, Lincoln pondered that. "It would be a nice gesture, one I'm sure he'd appreciate."

"That's what I'm thinking, too, so why then do I keep putting it off?"

Lincoln laughed. "Because you want to marry the man's only child, his *daughter*, and it's a scary thing to call him up and say, hey, I'm going to take her away from you forever, and I need you to be okay with that."

"I'm not taking her away from him."

"Aren't you? Haven't you already?"

"That wasn't my intention."

"Of course it wasn't, but it's the circle of life. I felt the same way asking Elmer for permission to marry his precious Molly. Like Patrick with you, he barely knew me. She'd gone away for a summer to help build houses for the poor in the South and came home with a flatlander who had lofty ideas about living overseas and getting out to see the world. And I wanted to take his daughter with me."

"What did he say when you asked him?" Will asked, fascinated to hear this for the first time.

"He told me that despite what Molly said to the contrary, she'd never be happy anywhere but here, and that I ought to think long and hard if I felt the need to take her somewhere else in order to be happy myself."

"So wait, you went to him planning to take her somewhere else? Away from here?"

Lincoln nodded. "I'd talked her into going to London for a couple of years, and she was on board with that. At least that's what she told me. But then I talked to Elmer, and he made me see that she was sacrificing her own happiness to serve mine. After that conversation, I changed my mind about wanting to go to England."

"But wait," Will said, "what about what *you* wanted? Didn't that matter?"

"Of course it did. Turns out I wanted her more than I wanted anything else, and it didn't matter to me where we were. But it mattered to her." Lincoln shrugged. "It was a no-brainer to change the plan to make her happy."

"Did I ask too much of Cam by moving her up here?"

"Not at all. She loves it here. Anyone can see that. And it's not just because you're here, although that's the number one reason. The place agrees with her. I know I speak for your mother as well when I tell you we couldn't be happier to have Cameron joining our family. She's an absolute gem, and knowing she loves you so fiercely is a tremendous comfort to us. That kind of love is all we've ever wanted for you—for all of you."

"Thanks, Dad."

"Go make that call. Your future father-in-law will appreciate the courtesy."

"All right." Will got up to return to his office. "Are you coming?"

"In a minute. I'm going to enjoy this beautiful day for a little while longer. I'll be right along."

"Okay then." Will cut through the store and up the back stairs to the offices on the second floor. Fortunately, no one was around in the reception area, so he was able to go directly to his office without having to talk to anyone. He closed the door and sat at his desk to dial the number he'd committed to memory while he worked up the nerve to actually call it.

Will was one of three people in the world who had the private cell phone number of one of the country's wealthiest businessmen. His daughter and personal assistant were the other two. Patrick had wanted Will to have the number in case Cameron ever needed him for any reason, and Will had been honored to be admitted into Patrick's small inner circle.

The phone rang once before Patrick picked up. "Will? Is everything okay?"

"Everything is fine. Do you have a minute?"

"Of course. Cameron is well?"

"She's great. She's with my sister this afternoon. They've become very good friends."

"That would be Hannah, right?"

"Yes, she's my older sister. They've really hit it off."

"I'm glad she's making new friends up there."

"She is, and Lucy's here a lot now that she's engaged to my brother."

"Cameron is delighted to have her there, of course."

"We all are. We never expected anyone would be willing to take on Colton and his mountain, but Lucy is equal to the challenge."

Patrick's hearty laugh echoed through the phone line, making Will smile and relax a little. "That she is."

"So the reason I called . . . what we talked about that night at your place . . . I wanted to let you know I plan to propose to Cameron in the next few days."

"Oh, well." Patrick's normally booming voice softened noticeably with those two words. "I'm sure she'll be thrilled."

"I hope so."

"She will. You should hear the way she talks about you—as if you walk on water."

Humbled to hear that, Will closed his eyes against the powerful punch of emotion that could still catch him off guard all these months later. "I love her, Patrick. I'll always love her. I promise you that."

"I know, and I'm extremely thankful she found you and is so very happy. I wish she were closer to me, but she still calls her dear old dad just about every day, so I can hardly complain."

"We'd love to have you come visit. Anytime." As he said the words, he tried to imagine Patrick Murphy bunking in the loft at their cabin while they shared a bed downstairs. That would certainly put a damper on the romance.

"I'll take you up on that one of these days. I assume she'll want to be married there."

"We haven't gotten that far, but we'll let you know as soon as we have any plans."

"Tell her to call me. After."

"I will."

"I appreciate the call, Will. Someday you might have a daughter of your own, and you'll understand just how much I appreciate it."

"I hope I get that opportunity. We'll talk to you soon."

"I'll look forward to it. Good luck with the proposal. Not that you'll need it."

"Thank you."

Will ended the call feeling good about the conversation with Patrick and more determined than ever to ask her sooner rather than later. The day after tomorrow he and Hunter would go to buy the ring. He'd ask her that night. He couldn't wait.

CHAPTER 22

It is not the strongest of the species that
survive, nor the most intelligent, but
the one most responsive to change.

—Charles Darwin

When Nina appeared at his door shortly after two, Hunter was ready for her. He'd pushed aside every other thought he'd rather be thinking about Megan to focus exclusively on his work for the last two hours. After another thorough scrub of the diner numbers, he was more convinced than ever that the investment was a bad idea. Despite that, he was pushing forward with the plan to acquire it anyway because that was what his grandfather wanted him to do.

Their conversation about risk had resonated with him in more ways than one. From a business standpoint, sometimes it made sense to take on a new project that had potential to pay off in the future. Not everything had to yield immediate results to be considered worthwhile.

The same could be said for his personal life. He was willing to risk everything—his heart, his well-being, his mental health—for this chance with Megan and would do whatever it took to make it work. Despite all her warnings, she was a risk well worth taking.

"Come in." He stood when Nina stepped into his office. "Have a seat."

"Thanks."

"Can I get you anything? Coffee? Water?"

"I'm good. I've already OD'd on coffee today."

Hunter walked around the desk to shut the door and then returned to his seat behind the desk. "Thanks for coming over."

"No problem. I wanted to talk to you anyway."

"About?"

She tilted her head and offered a smile. "What do you think?"

"So my family isn't the only one that feels the need to be overly involved."

"No, the Abbotts don't have the market cornered on interfering, although I imagine their sheer numbers can be somewhat intimidating."

"Somewhat," he said, laughing.

"All I'm going to say is that she matters very much to me, and underneath that hard exterior she shows the world is a woman who feels things deeply and hurts easily."

"I know that. You should know I love her, and I'd never hurt her. I only want to make her happy."

Nina blinked and shook her head as she laughed. "Okay, I didn't see that coming."

"Neither did I, but there you have it. I love her. I've loved her for quite some time, and being with her the last few days has only proven what I've known all along. We belong together. I'm working on convincing her of that, but I have no plans to give up."

"She's apt to make it difficult."

He shrugged. "I won't give up on her."

"Does she know?"

"That I love her? Not yet, but she will before too much longer. I don't believe in guessing games. I believe in absolutes—black and white. And I absolutely love her."

"I'm sorry." Nina sniffed and dabbed at her eyes. "I don't mean to bawl all over you, but she's my baby sister."

"I understand. I have a few of those myself."

"Yes, you do. I'm so glad to know you'll be looking out for her when I can't."

"I will. You have my word on that. Even if she tells me to go to hell, I'll still look out for her."

"She's not going to tell you to go to hell. She's been walking around with a big dopey grin on her face for days now. I've never seen her like that before, and it's because of you."

Hunter couldn't believe how happy it made him to hear Nina say that. A knot of fear he'd been carrying around in his gut seemed to loosen somewhat at that news.

"Why do you look so relieved?"

"I guess I've worried about this being sort of one-sided. I mean, she was so into my brother for such a long time—"

"She wasn't into him the way you think she was. He was her fantasy. As long as she had her mind set on him, or the *idea* of him, she could stay removed from real entanglements. You're the first real risk she's taken since we lost our folks, and I hope you know what a big deal that is for her."

"I do. I get it, and I'm being careful with her. I promise."

"That's all I could ever hope for." Laughing, she pulled a tissue from her purse. "I honestly didn't come here to cry all over you."

"It's more than fine," he said, smiling at her. "I'm glad we had a chance to talk before you leave."

"Speaking of me leaving . . . That's going to be hard on her."

"I'll be right there for her. Whatever she needs. She won't be alone."

"I think *I* might be a little bit in love with you, Hunter."

He laughed—hard. "If only I could hear those words from your sister."

"You will. Give her time. She knows you're special."

"She's mad at me right now because I suggested we might need to make some changes at the diner."

"Because it's a money pit," Nina said knowingly.

"That's one way to put it."

"I'm surprised you're still interested after reviewing the

information I sent over. No one would ever accuse you of being reckless."

"I'll be honest with you, Nina. If it were up to me and me alone, we'd pass. But my grandfather has convinced me to give it a try, and I'm willing to do that because he asked me to."

"I understand. Elmer is hard to resist, and I'm not his grandchild."

"Exactly. He has a way of bending us to his will with a smile and a wink."

"He's adorable."

"We love him madly, and he knows it." Hunter cleared his throat and dove into the tricky part of the meeting. "Here's the thing though. I can't, in good conscience, offer to buy you out of the diner in light of what the financials and the inspection yielded."

"Oh," she said, deflating.

"What I *am* willing to do is assume the remaining mortgage and put my grandfather's investment into making the necessary upgrades. That would relieve you of the debt and leave you free and clear of the place, but you wouldn't make anything on the sale. I'd totally understand if that doesn't work for you, but it's the best I can do under the circumstances."

"Done."

Hunter stared at her, shocked. He'd expected her to quibble about walking away without profiting on the business she'd put so much effort into. "Really?"

"Yes! You have no idea how badly I've wanted out of that place. It's been a drain on us financially, emotionally, even romantically because all Brett and I do is fight over it. We used a big chunk of my share of the insurance money from my parents to buy it, thinking it would be a nice job for me as well as a source of extra income. Except that's not what happened at all. I work *all* the time, and we can't seem to get ahead no matter what we do. I only stuck with it for as long as I did because of Megan."

"What do you mean?"

"She'd never admit it, but she loves it there. She loves the people and the routine and the family we've found for ourselves among the customers we see every day."

Hunter already figured as much from things Megan had said. It made sense that the diner customers would be like a family to the sisters who'd lost their parents at such a young age. The patrons filled a void for them, one that Megan would feel acutely if the diner were to shut down. He was more determined than ever to make sure that didn't happen.

"She mentioned her writing to me."

"Did she? That's significant. She doesn't talk about it much."

"I want to encourage her to pursue it, but I'm not sure how."

"You'll be the new owner of the diner. Help her with the management so she has time to devote to her passions."

"Plural? She has others?"

Nina laughed. "*You*, silly."

For the first time in recent memory, Hunter felt his face turn bright red, which was rather embarrassing for a man of his age.

"You might just be completely perfect for her, and you've been right across the street all this time. It's amazing."

"To me as well."

Nina stood and reached out to shake his hand.

Hunter did her one better by coming around the desk to hug her.

"Thank you for this," she said, returning his embrace. "For all of it."

"Trust me when I tell you it's entirely my pleasure."

"La la la, too much information."

He laughed.

"We'll have to sign stuff, I assume?"

"I'll ask my cousin Grayson to draw up the paperwork right away. We'll get it done before you leave."

"Thank you again, Hunter. You're saving my life in more ways than you know."

"Have fun in France. We'll take care of things here."

"I feel much better about going than I did before."

"We may even come to visit."

"That'd be great. We'd love it."

She left him with a wave, and Hunter sat back in his chair, chewing on the end of his pencil and thinking about taking Megan to France. Wouldn't that be something? He who hadn't taken a real vacation in years was suddenly coming in late to work—or not coming in at all—"forgetting" to shave and planning a trip overseas. He'd heard about life changing on a dime, but other than Caleb's tragic death, it had never happened to him.

Until that first life-changing night with Megan, his routine had been utterly boring and completely predictable, just the way he'd thought he liked it. But she'd made him want more. She made him want to bust out of his staid existence and shake things up like he never had before.

With that in mind, he left a message for his grandfather detailing the meeting with Nina, sent an e-mail to his father and siblings about the purchase of the diner, shut down his computer, turned off the light on his desk and closed his office door behind him.

"I'm taking the rest of the day off," he said to Mary, whose eyes bugged in surprise.

Before she could formulate a reply, he was headed down the stairs. He burst into the warm autumn sunshine, giving thanks for the clean getaway from the office. Leaving dust in his wake, he pulled out of the parking lot and headed for Megan's house, hoping he'd find her home but willing to wait for her if she wasn't there. He'd wait forever for her, if that's what it took.

CHAPTER 23

◆◆◆

A man should never neglect his family for business.

—Walt Disney

Finished with work for the day, Megan returned home and went straight for the shower to wash off the stink of onions and peppers that clung to her hair and skin after hours of hustling Butch's famous fried potatoes. The customers went nuts over them. Megan had grown to hate the smell of them even if she loved the taste.

Hoping to see Hunter later, she shaved her legs, too. Before he got a chance to touch those freshly shaven legs, however, they would be having a conversation about what he'd said earlier in regard to his plans for the diner once it changed hands.

If he expected her to be involved going forward, they were going to need to resolve a few things about what she would and would not be party to. The thought took her by surprise. Had she made a decision about staying in Butler, working at the diner and committing fully to her relationship with Hunter? When had that happened?

Still reeling from the realization, she stepped out of the shower, put her hair up in a towel and put on the cozy robe Nina had given her last Christmas. It wasn't quite time to put on the heat, but there was a definite chill in the air this time of year. Megan loved autumn in Vermont. She loved the color and the apples and the crisp air and the bright blue skies. The only thing she didn't love was that it led directly into the long and snowy winter.

The thought of facing another winter in the Northeast Kingdom had her wondering if she was crazy to stay here when she hated snow so much and could choose to live anywhere in the world now that Nina and Brett were leaving.

If Hunter hadn't come into her life the way he had, there'd be nothing at all keeping her in Butler. Except for the customers she saw every day at the diner who'd become family to her and Nina over the years. On Thanksgiving, they prepared a big turkey dinner for the people in town who had nowhere else to go, and the diner was filled to the rafters all day with thankful, happy friends.

On Christmas, Butch went all out with prime rib and baked stuffed shrimp that made Megan's mouth water just thinking about how good they were. His honey-baked ham and pineapple on Easter was another of Megan's favorite meals of the year.

For the holidays, they broke out fancy white tablecloths and candles on the tables. They spent hours decorating the diner to make it look more like a home than a restaurant. The sisters had taken pride in the role they'd played in the community, never more so than on holidays. They knew all too well how difficult that time of year could be without their parents. The diner patrons had helped to fill the void for them.

And Butch . . . He might not have much in the way of personality, but the man could cook like no one she'd ever known, and she would miss him if she didn't see him every day anymore. What would become of him? Where would he go? He didn't have anyone to call his own either. Their merry group of misfits had come together in a family that had become important to Megan—and to Nina, who'd spent most of the last few days in tears as customers poured into the diner to wish her well.

Megan had seen the fear on the faces of the people who'd come by to see Nina. Where would they go every day? What would they do without their diner "family"? What would *Megan* do without those people when she was already going to be without Nina in her daily life? The thought of moving away from them, away from the town that had always been her home, away from Hunter and whatever might be developing between them, made her feel sad in a way she hadn't felt since she lost her parents.

Sure, she'd love to be anywhere that didn't include six months of snow, but at some point she'd decided she'd rather put up with the snow than leave Butler and all the people who mattered to her.

Euphoric to have settled on a decision about her immediate future, she went to answer a knock on her door. Expecting to see Nina, she gasped in surprise at the sight of Hunter. "What're you doing here?"

"Took the rest of the day off." His hungry gaze shifted from her face to the V of her robe and then down farther before taking the same slow path back to her eyes. "May I come in?"

"Sure." With every nerve ending in her body on fire after his slow perusal, she stepped aside to let him by. "I should go put some clothes on."

He reached for her hand to keep her from escaping. "Please don't." Drawing her into his embrace, he kissed her. "Hi there."

"Hello, yourself."

"Am I interrupting anything?"

"Nope. I just got home and took a shower." She was thankful she'd had enough time to wash off the onions and peppers before he came by. As usual, he smelled like a high-end department store in New York City and looked like he'd stepped right out of an equally high-end men's fashion magazine. "I feel underdressed."

"I like you that way." He nuzzled her neck, which dislodged the towel from her hair. "Mmm, you smell so good."

"You really left work early to come see me?"

"Uh-huh."

She tilted her head to give him better access to her neck. "Isn't that sort of out of character for you?"

"Uh-huh."

Knowing he'd stepped so far out of his usual routine because he wanted to spend time with her sent a flutter of giddy happiness straight to her heart, which was already beating faster than usual thanks to his lips on her neck.

"Hunter?"

"Hmm?"

"We need to talk."

"Nothing good ever comes of those words."

"Please?"

"Okay." He withdrew from her neck reluctantly. "What do you want to talk about?"

"Come sit." She took his hand, led him to the sofa and sat next to him, curling one leg under her body so she could look at him while they talked.

"Are you naked under there?"

"Focus," she said, amused and aroused by his obvious interest in her.

"I am focusing. I'm one hundred fifty percent focused on you—all of you."

His warm hand caressed her inner thigh, which made her forget all about why she wanted to talk to him. Because she loved the way his hand felt on her leg, she didn't push him away but had to force herself to focus after lecturing him. "What you said earlier about the changes you want to make at the diner . . . I want to talk about that."

"Okay."

"If you buy the diner—"

"We are buying the diner. I just met with Nina, and we worked out a deal."

"Oh. I hadn't heard that."

"Happened thirty minutes ago. I'm sure she hasn't gotten the chance to talk to you yet."

"Right . . . Anyway, if I'm going to be part of it—"

He raised that brow that made him look sexy and rakish. *"If?"*

"I want to be part of it, but we need to agree on a few things."

"I'm listening."

"You can't raise the prices."

"Megan—"

"Hear me out." She took a deep breath, trying to keep her emotions out of the mix. "That diner is about so much more than coffee and eggs. It's about a community. It's about people who have nowhere else to be on a given day. It's about widows and widowers who've lost the most important person in their lives, but can come to the diner every morning and have coffee and toast with others who understand them. It gives people like your grandfather and his friends a place to 'check in' every morning. Not all of his friends have families like yours. If they don't show up, someone goes to find out why. If you make it too expensive, they won't be able to afford to come there, and what will become of them?"

As she spoke, he tucked strands of her damp hair behind her ears and ran his finger over her cheek. Despite the way his touch aroused her, she didn't allow him to distract her. It was important that he understand her feelings about the diner.

"You really care about these people, don't you?"

"Of course I do! They're family to me—and to Nina. We take care of them, and they take care of us. If we change what we're about there, it'll hurt people who've already had enough hurt in their lives."

"You make a very compelling argument."

"But?"

"No buts. I hear you, and I agree that raising the prices isn't the right thing to do in light of what you've told me."

"Really?"

"Yes," he said, smiling widely, "really. Why do you sound so surprised?"

"I thought you'd put up more of a fight."

"Why would I when you make very valid points?"

"So it's that simple? No price increases?"

"It's not that simple. The diner is operating in the red, which is not sustainable for the long term. Eventually Nina was going to have to do something about that or risk going under."

"So what's the solution?"

"I don't know yet, but I bet if we put our heads together we can come up with a plan that works for everyone—us as the owners, you as the management and the customers."

"I haven't yet agreed to be your manager."

"I know, and I'm not looking to put any pressure on you. You've got some big decisions to make, and I don't want to make them any more difficult."

She glanced down at the hand that sat on her leg like a branding iron. "You don't?"

He shook his head. "I want you to be *happy*, Megan. Whatever that takes, I'm onboard."

"I want to be here, and I want to run the diner and be with you, but I also don't want to miss out on an opportunity to make some changes."

"What kind of changes?"

"I hate the snow. It scares me and makes my life so complicated for months on end. I'd like to live somewhere that didn't get so much snow."

"Okay. What else?"

"I'd like to write more." She felt her cheeks get warm as she made that confession. Her desire to write had always been something she kept close to the vest because it felt private. Only Nina had ever known she liked to write, and now Hunter knew, too.

"What else?"

"I want to travel. I want to go places and see the world."

"Anything else?"

She couldn't seem to look at him as she shared this last one. "Someday, down the road, I might like to have a family of my own. Not right away, but someday."

"Okay. Is that everything?"

"For now."

"Look at me, sweetheart." His fingers on her chin compelled her to meet his warm, sexy gaze. "I can't do anything about the snow. That's a fact of life here in Vermont, unfortunately. But if you're willing to put up with that, along with my promise to drive you anywhere you need to go any time it snows, I can help you get all the other things you want if you give me the chance."

"As sweet as that is, it's not your responsibility to help me get what I want out of life, Hunter."

"What if I were to tell you that helping you to get the things you want would make *me* happy?"

"Why?" she asked, her voice barely a whisper.

"I don't know if you're ready to hear why."

CHAPTER 24

━━◆◈◆━━

Sometimes when you innovate, you make mistakes.
It is best to admit them quickly and get on
with improving your other innovations.

—Steve Jobs, co-founder of Apple, Inc.

He hadn't said the words, and he was right, she probably wasn't ready to hear them. Not yet. But she certainly understood what he was not saying. "You're a very nice guy."

"This is what I'm trying to tell you."

Her laughter broke the tension that had grown and multiplied during the intense conversation. His smile lit up his handsome face, and Megan couldn't resist him when he looked at her that way. She put her hand around his nape and drew him into a kiss. "He cooks, he irons, he bakes *and* he makes dreams come true."

"You forgot balances the books and makes you come multiple times every night. What can I say, babe? I'm a Renaissance man."

"And he's funny and cute and sexy and adorable."

"All those things? You shouldn't let a guy like that get away. You might regret it for the rest of your life."

"Yes, I'm quite sure I would."

He put his arms around her and kissed the top of her

head. "We're going to figure this out. We're going to see to it that you get everything you want and things you've never dared to dream."

"You make me believe all of that's possible."

"It is. I want to share with you something my brother Colton told me after he got together with Lucy. They've worked out an arrangement to split their time between New York where she lives and his mountain here. I told him that sounded kind of complicated and asked if he was sure they could make that work. He told me it didn't matter where they were as long as they were together. He said being with her made him a better man, that they were stronger together than they were apart, and because of that they were willing to do whatever it took to make it work."

"That's really amazing. They're so lucky to have found each other."

"So are we, Megan. You make me want to be a better man so I'll be worthy of you. You make me want to climb mountains if it'll make you happy or make you smile or laugh. I really love when you laugh."

Megan's eyes burned with unshed tears. "How can you be real?"

"I'm real, and I'm smitten, and I'm consumed with the desire to be close to you in every possible way. You're all I think about."

"For the record, there's no way you could be a better man than you already are."

"There's always room for improvement."

"While that might be true, I'm starting to think you might be perfect for me exactly the way you are."

"I can live with that."

She smiled as she kissed him, and let him take her away from all her worries and fears. Wrapped up in his arms, it was easy to believe that everything would be fine. He would see to that with her. Together, they'd be stronger than they were apart. She loved what Colton had said about Lucy and their relationship. That was what she wanted, too.

"What do you have planned for the rest of the day?" Hunter asked as he kissed from her lips to her neck.

"Nothing much."

He made her feel treasured and aroused and uncomfortable and adored with the way he held her and kissed her. She couldn't get enough of his kisses. Now that she had spent time with him, her fantasy crush on his brother seemed like a distant memory, completely eclipsed by the reality of Hunter.

"Want to hang out with me?"

"I might be persuaded to do that. What'd you have in mind?"

"We could go for a walk or a drive or anything you want."

With her hand flat against his chest, she looked up at him. "Could we maybe stay here?"

"We could do that, too." He kissed her, groaning when she drew his bottom lip into her mouth and ran her tongue back and forth over it. "You want to watch a movie?"

She shook her head.

"I could bake you some more cookies."

"Maybe later."

"So what do you want to do?"

Holding his hand, Megan stood and gave a tug to bring him with her.

"Where are you taking me?"

"I feel a nap coming on."

"I never nap in the middle of the day."

Wondering if he was for real, she turned back to him and caught the teasing glint in his eyes. "Oh, thank goodness. For a second there, I thought you weren't as smart as everyone says you are."

With his arms around her waist, he picked her up and carried her laughing into her bedroom, depositing her on the bed before joining her. "I'm every bit as smart as people say I am."

"That's a relief."

He pulled on the tie to her robe and revealed her to his heated gaze. Rising to his knees, he bent to kiss her belly.

Megan ran her fingers through his hair, loving the way he looked at her. Then he stopped and rested his forehead against her stomach. "What's wrong?"

"Nothing at all. I just want you so badly all the time."

"Come here."

He scooted up on the bed so he was lying next to her. "I'm here."

Megan knelt on the bed and unbuttoned the red-pinstripe dress shirt he'd worn to work. On the cuffs, she noted his initials, *HEA*, and laughed.

"What's so funny?"

"Do you know what HEA stands for?"

"Um, Hunter Elmer Abbott?"

"In romance it stands for happily ever after."

"I've never heard that before."

She released the buttons on his cuffs. "Your parents set you up to be happy the day you were born."

He caressed her face. "I just needed you to make it happen."

"Take this off," she said of his shirt.

Hunter sat up to pull off the shirt and the T-shirt he wore under it, and then pushed her robe off her shoulders, leaving it to pool around her hips. "I wish you knew how beautiful you are to me." He kissed her shoulder, along her collarbone and then down to the nipple that tightened in anticipation of the kind of pleasure only he could deliver.

Before she knew what hit her, Megan was flat on her back and he was worshiping her breasts with his tongue, lips, teeth and fingers. She could barely keep up with him as he moved from one erogenous zone to another, making her crazier by the second.

"Hunter . . . I . . ." Her words were stolen by the sweep of his tongue between her legs, by the tight grip of his hand on her bottom, by the powerful sensations that rippled through her body. She couldn't have spoken then if her life had depended on it. He had her on the verge of release so fast she nearly forgot to breathe before it was upon her, sweeping her up with the power of a wave that lifted her up and left her suspended before bringing her crashing back to earth, breathless and battered.

Megan was still trying to find her equilibrium when Hunter pushed into her, triggering a second wave that had her clinging to him as he pounded into her, taking as much as giving. He filled her so completely, stretching her to the point of exquisite pain that only fueled her desire.

And then he reached beneath her, grabbed her ass to lift her tighter against him. He was relentless and driven and out of control, and she loved everything about the way he absolutely possessed her.

"God, Megan." His voice was choppy and broken against her ear. "Megan . . . I love you."

The words penetrated the sensual fog, leaving her reeling as he drove them both to the finish line. Reaching for her hands, he lifted them over her head and captured her mouth in a deep, searching kiss as he pressed into her one last time, coming with a gasp of pleasure.

Megan wrapped her legs around his hips, keeping him buried in her while they throbbed with aftershocks and her mind raced with the implications of what he'd said.

After a long silence, he said, "I didn't mean to just blurt that out."

"You didn't mean it?"

"That's not what I said. I meant it. I do love you. I have for a long time, but before now, before the time we've spent together, I loved the *idea* of you. Now I love the reality even more."

She had no idea how to respond to such heartfelt words. Her emotions were all over the place with Nina leaving, the diner changing hands, her own life in flux and now this amazing new possibility with Hunter. "I . . ."

He laid a finger over her lips. "Don't say anything. Not now. It's still new to you, and I don't want you to feel pressure."

Looking to defuse the tension she saw in the set of his jaw, she raised her hips. "I'm feeling the best kind of pressure."

"I was rough with you. Again. I'm sorry."

"Don't be sorry. I loved it. I've never had sex like I do with you."

"Neither have I." Still holding her hands above her head, he kissed her. "You're ruining me for all other women."

Her brows furrowed as she looked up at him. "I told you not to do this. I told you not to fall for me."

"Couldn't help it."

Suddenly she had to get away from him or risk surrendering things she hadn't planned to give. "I need to get up."

Watching her warily, he disentangled himself from her and let her up.

Megan went into the bathroom and shut the door, leaning against it as her heart pounded with anxiety and fear. This perfectly wonderful guy was in love with her, and all she could think about was how it would end. What was wrong with her?

Hunter awoke some time later to near darkness in Megan's bedroom. How long had he been asleep? Pushing the hair back from his forehead, he checked his watch and learned it was nearly six thirty. They'd slept for hours. Their sleepless nights were catching up to both of them.

At some point, Megan had turned onto her side, and her bottom was pressed tight against his groin.

His body reacted predictably to her nearness, as well as the soft satin of her skin, the silk of her hair and the heat of her body. He was only human, and she was like a goddess come to life in his arms.

He'd known it would be like this with her. Just like he'd always known that if he got close to her he'd fall in love. And as expected, he'd fallen completely, totally and irrevocably in love. He really hadn't meant to blurt it out when he was deep inside her, but the words had tumbled forth in the heat of passion, and he didn't regret them. But the last thing he wanted her to think was that he loved her because of the sex. That was one of many reasons.

Her care and concern for the needy patrons at the diner had touched him deeply and told him a lot about what mattered to her. Because the customers were so important to her, he was glad he'd been able to help keep the diner open. And he'd been hugely relieved to hear her say she wanted to be part of it. Maybe that was why the words had come tumbling out, because he wanted her to know he'd make it worth it if she stayed with him.

She stirred and turned over, her hand landing on his belly, right above the tip of his hard cock.

Hunter held his breath, waiting to see if she was awake. He

didn't have to wait long before her hand slid down to stroke him. He nearly swallowed his tongue from the surprise and then the pleasure, the incredible, unbelievable pleasure of her touch.

"Someone is wide awake," she said in the sleepy, sexy voice he loved.

"It's all your fault. You had your very sweet ass pressed up against him shamelessly. What was he to do?"

Her quiet laughter thrilled him. He'd meant it when he told her he loved the sound of her laugh. He loved making her laugh. He loved the lighter side of her personality that she'd shown him repeatedly over the last few days. He loved the way she felt in his arms, the sound she made when she came and her responsiveness to his touch.

"In that case, I suppose it's only fair that I tend to him."

"You won't hear me disagreeing."

She pushed him onto his back and kissed his chest and abdomen while continuing to stroke him.

In the dark, he could barely see her, but he could feel her getting closer all the time to where he wanted her most. She made a wide circle around his cock, nibbling on the V-cut muscles on his hips and then shocking the shit out of him with a bite to his inner thigh. He nearly came all over her with that maneuver.

"Christ, Megan. Have some mercy, will you?"

Once again her husky, sexy laughter was nearly his undoing. "Is this what you want?" She wrapped her lips around the tip and sucked hard, making him see stars.

"Yeah," he said on a gasp, "more of that."

"More of this?" She stroked him with her hand and tongue.

"*Megan* . . . God, yes, more of that." He wanted more of everything where she was concerned. In fact, he could actually die happy with her lips tight around the head of his cock. And then she drew him in deeper and he forgot all about dying happy. He wanted to live and feel the way she made him feel every day for the rest of his life.

She took him on an incredible ride, culminating in an orgasm that originated in the deepest part of him, leaving him depleted and trembling afterward.

"Holy shit," he whispered as she sprinkled his chest with kisses. "That was . . . I have no words."

"You? At a loss for words? I don't believe it."

"Also your fault."

"I'll take the blame this time."

Hunter wrapped his arms around her. "Are you hungry?"

"I could eat something."

"Me, too. Want to go out or order in?"

"Order in."

Hunter left her in bed while he went to order pizza and salad. When he got back in bed to wait for the delivery, he loved the way she crawled into his arms, her head resting on his chest and her hair soft against his face. "May I say something?" he asked.

"May I stop you?"

"No," he said, laughing. "No chance of that."

"Then by all means, proceed."

"What I said earlier . . ." Every muscle in her body seemed to tighten at once. "I didn't say it to put pressure on you or to try to influence your decisions. I know you're thinking about a lot of things, and all of a sudden I factor into it—or at least I hope I do."

"Of course you do, but this wasn't supposed to happen. It was supposed to be fun."

"It hasn't been fun?"

"Yes, but . . . I told you I don't do serious."

"And I heard you. I promise you I did, but I can't help how I feel about you. It's as natural to me as breathing." He never blinked as he stared into her eyes. "I knew we'd be good together. I *knew* it."

"How did you know?"

"Because of the way I felt every time I saw you or talked to you."

"How did you feel?"

"Certain. Absolutely certain."

"You could have anyone you want."

"As could you."

"I doubt that."

"Then you aren't paying attention to the way your customers look at you."

"Most of them are eighty!"

"Not all of them. I've seen guys looking at you probably the way I do, and I wanted to kill them all. I wanted to tell them, 'You can't have her.'" He kissed her forehead. "'She's mine.'"

"Yours, huh?"

"Yes, mine. All mine."

"As a woman of the new millennium, that declaration ought to offend me, but it doesn't. I like being with you this way. I couldn't wait to see you tonight. I even shaved my legs hoping I'd get to see you."

He reached down to run his hand over satiny smooth skin. "I noticed." His hand moved from calf to thigh to buttock, where he lingered, squeezing and molding her cheek until she squirmed in his arms.

"Don't. The pizza guy is coming."

"Not before you do."

"Hunter!"

He flattened his hand on her bottom, letting his fingers wander between her legs.

"*Hunter*, come on."

"No, you come on." Holding her tight against him with one arm, he teased and coaxed with his other hand. "Better hurry up. Time's a-wasting." As he spoke, he caressed her clit in tight circles. "He'll be here *any* minute."

She gasped, and her legs tightened around his hand. "Hunter . . ."

"I'm right here, sweetheart. Let it happen." He captured her mouth in a deep kiss, the strokes of his tongue matching the thrusts of his fingers.

Megan came with a sharp cry just as the doorbell rang.

Hunter removed his fingers, licked them clean and said, "I'll get that."

She replied with a shaky laugh. "That's good, because I couldn't move if I had to."

He leaned over the bed to kiss her. "Luckily, you don't have to."

CHAPTER 25

—◆—

*Leadership is a potent combination of strategy
and character. But if you must be without
one, be without the strategy.*

—General Norman Schwarzkopf, U.S. Army

After spending the night with Megan, Hunter got up when she did to go home to shower, shave and get ready for work. He made a point of getting to the office early because he knew he'd been setting a shitty example lately. Working with his siblings took a certain amount of diplomacy to keep the peace, but Hunter had always insisted the family set the tone for the rest of the employees by showing up on time.

He'd been slacking in that regard lately—with good reason, but still slacking. He had a busy day ahead with a meeting at nine to discuss a new product line his dad wanted to introduce at the store, payroll due by the end of the day and August financial statements to be generated. He gave himself two weeks after the end of every month to close out the financials, and today was exactly fourteen days into the new month.

He'd made some headway on the financials by the time his brother Colton arrived in the office right before nine.

"What brings you down off the mountain?" Hunter asked.

"Dad asked me to come to the meeting this morning about the new product line. Remember the convention in New York last month? He asked me to report to you all about my findings, and let me say how much I'm looking forward to that."

Hunter laughed at the distressed look on Colton's face. "He's not serious about selling that stuff in the store, is he?"

"Um, I think he is."

"He's got to retire eventually, right?"

"He's not even sixty. Don't write him off yet."

"Is Lucy with you?"

"Nah, as much as she wanted to witness my mortification, she's got a new website going live today, so she stayed up at the cabin. She gets the best connectivity up there."

Hunter sat back in his chair. "Things are going well for you guys?"

"Things are great. We're making it work one day at a time."

"I'm glad for you."

"What's this I hear about you and Megan hot and heavy?"

"We've been seeing each other lately."

"That's great."

"Yeah, it is."

"Why do you not seem happier about it? I thought you'd been lusting after her for ages."

"I was, and I'm happier than I've ever been."

"So, then . . ."

"I know she likes me, and we're having a lot of fun together. I just don't know if she's thinking short-term fling or long-term relationship."

"Have you thought about asking her?"

"Yeah, I've thought about it. Just haven't been able to actually do it. I'm sort of afraid of what she might say."

"You love her?"

"Yeah."

"Does she know that?"

"She does."

"Then give her some time to get used to the idea. Keep

doing what you're doing. Keep showing up. That's what Gramps told me to do with Lucy, and it worked out pretty well for us."

"I can't believe I'm taking romance advice from you."

"Suck it up, big brother. You can't be the best at everything."

"I'm happy to defer to you on the topic of sex toys."

Colton winked at him. "Don't knock 'em till you've tried 'em."

"Eww, I don't want that visual in my head. Get out. Right now. Serious work is being done here."

"Yeah, yeah, yeah."

Much to Colton's dismay, the entire family turned out for his presentation. "This is right up there with my middle school nightmares about sporting a boner in front of the class during the science fair," he said at the outset, making everyone howl with laughter. "Did you really have to invite Mom and Gramps?" he asked his father.

"They're on the board," Lincoln said with a smile and a shrug.

"It's okay, honey," Molly said. "Dad and I can take it. You'd be surprised—"

"Under penalty of death, do not finish that thought," said Max, the youngest of the Abbott siblings.

Molly giggled behind her hand.

"I'm with him," her father, Elmer, said with a glare for his daughter. "Put a sock in it. Please proceed, Colton. You've got me all a-quiver with curiosity."

"Jesus," Colton muttered to more laughter from his siblings. "Here's the deal—there's a lot of money in them there sex toys, and they're being manufactured for people of all ages. Dad sent me to the convention because he was trying to push me together with Lucy by giving me a week with her in New York."

"That is not true," Lincoln said. "I was genuinely curious about the product line."

"Sure," Colton said. "Whatever you say. Anyhow, I found out some very interesting stats about the industry." He clicked a few buttons on a laptop on the conference table, and a professionally produced PowerPoint presentation came on the screen.

"Someone has been taking full advantage of his fiancée," Cameron said.

"Yes, we've had fun testing all the products," Colton said, to groans from everyone.

Landon, Lucas and Max threw wadded-up paper at him.

"Flag on the play," Lucas said, covering his ears.

"We can't unhear that," Charley said dryly.

"Nolan and I would be happy to be a focus group on this project," Hannah said, earning balled-up paper bombs from her younger brothers.

"Make it stop, Mom," Max said, hands over ears.

"Grow up, honey. You're going to be a father soon. Surely you're wise to how things work."

"I don't want to hear it from *them*," Max said.

"We should get hazardous-duty pay for this meeting," Ella said.

"Seriously," Will concurred.

"Does that mean we can't offer to be a focus group?" Cameron asked him, earning a playful scowl from her boyfriend.

"*Anyway*," Colton said, trying to get things back on track, "I met with Joyce, the owner of the company that produces this particular product line. She talked to me about the therapeutic uses of the products as well as the more straightforward uses."

"Straightforward," Lucas said with a snicker. "That's what I'm all about."

"Shut *up*, will you?" Charley gestured to her three youngest brothers. "They're far too young to be allowed in this meeting."

"Everyone shut up and let Colton finish," Lincoln said.

"Joyce and her daughter Amanda travel all over to retail outlets like ours to offer in-store workshops on the product lines for the floor teams as well as customers who want to learn more about them."

"You really think our customers will show up for how-to workshops about sex toys?" Hunter asked.

"We won't know until we try," Colton said. "It's a long, cold winter up here in the mountains. We might be surprised by how many of the locals would be interested."

"I don't see them coming to us for that," Hunter said.

"I do," said Wade, who oversaw the health and wellness portion of the business. "They buy all sorts of remedies from us, for everything from toe fungus to hemorrhoids. What's to stop them from trying these products, too?"

"How about the ladies on the floor?" Ella asked, referring to their in-store sales team, most of them grandmothers. "Won't it be embarrassing for them to have to answer questions about these products?"

"Not if we educate them properly," Lincoln said.

"So you're totally sold on this, Dad?" Will asked.

"I think we ought to give it a try. Give them some stats, Colton."

Colton flipped his presentation forward, skipping over photos of items that had Hunter thinking of Megan and focus groups, to a slide with bulleted statistics. "The sex toy and novelty business is a fifteen-billion-dollar—that's *billion* with a *B*—industry in the United States, and it's growing every year."

"No pun intended," Lucas muttered, earning him a glare from his father.

"People of all ages are using these products to spice up their love lives," Colton said, "to aid in their recovery from surgery and for other therapeutic purposes."

"What does your research show about where the sales are most often made?" Cameron asked. "Brick-and-mortar stores or online?"

"Mostly online, which is why Dad and I are proposing a small display in the store and a larger presence on the website, at least initially," Colton said. "Obviously, we'd revisit that plan when we have about six months' worth of sales data to analyze."

"I like it," Wade said. "I think we ought to at least try it and see what transpires."

"I'll tell you what'll transpire," Elmer said. "A whole bunch of harpies in this town are going to jump all over us for venturing into the porn business."

"That's hardly what we're doing, Gramps," Colton said.

"Still, that's how people will see it. I'm not voting against it. I'm just playing devil's advocate for a minute here."

"Dad makes a good point," Molly said. "We have the facts and figures in front of us, but it'll take a bit of a PR effort to make sure our customers have the relevant information."

"I agree," Wade said. "We can't just plunk this stuff down in the store in a town like this without proper preparation."

"Plenty of lube," Landon said gravely.

While everyone else groaned, Colton picked up one of the paper balls and threw it at Landon, hitting him in the forehead with laser precision.

"Does this require a vote?" Hunter asked.

"I don't think so," Lincoln replied. "It doesn't require a huge outlay of capital to take on the additional inventory. Is anyone violently opposed?" Hearing no opposition, Lincoln said, "Thanks for your work on this, Colton. We appreciate you taking one for the team."

"It was a tough job, but someone had to do it," Colton said gravely, to more groans.

"Holy shit," Max said, his eyes glued to his smartphone. "Did you guys hear Gavin Guthrie got arrested last night?"

A gasp went through the room.

"For what?" Hannah asked.

"He got into a fight at a bar out on 114."

Ella got up and headed for the conference room door.

"Ella?" Charley called after her. "Where're you going?"

Ella didn't reply.

"What the hell?" Charley asked the others. "What's up with her?"

"Leave her alone," Hannah said quietly.

"What do you know, Hannah?"

Hannah put up her hands to ward off Charley. "Nothing."

"Whatever it is, I'm sure she'll tell us when she's ready to," Molly said, sending the signal that the subject was closed—for now.

"While we're all here, Hunter, bring us up to speed on what's going on with the diner," Lincoln said.

All eyes shifted to him. He liked it better when they were making fun of Colton. "As you've all heard by now, Nina and Brett are moving to France, and the diner was up for sale. Gramps came to me and suggested we look into snapping it up while we could. His thinking and mine is that with the website coming online in the next couple of months, we'll see an influx of visitors to the store and the town. They'll need a place to grab a meal."

"What does our sudden purchase of the diner have to do with you and Megan dating?" Charley asked.

"He's *dating* Megan?" Lucas asked.

"Catch up, man," Max said. "Even I've heard about that."

"It's got nothing to do with me dating Megan," Hunter said with a pointed look for Charley. "We're talking to her about managing the diner for us, but nothing is set in stone."

"If she doesn't take the job, who will?" Charley asked.

"We haven't gotten that far yet," Hunter said. "We just came to terms with Nina yesterday, and there's some work we need to have done before we reopen."

"Assume you're talking to Noah about that," Will said of their cousin, the general contractor.

Hunter nodded. "He did the inspection for me the other day and will be handling the upgrades, too. We hope to get them done in the next week or two, so we're only closed for a short time."

"Dude, are you sure about Megan?" Landon asked. "She can be kinda—"

"I firmly recommend against finishing that thought, Landon." Infuriated, Hunter stood and gathered his belongings. "Whatever thoughts any of you have about her you can keep to yourselves. If I have my way, she's in my life to stay, so live with it."

He left the conference room, went into his office and shut

the door behind him. No way would he stand for anyone disparaging Megan, let alone members of his own family.

A quick knock preceded his mother's entry into the office. She closed the door and leaned back against it.

"Um, come in?"

She smiled. "I didn't want to give you time to tell me to go away."

"Go away."

"Not so fast. That was quite a speech just now."

"So what about it? I'm not going to let anyone speak poorly of her, especially people who don't even know her."

"Fair enough. You care about her, so you shouldn't have to put up with that. But you should know, they care about *you*. They're concerned about *you*."

"No one needs to be concerned about me. I'm fine. I'm happy."

"It's happened fast with Megan."

"Not from my point of view. It's taken forever."

"Still . . . Telling your entire family she's in your life to stay a couple of days after your first official date . . . That's fast. You're being careful?"

"You're not seriously asking me about safe sex, are you, Mom?"

Molly snorted with laughter. "That's the least of what I'm asking you. I'm far more concerned about your precious heart than I am about your . . ." She waved her hand as her face flushed with color.

"Precious penis?"

"Hunter! Stop it."

He laughed. "What? You went there. Not me. My heart is fine. It's in very good hands with Megan." Even as he assured his mother, a nagging sense of doubt plagued him as he remembered what Megan had said about not getting serious. He pushed that aside, not willing to entertain any scenario that didn't include her as a permanent part of his life. "No need to worry."

"I *am* worried. I'm worried what'll become of you if she disappoints you."

"I'm hardly a child. I've been disappointed before."

"This would be different."

Since Hunter could hardly tell her she was wrong about that, he didn't try. "Look, I appreciate what you're trying to do and why you're trying to do it. I don't need to be warned off her. Things are great with us. They're going to stay great."

"Be careful, Hunter. You're a good man, one of the best I've ever known."

"And you're not at all biased about that."

"Not one bit. I speak the truth. You put others ahead of yourself all the time. It's what you do. I don't want to see that come back to bite you. I think it's wonderful that you've found someone you care so deeply about. Just make sure you get back from her everything you deserve and then some."

"I hear you, and I appreciate what you're saying."

"Good. Bring her to Sunday dinner this week."

"I'll ask her. Now tell me . . . What's up with Ella walking out of the meeting like that after she heard about Gavin being arrested?"

"I have no idea."

"But I'm sure you plan to find out."

"Duh. What do you think?"

Hunter was still laughing at his mother's predictable reply when another knock sounded at the door. He was resigned to this day being a total loss. "Come in."

Hannah stepped into his office and closed the door behind her. "Everything okay in here?" She glanced from her mother to her brother.

"Everything is fine," Molly said. "How about you tell me what's going on with your sister and Gavin."

"Nothing that I know of," Hannah said.

"So why did she bolt out of here like that when she heard he'd been arrested?" Hunter asked.

Hannah seemed to be weighing whether she should tell them something.

"Hannah?" Molly said. "What do you know?"

"She has a soft spot for him. That's all I'm going to say."

"Ella has a soft spot for Gavin Guthrie?" Hunter asked, astounded. "For how long?"

"Quite some time now," Hannah said.

"How did this get by us?" Hunter asked.

"I know everyone in this family is always in everyone's business," Hannah said, "but I think we should leave her alone with this. It's a delicate situation. He's . . . He's still broken, over Caleb, and she's . . ."

"Fragile," Molly said. "Easily wounded. Kind, compassionate, caring."

"All those things," Hannah said, nodding. "Sometimes I think he might be the worst possible guy for her, as much as I adore him."

"You'll keep an eye on her?" Molly asked her oldest daughter.

"Always," Hannah said. "She talked to me about him once before. Hopefully, she will again if need be. I'll make sure she knows she can."

Molly hugged Hannah. "I love the way you all look out for each other. It's my proudest accomplishment as a mother."

"I wish we looked out for each other a little *less* sometimes," Hunter said.

"I'm sure you do," Hannah said, "but you're not getting off the hook that easily. Not after the way you tortured poor Nolan when we started dating."

"*Tortured* is such a strong word."

Molly laughed at their banter. "I'll let you two work this out the way you always do." She came around his desk to give Hunter a hug. "Love you."

"You, too, Mom. I heard what you said. Every word of it."

"Good. Don't forget it."

"How could I?"

Molly gave Hannah another hug on her way out of the office.

"What was that all about?" Hannah asked him when they were alone.

"She's worried about me with Megan. Too much, too soon. Over the edge."

"Does she have a point?"

"No, she doesn't. It's fine. Is it happening fast? Maybe, but it's hardly like we just met each other last week. I've known her for years. Wanted her for almost as long as I've known her. Now I finally get a chance with her and everyone is worried. I'm a grown man. I can take care of myself."

"We know that, Hunter. You're the most competent person any of us have ever known. You're almost good to a fault."

"What's that supposed to mean?"

"You take care of others at your own expense. You always have."

He didn't bother to tell her their mother had just said basically the same thing. "I don't do that."

"Yes, you do. Remember when Caleb died? You barely left my side for the first year, and in all that time I never saw you shed a tear despite what was a devastating loss for you, too."

"It wasn't about me then."

She challenged him with the same eyes that stared back at him in the mirror. No one had ever *seen* him as completely as Hannah did, and at times like this, her fundamental understanding of him made him pretty damned uncomfortable.

"I shed my share of tears over Caleb. I still do."

"I have no doubt you've grieved for him, but you never let me see that."

"It wasn't about me," he said again, more intently this time.

"Yes, it was. That's what I'm trying to tell you. He was my husband, but he was your best friend, and you had every right to be almost as devastated as I was. Even when it's about you, you put others before yourself. None of us want to see you get hurt when or if Megan decides she wants to be somewhere else or that she's not as serious about you as you are about her. Only a short time ago, she was still pining over Will. Has she really moved on from him? Those are the things that worry me."

Those things worried him, too, not that he'd ever admit that to Hannah or anyone else. Her words had struck at some of his deepest fears where Megan was concerned. "All I can tell you is that things are good with us. Really good."

"I'm happy for you. You know that, right?"

"Even if you wouldn't have chosen her for me?"

"I never said that, and it's not about who I want for you. It's about what *you* want and making sure you get it."

"I'm doing my best to get what I want and to make sure she gets what she wants, too."

"Does she know what she wants?"

"She . . . She's working on that."

"Make sure she doesn't get what she wants at your expense." She checked her watch. "I've got to run. Doctor's appointment in half an hour."

He stood and went around his desk to get the door for her. "Is everything all right with the baby?"

"Everything is fine. Routine checkup."

She gave him a kiss on the cheek. "Think about what I said."

Watching her go, Hunter wondered how he would think about anything else.

CHAPTER 26

———◆◇◆———

The important thing is not being afraid to take a chance. Remember, the greatest failure is to not try.

—Debbi Fields, founder of Mrs. Fields bakeries

Ella drove like a woman possessed, out of Butler, over the one-lane covered bridge, past her parents' home on Hells Peak Road, heading north. She flew by the road that led up to Colton's mountain and kept the accelerator pressed closer to the floor than she normally dared.

Gavin had been *arrested*. Arrested. Was he still in jail? Or had he been released? Was her middle-of-the-workday trip to his home at the logging company he owned a fool's errand? Would he want to see her if he was in some sort of trouble?

The last time she saw him had been at Hannah and Nolan's wedding in late July. That was almost two months ago—two long months of thinking about their kiss on the beach at the lake, how he'd told her he wasn't capable of giving her what she deserved, that if he had been capable, she'd be the only one he'd want.

Those words, reliving that kiss . . . She'd lost a lot of sleep over Gavin Guthrie in the last few weeks. The remarriage of his late brother's wife, even to a man Gavin loved and respected, had hit him hard. He'd admitted as much. Had he been spinning ever since? The thought of that, of him going through that kind of pain alone, brought tears to Ella's eyes. His agony over the loss of his brother was still so raw, so close to the surface even after all this time.

She wiped away her tears, determined to find him and offer him anything he needed. The Gavin she knew and loved—yes, she loved him—didn't get into fights in bars. And he certainly didn't get arrested.

Twenty minutes after she'd walked out of the office—and there'd be hell to pay for that with her family, not that she cared—she drove through the gates to Gavin's logging company, which was abuzz with workers and trucks and equipment. She paid no mind to any of that, heading directly to the log cabin he'd built for himself on the property.

She'd never been here before, but after hearing so much about the business, she knew exactly where to go. Pulling up in front of the house, she noticed his big pickup truck parked outside, but that didn't mean he was home. What if he was still in jail? Would she actually go there and post his bail? Absolutely.

Her hands trembled as she got out of the car, leaving her keys and purse behind as she went to his front door and knocked. She waited for several minutes before she knocked again. What was she doing here? This was none of her business, and he'd probably resent the interruption, if he was even home. A bead of sweat rolled down her back. Ella Abbott didn't sweat. This was ridiculous.

She was about to return to her car and regroup when the inside door opened to reveal Gavin, fresh from the shower and wearing only a pair of unbuttoned faded jeans. Water dripped from his dark hair and his usually gorgeous face was bruised and swollen. She gasped at the sight of him.

"Ella? What're you doing here?"

"I . . . um, I don't know. I shouldn't have come. I heard . . . I'm sorry." She would've turned away and left except he opened the storm door, grabbed her hand and half dragged her into the house, slamming the inside door closed behind them.

"Tell me why you're here."

"Gavin," she said softly. "Your face. Does it hurt?"

"It doesn't feel great, but the other guy looks worse." He attempted a cocky grin that turned into a grimace when his battered face fought back.

"Have you iced it?"

"Not yet. I just got home a little while ago."

Since she'd already invaded his privacy and his home, she didn't see anything wrong with going to his freezer, finding an ice pack and bringing it to him. "Put this on it."

"Why are you here?"

"Ice your face."

"Answer the question."

"I heard you got arrested, and I was worried."

"Worried. Not horrified?"

"Not horrified. What happened?"

"Some dude got mouthy with me, so I shut him up. The owner of the place called the cops, and they arrested both of us." He shrugged as if it were no big deal to have been arrested.

"You spent the night in jail?"

"Yep, arraigned this morning and charged with disorderly conduct. But don't sweat it. My lawyer is on it. I'll pay for the damage, and he'll get the charges dropped."

"Damage?"

"We busted up the place pretty good before the cops got there."

"Gavin . . . This isn't like you. Brawling in public . . ."

"How do you know what's like me? You don't know me."

Though his sharply spoken words cut her to the quick, she refused to be brushed aside like she didn't matter to him. She knew better. He'd told her otherwise that day at the lake when he'd kissed her. "I *do* know you, and this *isn't* like you."

He removed the ice pack from his face—his incredibly handsome, even when bruised, face. "Maybe it is. Maybe it's more like me than either of us thought. It sure felt good to pound the shit out of that bigmouthed asshole."

Ella crossed the room to where he leaned against the bar between his kitchen and a spacious family room adorned by one of the biggest flat-screen TVs she'd ever seen. Such a guy. She pushed the ice pack back onto his face, covering his hand with hers. "What did he say?"

"It's not worth repeating."

"Tell me anyway."

"Something about how we wasted our time in Iraq."

"Oh God . . ."

"Yeah, that's a bit of a trigger for me."

"I imagine it is. The poor guy didn't stand a chance."

"Whose side are you on anyway?" he asked with the hint of a smile.

"Yours. I'm always on your side."

He stared at her for a long moment before he withdrew his hand and the ice pack from under her hand. "Feels better now."

"That wasn't long enough."

"I'm getting a brain freeze."

"Your eye is swollen shut. Did you have that looked at?"

"No need. I can see fine." His one working eye looked her up and down, making her feel exposed and off-kilter, which was nothing new where he was concerned. "You look gorgeous as usual. Shouldn't you be at work?"

"I *was* at work, and then I heard what happened. I walked out of a room full of family members to come check on you, so don't brush me off like my concern doesn't matter to you. I know better."

"It does matter, El," he said with a tortured sigh. "And it's nice of you to come all this way to check on me and risk family scandal to do it. I appreciate it."

"But you don't want me here."

"That's not it, and you know it."

"Then what is it? Spell it out for me."

"I told you once already. You don't want me. I don't deserve you, not in my current condition."

"Don't tell me what I want or what you deserve. And what current condition?"

He paused for a long moment before his broad shoulders sagged. "It's been bad," he said so softly she almost couldn't hear him. "Since the wedding."

She knew he meant the grief, and the agony she saw on his face and heard in his voice touched the deepest part of her. "Gavin." She went to him, needing to touch him, to hold him, to offer any comfort he would take from her. Flattening her hands on his bare chest, she looked up at him, beseechingly. "Let me help."

He shook his head and sidestepped her, his rejection leaving her bereft. "You should go, Ella."

She turned to him, unashamed of the tears that spilled down her cheeks.

"*Fuck,*" he whispered. "Don't do that. Don't cry. Please don't."

"What do you expect me to do?" Angry now, she wiped the tears from her face. "You tell me you care about me, you kiss me, you rock my entire world, and then you walk away like it meant *nothing* to you, giving me some bullshit story about what you're *capable* of."

"It meant everything to me."

"Then *why* do you keep pushing me away?"

Dropping the ice pack on the counter, he came to her, using his thumbs to clear away new tears. "Because it's what's best for you." She shivered from his touch and not because one hand was freezing cold.

"I can understand why someone would be driven to punch you."

The uninjured side of his face lifted into a small, sad grin. "I'm not pushing you away because I don't want you. It's because I have nothing at all to give you."

"That's not true."

He stopped her heart when he framed her face with big, work-roughened hands, forcing her to look at him. "You deserve far better than some broken guy's scraps."

"You're not broken, Gavin. You're wounded but not broken."

"You don't know that."

"Yes, I do. You run a successful business. You're there for your friends and family when they need you. You help your parents put on the road race every year. If you were completely broken, you wouldn't be able to do any of those things."

"I've been spiraling lately. I can't let you be part of that."

"Then let me be part of *stopping* it." She put her arms around him, freezing when he winced.

"He got me in the ribs, too." Raising his arm, he showed her a huge bruise she'd somehow missed.

She put her hands on his hips, trying to ignore the rippling six-pack that made her want to kiss each well-defined muscle on his spectacular stomach. "Let me help."

"I can't. I've got to find my way out of this myself. Until I do, I can't let you in. I just can't."

"Why do you have to do it yourself? Why can't you let anyone help you? Why can't you let *me* help you?"

"Because if I'm going to destroy myself, I'm not taking anyone else down with me, especially not you."

His words brought new tears to her eyes. "Please don't say things like that. Please don't talk about destroying yourself. You have no idea how many people love you."

"Including you?"

A flash of blind rage caught her by surprise. "You haven't earned the right to ask me that."

"Fair enough." He kissed her forehead, lingering for a long, heart-stopping moment. "Go on, Ella. I'll be okay."

"I don't want to go. I want to stay. I want to be with you and hold you and . . ."

"Ella," he groaned. "Please . . . Don't do this to me. I can't. I just can't."

There was so much more she wanted to say. Maybe if she put her heart on the line and told him how desperately she loved him it would make a difference. But she couldn't seem to take that leap, no matter how badly she wanted to. She wouldn't guilt him into being with her. So without another word, she turned away from him and walked out the door.

Leaving him when he was so clearly in desperate need took everything she had and then some. In no condition to go back to work or to face her family, she went home to the apartment she rented in town from an elderly couple. She trudged up the stairs to her place, fumbled with her key in the door and, once inside, went straight to her bed, where she finally gave in to the sobs that overtook her.

He'd sent her away again, and this time her heart was well and truly broken.

Megan was long gone to work when Hunter woke up on Saturday morning, his body tired and aching from what he'd put it through during the night. But it had been so worth it. He lifted his arms over his head to stretch as erotic memories from the blissful night ran through his mind like the best movie he'd ever seen. He was completely gone over her and already counting the hours until he could see her again.

First he had to go to Rutland with Will to see a man about a ring. Even though he ached from head to toe, he went to the basement to get in a quick workout before he grabbed breakfast, a cup of coffee and a shower. Once again, he skipped the shaving portion of his morning ritual for the simple reason that she liked his stubble. If she liked stubble, he'd give her stubble.

He was dressed and ready when Will arrived shortly after ten. "Ready for this?" Hunter asked his brother when they were in Will's truck heading south.

"Yep."

"That's it? Just 'yep'?"

"Yep."

Hunter laughed. "It must be nice to be so sure."

"It is. I've done this once before when I wasn't as sure, and this is way better."

"Where does Cameron think you are today?"

"Helping you with something."

"You don't think she has any idea?"

"If she does, she's not letting on to me. She's been crazy busy with work and helping Hannah get ready for next weekend."

"What's your plan for popping the question?"

"I've been thinking a lot about that. When I asked Lisa, I

took her out to the property where my house is now and asked her, hoping she might want to live with me there. We all know how that turned out. I'd like to ask Cameron at home, but I don't want her to think she's getting the same thing Lisa got. You know?"

"I can see what you mean. Are you determined to do it there?"

"I wanted to do it in our place, the place we've made ours."

"I doubt she'll be thinking of Lisa and what you did for her when you're down on one knee asking her to marry you."

"What if she does though?"

"She's not going to. She'll be freaking out and crying and doing all that stuff women do when guys declare themselves. You'll be fine. You already know she's going to say yes."

"I want it to be special. Not just another night at home."

"You're going to be putting a diamond ring on her finger. That makes it special."

"I guess you're right."

"I usually am."

Will grunted out a laugh. "I walked right into that."

"While we're in Rutland, I need to hit the mall."

"Sure, no problem."

He'd be on the receiving end of no small amount of abuse when Will found out what he needed to get at the mall, but that was okay. If it meant seeing Megan decked out in silk lingerie, he was good with that.

"Did you get the message from Mom last night about what she wants us to wear to dinner tomorrow?"

"Yes! Denim shirts and khakis can only mean one thing."

"The dreaded family photo."

"Ugh. Does she think we don't know?"

"I'll never understand why we all have to dress alike. It's so goofy."

"We're far too old for that. We ought to protest."

"I'll let you handle the protest as the oldest."

"Gee, thanks."

They went to five different jewelry stores in Rutland before

Will found what he was looking for—an exquisite two-carat emerald-cut diamond in a platinum setting with smaller diamonds on either side of it. He'd wanted simple, classy and understated rather than the flashier style that was in vogue these days, and Hunter totally approved of his choice. The brothers had learned more than they'd ever wanted to know about color, clarity, cut and carat, but Will's pleasure at finding the perfect ring for Cameron was contagious.

While Will made the purchase, Hunter browsed the cases filled with dazzling gems and polished metals. One of the rings caught his eye—a square-cut yellow diamond that stood apart from the others with its unique color. He stared at it until his eyes began to water from not blinking. The weirdest feeling came over him, not unlike the feeling he got every time he looked at Megan.

"Help you with something?" one of the saleswomen asked.

"Could I see that one?" He pointed to the ring that had caught his eye.

"Of course." She unlocked the case and withdrew the ring he'd indicated, handing it over to him.

The moment the ring made contact with his hand, a charge of electricity traveled through his body, leaving him stunned by the power of the connection he felt to a ring, of all things. His gut hummed with awareness as he studied the incredible ring while the saleslady listed its attributes. As he stared at the yellow stone, he heard bits and pieces of what she was saying . . . just under three carats . . . an exceptional cut, a unique color.

"I'll take it."

"Oh," the stunned saleslady said. "Wonderful."

Like with Megan, he'd taken one look and known. He'd *known*. That was the ring she was meant to have.

Carrying a small shopping bag that contained the ring he'd bought for Cameron, Will joined him. "What're you doing?"

"I have no idea," Hunter said with a nervous laugh.

"Are you *buying* that ring?"

"It seems that I am."

"For Megan?"

"I believe so."

"Um, wow?"

"It's okay. You can say it. You can tell me I just started actually seeing her this week, and the last thing I should be doing is buying her a ring."

"What you said."

"I'm crazy, right?"

"Your words, not mine."

Hunter laughed at Will's obvious effort to refrain from saying the wrong thing. "Feels right."

"Then do it."

"I'm doing it."

"Okay, then."

"But I'm crazy, right?"

"I'd like to take the Fifth on that one."

"I am crazy—about her."

"Does this count as the most spontaneous moment of your life?"

Hunter handed over his credit card, trying to remember what the limit was on that card and hoping it was enough. "Without a doubt."

Twenty minutes later, the brothers left the store, each with a small silver bag in hand.

"Well, that turned out to be more interesting than expected," Will said. "And I expected it to be pretty damned interesting."

"Why are my hands shaking?" Hunter asked.

"Because you just spent thousands of dollars without first doing a thorough analysis and without consulting *Consumer Reports*?"

"I don't think that's why, although that's a good guess."

"Maybe because you just decided, while standing in a jewelry store, that you want to marry a woman you've been dating for less than a week, a spontaneous decision so contrary to your entire life before now that your closest brother is wondering if you've been abducted by aliens?"

"That could be it."

Will lost it laughing. "Do you think?"

"I should take it back, right? This was stupid and impulsive and irresponsible."

"It was all those things, but it was also perfect. If you could've seen the look on your face when you saw that ring . . ."

"Yeah, it was kind of perfect."

"Nothing says you have to go home and pop the question. In fact, I'd prefer if you could hold off for a day or two so Cam can have her moment."

"That shouldn't be a problem."

"Excellent," Will said, shaking his head and laughing at Hunter.

"I'd planned to hit Victoria's Secret and buy her something sexy. How'd I end up with a diamond ring?"

"You may be still asking yourself that question in thirty years."

"Probably so, but I'll never forget the way I felt when I saw that ring." He rested his hand flat on his abdomen. "I felt it here." He moved his hand to his chest. "And here."

"Then you did the right thing buying it."

"I hope you're right."

"I'm always right."

"Hey, that's my line."

"You've gone off the rails."

That might be true. In fact, it was absolutely true. But Hunter was discovering he rather enjoyed life off the rails. At least he was out of his rut.

CHAPTER 27

——◆◆——

I feel that luck is preparation meeting opportunity.

—Oprah Winfrey, TV personality and businesswoman

W ill returned home to an empty house. Even the dogs
were gone. Cameron must've taken them with her. In
the kitchen he stashed the groceries he'd bought for dinner
in the fridge and found a note on the counter.

*Over at Hannah's. Back by five. The boys are having a
playdate with their cousin Homer Junior.*

Love you, Cam

"Love you, too, baby." He checked his watch. She'd be
home in less than an hour. The house was chilly, so he started
a fire in the woodstove. Then he sat on the sofa, removed the
small velvet box from the shopping bag and took another
look at the ring, trying to picture it on Cameron's finger.

He thought about the time they'd spent together since the
night she slammed into Fred—and into his life with her
bruised face, dented Mini Cooper and the suede boots that
had nearly been lost to Vermont mud season. He recalled

her immediate fascination with his big family, wanting to know all his siblings' names minutes after they met.

Those first two weeks together had been like something out of a dream. Their attraction had been mutual and instantaneous. He'd brought her gifts from the store, beginning with the sturdy boots she needed to survive mud season, the moose pajamas she'd loved and a sweater she'd admired. From the beginning, he'd wanted to please her, and she'd always been easy to please.

Despite her fancy upbringing in a New York City penthouse with a billionaire father, Cameron was the most grounded, down-to-earth woman he'd ever known. She was everything he'd ever wanted—and then some. He couldn't wait to tell her so.

By five fifteen, he was pacing. It wasn't unusual for her to be late. She was forever doing something for someone, usually a member of his family, and they were all as in love with her as he was. By five thirty, he was worried. He used the house phone to call her cell, knowing it would be pointless if she was still in town where there was no cell service, but he tried anyway.

A clicking noise on the other end triggered full-on panic. "Cameron?"

"Will, I'm stuck—"

The connection died. "Goddamn it." With an awful array of scenarios running through his mind, he grabbed his keys and headed for the door, figuring he'd find her somewhere between his house and Hannah's. Then he remembered the priceless ring he'd left sitting out on the table and went back to grab it, just in case she made it home before he did. In his truck, he stuffed the ring box and the bag from the store into his glove compartment and tore out of the dirt road that also served as his driveway.

Heading for town, he hadn't gone far when he encountered Fred the moose standing across the road, blocking the way for one car: Cameron's black SUV. Laughing at the sight before him, Will put his truck in park, turned on his hazards and reached for the door handle. Almost as an afterthought, he grabbed the ring box from the glove compartment and jammed it into the front pocket of his jeans before he got out to go to her.

Walking around Fred's back end, Will gave the moose a wide berth. While he believed what everyone said about Fred being tame and harmless, he was still a wild animal, and unlike Hannah, Will was no moose whisperer.

With their heads out the window in the backseat of the SUV he'd insisted Cameron get to replace the impractical Mini, Trevor and Tanner went crazy barking when they saw him coming. "Hush, boys." For once they actually did as he told them to.

Obviously infuriated, Cameron leaned through the open driver's-side window. "Can you *believe* this? I've been stuck here for *thirty minutes! What* is his problem?"

"Dad thinks he has a crush on you, and really, I can't say I blame him."

"This is not funny, Will! I'm being *stalked* by a moose!"

Could she be any more adorable? "He's a cute moose, and it's possible he loves you as much as I do."

Fred let out a loud moo, which made them laugh.

"Told ya." Will opened her door and leaned across her to unfasten her seatbelt. He took her hand and gave a gentle tug. "Come here for a sec."

"What're you doing? We're in the middle of a road once again being held hostage by a freaking moose."

"I know where we are." They were in just about the exact spot where their lives, and Fred's, had come crashing together six months ago—and it was the perfect place for what he had planned. Once again, Will Abbott owed Fred the moose a tremendous debt of gratitude for his assistance. When he had Cameron out of the car, looking frustrated and pissed off, he put his arms around her and kissed her.

Seeming baffled, she glanced around them, probably looking for other cars that weren't coming. They had the road all to themselves. "Have you lost your mind? What are you *doing*?"

"I can't believe we're right back here where we first met with Fred as our witness."

"Our witness to what?"

"This." He dropped to one knee before her and took hold of her left hand, placing a kiss square in the middle of it. Then he looked up to find her other hand over her mouth and tears in her eyes.

"Will . . ."

"I love you more than you'll ever know, Cameron Murphy. The rest of my life won't be enough time to tell you and show you how much I love you. I want to spend every minute of what's left of both our lives together. I want to have blond babies with you and raise them together and work with you sitting on the other side of my desk, driving me wild just because you're in the room. I want to sleep with you and make love with you and do everything with you. Will you marry me, Cameron?"

"*Yes!* Oh my God, *yes!*" And then she was on her knees with him, kissing him while she cried. "Did you plan this? Did you get Fred to do this so it could happen here?"

"I wish I had that kind of imagination. This was all his idea." Will let her go long enough to pull the velvet box from his pocket.

"You even have a ring?"

"Where do you think I was all day?" He removed the ring from the box and slid it onto her trembling hand.

"Oh, Will." She sighed as she gazed at the ring. "It's beautiful! I love it."

"Do you? If·you don't, we can return it for something else—"

She kissed the words right off his lips. "It's perfect. You're perfect. Fred is perfect."

"Fred is a pain in the ass, but I love him anyway."

"So do I."

Fred's loud moo had them both laughing again.

Will stood and helped her up. "We probably ought to get out of the road before our engagement turns into roadkill."

"That would ruin the mood."

He hooked an arm around her waist and pulled her into his chest. "Nothing could ruin my mood right now. The woman I love has just agreed to spend the rest of her life with me." He kissed her. "Best thing to ever happen to me."

"To me, too," she said, blinking back more tears.

"You have to call your dad. I promised him you'd call as soon as it happened."

Her watery eyes widened in surprise. "You talked to him?"

"The day before yesterday to give him a heads-up."

"Thank you for that. I'm sure it meant a lot to him."

"He seemed to appreciate it."

"This was the best ten minutes of my entire life," she said, her hands on his face as she kissed him.

"Mine, too."

"Let's go home and make some calls."

"Oh man, I so thought that sentence was going to end differently than that."

Cameron laughed. "We'll do that, too."

Charley gave Ella a full day of ignoring her calls until Saturday night, when she took their friends Ben and Jerry to her sister's place for a showdown. It wasn't like Ella to go silent for this long. It also wasn't like Ella to walk out of a family meeting without a word to anyone. Something was up, and Charley was determined to find out what.

Using the spare key Ella had given her for emergencies, Charley let herself into the foyer of the house where Ella rented an upstairs apartment. She knocked on Ella's door. "Open up. It's me, Charley."

No answer.

Charley knocked again. "I've got presents. Your favorites— Cherry Garcia and salted caramel. Come on, Ella. I know you're home. Your car is parked outside." She knocked some more until she heard rustling inside the apartment. The door swung open, and Charley held back a gasp at the sight of her sister's swollen eyes and red nose. Had she been crying all this time?

"What're you doing here, Charley?"

"My sister lives here, and I haven't heard a word from her since sometime yesterday when she went running out of a meeting to go check on a guy I didn't know she cared all that much about. So I did what any good sister would do and bought ice cream."

"That's really nice of you, but—"

"I'm not leaving until you talk to me."

"This isn't the time to be your usual pain-in-the-ass self."

"Ouch. That hurt. Sticks and stones . . ." Charley pulled Ella's all-time favorite, the Cherry Garcia, out of the bag and pulled off the lid. "I could eat this whole pint myself, or you could help me."

Ella glared at her for another minute before she snatched the pint out of Charley's hand and took it with her into the apartment.

"Success," Charley whispered as she followed her sister, closing the door behind her.

In the kitchen, Ella produced two spoons, handing one of them to Charley. Ella dug into the Cherry Garcia while Charley took a couple of bites of the salted caramel, which was her favorite. She waited, hoping Ella would talk to her but prepared to be her "usual pain-in-the-ass self" if it came to that.

"Why aren't you doing what you do?" Ella asked.

Charley held back a laugh. "You told me this wasn't the time for what I do."

"Since when has that ever stopped you?"

"You wanna talk about it?"

"Not particularly."

"Okay then let's eat ice cream and watch the new episode of *The Bachelor*. I haven't seen it yet. Have you?"

"No, I haven't," Ella said.

Charley looked at her sister and was shocked to see tears on her cheeks. "Oh, El, what's wrong? Will you please tell me?"

Ella put down the pint and rested her hands flat against the countertop. "I don't want to talk about it. It's personal."

"I won't bust your balls or do any of the things I normally do."

Ella laughed through her tears. "Promise?"

"Yeah, I promise. You can tell me. I want to help."

After another long pause, Ella said, "It's Gavin."

"What about him?"

"I . . . I care about him."

Charley kept her expression neutral as Ella confirmed what Charley had suspected. "For how long?"

"I don't know. A long time."

"So you went there yesterday after you heard he'd been arrested?"

Ella nodded. "For all the good it did. He doesn't want me. Not like that anyway."

"How do you know that?"

"He told me."

"He said, 'Go away, Ella. I don't want you.'"

"Not in those exact words, but the message was loud and clear."

"Tell me exactly what happened. Leave nothing out. I'll be the judge of whether he doesn't want you."

Sighing, Ella took her pint and spoon and went to sit on the sofa in the living room. "It's a longer story than just yesterday."

"I've got all night, and I'm all yours." Charley followed, wondering if her sister was going to tell her the full story.

"I've had a crush on him for ages. Going back to when Hannah and Caleb got married."

"That was thirteen years ago, El. You've dated other guys since then."

"I know, but in the back of my mind, I always knew that if I could pick any guy I wanted, it would be him."

"And you never told anyone this?"

She shrugged. "What would be the point? Have you seen him? He's a freaking god. And I'm . . . well, he's a bit out of my league."

Charley stared at Ella, agog. "*How* can you say that? Have you looked in a mirror lately? Do you have any idea how incredibly gorgeous you are? I'd give anything for your long dark hair and your flawless skin. I got stuck with curls and crappy skin that requires boatloads of moisturizer to get through a day. You're effortlessly beautiful."

"You have to say that. You're my sister."

"Have you met me? I don't say nice things just to say them. I mean it, Ella. You are totally in his league. In fact, you might be out of his league."

That made Ella laugh even as new tears filled her eyes.

Seeing the normally unflappable Ella so undone was hard for Charley to fathom. How had she hidden such a huge secret for so long?

"We talked the day of Homer's funeral. That was a hard day for him. Homer was the last real tie to Caleb, and saying good-bye to Caleb's dog meant saying good-bye once again to his beloved brother. He's still so broken over losing Caleb, even after all this time."

"They were so close. I can't imagine what it's been like for him."

"And then Hannah got remarried a short time after Homer died, and he's been spiraling. His word." She wiped her tears. "His pain kills me, Charl. It guts me to see him struggling by himself when he doesn't have to be alone."

"So he knows how you feel?"

"He knows. He told me at Hannah's wedding if he had anything to give, I'd be the one he'd want to give it to."

"Whoa. When did that happen?"

"Remember when Nolan sang to Hannah?"

Charley fanned her face as she recalled the single most romantic thing she'd ever witnessed. The thought of her brother-in-law's beautiful gesture could still bring her nearly to tears. "How could I forget?"

"I saw Gavin escape down the stairs to the beach, so I followed him. We talked some and he admitted that even though he's thrilled for Hannah and Nolan, it was a very difficult day for him."

"You gotta give him—and his parents—credit for being there."

"They wouldn't have missed it. They love Hannah almost as much as they loved Caleb."

"Still . . ."

"I know. On the beach, we . . . he . . . We kissed, and it was incredible. Unlike any other kiss ever, and since then, all I can think about is what it was like to kiss him and how much I wish things were different. When I heard what happened the other night, I had to go to him. I had to see him." Wiping away more tears, she conveyed the gist of what'd transpired at Gavin's house the day before.

Charley listened to Ella's heartbroken recitation, trying to find the words her sister needed. She wasn't always known for her tact, but if ever there was a time for the right words it was now.

Ella wiped away a flood of new tears. "You can't tell anyone about this. I know we gossip like crazy fools in our family, but this isn't for public consumption. I couldn't take it if everyone knew."

Charley drew her sister into a hug. "I won't tell anyone. I promise." Holding Ella as she sobbed, Charley wished there were something she could say or do to fix things for her. But what was broken in this situation couldn't be easily fixed.

"I need to give up on him," Ella said. "I know that, but knowing it and doing it are two different things."

"Maybe he just needs some more time."

"It's been seven years, and he's worse off now than he's been since it first happened. He tells me I deserve better. I deserve someone who isn't broken inside, but I don't want someone else. I want *him*. I've always wanted him."

"I'm so sorry you've been suffering in silence over this."

"I haven't been completely alone with it. Hannah knows."

"She does? What does she say about it?"

"We haven't talked about it recently, but the one time we did, the day of Homer's funeral, she said she loves us both and would love to see us together. But even she knows I'm facing an uphill battle where he's concerned."

"It's so sad." Charley rested her head on the back of Ella's sofa. "The worst part, of course, is that Caleb died so young when he had so much living left to do. But the fallout for the people around him lasts a lifetime." She took hold of Ella's hand. "I don't have any words of wisdom for you. All I can tell you is I'm sorry you're hurting. I'm sorry he is, too, because he's a great guy. Caleb would hate that his death has ruined Gavin's life, too."

"It hasn't completely ruined it. He's poured his grief into building that incredible business, and he's been so good to his parents. But it's ruined some aspects of his life. That's for sure."

"The way I look at it, you have two choices. Continue to hope that he'll get to the point where he's capable of a relationship or give up and move on."

"I've been thinking a lot about those two options since yesterday."

"And?"

"It might be time to give up and move on."

"I hate to say that might be the right move because I know it's not what you really want, but Caleb's been gone a long time now, and Gavin's not getting any better. In fact, it seems he might be getting worse. I have to give him credit for not wanting to take my lovely sister down with him."

"How sad is it that part of me would rather go down with him than live without him?"

"It's not sad. It's love."

"Yeah," Ella said with another deep sigh. "Is everyone talking about me after I ran out of there yesterday?"

"Not really."

"Are you lying?"

"Not really."

Ella laughed. "I'm sure they're all abuzz over me having a thing for him."

"They'll leave you alone about it. I'll make sure of it."

"Aww, Charlotte Abbott. Are you finally growing up?"

"Make a thing of it, and I'll take it all back."

"Your secret is safe with me."

"Did you get Mom's message about denim day at dinner tomorrow?"

"I'm not going."

"You have to go! Mom's got Izzy coming to take the dreaded family photo."

"Cameron can Photoshop me in."

"Mom will never go for that. If you don't want everyone up in your business, you have to come and put on a happy face. Just for an hour or two."

"I don't know if I can."

"I'll be with you."

"Thanks for coming, Charl. It means a lot to me that you brought me Cherry Garcia and listened to my pathetic tale of woe."

"Happy to listen, but I'm sorry you're sad. Hey, you know what we haven't done in ages?"

"What's that?"

"A sleepover."

"You want to sleep over?" Ella asked hopefully.

Charley was pleased that Ella seemed to like the idea. "If you'll have me. I'll even let you watch *Pretty Woman* for the nine-thousandth time."

Ella took another huge spoonful of ice cream. "Maybe I should become a hooker. Things worked out well for her."

Charley lost it laughing. Ella's joke made Charley feel more confident that her sister would get past her heartbreak over Gavin. Eventually.

CHAPTER 28

——◆◇◆——

To win without risk is to triumph without glory.

—Pierre Corneille, French dramatist

Megan couldn't believe Hunter had talked her into Sunday dinner at his parents' house. He'd gotten her to agree to go when he had her hovering on the brink of an orgasm that he'd denied her until she acquiesced—a dirty trick of the highest order. She'd make him pay for that later. She couldn't wait. He'd returned from Rutland with a huge bag of silk lingerie that he'd insisted she model for him.

They'd made it to the third item before he was pulling the silky fabric from her body and making mad, passionate love to her.

After yet another incredible night with him, she could no longer recall what her life had been like before he declared himself to her, before he told her he'd been into her for years and had dreamed about being with her. He was completely irresistible as well as funny, sexy, thoughtful, smart, charming, caring and more than a little bossy when he wanted to be.

She couldn't get enough of him. Even the thought of Nina's looming departure on Wednesday couldn't dim the light that glowed inside Megan thanks to Hunter's love and attention. Nina and Brett had gone to spend some time with his family today. They'd invited her to come along, but she'd declined. There was no time like the present to start letting Nina go.

After Hunter got her to agree to dinner with his family, she began to regret not taking Nina up on her invitation. Wearing a denim shirt with khakis, Hunter looked as gorgeous as ever while he drove them from her house to his parents' barn on Hells Peak Road.

As they crossed the one-lane covered bridge, Megan's nerves went into overdrive. Everyone would be there. They'd all be looking at her and wondering what he saw in her.

"Whatever you're thinking, knock it off."

"How do you know what I'm thinking?" she asked, unnerved by how tuned into her he was.

"You're doing that thing with your hands."

"What thing with my hands?"

With his wrists propped on the steering wheel, he twisted his fingers around in circles. "You do it when you're stewing over something, and since we're on our way to my parents' house for dinner with my family, I assume you're stewing over that, which you shouldn't be."

"Stop doing that."

"Doing what?"

"Knowing me so well. You shouldn't know me so well yet. It's not right."

Hunter laughed, a sexy, gravelly sound that she'd come to adore, especially when she made it happen. "Hannah is a moose whisperer. I'm a Megan whisperer."

"Did you just compare me to a moose?"

"Not at all." He reached for her hand, wrapping his much larger one around hers. "Relax. I promise it'll all be fine."

"Easy for you to say. Your boyfriend's family isn't large enough to be a baseball team."

"Boyfriend?"

"Is that really all you heard there?"

"Did you say something else?"

"Hunter! I'm serious. This is very intimidating to me."

He pulled to the side of the road and put the SUV in park.

"What're you doing?"

"Giving you a minute to calm down and contemplating how soon I can trade in this freaking truck so I can get one that gives me access to you when I need it."

Megan needed him as much as he seemed to need her, so she unbuckled her seatbelt and crawled across the console, landing in his lap with an inelegant plop that made him gasp. "Sorry. Did I hurt you?"

"No," he said in a high-pitched, female tone. "I'll be fine."

"Stop it," she said, laughing.

His arms came around her, cuddling her, and all her worries disappeared like a wisp of smoke leaving a chimney. When he was holding her and looking at her with those incredible eyes, nothing could bother her.

"If you feel freaked out at dinner, look at me. I'll remind you why you're there."

"Why am I there?"

"Because I want you with me. I want you to know the people who matter to me—and not just know what they like to order at the diner, but really *know* them. I want you to be a part of the second most important thing in my life—my family. I want to spend every possible minute with you."

"You said your family is the second most important thing in your life. What's first? Your work?"

He smiled and shook his head. "No, silly. The most important thing in my life is the woman I love."

Megan closed her eyes and sighed. What else could she do? "She's a lucky girl, whoever she is."

"I hope you get to meet her someday."

Megan opened her eyes to find his dancing with mirth. "Very funny."

He sobered all of a sudden, looking sexy and somber at the same time. "I need to tell you something before we get there."

"What?"

"There's a very good chance that Will and Cameron got engaged last night."

"Oh."

"Are you okay with that?"

"I'm fine. I'm happy for him—for both of them."

"Are you sure?"

"Sure that I'm happy for them? Yes. Sure that I'm fine with it? Positive. But you're sweet to give me a heads-up and to be concerned about me."

"Of course I'm concerned about you. I'll always be concerned about you."

"How do you know that?"

He shrugged. "I just do."

"You're very certain about all of this."

"You have no idea how certain I am," he said with a mysterious smile. "Let's go to dinner."

"You're not going to explain that?"

After thinking about it for a second, he said, "Nope."

"It's not nice to tease me that way."

"You love when I tease you." He swooped in to kiss her, but she turned away.

"No kissing until you tell me what you meant by that."

"I'll get you to change your mind."

She lifted herself off his lap and back into her seat. "Give it your best shot."

CHAPTER 29

*To succeed . . . You need to find something
to hold on to, something to motivate you,
something to inspire you.*

—Tony Dorsett, former football player

Walking into the madness that was Sunday dinner at his parents' house, Hunter hoped he hadn't made a huge mistake by bringing Megan with him. Was it too soon in their new relationship to subject her to the Abbotts? Probably, but Sunday dinner was a big part of their routine and he wanted her to be a big part of *his* routine. And he wanted his family to know he was serious about her right from the beginning.

"Is there a Sunday dinner uniform that no one told me about?" she asked, gesturing to all the denim and khaki.

Hunter laughed at her observation. "Family picture. My mom gets a wild hair about pictures at least once a year, and she always makes us wear the same thing. This year it's denim. Last year it was black."

"The picture on your mantel is from last year."

"Yes," he said, pleased that she'd noticed. "We've got a few more family members this year."

"Mom," Hannah said as she helped in the kitchen. "Are Will and Cam coming?"

"They said they were when we talked to them last night."

"Can I help with anything?" Megan asked.

"Not a thing, honey," Molly said. "You're forever waiting on all of us. Today it's our turn."

Hunter sent his mother a grateful smile. He could always count on her to say the exact right thing.

Colton and Lucy arrived, followed by Lucas and Landon and then Max and his very pregnant girlfriend, Chloe.

"Lucas," Molly said, "go upstairs and iron that shirt right now. You're not ruining another family picture."

"Told you she'd make you iron," Landon said with a smirk.

"*She* is in the room, and *she* has a name," Molly said.

"He's been ruining the family pictures since the day he was born," Hunter said, earning a middle finger from his younger brother on his way out of the kitchen.

Hunter grabbed the finger and had Lucas's arm pinned to his back so quickly his brother never saw it coming.

"The *hands*!" Lucas screamed. "They're insured for millions!"

Hunter let him go with a shove that sent Lucas tumbling into the dining room. Then he brushed off his hands like he'd touched something undesirable.

"If you break my china, I'll kill you," Molly said.

"It was him." Hunter winked at Megan, who was trying hard not to laugh.

"Sure it was," Molly said. "Get out of my kitchen. You're in my way."

"You don't have to tell me twice." He took hold of Megan's hand. "Come see my old room."

"No girls in your bedroom," Molly called after him.

"I'm thirty-five, Mom. I have girls in my bedroom all the time."

"La la la, can't hear you."

"All the time," Landon said, rolling his eyes. "Dream on."

"I make them take numbers," Hunter said, as he led Megan from the kitchen before he could dig himself a deeper hole.

"*All the time?*" she asked.

"I have six younger brothers, sweetheart. I have to make them think I'm a badass, or I'll lose control of the whole situation."

"You did have the extra large box of condoms on hand," she said, surprising him with the witty comment. "I should've known."

He gestured for her to go up the stairs ahead of him. "An *unopened* box bought with you in mind."

"I bet you say that to *all* the girls."

"You're the only one who's ever spent a night in my bed."

Megan stopped halfway up the stairs and turned around, looking him square in the eye from the step above his. "Come on . . ."

"I'm serious. I never bring women to my house. I was involved with someone very casually for a couple of years. We hung out at her house. Never at mine."

"Why didn't you ever bring her to your house?"

"Because I didn't want people to see me bringing women there."

"Why?"

"You ask a lot of questions," Hunter said.

"That's not an answer."

"Because," he said with a sigh, "I didn't want you to hear I was bringing other women to my house. I didn't want to ruin any chance I might have with you by those kinds of rumors getting back to you."

"I didn't even know you were interested in me."

"I was hoping you'd find out someday, and I didn't want you to think poorly of me before you got to know me."

She put her hands on his shoulders and kissed him, "That's very sweet."

He wrapped his arms around her. "It's true." Without breaking the kiss, he picked her up and kept walking up the stairs, down a hallway to the last door on the left, which he opened and closed while continuing to kiss her.

"Put me down before you hurt yourself."

"You're light as a feather."

"Sure, I am," she said, laughing.

He laid her on his childhood bed, coming down on top of her. "Hey," he said, looking down at her.

"Hey, yourself."

"This is where all the magic happened."

She looked around him at the room that was exactly the way he'd left it when he went to college. "What're all the trophies for?"

"Cross-country and lacrosse. I was pretty good at both of them."

"Apparently. How did you end up with your own room in a family of ten kids?"

"Hannah and I both got our own rooms as the oldest. That's something the younger ones still bitch about to this day."

"They didn't give them your rooms when you moved out?"

"Nope. That's why this room is referred to as 'The Shrine.'"

Laughing, she said, "It's not easy being you around here, is it?"

"You're just figuring that out?" He kissed her lips and then turned his attention to her neck. "This is the first time I've ever had a girl in here. No way I would've gotten away with that with all the little eyes on me when I lived here."

"I bet there was no shortage of volunteers willing to risk it with you."

"A line out the door."

He loved making her laugh. He loved making her eyes light up with joy. He loved the rosy glow of her skin and the lips swollen from his kisses. He loved everything about her. "Megan . . ."

"Yeah?"

He wanted to tell her again, to say the words, to make sure she knew. But he was still afraid of scaring her off. "I've had my share of girlfriends, but I've never felt for anyone what I do for you."

"I . . . I want you to know . . . I'm falling for you, too. I really am. You're all I think about when we're not together, and every time we're apart, I can't wait to see you again."

He'd never been so happy to hear anything in his life. "I'm glad." Kissing her again, he said, "This is just the beginning."

"Percy's son called me about the office manager job in St. J earlier today."

"Oh. He did?"

"Uh-huh." She combed her fingers through Hunter's hair. He loved when she did that. "I told him I've already got a job but thanked him for calling."

Hunter nearly stopped breathing. "What job is that?"

She looked up at him almost shyly. "Running your diner, if you'll have me."

"Yes, I'll have you." He devoured her in a kiss that set his entire body on fire with desire for more of her. It didn't matter that they were in his childhood bedroom with his entire family downstairs. Nothing mattered beyond showing her how happy she'd made him.

A knock on the door had him moaning against her lips. "If you value your life, go away."

"Mom said to tell you it's time to eat," Lucas said. "And I'm telling her you've got a girl in there."

"Go right ahead, you little rat."

They could hear Lucas laughing as he walked away.

Hunter rolled off her onto his back. "I'm going to need an hour before I can go down there."

"I can make it go away a lot faster than that."

Before he could begin to gauge her intentions, she had his belt unbuckled and his pants unzipped. "Megan . . . Oh my God." All the air seemed to leave his body on a long exhale. The door wasn't locked. Anyone could walk in there and catch them. He didn't care. How could he care about anything else when her lips were wrapped around his cock as she licked, stroked and sucked him to the fastest orgasm in the history of the world?

"There," she said, running her tongue over her lips in the aftermath while he lay demolished and panting on the bed.

She put him away as efficiently as she'd taken him out and then patted his abdomen when she was done. "All better?"

"I've lost the ability to move my extremities."

"You've also lost your erection, so my work here is finished." She stood and reached for his hands, pulling him up. "Come on. You can do it."

He recovered his bearings enough to hook an arm around her waist. "That was the hottest thing *ever*. None of the fantasies I had in this room, and they were rather vivid, could've prepared me for you."

"Much more where that came from. We just have to get through dinner first."

Groaning, he followed her from the room. "How do you expect me to 'get through dinner' when you say things like that?"

"You can do it. Be strong."

Hands on her hips, he pulled her back against him, making her laugh when he pressed his reawakened erection against her bottom.

"You're on your own this time."

"We're going to give the term 'chew and screw' all new meaning today."

"You've got to pose for pictures before we can screw."

His loud groan made her laugh all the way down the stairs.

CHAPTER 30

———◄●►———

*Where there is an open mind, there
will always be a frontier.*

—Charles F. Kettering, inventor, engineer
and businessman

D inner with the Abbotts was every bit as loud and crazy
as Megan had expected it to be. Elmer had claimed the
seat next to hers, and Megan was thankful to have him on
one side and Hunter on the other, keeping a tight grip on her
hand under the table.

While chaos swirled all around her, Megan contended
with an emotional storm of her own as she realized she was
more than falling for Hunter. She'd already fallen. He'd
bowled her over with his special brand of humor, intelligence, intensity and sexiness as well as his unvarnished
ability to tell her exactly how he felt about her.

In her experience, men liked to talk a big game, saying
whatever it took to get a woman into bed. Once they'd had
what they wanted, inevitably they lost interest. Not Hunter.
The more time they spent together, the more adored and
loved she felt in his presence. The more she gave him in bed,
the more he seemed to worship the ground she walked on.

He released her hand and moved his hand down on her

leg until he encountered the hem of her dress. Dipping under it, he let his big, warm hand sit on her bare leg, all without missing a beat in the conversation he was having with his dad about his projections for the third quarter at the store.

The screen door in the mudroom slapped shut moments before two more yellow labs joined the party.

"Hey, Trev, Tanner," Lincoln said. "Come see your grandpa."

Dressed in denim and khaki, Will and Cameron came in right behind the dogs. At a fast glance, Megan could see they were glowing with happiness. She waited for the punch to the gut she'd experienced every time she'd seen them together, but it never materialized. Rather she experienced another feeling altogether when Hunter squeezed her leg and set off a throb of desire.

"Sorry we're late," Will said, "but we come bearing huge news."

"What news?" Charley asked.

Cameron held out her left hand, where a big diamond now resided.

The family erupted into cheers and shouts of congratulations and more than a few tears. Lincoln produced a bottle of champagne from under the table, indicating he and his wife had been told about the engagement the night before.

Everyone stood to hug and kiss the happy couple.

"Congratulations," Megan said to Cameron when it was down to her and Hunter.

Cameron surprised the shit out of her when she hugged her. "Thank you so much, Megan. I'm so happy to see you here."

Before Megan could begin to reply, Cameron was hugging Hunter, leaving Megan to come up with something she could say to Will.

"I'm really happy for you." *Lame, Megan. Totally lame.*

But Will just smiled and said, "Thanks, Megan."

Plates were produced for the newcomers, room was made for them at the table and talk turned to wedding plans.

"We don't want to wait," Cameron said. "We'll probably do something this fall at our place."

Elmer raised his glass of champagne. "We couldn't be happier to welcome you to the family, Cameron."

"Hear, hear," Lincoln said. The two men seemed rather pleased with themselves, and after hearing Hunter's stories about their matchmaking efforts, Megan could see why.

After dinner, their cousin Isabella arrived, camera in hand. She was introduced to Megan as the family photographer. "You're Isabella Coleman," Megan said, recognizing the well-known Vermont photographer. "We have some of your photos in the diner." Hunter had them at his house, too.

"That'd be me," Isabella said with a friendly smile. She had curly auburn hair that fell past her shoulders and bright green eyes.

"Thank you so much for coming on short notice, honey," Molly said, hugging her niece. "It's such a rare thing these days to have everyone in the same place at the same time."

"No problem, Aunt Molly. Anything for you."

"Everyone outside," Molly said.

Mumbling and grumbling, pushing and shoving, the Abbotts made their way through the kitchen and mudroom into bright September sunshine.

Isabella took a look around the yard and pointed to a spot near trees that were just beginning to show fall color. "The lighting will be perfect there."

"You're in charge," Molly told her niece. "And best of luck to you. You know what they say about herding cats."

Isabella grinned. "I got this."

Megan watched in amazement as people and dogs were arranged with military precision.

"Hunter, come on," Isabella said, pointing to the spot in the back row she'd reserved for him.

"Be right back," he said, kissing Megan's temple.

"Megan." Molly produced a denim button-down that she handed to Megan. "You, too, honey."

"What?" Megan glanced at Hunter and saw the warm, appreciative smile he directed at his mother.

Hunter took the shirt from her and held it out to Megan.

"You're part of our family now," Molly said. "We'd be honored to have you in the picture."

Megan blinked frantically as she moved robotically to put her arms in the sleeves of the shirt Hunter held for her. "I don't feel right about this," she said for his ears only.

Hunter buttoned the shirt over her dress and then kissed her cheek. "My mom wouldn't have invited you if she didn't want you in the picture. *I* want you in the picture. Okay?"

She nodded, unable to find the words to convey to either of them how much it meant to her to be considered a member of this incredible family. They had taken her in, surrounded her with love and affection and made her feel like she belonged even if they all knew she didn't. Not really.

Isabella put them on the far left side, Hunter behind her with his arms hooked loosely around her waist. Next to them, Will and Cameron stood in a similar position. Then came Colton and Lucy, Nolan and Hannah, who held her puppy, Homer Junior, in her arms, and then Max and Chloe.

Mimicking their siblings, Lucas and Landon wrapped their arms around each other, making kissing noises until their mother told them to shut up and stand still.

"She ruins all our fun," Landon said.

"That's my job," Molly replied. She was in the front row with Lincoln, Elmer, George and Ringo, Colton's dogs Sarah and Elmer, and Will's dogs Trevor and Tanner. Standing next to their parents and grandfather with the pets in front of them were Wade, Charley and Ella.

"Everyone shut up and look at me," Isabella said as she took a few practice shots, studying each of them with a critical eye.

Megan focused on breathing through the wide array of emotions that swirled around inside her as she was welcomed as an honorary member of a family she'd admired her whole life. She loved the way they bickered and laughed and made fun of each other and stood by each other, and being a part of that, even as a guest, was an amazing experience.

As if he knew how much his mother's gesture had meant to her, Hunter tightened his arms around her and nuzzled her neck between takes. "You're right where you belong, sweetheart. So smile and relax."

Did she belong here with him? It was starting to feel that way, and she couldn't deny that it felt good to be held by him, to be surrounded by his large and loving family. But what if she bought into it all and he lost interest in her? It'd happened before. It could happen again.

"Stop," he whispered in her ear. "Whatever you're thinking that's making your entire body go rigid, just stop."

Megan wanted to turn around so she could see his face, but she didn't want to ruin the photo Molly had so graciously invited her into, so she held her position. She was acutely aware of him behind her, of the heat of his hands on her belly, the press of his erection against her bottom and the scent she'd recognize anywhere as his.

Then he leaned forward and whispered in her ear. "I love you. I want you. I love that you're here, that I can hold you and touch you and tell you I love you rather than having to keep it to myself."

Megan's knees went weak, forcing him to tighten his hold on her to keep her standing.

"Come *on*, Izzy," Landon said. "I can't smile anymore. My face is gonna break."

"Your face is already ruining the picture," Colton said.

"Since I have the misfortune to bear the same face, I take issue with that," Lucas said.

"Couple more," Isabella said to groans from her cousins. The minute she said, "Okay, I think we've got it," Hunter took hold of Megan's hand and began walking toward his truck.

"Thanks for dinner, Mom," Hunter said.

"Wait." Megan tugged at his hand. "I need to say good-bye and thank you. And I need to give her the shirt back."

He released her. "Hurry."

One quick glance at his intense gaze told her what was on his mind. Removing the shirt as she went, Megan found Molly in the crowd and handed it to her. "Thank you, Mrs. Abbott, for dinner and for including me in the photo. That was very nice of you."

Molly hugged her. "I know this is going to be a tough week for you," she said softly so only Megan could hear her. "Please remember you're not alone in this world, Megan. Don't ever think you are." She drew back and kissed Megan on the cheek. "And call me Molly. Everyone does."

Contending with the huge lump in her throat, Megan managed to say, "Thank you." She received hugs and kisses on the cheek from Lincoln and Elmer before she turned to rejoin Hunter.

As she started to walk away, Homer Junior darted past her. Behind her, Hannah let out a cry. Megan turned in time to see Homer Junior trip Hannah, who was about to topple over. Megan reacted quickly, wrapping her arms around Hannah to break the fall with her own body.

The two women landed hard, Hannah coming down on top of Megan, who absorbed the full impact of the crash. Nolan let out an unholy cry as he dropped to his knees next to them. "Hannah! What happened?"

"I'm fine," she said. "Got my feet tangled up with Homer. Get me off poor Megan before I kill her."

"Are you sure you're okay to move?"

"Yes!" Hannah said. "Hurry up. I'm crushing her."

Nolan lifted Hannah, and then Hunter was there, hovering over Megan with concern etched into his handsome face.

"Are you okay, sweetheart?"

Megan drew in a deep breath and nodded.

He helped her up, brushing grass and dirt off her dress.

"Megan!" Molly rushed over to them. "Oh my goodness! Are you all right, honey?"

"I'm fine."

"I'm taking you to the ER," Nolan said to Hannah.

"No, you're not. I fell, Megan caught me and I'm perfectly fine. I'm far more worried about her. She took one for the team."

"I'm okay," Megan assured her.

"You were amazing." Hannah hugged her tightly. "I don't want to think about what might've happened if you hadn't done what you did. Thank you."

"I . . . um, sure. I just reacted. It was nothing."

"It was everything to us," Nolan said quietly.

"Come on, sweetheart." Hunter put his arm around Megan. "Let's go."

"Thank you again, Molly."

Molly stood with her arm around Hannah. "Thank *you*."

Megan left them with a smile and let Hunter walk her to the car. Now that she was moving, everything hurt.

"Tell me the truth, do you need a doctor?"

"No. Maybe a hot bath though."

"That I can do." He settled her in the SUV and belted her in. "You scared the hell of out me, but thank you so much for what you did for Hannah. I can't even think about the possibility of her losing that baby."

"I didn't really think about it. I just reacted."

He kissed her softly. "You were amazing, and you have to be hurting."

"Little bit."

"I'll take care of you." He kissed her again before he closed her door and went around to the driver's side. "What did my mom say to you?" he asked when they were driving away from the red barn.

"That she knows this'll be a tough week for me and I'm not alone. Far from it."

"It's true, you know. Nina might be leaving, but there're plenty of people who care about you who aren't going anywhere."

"It's good to know." She didn't trust herself to say anything more. They hadn't made plans for after dinner, but she wasn't surprised when he took her to his house rather than taking her home to hers.

She was surprised, however, to find another woman sitting in one of the chairs on his front porch. Apparently, so was he.

"Lauren? What're you doing here?"

The attractive dark-haired woman took in the sight of Hunter holding hands with Megan, her eyes narrowing with displeasure. "So *she's* my replacement? Kinda young for you, Hunter."

"Don't do this, Lauren. Please don't pretend we were more than what we were."

Megan tried to release his hand, but he didn't let her get away.

"Did I really mean so little to you that the minute something better came along, you forgot all about me?"

"Lauren—"

"It could happen to you, too," she said to Megan. "He could lose interest in you when a new flavor of the month comes along."

"I'll never lose interest in her," Hunter said sharply. "Not that it's any of your business, but I'm in love with her. I was never in love with you. I'm sorry if that hurts your feelings, but I was always honest with you."

"Were you? Or were you stringing me along until you got a better offer? It might not matter to you, but I fell in love." She was crying openly now, and despite the theatrics, Megan felt for her. Losing Hunter would hurt, and she'd only spent a week with him.

"I'm sorry," he said, tension rolling off him in waves. "I don't know what you want me to say."

"Forget it." Lauren came down off the porch, pushing past him in her haste to get away.

Hunter released Megan's hand to go after the other woman. "Lauren, wait. You shouldn't drive when you're upset."

"Leave me alone. I came here for answers, and I got them."

"Lauren!"

She got in her car and tore off down the street, leaving a cloud of dust in her wake.

Hunter stood at the end of the sidewalk, shoulders rigid, hands on hips.

Megan had no idea what she should do. Go to him and offer comfort or wait for him to say something? Though her inclination was to take a step back and give him space, she discovered a greater need to offer comfort, so she went to him, laying her hands on his back.

"I'm so sorry about that," he said. "I swear to you there

was never anything serious between us, and she knew it."
He turned then, his eyes imploring her to believe him. "I'm
supposed to be taking care of you, not the other way around."

"Is it okay if we take care of each other?"

He nodded, but she could see and feel his continuing distress as he took her into the house and straight upstairs to
the master bathroom, where he drew a bath for her. Then he
helped her out of her dress and held her hand while she
stepped into the warm water.

Kneeling on the floor next to the tub, Hunter winced at
the sight of a bruise already turning purple on her hip.
"That's going to hurt tomorrow."

"I'll be fine. All that matters is that Hannah and the baby
are okay."

"That's not all that matters. You matter, too, and I'm so
sorry you had to see that just now and to hear the awful
things she said. I'm not going to lose interest in you. I was
never interested in her the way I am in you. She knows that."

"It's not easy to lose the affection of someone like you."

"You'll never have to find out what that's like. I promise."

"You were with her for a while?"

"A couple of years. Usually one weekend a month when
her kids were with their dad. We were friends more than
anything. Or at least I thought we were."

"You slept with her."

"Yes. We had fun. We had laughs. We never talked about
anything past the current weekend. We didn't talk between
weekends. It was nothing like this, Megan. I can't stand an
hour without you in it, let alone weeks on end without seeing
or talking to you. After only a few nights with you, I already
know I want to spend every night with you."

"How can you already know that?"

"I knew it before I ever even kissed you. I knew you were
going to change my life forever."

She cupped his cheek, running her thumb over the light
stubble on his jaw.

He turned his face into her hand, kissing her palm.

"Everything about this is different. I've never told a woman I love her before you. I've never been in love, truly in love, the way I am with you."

"That wasn't supposed to happen."

"So you keep telling me."

"Hunter . . ."

"What, sweetheart?"

"There's something wrong with me."

"What? No, there isn't."

Her eyes filled and she closed them, trying to keep from crying. "There is. Why can't I say it back to you? You've been so amazing and wonderful and . . . You deserve someone who can say it back to you."

"Megan, sweetheart, I know you feel it. I don't care if you ever say it back to me. I can see it in the way you look at me, in the way you touch me, the way you make love with me. I see it. I *feel* it. I don't need the words."

"Lauren could give you the words."

"I don't want her. I only want you."

"What if . . ."

"Whatever it is, just say it so I can tell you how foolish you're being."

"What if you meet someone else—"

"I've already told you that's not gonna happen. I'm so blinded by love for you I can't see anyone else."

Smiling, she shook her head at his silliness even as her eyes filled again. "I told you it wasn't a good idea to fall for me. I tried to warn you."

His face lifted into a crazy sexy half grin. "Yeah, you did, and I decided you were worth the risk. So relax and go with it. Don't stress out about all the ways you think you're failing me. I've never been happier than I am with you."

"Don't you want more? Don't you want a wife and a family and all the things everyone wants?"

"I'd rather live in sin with you for the rest of my life than marry someone I don't love. I want *you*. I don't care how I get you as long as you're here with me."

"What would your family say if they knew you were so willing to settle for so much less than what you deserve?"

"I'm not doing that."

Her stomach ached from the sincerity she felt coming from him. What the hell was wrong with her that she couldn't give him everything he wanted and needed? Why did she have to be such a remote, untouchable mess?

"Whatever you're thinking, stop it." He ran his finger over the furrow between her brows. "You're going to get wrinkles."

"What if I can't ever say it?"

"Stop trying to think up ways to drive me away. It's not going to work."

"You're a glutton for punishment."

"If being with you is punishment, punish me, baby." And then he was leaning over the tub kissing her passionately and making her forget all about the many ways she was flawed. He didn't seem to care about any of that.

CHAPTER 31

———◆►◄◆———

Success is often achieved by those who
don't know that failure is inevitable.

—Coco Chanel, French fashion designer

Hunter hated seeing her so upset about her self-imagined inadequacies. To him she was perfect, exactly what he'd always wanted and so much more than he'd ever dared to dream. He'd meant it when he told her he didn't need the words. Maybe he was being a fool. Maybe he was on the path to disaster, but at least he'd go happy.

Watching her sleep, he let her silky hair slide through his fingers. He thought about the ring he'd bought for her and wondered if he'd ever get the chance to give it to her. If he worked up the nerve to ask her, would she turn him down? If he asked her and she said no, would that ruin everything between them?

He couldn't bear to think of that possibility. Did he wait until she was more secure in the relationship before he asked, or would a proposal tell her everything she needed to know about how serious he was? He wasn't sure, and he was never unsure. He always knew what to do in any given situation. Or he had until now, until he fell in love with Megan.

Even with all her foibles and fears, he wouldn't trade one

minute with her for a lifetime with someone else. Somehow he had to find a way to convince her he was in it for keeps.

He should go to sleep. Tomorrow, he was going climbing with his brothers—a long-planned day trip that he wished now he hadn't committed to. Tomorrow was also Nina's last day at the diner—they were opening to give Nina one last chance to see everyone before she left—and he wanted to be there to support Megan. He was truly torn between the plans with his brothers and his desire to be with her.

Will had just gotten engaged, and he was still going. They'd be back by sunset, and he could lend his shoulder to Megan then. Blowing off his brothers wasn't an option when they'd had these plans for weeks, unless he wanted to hear how pussy-whipped he was for the rest of his natural life. But oh how he wanted to blow them off.

For once, he was up before Megan to shower and grab some coffee that he took up to her when he woke her with kisses to her bare shoulder.

She came to with a groan. "Am I dead? Please tell me the truth because I feel like total death."

"You're very much alive and going to stay that way for at least ninety more years."

"I'm not going to survive this day. Everything hurts." She pulled back the covers to take a closer look at her hip, which had exploded in vivid shades of purple overnight.

"Oh, baby," he said with a sigh. "That's mean looking. We've got some stuff at the store for bruises. I'll get you some later."

She pushed herself up onto the pillows he piled behind her and took the coffee from him with a grateful smile. "I might still be here when you get back."

"You're more than welcome to be."

"I've got to go to be with Nina. She needs me."

"Will you need me?"

"I'll be fine."

"I'll stay home if you want me to."

She raised a brow. "And risk the relentless torment of your brothers? I wouldn't do that to you. I like you too much."

"That's good to know." He kissed her forehead and then her lips. "Take your time here this morning." He pressed a key into her hand as he kissed her again. "Use this to get in later. I'll meet you here when I get back."

"You're giving me the key to your house?"

"You've already got everything else. It's just a key."

"Thank you. You'll be careful up on the rocks, right?"

"Always," he said, touched by her concern. "I'll be back as soon as I can."

"I'll make some dinner."

"Don't bother if you don't feel like it. You need to take it easy. That was one hell of a fall you took. And did I say thank you enough yesterday for what you did for Hannah and the baby?"

She smoothed the hair off his forehead. "I did it for you, too. If she hurts, you hurt, and I don't want you to hurt. That's why I keep telling you—"

He kissed her, devouring her mouth with sweeping strokes of his tongue.

"Why do you never let me finish a sentence?"

"Because I don't want to hear all the ways you're not good for me. All I can see and hear and feel are the ways you're entirely perfect for me." He kissed her again, softer this time, lingering over the taste of coffee and Megan. "And on that note, I've got to go."

She grabbed his hand. "You promise you'll be careful, right?"

He kissed her forehead and then her lips again. He'd never get enough of those lips. "I promise."

Hunter had fully intended to keep that promise, but hours later, riding in an ambulance after his brothers had carried him out of the mountains, all he could think about was Megan and what would happen when she heard he'd fallen. The paramedics had him strapped down so tight he could barely breathe, even with the oxygen they were giving him.

Riding with him, Landon hovered over him, looking

anxious, dirty, sweaty and exhausted. Hunter wanted to ask his brother what had happened, but that would take energy he didn't have. One minute he'd been clinging to the side of a sheer wall of rock, busting balls with his brothers and having a fantastic time testing his physical and mental limits. The next thing he knew, he was on a makeshift backboard looking up at trees rushing by as his brothers made a frantic sprint back to where they'd left their trucks to meet the rescue.

He'd been pretty out of it for most of the sprint, but he'd been aware enough to know that Lucas and Landon, both paramedics, had been dead serious about getting him the hell out of there.

"He's trying to say something," Landon said to the other paramedic, who removed the oxygen mask over Hunter's face.

"What happened?" Hunter asked, every word causing him pain.

"Line slid through your hand, and you went down fast. Thankfully, it stopped you before you hit the ground, but you crashed into the wall hard on the way down."

That explained the unbearable pain in his entire body, but how could that have happened? They were always so careful. "How bad?"

"Hard to tell, but nothing seems broken except maybe your elbow. We've got it immobilized. We're worried about a head injury, too. You were out cold for a couple of minutes. Scared the living shit out of us."

"Aw, you do love me," Hunter said, even though the words cost him.

"Shut the fuck up," Landon said with a grunt that might've been a laugh.

The other paramedic smiled at their banter, and Hunter could see the relief on Landon's face. His younger brother looked away as he battled his emotions. Hunter hated to think about the ordeal he'd put his brothers through. "Megan."

"Mom's going to get her. They're meeting us at the hospital."

With the oxygen mask back in place, Hunter closed his eyes against the relentless pain in his skull. His parents must be freaking out, his grandfather . . . And poor Megan. He'd promised her he wouldn't get hurt. She'd never forgive him for this.

Megan knew something was wrong the minute she saw Molly Abbott come rushing into the diner, her face ashen and her eyes wide with fear.

She wanted to run from whatever Molly had come to tell her, but there was no way out of the diner except through Molly.

"Megan, honey, there's been an accident."

The coffeepot in her hand crashed to the floor, smashing into a million pieces. Megan's heart did the same thing, shattering into as many pieces at the thought of Hunter hurt or worse. "No," she whispered, taking a step back. If she didn't let Molly say the words she wouldn't have to hear about something happening to him.

"Honey, he's hurt, but he's going to be okay."

"No, please."

Nina came to her side, putting her arm around Megan's shoulders. "Megan, it's okay. Molly said he's alive but hurt, and he needs you."

"He's asking for you," Molly added.

"I can't." This was exactly why she'd told him she couldn't get involved. Something always happened to the people she cared about. They died, they moved away, they got hurt, they left. At the thought of Hunter being hurt, pain cut through her like a knife, leaving her bleeding inside.

"I thought you were made of better stuff than this, Megan," Molly said, her disappointment coming through loud and clear.

"I'm not. I told him that. I told him I couldn't do this. I *told* him." She was sobbing so hard she couldn't breathe.

"I'll talk to her," Nina said to Molly.

"Don't bother," Molly said as she turned and left the diner.

Megan wanted to call after her, to tell her to wait, to take her to him, to tell him . . . To tell him what? That everyone had been right about her? He was too good for her?

"Butch," Nina said. "Take over out front. I've got to get her out of here."

"I don't know what to do," Butch said, frazzled by Megan's tears and Nina's instructions.

"Just shut the place down," Nina said. "We're done here anyway." She hustled Megan out the back door and into her car, driving home with one eye on the road and one eye on Megan. "You going to tell me what that was all about?"

"He promised this wouldn't happen," Megan said between sobs. "He *promised*."

"What did he promise?"

"That he wouldn't get hurt! He wouldn't leave. He promised."

"Megan, it was an accident. He didn't do it on purpose. He's not leaving."

The thought of him hurt, in pain . . . She couldn't bear to think about it. "This is why I told him I couldn't do it. I tried to tell him, and he didn't want to hear it."

Nina pulled into the driveway and shut off the engine. "It's your life, and I'd never presume to tell you how to run it, but you're going to regret this. If you don't step up for him when he needs you, you'll be sorry. He's a great guy, and he loves you. If you let him get away, you'll have to live with that for the rest of your life."

"I never wanted him to love me! I told him not to! I told him he could do better."

"*Why* would you say that?" Nina produced a tissue from her purse and used it to wipe away a flood of tears on Megan's face.

"I don't want him to love me, and I don't want to love him. I never wanted that, and I kept trying to tell him, but he was relentless."

"Megan, honey, the reason you're freaking out right now is *because* you love him."

"No, I don't."

Nina took Megan by the chin and forced her to meet Nina's determined gaze. "Yes, you do, or you wouldn't care so much that he's hurt."

"It brings it all back. The night they came to tell me about Mom and Dad." She'd been home alone, waiting for them to get home and wondering what was taking so long. And then the police were at the door with the snow swirling all around them, bringing news that would shatter her world and change her life forever.

"I never wanted to feel that way again." Her eyes and chest ached from the emotional firestorm. She felt like her heart had been wrenched from her chest and stomped on.

"I know, honey. I understand better than anyone. But you can't hide out from love for the rest of your life because you're afraid of what you might lose. That's no kind of life for someone who has so much love to give."

She released a deep, shuddering sigh. "I messed this up, Nina. I should've gone with Molly."

"Stay here. I'll go inside and make some calls. I'll find out where they're taking him."

Megan sat in the car, staring out the windshield, aching. She would go to him. She'd make sure he was all right, and then she'd tell him she couldn't do this anymore.

The next few hours passed for Hunter in a sea of pain and discomfort. After arriving at the Northeastern Vermont Regional Hospital, he was poked and prodded and X-rayed and CT scanned. Since Landon was well known by the ER doctors, they allowed him to stay with Hunter through it all. After a thorough evaluation, the doctors decided there was no need to transport him to the level-one trauma center in Burlington.

They brought in an orthopedic doctor to set his fractured elbow and diagnosed a moderate concussion among other contusions and lacerations, one of which was on his leg and required ten stitches.

"Can he go home tonight?" Landon asked.

"We'd like to keep him for observation for at least twenty-four hours," the ER doctor replied.

They gave him something for the pain, and by the time he came to, he was in a dark quiet room with his mother hovering over him, stroking his hair.

"There you are." Molly's smile was bright and reassuring

even if her eyes told the true story of how afraid she'd been. "You gave us quite a scare, my love."

"Sorry." His mouth and throat were so dry he could barely speak. "Is there water?"

Molly helped him drink through a straw from a cup of ice water that was about the best-tasting thing to ever cross his lips.

"Did someone tell Megan?"

"I did, but she said she couldn't come."

Hunter understood immediately. "She's probably freaking out. I promised I wouldn't get hurt."

"Hunter . . ."

Closing eyes that refused to stay open, he squeezed the hand his mother had wrapped around his. "Don't say it, Mom. I know exactly why she isn't here. I get it."

"I'm glad you do."

He forced a smile for her behalf even as his heart broke for Megan, who'd probably flipped out after hearing what'd happened. In light of what she'd been through, he didn't blame her for that. Not one bit. As soon as he was able, he'd find her and make sure she knew he was fine and wasn't going anywhere.

"Everyone is here," Molly said. "Dad and Gramps are pacing the hallway, and Hannah was with me until a few minutes ago when Nolan made her go and get off her feet for a while."

"Good," he said, drifting, comforted to know his family was with him.

The next time he woke up, Megan was there, looking down at him with those adorably furrowed brows.

"Hey," he said, thrilled to see her, but concerned about the fear he saw in her gorgeous blue eyes.

"Hey, yourself." She wiped her cheeks. Was she crying? He couldn't tell in the dim light.

"Sorry about this. I promised it wouldn't happen."

"Yes, you did."

"Are you okay?"

"Why are you asking me that? *You're* the one in the hospital bed."

"Because I care more about you than I do about myself."

"Don't say that." Her eyes filled with tears. "I wanted to make sure you're okay, but I have to go now."

Though it caused his IV to pinch and pull on his skin, he reached for her hand before she could withdraw it. "Stay with me. I need you."

She shook her head. "I can't."

"Megan, look at me."

"No, I can't look at you. I can't let you tell me again that you love me, and you'll never leave me when we both know you can't keep those kinds of promises."

"I do love you, and I can promise I'll never leave you because I want to. This was a freak accident. Shit happens. I'm a little banged up but mostly fine."

"You could've been killed."

"But I wasn't."

"You do this stuff . . . rock climbing and snow patrol and skiing and snowmobiling . . ."

Though every movement caused pain to ricochet through his head, Hunter felt like he was fighting for his life far more than he had earlier on the mountain. Any chance he had at being happy rested in her fragile hands. "I like to do all those things."

"They're all dangerous."

"They're fun."

"I can't live in fear of something happening to you. I can't do it."

"Nothing's going to happen to me."

"How can you say that when *today* something happened to you?"

"Today was a bad day. Tomorrow will be better. That's life, sweetheart."

"I'm so afraid of everything, Hunter. I don't want to be, but I am."

"You've had good reason to be afraid, but you can't live in fear of what *might* happen and miss out on what's happening right in front of you. If you leave me, you'll ruin my life. Is that what you want?"

"Don't put that on me after I told you from the beginning that I didn't want this."

"I can't help how I feel any more than you can."

Hannah poked her head in the room. "Everything okay in here?"

Hunter looked up at Megan, seeking a verdict.

"He's feisty," Megan said after a long pause, during which he died a thousand painful deaths. "I guess that's a good sign."

Hunter's chest, which had been tight from not breathing, loosened and allowed in the oxygen he desperately needed. She wasn't going anywhere. Not right now anyway, but the battle for her heart was far from won.

CHAPTER 32

———◦‹›◦———

The only way around is through.

—Robert Frost, poet

Hunter was released from the hospital late the next afternoon with orders to take it easy for a week while he recovered from the concussion. The fractured elbow would take longer to heal, but at least he was in a soft cast that could come off for showers. Every inch of his body hurt, but he kept quiet about that so they'd let him go home.

Megan had been by his side since the night before, but he'd been painfully aware of the distance between them. It seemed she was there because she felt she *should* be rather than because she *wanted* to be. She hadn't said a word to that effect, but he'd felt the vibe just the same.

He understood why his accident had hit her so hard. After years by herself, she'd finally taken a big chance and allowed someone new into her life and her heart. Just when she'd begun to have some faith in their relationship, his accident had her reconsidering everything.

That was all right. As long as he understood the *why* of it, he could figure out the next steps.

Megan drove him home in encroaching darkness in his SUV with Hannah and Nolan following behind. Hannah had insisted on coming with them to help him get settled, and Hunter hadn't protested because he knew she needed to fuss over him. He'd give her an hour and then send her on her way. He wanted to be alone with Megan.

However, a short time after they had him settled—painfully—on his sofa, propped up with pillows and covered with a warm blanket, Megan announced that she had to leave.

"Where're you going?" Hannah asked her with noticeable hostility.

"Home."

"How come?"

"Because I live there."

"It's okay, Han." Hunter reached out to Megan. When she reluctantly—or so it seemed to him—took his hand, he drew her down for a kiss. "See you tomorrow?"

"Uh-huh."

He released her and watched her every move as she gathered her things and scurried out the door without another word to anyone.

"What the hell is her problem?" Hannah asked, visibly annoyed.

"I know exactly what her problem is, and it's not your problem."

"It shouldn't be yours either."

"Let me worry about me. You worry about you. In fact, you should go home and get some rest. You look like hell."

"Thanks a lot. Let's see how you look when I fall off the side of a mountain and nearly crack open my skull."

"Are you planning to do that any time soon? I wouldn't recommend it in your delicate condition."

For the first time in their lives, Hannah seemed genuinely furious with him. "Wake *up*, will you? She's being a shit, and you're acting like it's no big deal!"

"It isn't. I understand completely why she's upset, and as soon as I'm able to, we'll deal with it. In the meantime, butt out. That's an order."

"Hannah," Nolan said, "maybe we ought to go and let Hunter get some sleep."

"I'm not going anywhere. He can't be alone."

"Yes, I can. I'm fine, except for my blood pressure, which is rising by the minute."

"His *girlfriend* should be with him tonight. That's where she belongs."

"Hannah," Hunter said again, the warning unmistakable to everyone except her, apparently.

"Don't 'Hannah' me. You know I'm right." She plopped down on the other sofa, kicked off her shoes and put her feet up. "I'm not going anywhere," she said with a mulish look for her husband, who sighed as he sat in the rocking chair. "You don't have to stay. I can handle him." She used her thumb to gesture at Hunter.

"Where's Mom when I need her?" Hunter asked. "She could get you out of here."

"She's exhausted from worrying about you, so Dad took her home to get some sleep. I'm sure she'll be here to hover first thing in the morning."

"Excellent," Hunter said, resigned to being fussed over by everyone other than the one person he wanted fussing over him. If only he weren't so damned exhausted and still drugged up. He'd be at her place by now, fighting for them the way he always had. That wasn't in the cards tonight. But tomorrow . . . Tomorrow he'd get someone to take him to her so they could fix this before it got any worse.

Megan was relieved to see the lights off in Nina and Brett's house, where they were camping out on an air mattress for their final nights in Butler before they left for France. The house was empty and would be turned over to the new tenants at the end of the week. Nina had told her they were a newly retired couple who were thinking of relocating to Vermont but wanted to experience a winter before they committed to anything permanently.

Nina assured her they were nice people. Megan was sure they were, but what did it matter? They weren't Nina and Brett, who would be living thousands of miles from her by this time Wednesday. She trudged up the stairs, unlocked her door and nearly jumped out of her skin when Nina appeared on the other side.

"What the hell, Neen? Are you trying to give me a heart attack?"

"Nope. Just waiting for you to get home."

Megan flipped on a light, which made both sisters wince from the sudden brightness. "How did you know I was coming home?"

Nina gave her that knowing look she did so well. "You were primed to bolt before he ever left the hospital. When we went to see him this morning, he told me you'd be home later and you'd be upset. I promised him I'd be here for you."

"It's irritating that he thinks he knows me so well."

"He does know you that well. He knew you'd be out of there the minute you could."

Megan flopped down on the sofa. "I'm a horrible person."

Nina sat next to her. "No, you're not. You're reeling from what happened, which is understandable. To a point."

"What does that mean?"

"It means it's okay to be upset about what happened to him. It's not okay to walk away from him when he needs you. That's not okay, Megan, and if you care about him, which I think you do, you need to be with him right now. Not hiding out. I thought those days were over."

"So did I until I heard he got hurt and I was suddenly right back there."

"You had a scare, and you reacted emotionally. I get it. But now you have to 'man up,' so to speak, and do the right thing. He's in love with you, Meggie. How do you think it made him feel to see you leave tonight?"

Megan pressed the heels of her hands to her eyes. "It's all too much for me. I knew it would be. I told him that. He overwhelms me."

"He loves you."

"I didn't want him to."

"You love him."

"I didn't want to."

Nina laughed and put her arms around her. "Tough shit,

kid. You've fallen in love with a wonderful guy who loves you right back. It's time to step up for him the way he would for you. Where do you think he'd be right now if you'd been the one who got hurt?"

Megan knew exactly where he'd be, and the realization had her standing to go into her bedroom.

Nina followed her. "What're you doing?"

"Packing." She threw clothes and pajamas and some of the silky underwear Hunter had bought her into a bag. From her bedside table, she grabbed her e-reader and tossed it into the bag. "I'm going back over there."

"He'll be happy to see you."

"I know." Megan hugged her sister. "Thank you."

"It's okay to love him, Meggie."

"I'm starting to believe you might be right about that."

"I can delay my flight for a few days if you think you'll need me."

"Absolutely not. There's no need for that."

"Are you sure?"

"Positive. Go. Have a wonderful adventure, and don't worry about me."

"Right . . . That would be like telling me not to breathe." She hugged Megan again. "We sign the papers for the sale of the diner first thing in the morning, and then we'll stop by Hunter's to see you on our way out of town." They were going to Boston tomorrow and would fly to France from there on Wednesday.

"I'll be there."

Megan followed Nina down the stairs, said goodnight to her sister and got into her car to drive the short distance to Hunter's house. She knew he'd be glad she'd come back, but beyond that she didn't know what to expect. All she knew for certain is that she needed to be with him. With the world spinning wildly out of control around her, one touch from him calmed and quieted the chaos in her mind.

She could do this. She *would* do this. She would try her best to be what he needed and deserved. Using the key he'd given her, she let herself into the house, which was lit only by the light he left on all the time in the kitchen. The living room was deserted, so she started up the stairs only to encounter Hannah on her way down.

"So you came back."

"I did."

"Good."

"You're pissed with me."

"I'm baffled, Megan. Truly."

"I . . . I care about him. I really do. I've never cared about anyone the way I care about him. I'm sorry if I'm not handling it the way you would."

Hannah sighed, and some of the rigidity seemed to leave her posture. "It's good that you came back."

"Is he . . . He's okay?"

Hannah nodded. "He was in some pain, so we gave him another pain pill before we got him up to bed. He's likely to be out of it for a while."

"That's okay. If you want to go home, I'll be with him if he needs anything."

"And you won't suddenly decide to leave in the middle of the night?"

Megan shook her head. "I'm not going anywhere for as long as he needs me."

"That could be a really long time. Are you prepared to stay that long?"

Megan looked up and forced herself to meet the challenge in Hannah's direct gaze. "Yeah, I am."

"Fine, then we'll go, but we'll be back in the morning."

"I'll be here."

"Megan . . . You don't have to handle this the way I would, but I'm asking you, as someone who loves him with every fiber of her being, please be kind to him. He's one of the best men I've ever known, and if he loves you, that makes you very, very lucky."

"I know that, Hannah, and I will be kind to him. I'm sorry if you thought I wouldn't be. Hunter's accident triggered some unpleasant memories for me, which isn't his fault. That's all on me. I'm dealing with it."

"I understand all too well how the past can overshadow the present, and I'm here if I can help."

"That's very nice of you. Thank you."

Hannah went back up the stairs so Megan could get by. "I'll see you in the morning. Feel free to call if you need us during the night. Hunter has the number."

"I will, but we'll be fine." As she left Hannah in the hallway and went into Hunter's room, a sense of calm came over her. They would be fine. All she had to do was stop teetering on the edge of the cliff and just jump. The thought nearly made her laugh. *All* she had to do . . .

A night light cast a warm glow over the room, which was how she could see Hunter sleeping on a pile of pillows with one propped under his casted left arm. His other arm was thrown over his head, leaving his magnificent chest bare to her greedy stare. He was so beautiful, inside and out, and Hannah was right that Megan was lucky to have won his heart.

She went into the adjoining bathroom to change into pajama pants and a tank. After brushing her teeth, she moved gingerly to get into bed next to him, wanting to be nearby if he awoke during the night and needed her.

He never stirred as she got settled.

Lying on her side, she watched him intently, each rise and fall of his chest a reminder that he was alive and well, if a bit battered at the moment. Unable to resist the need to touch him, she rested her hand flat against his chest, the steady beat of his heart serving as further proof.

Reassured, she snuggled closer to him, mindful of his injuries but needing the warmth of his body to further remind her that he was there, he was fine, he loved her. She released a deep breath along with all the tension that had knotted her up since the minute she heard he'd been hurt and drifted off to sleep.

The second the pain pill wore off, Hunter was awake and aware of every one of his injuries, especially his head and elbow, which throbbed relentlessly. Shifting to find a more comfortable position only made things worse until he realized he wasn't alone in bed.

She'd come back to him. The realization nearly trumped the pain that had woken him in the first place. He wrapped his uninjured arm around her, willing to bear the fiery blast of pain to bring her closer to him.

Her eyes popped open. "Are you okay?"

"I'm much better now that you're here."

"I'm sorry I left before. I'm sorry for everything that's happened since you got hurt. I should've come to the hospital with your mom, and I should've stayed with you tonight, and I should've—"

"Stop, sweetheart. You don't owe me any apologies. I know it was hard on you to hear I'd been hurt, and the fact that you freaked out actually makes me happy."

"How?" she asked, baffled.

"It means you care."

"Hunter," she said on a long exhale, "of course I care. I care too much. That's the problem."

"It's never a problem to care too much about someone."

"It is if you're me and live in constant fear of the people you love disappearing in the blink of an eye."

"The people you love . . . Does that include me?"

"Are you fishing?"

"Damn right I am."

"It does include you. I figured that out right about the time your mother told me you were hurt."

"Then it was well worth falling down the side of a mountain if it moved things along for us."

"I'm going to pretend you didn't just say that."

He laughed and then grimaced. "Laughter is not my friend. Makes my brain feel like it's exploding."

"Can you take another pain pill?"

"Not for a couple of hours."

"Shouldn't they last longer than they do?"

"You would think."

"So what do we do until you can take another one?"

"Talk to me?"

"What do you want to talk about?"

His eyes closed, and for a second she thought he might be drifting off again. "Let's talk some more about the moment you knew you loved me. Tell me that story again. I love a happy ending."

She chuckled at his shamelessness. Even when injured and in pain, he was all about her. But thinking about Molly coming into the diner, her face bleached of all color, her eyes wide with fear and panic, had Megan spiraling down the rabbit hole again.

"Hey," he said, squeezing her hand, "where'd you go?"

"I took one look at your mom, and I knew something had happened to you. I dropped the coffeepot on the floor and it smashed into a million pieces. I remember thinking my heart was doing the same thing at the thought of you being hurt. I reacted badly. Molly wanted me to come to the hospital with her. She said you were asking for me, but I couldn't move. I couldn't bring myself to go there, to see you hurt or worse . . . I couldn't do it. Your mom was disgusted with me, and for good reason."

"Don't worry about her. I took care of it."

"What do you mean, you took care of it?"

"I explained to her that I'd promised I wouldn't get hurt, and you were right to be upset with me for breaking my promise."

"Hunter . . . It wasn't your fault you couldn't keep your promise. It's not like you fell off the side of a mountain on purpose."

"Definitely not."

"Your mom got to see a side of me I'm not proud of. Hannah saw it, too, so now they're both filled with doubts about whether I'm good enough for you."

"All that matters is that *I* think you're good enough."

"Even after I nearly bailed on you when you needed me?"

"You didn't."

"I thought about it."

"But you didn't do it. You're right here, which is exactly where you belong."

"I'm starting to believe that might be true."

He kissed the back of her hand and the inside of her wrist, his rough whiskers against her sensitive skin sending a tingling awareness rippling through her body. "It is true. I'm sorry my fall upset you. I'm sorry you had to hear that kind of news and that it caught you off guard. I'd never do that to you intentionally. I hope you know that."

"I do."

"What're we going to do about all these fears that are holding you back from enjoying life to the fullest?"

"They're not doing that."

"Yes, they are, and I want you to be able to enjoy every single minute we spend together without worrying all the time about how it's going to go bad. It doesn't *always* go bad."

"It does for me."

"Not this time." He continued to kiss her hand and wrist, setting her on fire with only the touch of his lips and the brush of his whiskers. "This time you're going to get everything you want and need. All you have to do is stop being afraid and let go of the things you can't control."

"That's easier said than done."

"You're right. It is. But things are going to happen, upsetting things, difficult things, sad things. That's life. The good news is there're also plenty of happy things and joyful moments. I want to experience all of them with you—the highs, the lows and everything in between. I want you to have faith that I'll always be right there with you. And I want you to have faith that I'll always love you no matter what. I want us to live together and sleep together and work together at the diner and make beautiful babies together and watch them grow up together and then grow old and cranky together."

Megan laughed even as a sob erupted from her throat. His incredible words had her emotions spinning out of control again. "Are you proposing to me?" she asked, teasing.

"Maybe I am."

She gasped. "Hunter . . . Don't. You're high on pain meds. This is no time to be having that kind of conversation."

"Maybe it's the perfect time."

"Stop it. You should try to go back to sleep for a while."

"Megan, look at me."

She forced herself to make contact with those beautiful brown eyes that looked at her with nothing but love.

"I love you, and I want to spend the rest of my life with you. Will you spend the rest of yours with me?"

There she was again, hovering on the edge of that cliff trying to decide whether to take the leap. She thought about what he'd said about the highs, the lows and everything in between. Life would happen whether she was with him or not, and if she had to go through it, she'd much rather go through it with him by her side, always assuring her that it would all be okay.

He studied her intently, probably trying to gauge her reaction to his question. "Megan?"

"Yes, Hunter. I want to spend the rest of my life with you."

"Really?"

She bit her lip and nodded.

"Why?" he asked with that small sexy smile that left her breathless.

"Because I love you, and I don't want to be anywhere but where you are."

"Good answer, my love." With his hand curled around her nape, he drew her into a sweet, lingering kiss. "Do me a favor?"

"Anything."

"There's a small silver bag in the top drawer of my dresser. Will you get it for me?"

"Now?"

"Right now."

"Okay." She moved slowly to disentangle herself from him and get out of bed without jostling him. In his dresser she found the bag but couldn't make out the words on it in the faint glow of the nightlight. She delivered it to him.

"Thanks. Now come back to bed."

Curious about what was in the bag, she got back into bed the same way she'd left—carefully.

"Closer."

She scooted over until she was pressed against his side.

He put his arm around her and handed her the bag. "Help me out, will you? I can't do much with only one hand."

Her heart beating fast, she withdrew a small velvet box from the bag and looked at him. "What is it?"

"Open it and find out."

She flipped open the box and let out a gasp at the incredible ring nestled in dark velvet. "Hunter . . . what . . . when did you . . . Oh my God!"

"Turn the light on so you can see it."

Her hands were shaking violently, but she somehow managed to turn on the bedside light. That was when she saw that the diamond was yellow. Her favorite color. He'd remembered that. Of course he had. Tears streamed down her face as it settled in on her, finally, that he really did love her as much as he said he did. And looking down at the incredible ring he'd chosen for her, she believed, really believed, that he always would.

"Do you like it?" he asked hopefully.

"It's . . . *yellow!* Oh my God, Hunter. It's the most beautiful ring I've ever seen."

"Put it on."

She looked over at him. "Are you sure?"

"Never been more sure of anything in my life. You?"

"Same."

"Then allow me." He held out his hand.

With trembling fingers Megan freed the ring from the velvet and handed it to him.

He slid it onto her ring finger and then brought her hand to his lips to kiss the back. "Perfect. I knew it would be." He looked up at her. "You're really going to marry me?"

"You really want me to?"

"So bad. So, *so* bad."

"Then how could I say no?"

Smiling, he kissed her like a man who was perfectly healthy rather than recovering from serious injuries. He kissed her until she pulled back from him, reluctantly, and only because she was concerned about him overexerting himself.

"The minute I feel better, we're celebrating. You got me?"

"I got you. We'll definitely celebrate."

"Every day for the rest of our lives."

Megan had taken the leap and landed exactly where she was always meant to be.

The following Saturday, Hunter and Megan made their first appearance as an engaged couple at the grand opening of Guthrie House. His arm was still in a sling, but he was feeling better every day, and he had Megan to thank for his speedy recovery. They'd spent just about every minute of the last week together, holed up in his house, watching movies, eating the staggering amount of food his family had brought over and playing board games. Citing his unfair advantage, she absolutely refused to ever play Monopoly with him again after he thoroughly kicked her ass.

They laughed, they talked, they whispered deep into the night about their plans for the future. They celebrated her twenty-eighth birthday with a cake they made themselves and fought endlessly about the newly renamed Green Mountain Diner, which was closed for two weeks while his cousin Noah completed the renovations. Hunter let her win every argument because, for the first time in his life, he didn't care if the business was ever profitable. All he cared about was her happiness.

And she fairly glowed from happiness. In the time they'd spent together, just the two of them, he'd watched her let go of the worries that had dogged her for so long. The ring he'd given her and the promises he'd made seemed to have freed her from the past.

One afternoon, while he took care of paperwork Will had brought him from the office, she had done some writing, and he'd found himself staring at her as she lost herself in one of her stories. Watching her was far more interesting than concentrating on work.

Now, surrounded by his family and Caleb's as they celebrated the opening of Guthrie House, Hunter felt like things were getting back to a new version of normal that included Megan, which was the best kind of normal.

Hannah came in from the backyard where Caleb's Sultans

had gathered around the fire pit. "I haven't even gotten to talk to my own family today."

"Everything's been great, Han," Will said. "You and Cameron throw one hell of a party."

"Yes, we do," Hannah said.

"Couldn't agree more," Hunter said.

His sister came over to kiss his cheek, and then she did the same to Megan. "How's our patient today?"

"Much better," Megan said. "Full of piss and vinegar."

"Just the way you like me," Hunter said.

"Yeah, he's fine," Hannah replied. "Good job, Nurse Megan."

She smiled at Hannah. "Thank you."

Molly came into the kitchen. "Anyone still need a tour of what Hannah has done with the rooms upstairs?"

"I'd love to see it," Megan said. To him, she said, "Can you live without me for a couple of minutes?"

"Only a couple."

Megan kissed him and patted his chest. "Be right back."

His mother watched them, her expression unreadable. Hunter wondered what that was about.

Megan followed Molly upstairs where the doors to the bedrooms were open for visitors to tour. She ducked her head into the first room, which had been decorated in shades of dark green and burgundy with an antique four-poster bed and matching vanity. "This is lovely."

"Hannah decorated that room herself from items she kept from when Caleb's grandmother owned the house," Molly said.

"It's beautiful. This is a wonderful thing she's doing here."

"We're very proud of her, but then we're proud of all our children." Her tone was polite, as always, but Megan noted a hint of frost and couldn't blame Hunter's mother for being annoyed with her. She'd be annoyed with her, too.

"Mrs. Abbott—"

"Molly."

"Molly . . . I want to apologize for what happened that day in the diner." Megan clasped her hands together and forced herself to look her future mother-in-law in the eye. "Hunter's accident . . . It was . . . I was . . ."

Molly put Megan out of her misery by squeezing her arm. "I know. It was for me, too. For all of us."

"I behaved badly and gave you the impression that I didn't care enough about him to go to him when the opposite is true."

"I know that now. I can see how happy he is with you. We've all seen that."

"I've been hoping for a chance to tell you how sorry I am for the way I reacted."

"Thank you for that, and you were forgiven the moment you came to the hospital. You should know that when we told him you weren't coming, he immediately understood."

Megan smiled. Of course he did. "He gets me. He might be the only person who does."

"I've never seen him so happy. Thank you for that, too."

"It's always going to be important to me that he's happy. And safe. No more rock climbing." Megan shuddered at the memory of that awful day.

"Good luck with that one, honey," Molly said with a laugh. "I've been trying to get them all to stay off the rocks for as long as they've been old enough to climb them. Abbott men need to climb things. And ski down things. And rappel from things."

"Ugh, stop. You don't want me to change my mind about him, do you?"

"No, I certainly do not." Molly hooked her arm through Megan's. "Come on, let me show you the rest."

Walking home from Hannah's party, his arm around Megan, Hunter was as happy as he'd ever been, despite the emotional event they'd just attended.

"What an incredible thing Hannah is doing there," Megan said. "It's hard to believe everything she's been through when she seems so happy and at peace now with Nolan."

"It's been a very long journey to get there. You can relate in many ways."

"Yes, I guess I can. I give her tons of credit for channeling her grief into something so productive."

"I do, too. And Caleb's parents as well. I think it's amazing that they've stepped up to run the inn for Hannah. I haven't seen them so excited about anything since we lost Caleb. It's good to see everyone moving on." During the last week, while he recovered from his injuries, the rest of the family had helped Hannah move out of the home she'd shared with Caleb and into her new home with Nolan.

"Your family was really nice to me today," Megan said.

"Why wouldn't they be? You're going to be an Abbott before too much longer."

"I wasn't sure if they'd be happy for us or worried for you."

"They're happy, sweetheart. They're happy because *I'm* happy."

"Are you?"

"How can you even ask me that after the best week of my life?"

"Only you would say that after suffering a concussion and a fractured elbow, not to mention stitches."

He pulled her in tighter against him, kissing her temple. "My *fiancée* made me all better with her company, her excellent nursing skills and her sponge baths."

"Ha ha, very funny. What sponge baths?"

"Maybe I just dreamed that. My dreams have been pretty vivid since my *fiancée* has denied me access to her delectable body this week."

She giggled from the kisses he rained down on her neck without missing a step on their walk. "Only because you were recovering."

"I'm all recovered now, but I'm about to have new injuries if I can't make love to my *fiancée*. You wouldn't want that, would you?"

"Definitely not. I like you healthy and available to me on a moment's notice."

His low growl set her on fire. "Walk faster."

They arrived at his house a short time later, and Hunter directed her straight up the stairs to the room that had become theirs, rather than his, over the last week. "Get naked," he said without preamble.

"Tell me what you really want."

"I want to be inside you. Right now."

Her face flushed with the color he'd come to expect when he spoke bluntly to her about what he wanted from her in bed. "Well, then . . ." She drew her dress up and over her head, leaving her only in the matching silk bra and panties he'd bought for her. "You were right about the silk, by the way."

"Told ya."

"You didn't have to buy out the store to prove your point."

"It was an excellent investment, and as beautiful as you are in red silk, that's not naked."

"I don't see you getting naked."

"I'd rather watch you, and besides, I need help." He gestured to his arm in the sling.

"You're milking this injury."

"For all it's worth."

Still in her bra and panties, she approached him with a playful glint in her eyes and began to unbutton his shirt. Her nearness was making him crazy, as it had earlier in the day when she'd helped him shave off a week's worth of whiskers. He hadn't had time then to fully indulge in his desire for her. Now nothing would keep him from finally holding her and making love to her after a week of wishing he could. His head still protested when he moved too fast, but he was willing to risk it to be able to touch her.

She pulled his shirttails from his pants and helped him take it off around the cast that held his left arm immobile. Next came the T-shirt he'd worn under it. Then she was tugging at his belt and unzipping his black dress pants, which fell into a pile at his feet.

Hunter kicked off his shoes and stepped out of the pants before hooking his arm around her waist and drawing her in close to him. "Hey."

"What's up?"

"I am."

She laughed and wrapped her arms around his neck, bringing her entire body into tight contact with his.

He wanted to beg for mercy. "Megan . . ."

"Yes, Hunter?" she asked, her voice breathy and sultry.

"Don't play with me. Not now."

"I thought you wanted to play."

"That's not what I want and you know it. Get a condom."

"No." She backed him up until his legs connected with the edge of the bed, forcing him to sit or fall over.

The damned cast on his arm made him feel off balance all the time, but Megan decked out in red silk made him positively dizzy. Then her one-word answer penetrated his lust-addled brain. *"No?"*

"We don't need a condom."

"We most definitely *do* need one."

"No, we don't," she said with a smug smile.

"Explain. Immediately."

"The other day when I went to the store?"

"Uh-huh."

"I also went to a doctor's appointment where I received a three-month birth-control injection that's effective immediately."

"And you were going to tell me this when?"

"As soon as you were well enough to take full advantage of this development."

"I've never had sex without a condom."

"Never?"

"Not once. Ever."

"Oh boy. This is going to be fun."

"It's probably going to be fast," he said with a chuckle. Wrapping his arm around her, he nuzzled her belly. "I've never made love to my *fiancée* before either."

"Mmm," she said, her fingers sifting through his hair, "you do like saying that word."

"It beats *lover*, right?"

She gave his hair a playful tug that drew a snort of laughter from him.

"Put me out of my misery, baby."

"Let's get you comfortable first."

"There's only one way that's going to happen."

She sat him up against a stack of pillows, placing one under his injured arm. "Good?"

"Getting there. Get these boxers off me."

"Gladly." She helped him out of his underwear, removed her thong and then climbed on top of him, straddling his lap, still wearing the bra. "Is this what you wanted?"

"You know it is. I feel like it's been forever since I was able to hold you this way." He ran his hand up her back, tangling it into her hair and bringing her down for a deep, passionate kiss. "I want you right now."

She reached between them and guided him into her, sinking down on him slowly, going for maximum effect.

His head fell back on the pillow and his body arched into hers. "God, Megan . . . So hot."

She moved slowly, trying to draw out the pleasure for both of them.

With his one free hand he released the front clasp of her bra, pushed it aside and cupped her left breast, running his thumb back and forth over her nipple. "Love you so much."

Megan leaned forward to kiss him. "Love you, too."

"I can't get enough of those words from you. Say it again." His hand moved from her breast to her ass, pulling her tightly against him as he surged into her.

"I love you, Hunter," she said, her voice breaking on his name as his deep strokes triggered her orgasm. "I love you."

He was right behind her, lifting his hips as he pushed down hard on her. He got a lot done with that one working arm.

She collapsed on top of his heaving chest and closed her eyes as his arm came around her, holding her close to him. "What do you think of sex without a condom?" she asked after a long period of quiet.

He immediately came back to life, hardening inside her. "Any questions?"

"None," she said laughing. "All my questions have been answered to my extreme satisfaction."

Hunter looked up at her, his gaze full of love. "Mine, too, sweetheart. Mine, too."

EPILOGUE

——◀▶——

*Winners take time to relish their work, knowing
that scaling the mountain is what makes
the view from the top so exhilarating.*

—Denis Waitley, motivational speaker

Lincoln Abbott found an unopened bottle of champagne in Hannah's kitchen and took it and two glasses with him onto the back porch, where family and friends had gathered after the grand-opening celebration for Guthrie House. It had been a wonderful day of friends and family and reminiscing about the incredible young man they'd loved and lost in Iraq.

He'd never been prouder of Hannah, who continued to honor her late husband's memory even as she moved forward into a new life with Nolan. Lincoln found his father-in-law sitting by himself at the far end of the screened-in porch and took a seat next to him.

"What's the good word, my friend?" Elmer asked.

Lincoln popped the cork on the bottle and caught the bubbly in one of the glasses, which he handed to Elmer before filling another for himself. "The good word is another engagement to our credit that needs to be celebrated."

"Another one in my column." Elmer touched his glass to

Lincoln's. "And I've got to say, our boy Hunter has never seemed happier in his life than he was today with Megan by his side. They make a beautiful couple."

"Indeed they do. As would they." Lincoln gestured to the yard, where Ella was sitting with her sisters, trying not to stare at Gavin Guthrie and failing miserably, as she had all day.

"Two of them have been circling the wagons for a while now," Elmer said. "That boy worries me though. Getting into fights and getting arrested . . . Ella doesn't need those headaches."

"The guy he fought with said we wasted our time in Iraq," Lincoln said quietly so no one would overhear him.

"Is that so? Well, then good for Gavin for beating the crap out of him."

"Thought you'd agree."

"He's wounded, Linc. All you gotta do is look at him to see that."

"If anyone is strong enough to help heal those wounds, it's our Ella."

"This is true." Elmer eyed him suspiciously. "What've you got up your sleeve?"

"I've been thinking about clearing out some of the back acreage behind the barn." Lincoln kept his gaze fixed on his gorgeous daughter. "I bet Gavin would be the perfect man for that job."

"You'll keep a close eye on her, won't you?"

"Don't I always?"

"That you do." Elmer held up his glass. "In that case, let's go for number five."

Lincoln touched his glass to Elmer's. "To number five."

ACKNOWLEDGMENTS

Thank you for reading *And I Love Her*. I hope you enjoyed Hunter and Megan's story as well as a visit with the Abbott family! Up next from the Green Mountain series is *You'll Be Mine*, Will and Cameron's wedding novella, part of the *Ask Me Why* anthology that's out in July 2015.

A very special thank-you to "Jack's" Team: Julie Cupp, Lisa Cafferty, Holly Sullivan, Isabel Sullivan, Nikki Colquhoun and Cheryl Serra for all your help and encouragement, and to my family, Dan, Emily and Jake for their support.

Thanks to my agent, Kevan Lyon; my editor, Kate Seaver, and the entire Berkley team for all their hard work on the Green Mountain series.

If you enjoyed *And I Love Her*, consider leaving a review at Goodreads and/or the retailer of your choice. Your reviews help other readers to discover the Green Mountain series, and I appreciate them so much.

When you finish the book, dish about the details, with spoilers encouraged, in the *And I Love Her* readers group at facebook.com/groups/AndILoveHer/. If you haven't yet joined the Green Mountain series reader group, you can find it here: facebook.com/groups/GreenMountainSeries/. Also, if you're not on my newsletter mailing list, you can join at marieforce .com for regular updates about new books and possible appearances in your area.

Thanks so much for reading!

xoxo
Marie

A DAY IN THE LIFE
A Green Mountain Short Story

CHAPTER 1

————◆————

Hunter Abbott loved to sleep in on Sunday, his favorite day of the week. It was the one morning he didn't have anywhere to be, no one looking to him to solve all their problems, no one needing him for anything until late-afternoon dinner with his family. Lately, he loved his Sundays even more because of his Saturday nights with his fiancée, Megan.

Since she'd moved in with him a couple of weeks ago, every day felt like Sunday. Hell, every day felt like Sunday and Christmas and his birthday all rolled up into one big dose of perfection. Sleeping with her in his arms every night was the best thing to ever happen to him. If only she didn't have to be up and out so early to get to the diner.

So far she seemed to love her new role there, managing the business and making it her own. She'd even implemented one of his ideas by offering prepared takeout meals during the day rather than staying open for dinner service. That one small change had resulted in a significant boost to the bottom line, which Hunter kept a close eye on as the chief financial officer for his family's businesses. It also got her home much earlier in the day, which suited his desire to spend every possible minute with her.

Thanks to his grandfather, the diner was now one of their family businesses, and Hunter was looking forward to watching it grow under Megan's leadership. Fortunately, the waitresses who'd once covered the dinner shift had been willing to move to mornings, so she hadn't had to hire new help.

It was all working out rather well so far, and she seemed happy, which was the most important thing to Hunter. He was happy if she was happy, although he'd be a lot happier if she didn't have to get up so damned early every day.

Shifting onto her pillow, he breathed in the jasmine scent of her shampoo and thought about their night together. He was officially addicted to her and couldn't get enough of everything about her. From talking to laughing to cooking to working to sleeping to making love to driving in the car . . . It didn't matter what they did as long as they did it together.

The ringing phone jarred him out of his thoughts to wonder who would be calling him so early on his day to sleep in. He reached for the extension on the bedside table. "Hello?"

"Hunter." The frantic way Megan said his name had him sitting up in bed. "I need you."

"What's wrong?"

"Paige and Delia are both sick and Petey, the dishwasher, got arrested last night. I thought I could handle it on my own, but we're getting killed with leaf peepers. Can you come?"

He was up and moving before she'd finished talking. "I'll be right there."

"Thank you." The line went dead.

Tossing the phone on the unmade bed that would stay that way for once, he ran for the closet to find jeans and a T-shirt. He splashed water on his face, brushed his teeth and ran a comb through his hair and was out the door less than five minutes after she called.

He parked in the lot behind his family's store and jogged across Elm Street, where patrons were in a line outside the door. He'd never seen that before. Since there was no way to push through the crowd at the front door, he went around to the back and in through the kitchen.

"Good of you to show up, CFO," Butch grumbled, calling him by the nickname he'd bestowed upon Hunter after the Abbott family acquired the diner.

"What can I do?"

Butch gestured to a mountain of dishes surrounding the deep sink. "Better start there. We're almost out of plates."

Was it his imagination or did Butch seem to relish the idea of putting him on dish duty? Whatever. After growing up with nine younger siblings, Hunter certainly knew how to do dishes. He started with the plates and moved as fast as he could to get them clean.

Megan came in with an armload of dirty dishes. "Thank God you're here." She stole a quick kiss as she deposited the dishes and spun around to head back into battle.

Hunter washed dishes until his hands were sore and his back ached, but he never stopped, even when the elbow he'd fractured in a recent climbing accident began to fight back against the constant activity. The cast was long gone, his elbow was healing well according to his orthopedic doctor and he'd been undergoing physical therapy to get it working properly again. He probably shouldn't be putting it through such a workout, but he tried not to think about what it would feel like later as he kept working.

"CFO," Butch barked at him. "Grab a bin and start busing. We need tables, man."

Judging by the gleam in his eyes, Butch was definitely enjoying giving him orders.

Hunter dried his hands and took a bin with him into the carnage that was the diner. "Holy shit," he whispered as he took in the sight of dirty tables everywhere he looked. He started at the far end and filled the bin with the dishes from two tables. When he went to pick it up, his elbow fought back, and he nearly dropped it.

From out of nowhere, Megan swooped in, grabbed the bin and carted it away without a word to him.

Wow, talk about feeling like a useless dick! He wiped down the table and moved on to the next one.

Megan returned with an empty bin, handing it to him with a saucy smile before she went to seat new customers at the table he'd just cleaned. She seemed to be everywhere, acting as hostess, waitress and cashier all at once while also doing the heavy lifting for him. Despite the crazy day, she never lost her smile or her sparkle as she moved effortlessly from one task to another. She was in her element here and kept everything running smoothly even in the midst of madness.

"CFO!" Butch barked through the window that separated the kitchen from the restaurant. "Need more plates!"

Hunter finished the table he was clearing, wiped it down and was able to cart a lighter load of dishes to the kitchen by himself this time. Thank goodness his elbow didn't decide to suddenly give out. He could only imagine what Butch would have to say if he dropped a bin full of dishes.

Back at the sink, he had twenty plates washed and stacked next to the grill within ten minutes.

Megan came rushing into the kitchen. "Need mugs, stat."

"On it," Hunter said, falling into a groove now.

"Silverware, too," Megan called over her shoulder.

Hunter was sweating as he worked harder than he ever had in his life over the next hour. He rotated between dish-washing and busing as the people kept coming and coming. Surely they'd fed everyone in a ten-mile radius by now, hadn't they? He'd be hearing the ring of Butch's bell and his bark of "Megan, pickup" in his sleep.

"Are we having fun, boys?" Megan asked when she came into the kitchen with more dishes.

"Best day I ever had," Butch said sarcastically.

"Time of my life," Hunter said with equal sarcasm. For once he and Butch were in total agreement about something.

By the time the rush began to die down, it was after noon and Hunter felt like he'd run a marathon. His lower back ached, his recently concussed brain throbbed and his elbow might never bend correctly again. How did Megan do this every day? He had a whole new respect for her, Butch and the others who worked here. His job was a piece of cake compared to theirs.

At the thought of cake, he realized he hadn't eaten anything all day and was absolutely starving. Since Butch was still frantically filling orders, Hunter didn't dare ask him for food. In two hours, they'd close down and he could eat then. If he lived that long.

Megan couldn't remember a busier day at the diner than this one had been, and it figured that her two waitresses, who were roommates, had caught the same bug, on the day that Petey, her dishwasher, had been arrested for disorderly conduct. After the diner closed, she'd have to see about getting him out of jail. Or she'd send Butch.

She smiled at Hunter as he hauled yet another bin full of dirty dishes into the kitchen. She'd owe him big for this. Her adorable, sexy, *GQ* fiancé reduced to washing dishes and cleaning tables. Wait until his family heard about his shift at the diner.

The next time she looked up, Hunter's grandfather, Elmer Stillman, was coming through the door with his best friends Cletus and Percy.

"What in the devil is going on here today?" Elmer asked after he'd given her a kiss on the cheek. Ever since she'd accepted Hunter's proposal, he'd treated her like a member of his family, and she loved him for it.

"The leaves are what's going on here. We're at peak this weekend."

"Damned peeper season," Cletus muttered under his breath. "Never had to wait in a *line* to get in here before."

"Sorry you had to wait, boys," Megan said as she poured coffee for them, hoping to soothe their ruffled feathers. "Wait till you see the hottie busboy I've got working today." She left them with a smile and moved on to refresh coffee at other tables.

Hunter chose that moment to come out of the kitchen looking sweaty and disheveled and absolutely adorable. She loved him more all the time, never more so than right now as he pitched in to help her out of a pinch.

"Are my eyes deceiving me?" Elmer asked his grandson.

"I wish they were."

"Oh, how the mighty have fallen," Percy said with a grunt of laughter.

Hunter's good-natured grin never faltered. "Yeah, yeah. I'm taking one for the team today, and it's all your fault, Gramps. It was your idea to buy this place."

"I knew you were the right man for the job," Elmer said.

"He's saving our lives," Megan added. She took a closer look at Hunter. After spending a full week with him following his climbing accident, she'd learned to tell when he was in pain. "Are you okay?"

"I'm good."

"Did you eat anything?"

"Not yet."

"Hey, Butch," she called. "Get me a grilled corn muffin stat."

"Fill out a slip."

"Kiss my ass."

Hunter let out a low growl that made her laugh. "No one kisses your ass but me."

Elmer raised his hands to his head. "My ears, my ears."

Megan introduced Hunter's ribs to the sharp end of her elbow. "Not in front of the customers, Abbott. Get back to work."

He leaned in close to her, so only she could hear him. "Revenge is a bitch, my love."

Megan's entire body flushed with heat as she thought about his particular brand of revenge.

"Whatever he said made her blush," Percy said.

"Better that we couldn't hear it," Cletus said.

"When are you two kids tying the knot anyway?" Percy asked.

"Mind your business," Elmer said.

"It's fine." Megan rested her hand on Elmer's shoulder. "We're hoping to set a date soon." They didn't want to wait to get married, but hadn't been able to settle on a date despite weeks of going round and round about when to do it. She hoped they could figure it out soon because she couldn't wait to be married to him.

Nolan and Skeeter came in from the garage, stopping short in their tracks when they saw Hunter clearing tables.

"Well, if this don't beat all," Skeeter said.

"No kidding," Nolan said. "I've got to get Hannah over here to see this. Can I use the phone, Megan?"

"You know where it is." The words were no sooner out of her mouth than the phone rang. "Take an order while you're at it, Nolan."

He waved to indicate he'd heard her.

With hardly a lull between the breakfast rush and lunch, they got busy again and had no time for the usual tomfoolery with the patrons.

Hannah arrived about twenty minutes after Nolan called her and went straight into the kitchen to see her twin brother washing dishes. Because Megan was right behind her with another full-to-overflowing bin, she got to watch Hannah whip out a camera and take some pictures.

"Go away, Hannah," Hunter growled at her.

"In a minute," she said, snapping away.

After she'd had her fun at her twin's expense, Hannah went to join her husband and Skeeter in one of the booths.

"CFO," Butch said, ringing the bell, "your muffin's ready."

"Took long enough," Hunter said.

"I had real customers to take care of first."

Hunter downed the muffin in four huge bites.

Megan handed him a large carryout cup of coffee, fixed with cream and two sugars the way he liked it.

He guzzled the coffee. "Thank you, Jesus—and Megan."

She went to him and leaned against him, resting her hand against the damp fabric on the back of his T-shirt. "Are you okay? Really?"

"I'm fine, babe." He kissed her.

"I'll rub all your sore muscles later."

His brown eyes widened with pleasure. "I'll wash your dishes anytime for that kind of service."

"Thought you might say that."

"One muscle in particular is *really* aching."

She pinched his rear. "You are so predictable, CFO."

"Only Butch is allowed to call me that. It's his pet name for me."

Butch grunted behind them. "Pet name. Whatever. Try pussy name."

"I'm wounded," Hunter said.

"Be nice to him, Butch," Megan said on her way out of the kitchen. "He owns the place."

"I wasn't nice to your sister when she owned the place."

"At least you're consistent," Hunter said, amused by Butch's gruffness. During his five-minute "break" the dirty dishes seemed to have given birth to more. He dove in and kept at it until the dishes stopped coming shortly after two. Thanks to Hannah's big mouth, most of his family stopped by before closing to take their digs at the diner's new dishwasher.

When they finally and blessedly ushered out the last of the customers at two thirty, he helped Megan clean up the disaster that was the diner. They scrubbed tables and seats, the counter and then the floor. They even had to wash windows where little fingers had smeared maple syrup on the glass.

By four o'clock, they had refilled the creamers as well as the sugar, salt and pepper shakers and prepared for Tuesday morning when the diner would reopen. It was usually closed on Mondays.

"Is that everything?" Hunter asked Megan.

"Everything except for this." She put her arms around him and hugged him tightly.

"I stink like shit," he said, even as he returned her embrace.

"You couldn't possibly stink like anything other than awesome." She nuzzled into his neck. "Thank you so much for this. You totally saved my bacon in every possible way."

"I can't believe you do this six days a week."

"It's never like this."

"If it's even half of this, I still don't know how you do it."

"You get used to it after a while."

Butch rang the bell loudly and then grumbled with laughter when they sprang apart. "Made you lovebirds some lunch." He pushed two turkey club sandwiches with fries and pickles through the window. "Good job today, CFO. You might not be as much of a pansy as I thought you were."

"Aww, thanks, Butch, but I'm taken."

"Eww. You're not my type."

Megan giggled at their banter. She brought the plates to the counter, poured a tall icy Coke for him and a Diet Coke for herself and sat next to him on one of the stools.

"Don't get any ketchup on my clean counter," Hunter said.

"I'll do my best not to make a mess."

"I've never been so hungry in my entire life."

"Real work will do that to ya, sissy boy," Butch said.

Hunter laughed. "You're right about that. I've got it easy compared to you guys."

"All you eggheads should do some time in the trenches to see what it's like."

"One of my business professors at UVM used to say that same thing. He'd tell us there's something to be said for getting your hands dirty." He took a closer look at the mess of shredded skin and blisters on his hands. "Nothing like a good dose of dishpan hands to better understand the business."

"I got something that'll fix you right up." Butch disappeared into the kitchen and returned with a tub of something yellow and greasy. "Put that on them. Be good as new tomorrow."

"Thanks, Butch," Megan said for him. "Will you go see about getting Petey out of jail?"

"Yeah, I'll take care it. Stupid kid needs to start using his brain instead of his mouth."

"Do you need money to post the bail?"

"I got it."

"Thanks for that and for busting ass today. See you Tuesday?"

"Where else would I be?" He waved as he headed out the door.

"Pleasant sort of guy," Hunter said when they were alone.

"He's an acquired taste."

"I'll take your word for that."

"You earned his respect today—big-time. If you hadn't, he wouldn't have made lunch for you. That's his way of saying you're okay, sissy boy."

Scowling playfully at her use of Butch's term, Hunter said, "I feel all warm and fuzzy inside."

She leaned in to nibble on his earlobe, and he went instantly hard. "I've got other ways of making you feel warm and fuzzy inside."

"Let's get out of here."

"Not until you wash those dishes," she said with a smile.

CHAPTER 2

——◆◆◆——

Hunter was dying. That was the only possible explanation for the fact that his entire body was on fire, and not in a good way. And all he'd done was drive home from the diner after washing their lunch dishes like the boss demanded.

Megan was right behind him, pulling into the driveway a few minutes after he did. She approached his car and knocked on the glass.

Hunter was able to marshal the strength to push the button to lower the window, wincing at the pain in his hands. They'd never be the same even with Butch's miracle cure.

"Why are you just sitting here?"

"Because I can't move."

"Aww, poor baby! Are you sore?"

"Sore, exhausted, depleted and aware of how easy I have it the rest of the time. I thought I was in good shape. How can a few hours of manual labor destroy me?"

"Um, maybe because you recently sustained some rather major injuries and haven't been working out as much as you usually do?" She pulled open the door, reached over him to unbuckle his seatbelt and gave a gentle tug to get him out of his SUV. "Let's go take a nice hot bath."

He moaned from the idea of it until it occurred to him that he'd have to climb multiple stairs to get to the tub. Would she think less of him if he crawled up the stairs?

"I shouldn't have called you," she said regretfully. "You've been doing so great that I forget sometimes that you were hurt pretty badly not that long ago."

"I'm fine, or I was until I worked in your sweatshop for a few hours." With her arm around his waist and his around her shoulders, they went up the stairs to the porch. "You have earned my endless, undying respect for what you do every day."

"Does that mean I can expect a foot rub after work every night from now on?"

"If you so desire."

"I do." She slipped her hand into the back pocket of his jeans and gave a little squeeze that had him forgetting all about how sore and tired he was. "I desire."

"I may not be able to service you today."

"I can't believe I'm hearing this. Even when you had a concussion you wanted to 'service' me."

"This is what happens when you set your sights on an older man."

"Older," she said with a snort. "You're only thirty-five. Stop acting like a geriatric."

"I feel like one after my shift at the diner."

"I'll fix you right up with a hot bath and a rubdown."

"I'm feeling better already."

"Is all this moaning and groaning a ploy to get my hands on you?" she asked as she propelled him up the stairs with her hands cupping his ass.

"Whatever it takes."

"You know you don't have to resort to tricks to get my hands on you. They're always happy to be on you."

"No tricks, baby. I'm sore and tired as hell. Butch might be right about me."

"No, he isn't. You're a stud, or I wouldn't love you so much."

"So you only love me for my hot bod?"

"It's one of the many reasons I love you."

"Oh, do tell." He turned to her after he'd started the water in the tub. "This I've got to hear."

She tilted her head and eyed him lovingly. "I love your sexy face, your sexy brain, your sexy mouth, your sexy bod, your sense of humor, your loyalty to your family, your business sense, the way you came running when I said I needed you and especially the way you refused to give up on us even when I was acting like a stupid idiot."

He laughed at that last one and then kissed her. "You never acted like a stupid idiot."

"Yes, I did. I refused to believe something so good could be real, and that was stupid. Because it's real, and it's incredible, and I love you because you're the best thing to ever happen to me."

"Megan," he whispered, drawing her into a much more serious kiss. "I never thought I'd hear you say such things about me. For the longest time all I could do was wish and hope for what I have right now. And it's all because of you. When you called me earlier? I was thinking about how much I love living with you and sleeping with you every night. I had a lot of fantasies where you're concerned, but none of them came close to touching the reality of what we have."

She wrapped her arms around his waist and rested her head on his chest. "Love you. Thank you so much for what you did today."

"It was my pleasure."

"Now you're just lying."

"Yes, it was. I got to spend the day with you rather than waiting for you to get home from work. Being there with you was better than waiting for you."

"You must *really* love me."

"I *really* love you. Now, let's take that bath."

After a long soak in the tub and the rubdown Megan had promised him, Hunter fell into a deep sleep. He woke in a darkened room with Megan propped on one hand, looking down at him.

"You're back."

He rubbed his hand over his face, which was when he remembered his hands were destroyed. "What time is it?"

"Nearly seven."

"Damn." He shifted to find a more comfortable position and immediately regretted moving. If one shift at the diner could so thoroughly kick his ass, he'd be spending a lot more time in his home gym starting tomorrow. Or maybe the day after. "Did you sleep?"

"A little. Mostly I watched you sleep."

"That must've been fun."

"It's very entertaining. You do this cute thing with your mouth. I could watch that all day."

"What cute thing?"

She moved her lips from side to side, which was all it took to wake up another part of him.

"Come here," he said, reaching for her with both arms, including the one that didn't want to bend.

She came into his embrace, molding her naked body to his, making him forget all about his aches and pains.

"I have a surprise for you," she said.

"What kind of surprise?"

"The kind you have to get up and get dressed for."

"I like the naked kind of surprises better."

"You'll like this one, too." Lifting her head from his chest, she bit her lip and glanced at him shyly. "At least I hope you will."

"Why do you seem nervous?"

"Because I did something that affects both of us without talking to you about it first."

"And you did this because you wanted to surprise me?"

"Uh-huh."

"Whatever it is, I'm sure I'll love it."

"How do you know that?"

"Because I love you, and if you went out of your way to arrange a surprise for me that you thought would make me happy, then I already love it."

"I hope you're still saying that when you see what it is."

Curiosity piqued, Hunter got up slowly and painfully. It was daunting to realize he wasn't as recovered from his injuries as he'd thought if a few hours of hard work could turn him into the Tin Man pre-oilcan.

Megan came into the bathroom with a glass of water and two pills, which she dropped into his hand.

"Thank you, sweetheart."

"I feel bad that you're so achy."

He took the pills and washed them down with a drink of water. "Don't feel bad. It's just a heads-up that I wasn't as recovered from the fall as I thought I was. Not to worry though. I'll be back to fighting form in no time."

"No more rock climbing for a while though, okay?"

"Ice season is coming soon, so we'll be abandoning the rocks for other pursuits."

Her brows furrowed. "Other dangerous pursuits."

"Nah, we're old pros."

"Seems I've heard that before . . . Right around the last time you went rock climbing . . . Ringing any bells?"

Laughing, he kissed her nose and then her lips. "I love your sarcasm."

"I love your body, especially when it's all in one piece."

The doorbell rang.

"Showtime," she said. "I'll get that. Come down when you're ready."

Since she was wearing a Vermont sweatshirt and flannel pajama pants, Hunter put on sweats and a long-sleeve T-shirt, wincing at the pain in his elbow when he jammed his arm into the sleeve. Praying for the pain pills to kick in quickly, he went downstairs slowly, like the old man he was.

In his living room were Dude Danforth and her "boy-friend," Skeeter.

"Recovered from your shift as a busboy, Hunter?" Skeeter asked.

"Not really." He glanced at Megan, wondering what was going on and why Skeeter and Dude had stopped by.

"Ready for your surprise?" Megan asked warily.

"Sure thing."

"Be right back," Dude said.

"You're gonna love this, Hunter," Skeeter said with a big dopey grin.

"It's not a cat from your freezer, is it?" Everyone in town knew about the dead cat Skeeter had left in his mother's freezer. For ten years.

Skeeter laughed. "Nah, that was a onetime case of forgetfulness that no one's ever gonna let me forget."

"Can you blame us?".

Dude came back in carrying a bundle close to her chest.

Next to him, Megan fairly vibrated with excitement and nerves.

"You want to tell him, Megan?"

"Okay," she said, turning to face Hunter.

Whatever she had to tell him, he decided right then and there, he wanted to see her eyes glow with that kind of excitement every day for the rest of their lives.

"A week or so ago, Dude came into the diner and told me that one of the puppies in Homer Junior's litter had been returned because the family had to move to another home, and they weren't allowed to have dogs there. She said she could only think of one person who should have this particular puppy—you."

"You got me a puppy?" He loved dogs and had been thinking about getting one of his own for some time now.

"Not just any puppy," Dude said.

"Homer Junior's twin," Megan said.

Dude removed the squirming body from the lightweight blanket that covered him, revealing Homer Junior's identical twin, right down to the all-brown face with the white circle over his left eye and paws in brown, black, white and white with brown spots.

"Oh my God." Hunter took the wiggling little body from Dude. "Are you sure this isn't Homer Junior?"

"Positive." Dude beamed with pleasure at Hunter's reaction to the puppy.

"I can't believe you got me the twin of my twin's dog."

With the puppy in his arms, he kissed Megan. "Best surprise ever."

"Really? You're not mad?"

"How could I be mad when—" He held the puppy away from him to reveal a huge patch of puppy pee on his T-shirt. Holding the little body up in the air, Hunter looked him in the eye. "*Really?* We just met!" The puppy seemed to grin at him, making him laugh as he fell madly in love.

Megan shook with silent laughter.

"There's goes my nice, clean, orderly house," Hunter said.

"A house that's too clean means a life not being lived to its fullest," Skeeter declared.

"Now you sound like my grandfather," Hunter said.

"We brought him a bed and some food to get you through tonight," Dude said. "I've also got a crate in the truck if you want it."

Hunter glanced at Megan who shook her head.

"No crate," Hunter said. "Hannah would never forgive me."

"For what?" Hannah asked as she came into the living room holding Homer Junior, with Nolan following behind her.

"If I put him in a crate," Hunter said.

"No crates," Hannah said emphatically, squealing as she caught sight of her puppy's twin.

"You'll regret that when he's tearing up your house," Nolan said.

Hannah rolled her eyes. "Don't listen to him. These are the best-behaved puppies in the universe."

"*Right,*" Nolan said with an eye roll of his own.

"Mine's already peed on me," Hunter said.

Dude scratched the puppy behind his ears. "That's him deciding you're his person."

"Am I your person, little buddy?"

The puppy let out an adorable little yelp that had Homer Junior straining to get free of Hannah so he could say hello to his brother.

Hunter put his puppy down on the floor so they could romp.

They fell into a gleeful wrestling match that had everyone laughing at their antics.

Hannah waved her hand in front of her face, as if she were trying not to cry. Thanks to pregnancy hormones, she cried at commercials these days, or so Nolan said. "They remember each other."

"I knew they would," Dude said proudly.

"Did you know about this?" Hunter asked his sister.

"Megan clued me in the other day. She wanted me to bring Homer over so you'd believe you had his twin and not him."

"These are the only two from that litter who had this same exact coloring," Dude said.

"Just like us and our litter," Hunter said to Hannah.

"Exactly," she said, laughing.

"Good surprise?" Megan asked.

Hunter put his arm around her and drew her in close to him. "Awesome surprise."

"Don't get puppy pee on me."

"We're in this together, sweetheart."

Shrieking, she twirled out of his embrace.

"What're you going to name him?" Hannah asked from her post on the floor with the dogs.

"It's got to be an H name," Nolan said. "Can't be anything else."

"How about Hector?" Hannah asked.

Hunter wrinkled his nose. "He's not a Hector." He picked up his new buddy—and he knew this one was his because he wasn't wearing a collar. *Note to self: Don't get a red collar or you'll never be able to tell him apart from his brother/cousin.* Hunter looked him in the eye, falling more in love by the second with the sweet face that looked back at him. "Horace."

"The nickname for that would be Hor," Nolan said. "The other dogs at the dog park are likely to be ruthless with that name."

Hunter looked up at Megan, seeking her approval.

She smiled and nodded. "We'll take our chances."

* * *

Later that night, in bed with Megan tucked up against one side of him and Horace snuggled up against the other, Hunter thought about how much his life had changed in the last few months. He'd gone from living a boring, somewhat staid existence, to falling in love, getting engaged, moving Megan into his house, even working at the diner and now adding Horace to their little family.

"What're you thinking about?" she asked in a sleepy voice.

"Everything that's happened in the last few months. Hard to believe how much has changed."

"I wouldn't believe it myself if I hadn't had a front-row seat."

"All good changes. The best kind of changes."

"Mmm."

"We need to set a wedding date," he said.

"I've been thinking about that. What do you say about Christmas?"

"I love Christmas. What's not to love about Christmas?"

"It's been a tough time of year for me since my parents died. A wedding could give me some new memories of the season. Plus Nina and Brett will be home. What do you think?"

"I think," he said, shifting slightly so he could kiss her while trying not to wake the puppy, "that's a fantastic idea."

"The weather might be an issue though."

"Always a concern, but as long as we can get Nina, Brett and my family there, which shouldn't be a problem, I'd be happy. How about you?"

"That's all I need."

"Where do you want to do it?"

"This is the part I feel sort of weird about."

"How do you mean?"

"I'd love to do it at your parents' house if you don't think they'd mind. They've got that huge, beautiful family room with the fireplace. I bet your mom goes all out with the tree and the decorating. I can't think of anywhere better, unless it would be too much to ask of them."

"They'd love it. I don't even have to ask to know they'd be all for it."

"Still, we're going to ask before we make any firm plans."

"We'll ask. They'll say yes—emphatically—and we'll make our plans."

"You really like the idea of doing it there?"

"I love it. Almost as much as I love you." He kissed her, lingering on the sweet softness of her lips. "This turned out to be one hell of a Sunday."

In the darkness, he felt her smile against his lips. He fell asleep with a smile on his face, which was the only part of him that didn't ache like hell. Well, that wasn't entirely true. His heart was in pretty good shape these days, too.

Turn the page for a sneak peek at

YOU'LL BE MINE
Will and Cameron's wedding novella

Available July 2015 from Berkley
in the Ask Me Why *anthology!*

A t exactly one forty-five two days before her wedding to Will Abbott, Cameron Murphy shut off her laptop and left it in the office she shared with her fiancé. She wouldn't need the computer for the next two weeks. When she returned to the office, he'd be her husband and they'd be back from their honeymoon.

Filled with giddy excitement, Cameron turned off the office light and closed the door behind her. Will was already gone for the day, off doing last-minute wedding errands while she finished up at work.

Their office manager, Mary, stood and came around her desk to give Cameron a hug. "Enjoy every minute of this special time," she said, nearly reducing Cameron to tears.

"Thank you so much, Mary. I'll see you tomorrow night, right?" She was one of a few special friends invited to join the family for the rehearsal dinner Will's parents were throwing for them at their home.

"Wouldn't miss it for all the world."

"I'll see you then."

Cameron skipped down the stairs and into the store, where

she was greeted with more hugs and good wishes from the employees. While no one would mistake her little old nuptials for a royal wedding, it sort of had that feel to it. In Butler, Vermont, the Abbott family was royalty. With a family of ten children and businesses that employed numerous members of the local community, an Abbott wedding was big news.

She accepted a hug, a kiss, best wishes and a cider donut from Dottie, who ran the donut counter. After talking wedding plans with Dottie and the other ladies for a couple of minutes, Cameron took her donut to the front porch of the store to enjoy it in relative peace. With only two days to go, she was confident she'd fit into her dress, so she sat in one of the rockers and ate the donut in guilt-free heaven.

She'd no sooner sat down than who should appear on a leisurely stroll down Elm Street but her very own stalker, Fred the moose. Cameron sank deeper into the rocker, hoping Fred wouldn't notice her. In all her years of living in New York City and after scores of first dates, she'd never had an actual stalker until she came to Vermont and slammed her Mini Cooper into Fred, the Butler town moose. Will's dad, Lincoln, had recently concluded that Fred had a crush on her.

Fantastic. A moose with a crush. With her dad due at two and Patrick Murphy always on time, the last thing she needed was yet another mooseastrophy. Fortunately, Fred didn't see her sitting on the porch and continued on his merry way, leaving Cameron to breathe easier about Fred but not about her dad's pending arrival.

The thought of her billionaire father in tiny Butler had provoked more nerves than anything else about the upcoming weekend. Marrying Will? No worries at all. Getting through the wedding? Who cared if it all went wrong? At the end of the day, she'd be married to Will. That was all she cared about. But bringing Patrick here to this place she now called home?

Cameron drew in a deep breath and blew it out. She hoped he wouldn't do or say something to make her feel less at home here because she loved everything about Butler and her life with Will in Vermont. She'd experienced mud season— along with a late-season blast of snow—spring, summer and now the glorious autumn, which was, by far, her favorite season yet.

How could she adequately describe the russet glow of the trees, the vivid blue skies, the bright sunny days and the chilly autumn nights spent snuggled up with Will in front of the woodstove. The apples, pumpkins, chrysanthemums, corn husks tied to porch rails, hay bales and cider. She loved it all, but she especially loved the scent of woodsmoke in the air.

Cameron couldn't have asked for a better time of year to pitch a tent in their enormous yard and throw a great big party. All her favorite autumn touches would be incorporated into the wedding, and she couldn't wait to see it all come together on Saturday. At Will's suggestion, they'd hired a wedding planner to see to the myriad details because they were both so busy at work.

At first, Cameron had balked at the idea of hiring a stranger to plan the most important day of her life, but Regan had won her over at their first meeting and had quickly become essential to her. No way could Cameron have focused on the website she was building for the store and planned a wedding at the same time.

She glanced at her watch. Three minutes until two. Patrick would be here soon, probably driven in the town car he used to get around the city. Under no circumstances could she picture her dad driving himself six hours north to Vermont. Not when there were deals to be struck and money to be made. Time, he always said, was money.

He'd shocked the hell out of her when he told her he wanted to come up on Thursday so he could spend some time with her and Will before the madness began in earnest. Her dad would be sleeping in their loft tonight, and Will had already put her on notice that there would be no sex while her dad was in the house. She couldn't wait to break his resolve.

The thought of how she might accomplish that had her in giggles that died on her lips at the familiar *thump, thump, thump* sound that suddenly invaded the peaceful afternoon. *No way. No freaking way. He did not.* If this was what she thought it was, she'd have no choice but to kill him. Warily, she got up from her chair and ventured down the stairs to look up at the sky just as her father's big, black Sikorsky helicopter came swooping in on tiny Butler, bringing cars and people to a halt on Elm Street.

One woman let out an ear-piercing scream and dove for cover in some bushes.

Amused and aggravated, Cameron took off jogging toward the town common, the one space nearby where the bird could land unencumbered. As she went, she realized she should've expected him to make an entrance. Didn't he always?

Nolan and Skeeter were outside the garage looking up when she went by.

"What the hell was that?" asked Nolan, who would be her brother-in-law after the wedding.

"Just my dad coming to town."

"Holy Moses," Skeeter said. "Thought it was the end of the world."

"Nope, just Patrick Murphy coming to what he considers the end of the earth. Gotta run. See you later."

"Bye, Cam," Nolan said.

"I assume that's with you," Lucas Abbott said, gesturing toward the town common with his thumb, as Cameron trotted past his woodworking barn.

"You'd be correct."

"That thing is righteous. Does he give rides?"

"I'll be sure to ask him."

"Nice."

Cameron sort of hated that everyone in town would know her pedigree after her father's auspicious arrival. Maybe they already knew. In fact, they probably did. The Butler gossip grapevine was nothing short of astonishing. If the people in town knew who she was, or more importantly who her father was, no one made a thing of it. After this they probably would, which saddened her. She loved her low-key, under-the-radar life in Butler and wouldn't change a thing about it.

But she also loved her dad, and after thirty years as his daughter she should certainly be accustomed to the grandiose way he did things. She got to the field just as he was emerging from the gigantic black bird with the gold *PME* lettering on the side: Patrick Murphy Enterprises. Those initials were as familiar to Cameron as her own as they'd always been part of her life.

Hoping to regain her breath and her composure, she came to a stop about twenty yards from the landing site and waited for him to come to her. Hands on hips, she watched him exchange a few words with the pilot before shaking his hand, grabbing a suitcase and garment bag as well as his everpresent messenger bag, which he slung over his shoulder. Wait until he experienced Butler Wi-Fi, or the lack thereof.

As he came toward Cameron, a smile on his handsome face, she felt her heart soften toward him, as it always did, no matter how outrageous he might be.

She took the garment bag from him and lifted her cheek to receive his kiss. "Always gotta make an entrance, don't you?"

"What's that supposed to mean?"

"The *bird*, Dad. You scared the hell out of everyone. They thought we were being attacked."

He looked completely baffled. "I told you I'd be here at two."

"I was watching for a car, not a chopper."

Recoiling from the very idea, he said, "I didn't have six hours to sit in traffic on the Taconic. As it is, my ass is numb after ninety minutes in the chopper."

"We do have airports in Vermont, you know."

"We checked on that. Closest one that could take the Lear is in Burlington, which is more than two hours from here. Time—"

"Is money," she said with a sigh. "I know."

"For the record, I'd like to point out it wasn't my idea to move you out to the bumfuck of nowhere."

Cameron laughed at his colorful wording. "This is *not* the bumfuck of nowhere. This," she said, with a dramatic sweep of her arm, "is the lovely, magnificent town of Butler, Vermont. Home sweet home."

"It's as charming as I recall from the last time I was here for Linc's wedding."

"Are you being sarcastic?"

"Me? Sarcastic?"

"Your sarcasm notwithstanding, it's great to see you and to have you here. I know it's not what you're used to, but I think you'll enjoy it."

He stopped walking and turned to her. "You're here. That's all I need to enjoy myself, honey."

Cameron let the garment bag flop over her arm so she could hug him. "Thank you so much for coming, Dad."

He wrapped his arms around her. "Happy to be anywhere you are."

They stashed Patrick's bags in Cameron's black SUV. "Where'd you get this beast?" he asked.

"Will insisted I trade the Mini for something built for Vermont winters. I don't love it, but as I haven't survived a winter here yet, I'll take his word for it." She took Patrick's hand, eager to introduce him to all her new friends. "Come see the store."

He followed her up the stairs to the porch and into the Green Mountain Country Store in all its glory.

"Wow." Patrick looked up at the vintage bicycle fastened to one of the wooden beams above the store. "I feel like I just stepped into an episode of *Little House on the Prairie*."

"Isn't it amazing? I'll never forget the first time I came in here. It was like I'd been transported to anther century or something." She looked up at him as he took in the barrels full of peanuts and iced bottles of Coke and products from a bygone era, a simpler time, hoping he'd see the magic that she experienced every time she came through the doors to the store. "That's dumb, right?"

"Not at all. It's quite something. I'm wondering how in the name of hell you build a website for a place like this?"

Cameron laughed. "Slowly and painstakingly."

"I can't wait to see how you've captured it."

She tugged on his hand. "Come meet Dottie and have a cider donut."

"Oh, I don't think—"

"You have to! Your visit won't be complete without one."

She led him back to the donut counter, where Dottie was pulling a fresh batch from the oven. "Perfect timing. Dottie, this is my dad, Patrick, and he's in bad need of a donut."

Dottie wiped her hands on a towel before reaching across the counter to shake Patrick's hand. "So nice to meet you, Patrick. We're all very big fans of your daughter."

"As am I."

"Can I get one of those for him?"

"Of course! Another for you, sweetie?"

"Absolutely not! I've got a dress to fit into on Saturday, so don't tempt me." To Patrick, Cameron added, "Dottie is the devil when it comes to these donuts."

"Why, thank you," Dottie said with a proud smile as she handed over a piping-hot donut to Patrick.

Both women watched expectantly as he took a bite.

His blue eyes lit up. "Holy cow, that's good."

"*Right?*" Cameron said, pleased by his obvious pleasure. "I limit myself to two a week or I wouldn't fit through the doors around here. Come on upstairs and check out the office. See you later, Dottie."

"Bye, Cam. Nice to meet you, Patrick."

"You, too."

He followed her through the store, stopping to look at various items as they went.

"That's Hannah's jewelry," Cameron said of the pieces that'd stopped him for a closer look. "She's Will's older sister, twin to Hunter, who's the company CFO."

"She does beautiful work."

"I know! I'm a huge fan. I have a couple of her bracelets. Helps to have friends in high places."

"I'm glad you're making friends here."

They proceeded up the stairs to the offices on the second floor. "So many friends. And now Lucy's here a lot, too, which makes it even better."

"Back so soon?" Mary asked when they arrived in the reception area. "I didn't think I'd see you here again for at least two weeks."

"I wanted you to meet my dad, Patrick."

Mary came around her desk to shake his hand. "So nice to meet Cameron's dad. We adore her here."

"So I'm hearing. Nice to meet you, too."

"This is our office," Cameron said, throwing open the door and turning on the lights so her dad could see her workspace.

"*Our* office?"

"Mine and Will's."

"You two *share* an office? They didn't give you one of your own?"

"We tried," Mary said. "Those two kids are inseparable."

Cameron blushed and shrugged. "What she said. Besides, if I'm in another office, how am I supposed to play footsie with him during the day?"

"Ugh," Patrick said with a grunt of laughter. "TMI. I'd go crazy sharing office space with anyone, especially such a small one."

"Not everyone can have an acre in the sky to call their own," Cameron said disdainfully.

He tweaked her nose. "It's not a full acre, and I do need my elbow room."

"You're a spoiled, pampered brat, and we all know it."

Mary laughed at their sparring.

"Don't listen to her, Mary," Patrick said with a wink that had Mary blushing to the roots of her brown hair. "We all know who the spoiled brat is here."

"Yeah, and it's not me."

"I'm afraid I have to side with your daughter, Patrick. There's nothing spoiled about her. She works harder than all of us put together."

"Thank you, Mary. I'll make sure Hunter hears about your fifty percent raise."

They left Mary laughing as they went back downstairs.

"What's her story?" Patrick asked.

"Who, Mary?"

"Yeah. She's adorable."

"Dad . . . Don't. She's a really nice lady. Leave her alone. She wouldn't stand a chance against your brand of charm."

"Why can't I have a little fun while I'm in town?"

Cameron stopped on the landing and turned to him. "She's off-limits. I mean that."

"Don't be so touchy, Cam." He kissed her cheek and proceeded ahead of her into the store.

She watched him go with a growing sense of unease. She'd have to keep an eye on him this weekend and keep him far, far away from Mary—and all the other single women in Butler.

THE Vermont
COUNTRY STORE®

FEEL LIKE A KID
IN A CANDY STORE

In 1946 we opened our store in Weston, Vermont, and it still looks very much the same today as it did then. We are stocked to the rafters with thousands of practical and hard-to-find goods.

THREE WAYS TO SHOP—ONE GREAT EXPERIENCE

RETAIL LOCATIONS

WESTON | **ROCKINGHAM**
657 Main St • Route 100 | 1292 Rockingham Rd • Route 103

OPEN 7 DAYS A WEEK • 802.824.3184

SHOP OUR CATALOG
800.564.4623

SHOP ONLINE
WWW.VERMONTCOUNTRYSTORE.COM

The Orton Family Business Since 1946

M1409OA1213